To Joan,

R. Scott Reid

THE CORPORATE VEIL

a novel

R. SCOTT RICKS

LONGSTREET PRESS

Atlanta

FOR MAGGIE AND FRANCES,
MAY YOU GROW TO FIND THAT THE WORLD
IS A BETTER PLACE WHEN VIEWED FROM
THE HEART THAN THROUGH THE EYES.

LOVE, DADDY

Published by
LONGSTREET PRESS, INC.
2974 Hardman Court, Atlanta, Georgia 30305
www.longstreetpress.net

1st printing, 2003
ISBN: 1-56352-720-0

Printed in the United States of America

Jacket and book design by Burtch Hunter Design LLC
Back cover author photo by Marsha Perry
Flap author photo by Carol Bryan

ACKNOWLEDGMENTS

THERE WAS A point in my life when I believed a book was a simple affair. Those days are gone. I always thought a book had three simple parts, a writer came up with a story and put it on paper, the editor corrected misspellings, changed sentence structures and added comas, and then a publisher printed the book and hoped that it sold. If only it were so simple. The only part that I had right was that it took a great deal of effort by many different people to make a book come together, but none of their jobs are simple.

An editor has the daunting task of harnessing someone else's thoughts and making them clear to the rest of the world. When John Yow read my first draft of The Corporate Veil he confirmed the feeling that I had all along, my story was intriguing, but I needed help getting those thoughts to paper. I assured John that my imagination had been outrunning my talents for the majority of my life and that this was just the latest episode to see if I could overcome this constant dilemma. We rolled up our sleeves for my first official writing class and got to work. John taught me that the idea of a good book is for the writing to disappear to where only the intrigue of the story remains. If this book does that for you, it's because of John Yow.

When I began to look for a publisher for *The Corporate Veil* I had no idea how hard it was just to get someone to read a manuscript, much less offer to publish it. I soon found that completing a book was much easier than convincing someone to spend money on it. Publishers must wade through countless numbers of submissions looking for that undiscovered gem, often only to be rewarded by a world that is a constant gamble and bearing the entire financial burden if a book does not sell. I am thankful to Scott Bard and the employees of Longstreet Press for finding something in me that they viewed worthy of the risk. I hope I can live up to their expectations.

As for the third part of a book, the author, I can only say that I am the product of the wonderful people that surround my life and even though I could write an entire book thanking them, I'll try to be brief. To my mother,

Doris Ricks, who has always been there for spiritual guidance and as a moral compass. I love you very much. To my father, Roger Ricks, who paid for the majority of my education and never let me settle for less when I could do more. It wasn't always easy being your son, but I'm a better man because of it. To my sweet sister, Karen Ricks Tautan, my dearest and oldest friend. There will always a special place in my heart for you. To Bob and Barbara McLendon, who have accepted me into their family and indeed made me feel like their son. To my extended friends and family who have been such a strong part of my nurturing. There's a little piece of each of you within me. To Steve Bowden, co-founder (and only other member) of the Childersburg Literary Society. I hope you can look with pride on how our little project has started. To the dedicated employees of my companies and their affiliates, who have managed to grow a thriving business despite the many shortcomings of their boss. To the men and women at Brasfield & Gorrie, American Cast Iron Pipe, Imery's, O'neal Steel, Namasco Steel and the many other customers and vendors that, next to my employees, have been the biggest part of my success. Many of my closest friends work for these fine companies and I am truly grateful for your support. To my law school pals Pat Davenport, Wes Tibbals and Joe Herring, who proofread the original storyline to check for legal errors. Thanks for being there for me, I hope someday I can do the same for you. To my longtime partner and best friend, Jim Landers, who every day continues to teach me a new lesson in loyalty. To my beautiful wife, Jennifer, who has sometimes taken a backseat to allow her husband to chase his dreams. I am often praised by my family, friends and peers for having accomplished a great number of things in such a short lifetime, but no matter what I have done in the past or will do in the future, convincing you that I was the one will always be my greatest achievement. I love you more than words can say.

And finally, thank you to anyone who spends their precious money or time on this book. It was written with you in mind. I hope I prove worthy of your effort.

Sincerely,
R. Scott Ricks

THE
CORPORATE
VEIL

ONE

THE TINY SHACK stood like a tombstone against sil-
houettes of tall slender pines, marking the death of a life gone wrong.
Moonlight reached through the forest and placed shadows on the
outside walls, highlighting the emptiness of its soul. No love filled its
rooms. It offered no comfort to inhabitants or guests. Devoid of
human decency, the tiny shack had witnessed the most horrific acts
of man. And even now, on the stillness of the air, through the stifling
humidity of the summer heat, the past and present echoes of a child's
tears could be heard between the pauses of the nighttime symphony
played by an orchestra of whippoorwills and katydids. The tiny shack
in the trees was a house. It had never been a home.

Outside in the sandy soil of the front lot Douglas Watkins slipped
a key into the black 1985 Crown Victoria and thought to himself how
easy the killing had been. He had killed before, in Vietnam as a nine-
teen-year old enlisted infantry solider, but somehow that was different. As an invincible teenager on the other side of the world he simply began shooting into the thick roughage of the Vietnam jungle and
never actually saw the agonizing faces of those he killed or maimed.
But the experience of creating death had changed him, making the
man in him coarse and hard. By the end of his tour of duty the invin-

cible teenager was gone, no longer convinced of his own immortality having witnessed the end of so many friends who met their fate at his side. He was terrified under the circumstances of the jungle, it was only human nature to be. But this killing had been different and he was surprised at the calmness that had come over him. He felt no remorse for his victim.

He had been close, able to see the prey's face as it turned away and headed back into the dirty little shack. He felt the skull crack under his swing and knew that one blow had done the trick. The sweet spot of the bat found its mark and his aim was true. The victim fell to the floor in a puddle of blood and never moved. And now, just minutes later, his hands were no longer shaking and his knees were no longer weak. His breathing slowed and his head was clear.

Watkins opened the car door, which made a low squeak as time weighed heavy on its hinges. He sat on the ragged bench seat of the Crown Vic and swung his legs inside. His large chest and stomach prohibited easy entry and he tilted the steering wheel completely forward to secure himself underneath. Usually, he lifted the wheel when getting out of the car to make it easier to get back in. But moments ago the tension had been too high to perform his normal routine of exit. After all, he wasn't getting out at a store or in front of his office, but in front of a little shack in a pine tree thicket—which he would turn into murder scene. But now the anxiety was gone. The deed was done and there was no one within miles to notice.

He removed his hat and glasses and wiped the sweat from his forehead with the handkerchief he still held in his hand. It had made a nice batting glove. For a man of his size, even at night the Alabama heat was almost unbearable in July. He sometimes wondered how he'd lived here all of his life.

Replacing his hat and glasses he cranked the car. The old fan belt screeched and whined under the hood. The car's paint was now a pale faded black and showed the wear and tear of years as government transportation. The emblem on its side was peeling away and the vehicle looked as gruff as the man who drove it.

Placing his right hand on top of the passenger seat headrest, he looked over his right shoulder and turned the large four-door car around to return down the dirt road he'd traveled only ten minutes earlier. No need to turn on the lights. The south Alabama night was clear, and a full moon gave plenty of light for him to see.

"Damn it's hot," he thought aloud, and wiped his forehead again, though seconds later new beads of sweat began to reappear above his thick eyebrows. He took notice of his hands on the steering wheel. Driving to the crime scene moments before, his nervousness forced him to make a conscious effort to refrain from gripping the steering wheel so tight that his knuckles turned white from the pressure of his grasp. He had tried to relax by slumping in his seat and driving with only his wrist on the top of the wheel. But now he held the wheel without choking it, allowing the blood to flow freely over his knuckles and through his large fat fingers.

The long dirt road passed slowly underneath the Crown Vic and he was careful not to sling the mud of the road onto its fenders. The tall loblolly pines created a dark barrier on either side of the road— just as they created a livelihood, for better or worse, for just about everyone in the surrounding towns. Most folks within 40 miles worked either directly or indirectly on turning those trees into paper. In this particular stretch of the forest the trees were nearly fifty feet tall now, and he knew that soon this land would be prime hunting ground. The paper mill was sure to cut down the timber for pulp in the next few months. Clear-cut property was much easier hunting. It was tough to kill deer in pine thickets. Big bucks run the dogs in circles without ever crossing the roads to give the hunter a clear shot.

The pines towered over the road creating shadows even at night, but luckily the Alabama moon against a backdrop of darkness and stars shone brightly at the end. He continued to drive without the assistance of his lights as he progressed further into the forest. He didn't want to risk the slightest chance that maybe a coon hunter training a puppy would take notice of his headlight beams through the pine trees. He'd been careful to listen for a hound barking before entering the tiny shack to do his deed. Hearing nothing, he assumed he was alone—that is—except for his victims.

Even though it had rained most of the afternoon there wasn't a cloud in the sky, the summer thunderstorm disappearing as quickly as it had arrived. The glistening stars illuminated the night sky, while the moon at the end of the road reminded him of a lighthouse leading the sailor home after a long period at sea. He was relieved. Just like the sailor who anticipated shore, he anticipated the warm reception that would greet his night's work and then the quiet, sleepy calmness that would soon be his and his colleagues. He had done a good thing and he knew it. No need to feel guilty.

He rolled slowly down the road past the Shady Pines Baptist Church and took notice of the bright white paint that colored its walls. "Well, the niggers built that one back purty good," he said out loud. A smile creased his thick lips as he remembered the night when he and some of his friends from town set fire to the church. Dressed in the traditional white, just for the nostalgia of the moment, he could still see the bright orange flames licking the dark sky as the wind from the fire swayed the tops of the surrounding pines. He was old enough to remember a time when their kind knew their place in society, and he wished more people would continue to support the principles that his father and grandfather had passed on to him. Besides, had Reverend Stevens known his place and not complained so loudly about the discrepancies in the hiring practices out at the paper mill, bringing in all of those EEOC lawyers and such, there would've been no need to burn down his nigger church.

And as for Calvin, the dead man in the tiny shack, if he had remembered his place within the operation, he would have never asked for a larger share or made threats against Watkins and his colleagues, and consequently there would have been no reason to kill him. In his mind Watkins was a reasonable man. He treated blacks fairly if they didn't cause trouble, and he was no longer bitter about the fact that some in town were more educated and wealthy than himself. It was only those who didn't adhere to the natural order of things that had to be dealt with. Watkins knew the world had changed on him, both black and white, and by his thinking it was not for the better. And because of this change churches had to be burned and people had to be killed, until society opened its eyes to understand and remember how things were supposed to be.

In big cities across the South, politicians both white and black could preach all they wanted about equality, and they could pretend that the two races could live in harmony. But Watkins understood that complete coexistence wasn't possible and he knew he wasn't alone in his beliefs. After all, it was the trend of black church burnings in Birmingham in 1998 that gave him the idea of how to take care of the Reverend.

Unfortunately for Watkins, when he remembered the night of a year or so ago when Shady Pines Baptist went up in flames, he also thought of the morning after. He could still see Americus Kirkland, pompously waving his arms while standing on the courthouse steps at a press conference addressing the local paper, a Montgomery television station and a few spectators, who, noticing the TV cameras, stopped to hear him speak. Americus in all of his dramatic flare and arrogance pledged to personally pay for the materials needed to build back the church, and would conduct his own search to find out who was behind Satan's work. To Watkins, Americus was a pitiful excuse of a white man, actually giving money to pretend he cared about what happened to blacks, especially when there was no reason for him to. Watkins' position forced him to play a masquerade, but Americus certainly wasn't trying to win any elections. He just liked the attention.

Through years of practice Watkins had become quite good at the charade. When he began his profession over thirty years ago he didn't have to hide his true feelings, but again the world had changed.

He thought of his own response to the reporter's questions, asking if he would support Americus' mission to find the arsonist. He thought it a great quote. "I fully support my fellow Christians both black and white," Watkins had proudly proclaimed, "and intend to give my full time and support to find out who is behind this dreadful incident." He grinned again at the possibility of those liberal losers in the press actually believing his answer.

He wondered when the girl would wake up and discover her father's dead body. He had always heard that blacks hated being in a room with a corpse. He hoped it wouldn't be in the middle of his coffee and breakfast. He was awfully grumpy when he didn't get to eat. Maybe she would not seek help until after lunch or do something even better like run away.

"Damn," he said aloud, "wouldn't that be great?" It would make her look even more guilty if she were to flee the scene. He wiped his sweaty forehead again.

He knew his partners were going to be ecstatic with his impromptu decision to change the plan. Now they were rid of Calvin without killing the girl. His idea had been so obvious when he entered the shack, the girl unconscious with bruises on her face and blood oozing from her lip. Calvin had beaten her up pretty good. How could anyone not believe that she finally stood up for herself and retaliated?

He didn't think the girl was stupid enough to run, but perhaps she would be that scared. Being faced with murder can be an extremely frightening proposition and he knew she clearly understood the kind of justice she would get in his town. She knew Watkins well. In the past, when she tried to run away, he was the one who found her walking down the dirt roads and took her back to Calvin. He only wished Calvin could have waited until he was gone before beginning to beat the child. Even if she did run away and they couldn't find her, everyone would assume she was the killer and their problem was still solved.

But if they did find her, she probably wouldn't go to prison for long anyway. To him it was such a waste for something that pretty to have nigger blood coursing through her veins. His thoughts of what he'd like to do to her on previous visits to the shack were vivid, and he had even thought about having a little fun before taking her back to Calvin when he caught her running away. But if some of the boys ever found out he raped a black girl he would be disgraced. Besides, he was quite sure from the rumors circulating town that Calvin had already broken her in, and even a man as rough around the edges as Watkins found such behavior sickening. He could not imagine a father raping his own child, but then that's what you get with those kind of people.

He was almost back out to the paved road, if you could call it that. The county road that had more potholes than pavement. It was only a couple of hours before sunrise, so he pulled beside the river that paralleled the road and listened to a whippoorwill call while he cleaned the dirt from underneath his fingernails with a pocketknife. Even in the moonlight he could see how removing the dirt left tiny white lines beneath his nails, scratches by the tip of the blade. His mind went back to the killing. Easy. Nothing to it.

The river was up a little due to the afternoon rain, but continued to drift slowly south carrying muddy water and trash thrown on its banks by youngsters and fisherman. If there was no more rain the water level would be normal again by tomorrow afternoon, but the trash would cling to the branches of trees and bushes overhanging the river. Prisoners from the county lockup would be on detail for the next couple of days cleaning the rubbish from the river's banks, just so someone could come down the next day and trash it again. Not much difference between himself and the prisoners. Both cleaned up trash. But after he cleaned up, the trash was gone for good. He was in control now. Let this be a lesson, he thought, on just exactly who's in charge and has the power to make things right.

He stepped out of the car and checked himself for splatters of blood, then dusted the front of his uniform's shirt and pants. When

he felt sufficiently clean he repeated the ritual that allowed him to get
his tremendous stomach underneath the steering wheel. He reached
into his back pocket and pulled out a package of Levi Garrett. With
his left hand he pulled a large wad of the shredded tobacco from the
pouch and placed it inside his right cheek, gathering in all of the
loose edges with his forefinger until all was firmly packed in. He
cranked the Crown Vic, which once again made a shrieking sound as
it started.

"'Bout time for a new car," he mumbled.

He believed this time he could get one too. There were a lot of
people in town who owed him plenty. He had taken care of their little mess and quite proud of himself, he'd taken care of it for good.

The curiosity—if in fact anyone cared about what happened to
the girl—would last for a month or two until the trial was over.
Perhaps there would even be an excuse to burn a church or two.
Given Calvin's background, Watkins was interested in how the town
would react. He relished having caused a little havoc for the 'other
side.'

Thirty minutes before sunrise he slowly pulled the car back onto
the dirt road, drove about two hundred feet, and turned left onto the
paved highway heading back into town. He reached into his shirt
pocket, pulled out his sheriff's badge and replaced it on his chest. He
would need it in a couple of hours.

TWO

SAM HUNG HER head out the window of the 1983 Ford pickup truck, while Spencer Michael Thompson—Spence for short—sat behind the wheel driving down Interstate 85 through Georgia. With the windows down, Sam loved to feel the wind in her face, sitting to the far right of the passenger seat to get the full effect of it blowing across her ears. It didn't bother her that the air conditioning in the old black pickup was broken. Occasionally her eyes watered from the wind, causing her to turn and face it even more. She was good tempered, very loving and showed Spence undying devotion. In his mind this was only because Sam was a dog, for no human was capable of such dedication. To be exact, Sam was a registered pointer. She was never a show dog or entered into field trials, but when it came to finding quail "Thompson's Samantha Baby" had few equals. So far in his life, Sam was the only female Spence considered worth the effort.

Their trip had originated on the sunny pebble beaches of the Atlantic East coast at his best friend's family beach home on Edisto Island, sixty miles south of Charleston, where Spence had spent a two-week vacation. Before that Spence had an even longer oat-sowing stint on a two-month backpack tour of Europe, a gift from the father of the same best friend and law school pal, Wesley Peale

McCain. Spence had never been given the chance to travel so he graciously accepted the token of Jack McCain's generosity. He also undertook the burden of keeping Wes sober for at least part of the excursion and free from any sexually transmitted diseases. He accepted his challenge knowing it would not be an easy task. For like Spence, Wes loved life, and himself, unreservedly.

The two friends were quite different in their backgrounds, mannerisms and degrees of loudness—Wes being the obnoxious one. So it happened on more than one occasion at a party in law school that Spence, in his more subtle approach in a quiet corner with a potential female catch, would look up to see Wes streaking through the same crowded room sporting nothing but running shoes. But no matter how different their approach may have been, their credo was still the same: *Life is short. Look out for number one and have fun.* In the pursuit of fun they had spent the three years of their legal studies playing sports, drinking beer, and chasing women. Unlike Wes, however, Spence was a man of limited resources and there was only so long he could afford to continue his lacksidasical days of law school, living off government loans.

The ragged Ford pick-up progressed slower than most of the other vehicles traveling on the highway. Occasionally Spence would catch himself driving only 60 MPH in the left passing lane of the 70 MPH interstate. Had Wes been behind him, he would have been cursing up a storm and blowing his horn. Spence was not typically a slow driver either, but today he was not in a hurry. He took the time to enjoy himself and feel the sun on his face and forearm, which hung from the window of the truck. Like Sam, he was almost enjoying the fact that the air conditioning didn't work, forcing him to ride with the windows down and giving him a chance to appreciate the hot summer climate of the South, even though the wind could not keep him from sweating. He missed the heat while in Europe and was glad to be back home—headed to what he hoped would be his new permanent hometown.

Tim McGraw sang on the portable radio positioned on the seat between he and Sam, while Spence gently tapped his thumb on the steering wheel to the beat of *I Like it, I love it*. The radio in the old truck had been broken since Spence purchased it in law school and he found that the thirty-dollar portable one from Wal-mart worked just as well as a car radio for far less cost. Occasionally he would spin the antennae around to get a better signal, but he did not mind the chore. He did wish he had preset channels.

On the passenger-side floorboard sat a little red cooler with the initials 'SMT' written on the side in large black ink. Spence flipped open the lid and pulled one of the four Budweiser bottles—two of which were already empty—from the cold ice and water. He unscrewed the top and threw the cap out the window, worked the beer into a University of Alabama hugger and then wedged the hugger between his legs. He reached over and rubbed Sam on top of her head, which dried the icy water from his hand and gave her a cool treat over her ears as he scratched. "Not too much longer now girl," he told her.

At one o'clock Spence made it past Hartsfield International airport just south of Atlanta and knew he was leaving the city behind. There were no more streetlights on either side of the highway and the road's surface began to worsen. In about three hours he would be at his new home in Monroe, Alabama, seventy miles south of Auburn in Crawford County. Although he'd lived in Alabama for all of his twenty-five years, he had only been to Monroe on a few occasions. Nevertheless, he now envisioned it as the place where he would grow old and, of course, make tons of money along the way.

He'd come a long way in a short time—a long, long way. Just a few years ago he'd been in high school in Decatur, living with his mother and her numerous redneck boyfriends in one small apartment after another. Sandra Kirkland was the victim of her own bad decisions. She married Spence's father at the age of seventeen in an attempt to get the attention she never got from her own father, who always seemed to be more concerned about her older brother and his success. Yearning to get out of the small town of Monroe, she was happy to move to Birmingham and the promise of a new life. But her new husband was disappointed when her father's affluence didn't follow them to their new life in the city. He refused to work, kept late hours, and acquired new friends, both male and female. He was gone before Spence turned a year old and neither Spence nor Sandra ever heard from him again. Spence was in middle school when Visa came looking for someone to pay off the dead man's credit cards.

Sandra never recovered from being abandoned and refused to return to Monroe to hear the "I told you so" from her father. When the old man Kirkland died a few years after Spence's father had deserted them, Sandra inherited several hundred thousand dollars. But by then she was living a lifestyle that guaranteed it would never last. New boyfriends came and went—all unemployed losers. Early on, Sandra tried to be a good mother, taking Spence to boy-scout meetings and pee-wee football games, but the years of physical and mental abuse by the men she had chosen eventually numbed her to her son's needs. She became an alcoholic and rarely stayed home at night, moved from job to job, and spent most of his high school years embarrassing Spence. He remembered the only time she came to watch him play football. Late for kickoff, she got into a fight with another woman in the stands after a drunk Sandra spilt her bourbon-laced coke down the woman's back while making her way across the bleachers. Eventually both women were escorted out of the stadium by the local police and thus concluded the only awareness that most of his high school friends had of Spence's mother.

No doubt it was the neglect he suffered from his mother that—at least in part—caused Spence to turn all of his attention to sports and especially football. For Spence, football was the way in, and ultimately, his way out. It wasn't difficult to see that the harder he tackled the quarterback the more back slaps he got from the guys and the more looks he got from the girls. Without football he was just another guy who lived on the wrong side of town, but with it, even the bankers in Decatur were glad to see him at their door to pick up their daughters.

Spence found football as his way out of a life he had grown to despise with his mother and her friends, who to Spence, always seemed to make him the object of their ridicule. One of his most vivid memories as a child was one night when his mother and her current loser, a biker named Chuck, came home with a half dozen other boozed up non-socialites. Seven-year old Spence was watching cartoons on the living room sofa at 11:00 P.M. when they came through the door. He didn't see their lights coming through the window, or he would have run to his room and pretended to be asleep so he didn't have to face them. Once in the living room, Chuck and another biker friend immediately began to make fun of the youngster's choice of entertainment by doing their best impressions of Donald Duck, but using language that Walt Disney never intended for his characters to use. As Spence got up to leave the room, the second biker grabbed him in a bear hug and said, "Come on little buddy, let's wrassle." Spence had never forgotten the smell of the biker's musty leather jacket soaked with cigarette smoke and the cheap wine on his breath as the man pinned him to the ground and made him say "uncle." Spence relented quickly, just wanting to get out of the room, but Chuck decided it was his turn to play roughhouse with the child. He blocked the doorway to Spence's room and dared him to try and make it past. Spence took a running start and tried to elude the drunk, but Chuck tackled the youngster and slammed him to the floor, wrenched his arm behind his back and demanded that he say "uncle." Even at seven, Spence didn't want to let the redneck get the better of him and refused to give in. "Say uncle," Chuck demanded again, but Spence became even more angry and though the tears began to surface in his eyes from the pain and humiliation, he was able to catch his breath long enough to repeat a phrase he'd often heard his mother say to Chuck: "You go to hell."

"What'd you say to me kid?" Chuck asked, increasing the pressure.

"You heard me."

"Why you little!" Chuck twisted Spence's arm until he let out a scream. Finally, his mother came to his rescue. She slapped Chuck on the back of the head and said, "let'im up," as she passed by headed to the kitchen for another bottle of wine. Chuck gritted his teeth and gave one more twist before he let Spence go.

"Go to bed Spence," his mother shouted from the kitchen.

Spence wiped the tears from his eyes and stared at Chuck as he started towards his room. If he had been able, he would have killed him.

"You little cuss," Chuck mumbled as Spence passed by.

If he didn't sufficiently hate Chuck up to that point he certainly did after that night. From then on he always viewed his mother's boyfriends with certain skepticism, even if they were nice to him.

Most of Sandra's beaus, however, chose to ignore young Spence, following the lead provided by his mother. But every so often came the rambunctious one who wanted to get drunk and anywhere from physically rough to down right violent. The pattern continued until Spence's junior year in high school, when the teenager began to spend three hours a day in the weight room. One of his mother's more unfortunate boyfriends, Jerry, an overweight sometimes plumber, made the mistake one night of coming over drunk and, thinking Spence was still a helpless kid, began to use Sandra as a punching bag. He awoke the next morning to find himself in the bushes next to the parking lot outside of Spence's apartment. Jerry didn't remember what had happened, but the discoloration around his eye and the way it pounded every time his heart beat told him his evening had not been pleasant. Jerry never came back, which was fine with Sandra, who had someone waiting in the shadows to replace him anyway. That was the first time Spence had ever been in a fight, and it gave him an even bigger rush than blindsiding a quarterback. He often thought about trying to find Chuck, just to see if the aspiring

Hell's Angel wanted any part of the "little cuss" now.

For the most part, Spence came and went as he pleased during those high school years and his mother never asked where he was or what he was doing. After she was thrown out of the stadium, she never again saw him play football and never met any of his high school girlfriends, mainly because Spence had been too embarrassed to bring them around. He had only seen his mother once since he left for college. His sophomore year he felt a void and the same instinctive feelings that caused him to defend her from Jerry. Concerned to know if she was all right, or if one of her boyfriends had finally killed her, he borrowed a friend's car and drove back to Decatur, only to find she was as cold as before, never offering to change her nightly plans to spend time with her son. He hadn't seen her since.

Spence was offered a scholarship to play at Troy State University, where he lettered three years as a reserve linebacker. Although he was not as talented as many of his teammates, he perhaps could have starred as a Troy State Trojan. But despite his natural gifts and 6' 1", two hundred twenty pound frame, by this time in his life Spence approached football like he did most everything else—selfishly. He knew he could not make the NFL and knocking himself out for the good of the team never held much allure. He remained on the team to keep his scholarship, which also guaranteed good grades with minimum effort and plenty of attention from young sorority girls. Like people, football was a means to an end, and to Spence Thompson, only he and those who could help him get what he wanted were important. As for everybody else, Spence was perfectly polite—and utterly unconcerned.

Spence, however, was smart enough to notice that if he was courteous to people they tended to respond in the way that he wished. When he made it a habit of saying "yes ma'am" and "yes sir," his professors and the boosters of the Troy State football program became increasingly willing to help such a nice young man.

He avoided trouble in college and luckily it avoided him. There were no fights in bars or DUI's, because he knew he could not afford to lose his scholarship. Besides, he didn't have a car to drive anyway until he began earning money as a clerk for a firm in law school to buy the old black truck. In addition to the benefits of being polite, there was another important lesson Spence learned in college by watching the financial boosters of the school. The richer you were the better you were treated and Spence decided that after football he would get his admiration the old fashion way—by purchasing it.

Spence's first trip to Monroe had been with his mother some four-teen years earlier when Sandra, shut out of her family by choice, decided to drop in on Thanksgiving dinner and brought along her awkward eleven-year old son. Most of his relatives, whom he had never seen before, refused to acknowledge his presence—except for Sandra's older brother, Americus. Spence remembered how his uncle, white-haired even at the age of forty-nine, embraced him in a hug, like the two were long lost father and son. He remembered how they went to the backyard after dinner and threw the orange rubber foot-ball that Spence took everywhere he went. He remembered his uncle introducing him to quail hunting, when the two took a quick hunt-ing excursion on the family farm in the late November afternoon and Americus let the lad fire his first shotgun. He recalled sitting on the porch swing that night while Americus sipped from a glass of bour-bon and wondering why this wealthy, southern gentlemen was offer-ing advice and telling him that if he ever needed anything, all he had to do was call. From that day on, Spence kept in touch with his uncle, who remained, until Jack McCain came along, the only fatherly role model Spence would ever have. But he never asked for any favors. He somehow sensed that it would be wise to save his markers until the right moment arrived. Part of the reason he accepted the scholarship to Troy State was so he would only be an hour away from his uncle, who attended every home game. Like Spence's mother, Americus also liked a laced drink at a football game, but he knew how to handle himself and was always one of the more popular spectators in the stands.

Americus was the only person, besides the date he borrowed from a married man in Monroe for the evening, that attended Troy State's graduation ceremony on Spence's behalf. And it was also his uncle who convinced Spence to go to The University of Alabama Law School and promised him a job when he finished.

Spence was heading into a new town with a brighter future in front of him, but in a way he was disheartened at the end of an era in his life. He loved law school, disappointed to know that someday it had to end. The girls looking for a man with a nice income made easy targets and other than making fun of those who took school a little too seriously and seemed to age ten years in three, there was little for he and Wes to do besides enjoy themselves. They were the lucky ones who already had jobs when they finished their studies, Wes with his father and Spence with his uncle. Americus told his nephew that his grades didn't matter. Less than two weeks after law school no one would ever be concerned about them again. Not that Spence was concerned in the first place. He had no idea what his cumulative GPA was, nor did he ever bother to find out about his class ranking. He assumed it was somewhere near the bottom and he spared himself the embarrassment of going to the registrar to ask. He approached his grades like most everything else—without concern. Americus promised that all Spence needed to do was pass the bar and he would teach him the rest. Not wanting to disappoint his uncle, Spence studied feverishly for the bar exam, but again, once he found out that he passed, he never took the time to learn where his score ranked among the other potential attorneys. According to Americus such information was useless in Monroe, where the practice of law left plenty of time for quail hunting and weekend trips to Atlanta, without all the hustle and stress of big time law firms.

Spence had seen how the top students in his class exhausted themselves trying to win positions at the top firms in Atlanta and Birmingham. Why work so hard to get a job where you could work eighty hours a week and make fifty thousand dollars a year, while making the partners a quarter of a million? And for icing on the cake, if the stress, divorce and alcoholism didn't kill you by the age of forty, then the worrying and wondering of whether or not you would ever make partner surely would. Spence believed that the quiet life of Monroe, Alabama was going to suit him just fine.

The landscape from Atlanta to Montgomery was flat and dry in the heat of the summer. Around LaGrange, Georgia the highway median was adorned with crépe myrtles and small colorful flowers, a lasting legacy of Lady Bird Johnson's Highway Beautification program. He admired the beauty of the terrain that was unmistakably the Deep South. Americus had promised Spence a big surprise when he got to Monroe, but even this did not speed up the old ragged truck. They continued at their gentle pace while the rest of their fellow travelers zipped by. Occasionally, a car full of children would smile at Sam with her head out the window. It was summer in the South and Spence wasn't bringing any extra troubles with him to his new life in Monroe. The radio talked of droughts hurting farmers and the layoff of factory workers at large companies, but as far as he could tell, life couldn't get any better for Spencer Michael Thompson. And that was all that mattered.

THREE

THE CRAWFORD COUNTY courthouse was a legacy of the early twentieth century South. A square red brick building with decorative masonry work on its outside walls, it had four large white pillars that elevated thirty feet into the air at both the north and south entrances. The east and west walls were adorned by large windows with triangular brick patterns over the eaves like the windows of the White House in Washington. On top of the structure sat a white dome with an unworking clock centered at the front, frozen in time at 2:30 for nearly fifteen years. Located in the middle of the town square, the courthouse no longer housed most of the county's important business, but it was well maintained as a source of pride for the people of Monroe and their past.

Spence parked the black Ford truck in one of the parking spaces on the town square. Across the street was the office of his uncle, Americus Kirkland. Casually dressed in blue jeans and a Abercrombie & Fitch T-shirt, the town's newest lawyer walked unnoticed into his office.

Americus' law office was a two-story structure that, like the others surrounding the town square, was completely different from the building on either side of it. It was solid red brick with a pointed roof, and Spence was sure that it had looked very stately at one time. Now, it just looked old. The buildings on either side were white with decorative trim and in bad need of a paint job. One had a pointed gabled roofline while the other was flat. There was nothing symmetrical about the buildings of the town square, and in fact, it was as if the designer tried to be as arbitrary and unbalanced as possible. But like most small southern towns, the people of Monroe made it all blend together and seem natural.

As Spence opened the door, a bell rang down the hall to let Kathy, Americus' latest secretary, know that someone had entered the building. Americus had a reputation for high turnover in his secretarial positions and finally decided to hire one that would not tempt his passion for trashy-looking women. From her upstairs desk, Kathy put down her "Shape" magazine and hoisted her five-foot-one-inch, two-hundred-pound body up and out of her office and towards the rail overlooking the lobby. The downstairs lobby had a receptionist station immediately to the right of the doorway, which would have been perfect for Kathy to welcome guests. But Americus was a businessman and always looking for the upper hand. He preferred for his clients to enter the lobby below, have Kathy come find out who they were, and if he wanted to see them, he would come out and greet them from the rail. They were forced to look up at him until he mercifully asked them to come up the curved staircase and into his office. Americus was certainly not the most organized lawyer in town and his office management skills were only adequate at best. But he did understand that in the business world perception meant so much more than reality, and he seldom missed an opportunity to press his advantage.

As Kathy waddled to the front she immediately felt the blood rush to her face when she peered over the handrail and found Spence looking back at her. Her expression made no secret that she didn't expect such an attractive man to grace the elderly building. The rush of color in her face clearly showed all of her imperfections, a hard task through her seemingly inches of makeup. She stared at Spence over the rail with a mischievous smile as a flood of improper thoughts ran through her mind. After an awkward five to ten seconds, Spence finally broke the silence and Kathy's blush.

"Hello, you must be Kathy?"

"Please, God, tell me you're Spence," Kathy gushed.

"Yes, as a matter of fact I am," Spence said, then waited another eight to ten seconds for a reply, while Kathy stood hanging her large chest over the rail of the second floor, gazing down at Spence and continuing to shake her head with the big smile on her face.

"Is my uncle here?"

"Of course he is, of course he is, Honey," Kathy said, hurrying down the curved staircase, something she never did. She thought it was stupid that Americus had her greet clients from the second floor, and she never actually came down to escort them up the stairs. But such a fine specimen was evidently more than a single woman in Monroe could take. She ran down, expending more energy than she had in a month, grabbed him by the left arm and began to drag him up the stairs. "You're going to be real happy here," she exclaimed. "I'm going to make sure of that, Honey. You just ask me if you need anything. Anything at all, okay? I'm a full service secretary. You hear that, Honey, a full service secretary. We're real professional around here, but"—she lowered her voice seductively— "we're like, intimate too."

Spence began to feel a little uneasy about what Kathy's definition of intimacy might be, but was able to mutter, "Okay, I will," as she escorted him up the stairs, down the hall and into Americus' office.

When Spence and an out of breath Kathy reached the doorway of Americus' office, they found the old gentleman reclined in his large leather chair, asleep, with a burning cigar in the corner of his mouth. Even in a slumber, Americus would occasionally give a big inhale on the cigar, and exhale through his nose. Spence watched in amazement for a few seconds, then asked, "Are y'all always this professional?"

"Americus!" Kathy scolded at the top of her lungs. "Wake up! Your nephew's here!"

At the sound of Kathy's voice, Americus jumped in his chair, and the lit cigar fell from his lips to his lap. Unable to gain control of the cigar, he tried to unseat himself from the large leather chair, but his lanky legs were trapped underneath the opening in his desk. With a loud scream, he finally rolled out of the chair and onto the floor, where he sat up on his knees and furiously dusted the crotch of his pants to remove the ashes. The still lit cigar rolled to the base of the wall and began to burn a mark on the carpet. Americus reached out and grabbed it, stuck it back in his mouth and glared at Kathy.

"Damn it, Kathy, is it necessary to scream that loud?"

"That's no way to greet your new employee. What kind of impression are you trying to make? I just got through informin' him of how professional we are around here, and then we come in here and find you drooling cigar smoke." Kathy shook her head as she lectured her boss. "Maybe if you didn't spend so much time with that floozy across town, you'd get some sleep at night and wouldn't be sleeping on the job."

"You're the highest paid secretary in south Alabama, especially for your skill level, so I must be taking care of business," Americus yelled back.

"Should I come back later?" Spence asked, worrying that the argument would escalate.

"Of course not, ma boy," Americus exclaimed, as he picked himself off the floor and widened his trademark grin, "This kind of thing is normal around here. Don't worry, you'll get used to it. I know you must be tired from all the driving you've been doing. Come in, take a load off."

As Spence entered the office, Kathy placed a short fat finger on his chest and said, "Remember, Honey, anything." She then gave the most seductive smile she was capable of, and attempted to strut off.

Spence entered the office and took Americus' hand, who returned a firm handshake. Americus Kirkland was a thin man, about five feet eleven inches and a hundred fifty pounds. He had thick white hair, except for some black that remained around the roots, a mustache to match, and his face was always tan even if he hadn't seen the sun in months. A bowtie was standard attire and his clothes were usually wrinkled—from sleeping in them on a regular basis. His shoes were old and ragged and his shirt stained, but somehow he still had a sense of style about him. A Southern aristocratic charm that had been his birthright, and no matter what his appearance, he was always elegant. Spence had always been a firm believer that the clothes made the man, but Americus' style came from something inside, from his heritage, and it was something that even Armani runway models couldn't imitate. Americus' father had been a dreamer, and in fact had taken his dreams all the way to the state capitol, as an Alabama State Senator for twelve years. This was about all Spence had known of his grandfather. This, and that he wanted his first-born son to be named America, in recognition of his great patriotic pride. Even though it was still an awkward name, Spence's grandmother bargained with the elder Kirkland for the name Americus, who was grateful, though most people now believed him to be named after a small southwest Georgia town. Naming him aside, Grandpa Kirkland had big dreams for his son and education and law school were never an option. Spence often wondered if Grandpa Kirkland were still alive would he be disappointed in Americus for not having made the White House yet. Probably not. After all, both U.S. Senators from Alabama as well as the state's governor recognized his voice when he called them on the telephone, which he did often.

"How've ya been my boy?"

"Fine, sir, and you?"

"Wonderful, wonderful. Just getting prepared for your arrival. I've got some good things happening for you and we'll get them started with a little drink."

Bourbon was Americus' second most favorite pastime, nestled

right between cigars and women. He walked over to the fully stocked bar he kept in his office and pulled out a bottle of Crown Royal.

"On ice or straight up?" Americus asked.

Spence thought better of asking for a little Coke in his drink, deciding he would start now with the transition from law student to lawyer. He did not know of any lawyers who drank bourbon and Coke and being able to handle your whiskey apparently came with the profession.

"A little ice, please," Spence responded and then quickly added, "with a splash of water," in fear that he would cringe at his first attempt of straight liquor.

Americus frowned at his nephew's weakness. He poured himself a straight shot, drank it, and poured another before getting around to Spence's drink.

"So, ma' boy, whadaya think of Kathy?" Americus asked handing Spence a glass.

"Well, I really don't know. I'm sure she's a wonderful secretary."

"She sucks," Americus responded, taking a sip of his drink and leaving Spence to wonder if the statement was to be interpreted in its most literal sense. "But she's fat and ugly, so that's the trade off," Americus finished.

"Not much of a trade off."

"Oh ma' boy, contraire, contraire. Business lesson number one that took me thirty years to figure out is never to hire an attractive secretary. There'll be plenty of time for frolicking, but when it comes to work, that's exactly what it should be. Work. If you play while you work then you will spend more time working when you should be playing. Understand?"

Spence nodded his head in agreement and took a drink. It was awful.

"Remember now, Spence," said Americus, getting down to business, "it's just like I told you. Contrary to the name, this is not really a law firm. It's a business, and I'm a businessman. The most dangerous

kind, one with a law degree. I don't do trials or cases. If the need aris-
es, I hire another attorney. My business is real estate, loans, banking,
and I get business from all over the state. I'm sure you've had professional responsibility, which taught you not to solicit clients. Well, forget about it. I am always looking for new clientele, and I keep them
very happy with extra perks, if you know what I mean." Americus
raised his eyebrows. "Repetitive business, easy repetitive business,
that's what we're looking for and I've got plenty of it for you to start
on. Let those other lawyers sweat with trials and such. I've got steady
income and enough warehouses from Mobile to Birmingham that if I
didn't feel like getting out of bed this morning I would've made
$2,000 today. Understand what we're doing, son?"

"Sounds like we're getting rich."

"Correction, ma' boy, you're getting rich. I'm already there. C'mon
I've got some things to show you."

Americus poured himself another drink, ran his fingers through
his thick white hair and motioned for Spence to follow him out of the
office and back into the hallway, past Kathy and her "Shape" magazine. She pretended not to notice them coming her way, but when
they passed she tilted her head sideways to get a good long stare at
Spence from the back. They turned down the hall and into a spacious
office with Spence's name on the door.

"This is your office, ma' boy. Whadaya think?"

The office was big and, of course, outfitted with a well stocked
bar. It had cherry-wood finished cornice board that ran from the
floor to about three feet up the wall and then capped with more
cherry molding. From the center molding to the ceiling the walls
were freshly painted white with thick crown molding at the top.
The ceiling had a decorative chandelier and a centerpiece medallion
from which it hung. The carpet was bright red, thick and new. The
desk and credenza were rich, dark mahogany and a big leather chair
sat between them. There was a new Compaq computer on the corner of the credenza, already running with the screen saver flashing

stars. It was perfect.

"You've got to be kidding me," Spence said, unable to suppress his smile.

"A man can't work in those dreary little places where they make associates bill hours in Birmingham and Montgomery, especially not a businessman lawyer. C'mon I've got some other things to show you."

Spence took one more look around, appreciatively inspecting every corner of his new office and then went back down the hall where Americus was giving Kathy some instructions.

"If Wilson calls from First National, tell him I'll do whatever he wants to do on the Taylor closing. Understood?"

"Of course I understand. I hope you don't think you could give me something I couldn't do?"

"Of course not, my dear. And Spence, why will I do anything that Mr. Wilson wants?"

"Because he's the client...customer...whatever."

"See how fast he learns, Kathy. That's something you might want to pick up on. We won't be back this afternoon." Americus finished off his drink and sat his glass on the corner of Kathy's desk. Spence did the same, except his glass was still half full. He looked at Kathy to give her a smile.

"Bye, Honey. I'll see you in the morning," Kathy tried again.

"I'm looking forward to it," he answered.

Spence and his uncle left the law office through a back door as the same bell rang down the hall. In the back alley Americus' black Mercedes stood ready with what seemed to be at least three inches of dust on its hood and trunk. Once in the car, Spence barely had time to fumble for his seatbelt before Americus jammed the car into gear, stomped on the gas, and left a big cloud of dust on the dirt surface of the alley. Now even more concerned, Spence furiously tried to find the buckle of his seatbelt and finally came to the conclusion that it was hopelessly stuffed behind the seat and he had no chance of sur-viving what was sure to be a hellacious crash. Meanwhile, Americus drove through town like he was practicing for the Talladega Super Speedway. In fact, Spence noticed that with his slight of build, white hair and mustache, the old man slightly resembled Richard Petty. All he needed was a cowboy hat adorned with a feather.

The whole time Americus was talking as fast as he was driving, about being a businessman and not a lawyer, keeping clients happy, and not sleeping with your secretary. Spence was barely paying attention to Americus, but was wholly interested in his new town.

Monroe, like many small Southern towns, seemed quiet yet busy. It was old, but technology was in evidence. Citizens here had cellular phones and beepers, and most people knew what you were talking about if you mentioned the Web, or at least they knew it had something to do with a computer. It was a town of many types of people—black, white, and even a Vietnamese family that ran a Chinese restaurant—and a wide assortment of characters living within its borders. Anything from wife beaters, alcoholics, gays and lesbians, drug addicts, to a few condemned souls who were brave enough to admit they were atheist. And contrary to the prevailing view of small Southern towns, whites and blacks lived in harmony for the most part. They worked together, went to school together, played on the same sports teams together, shopped at the same stores and it was not uncommon nor frowned upon to see them walking down the street together, provided there was a good explanation. There were seldom fights between the two that could not be explained as just boys being boys. It was a town where you could shake a man's hand in public and not have to worry about what color his skin was or what others would think. On the other hand, interracial relationships were frowned upon by both races. The two races had their own favorite restaurants and—the most notable holdover from segregation—their own churches. And there were always those who blamed everything on the other race and who privately went about the business of making life miserable for the "other side." It was like a lot of small towns, and that suited Spence just fine. His approach to the cause of ending racism was just like his attitude toward any other issue that did not benefit him directly—unconcerned.

"You understand, ma' boy…" Spence quickly came to the realization that Americus had never ceased talking and that there was presumably some wisdom to be learned from the lecture. "It's always good to keep them satisfied," Americus continued, "but it never hurts to have a little dirt on them as well. You've got to know if they're a closet drinker, or who they're seein' across town while her husband's on the night shift out at the mill. You follow all that and you'll do fine. And don't forget, sincerity is the key to trust, so you've really got to learn how to fake it."

Spence wasn't sure what he was answering too, but he nodded in agreement. The black Mercedes was about five miles out of town now and traveling on a road that would've been in better condition had the county never paved it at all. The dust of a dirt road would be a nice trade-off for the bumps and potholes. There were deep pine woods on each side of the road, just like the forest Spence had seen during his last hour of driving into Monroe.

In a break in one of the tree lines, Americus turned down a dirt road that cut back almost one hundred eighty degrees from the direction they had just come. On the right was the same pine thicket they passed on the paved road, but on the left was an open field with a tree line in the distance. About a quarter of a mile down the road, Americus turned the Mercedes onto a graveled driveway and proceeded through a white fence surrounding a house that was old, but freshly painted and in pretty good shape judging by its age. Spence thought it was in better condition than the house he remembered Americus was living in, although it was a quarter of the size.

"Whadaya think, ma' boy?"

"This is nice, Unc, but I didn't know you'd moved since my last visit."

"Me? Move? Good Lord, no, boy. This is your house."

"My house? I can't pay for this!" Spence's voice suddenly grew with excitement. " I've got student loans to pay for and I need a new car if I'm going to have to shmooze with clients. I thought maybe I could stay with you for a few days, until I could get an apartment or something." Spence shook his head, "There's no way I can pay for this."

"Relax, it's already paid for. I own it and I'm selling it to you for a fixed payment with no interest. You can pay me whatever a month you can afford and if you miss a payment, then you just miss a payment."

Spence's excitement soon turned into a calm smile. He stepped out of the Mercedes and stared a moment at the front of the house. It was a traditional white farmhouse with green shutters and a porch that ran the entire length of its front side. A garage, an obvious later addition, stood attached to the right. Spence walked around the front of the car and followed the walkway to the wooden steps and the porch.

"Go on in. It's open," Americus said, still standing beside the Mercedes.

"You mean you left my house unlocked," Spence said back.

He pushed open the door that led him into a large living room with a marble fireplace—a room bigger, he was pretty sure, than his last apartment. He walked to the middle of the room and admired it. Seeing the hallway to the left, he entered and turned to go to the master bedroom at the end of the hall. He passed the bathroom, the only part of the house showing its original age, with a pedestal sink and ceramic tile floor. But still, it was clean and serviceable. The hardwood floor squeaked every time Spence took a step until he made it to the end of the hall. The bedroom was large with a big window on each of the two walls facing the outside. There was a bed against one wall, the only piece of furniture in the house that Spence had seen. Spence walked to the window facing the back of the house and stared at the large tract of clear-cut land immediately behind the fence. The land was beautiful and he could see himself and Sam quail hunting in the early morning sun. Suddenly he remembered: he had forgotten that Sam was still in the bed of his truck outside the courthouse.

He could see her wagging her tail excitedly at the prospect of getting some attention whenever anybody passed by. His concentration came back to the house. Sam would be just as excited as he was.

"So, I take it you like the house," Americus had entered the room and was now standing just a few feet directly behind Spence.

"Jesus, you scared me. I didn't even hear you coming. How did you walk through the house without the floors squeaking?"

With a slight deviousness in his eyes, something Spence did not know Americus was capable of, he replied, "Ma' boy, you'd be surprised at what this old man is able—and willing—to do."

"I bet I would," Spence answered, and the two stood there for a second grinning at one another.

Americus turned for the door, "I've got to go now," he said. "It's almost happy hour, which I never miss. My maid, Miss Ophelia, will be by every Monday and Thursday to clean for you. There's a new Eddie Bauer Explorer in the garage. If it's not the color you like, take it back and get what you want. Even though I co-signed for the car, unfortunately for you, you'll have to make payments on this one. I've also arranged some credit for you at the furniture store in town. Don't worry about a washing machine Miss Ophelia will take care of your laundry. But college football will be starting in almost a month, so if you expect to have company in these parts on Saturdays, I suggest you get a television."

"Unc, how can I…"

"Make me some money, ma' boy. I'm a businessman, remember?"

FOUR

SHE SAT ON the cot in her orange county-issued clothing and peeled gray paint from the wall, continuing in a spot her predecessors had started before her. Her face was still hurting from the large bruise on her left eye and she could feel her pulse in the wound every time her heart kept its rhythm, which at this moment was faster than normal. The events shaping her life in the past few days were coming more into focus, but she still couldn't believe she had committed the act she always thought herself incapable of. She never had the strength, physically or mentally, and in fact knew she wouldn't have been able to do it, had it not been for... for what? That was the part driving her crazy. What caused her to do it? Where did she find the strength? The night had begun as such a normal event. He would beat her, sometimes to unconsciousness, and then she would either awake to find what else he had done to her, or if she remained conscious, flee into the nearby pine thickets and wait until he was asleep to return. She remembered him coming home, the beating, but then nothing. How did she get back inside after she did it? How did she get to the bat that always remained on the porch?

Angela Chauncey sat in her Crawford County jail cell pondering all of these questions and considered how bleak her future now seemed. Not that she had a bright future to begin with, but she had certainly hit bottom now. Or had she? At least he was out of her life, whatever life that promised to be from now on.

She was in a place surrounded by strangers with no one left to turn to in the entire town, even though she had lived in Monroe all of her life. They told her she could make a phone call, but she had no one to call, not even a preacher. She was alone in part because of the color of her skin and because of her father's past that followed behind her, though she had chosen neither. The skin, with all of its creamy rich beauty, had been a curse, and her family background, even though she was a descendent of some of Alabama's oldest money, had done even more to seal her fate.

She was the daughter of Calvin Chauncey, perhaps the greatest baseball player ever born in Crawford County. So good were Calvin's skills that he became the first black player from the county to receive a scholarship to play at The University of South Alabama. Calvin was an incredible athlete and not unintelligent, but he failed to abide by the unwritten conditions of his scholarship, which mandated that he stay away from the white females who attended the university. Perhaps it was this very unwritten law, which did not conform well to Calvin's rebellious personality, that caused him to actively pursue one of the most coveted prizes of all, the equally rebellious Leigh Anne Jenkins, daughter of wealthy Mobile lawyer, Thomas Jenkins. The two met while on the campus of South Alabama, and soon, in an open declaration of defiance, he to the white race and she to her father, began publicly seeing one another. When Leigh Anne's father forced her from the South Alabama campus to attend Judson College, an all female school in Marion, it was Calvin who came to rescue her and his child she carried in her womb. This meant the loss of his scholarship and a return to Monroe, where he and his new bride moved into a little shack deep in the pine trees that provided wood chips for the new NAPCO paper mill. The mill in turn provided Calvin with a job. But after the baby was born, he began feeling that he'd made a mistake by giving up his athlete's life just to spite the white man, who didn't seem to be concerned with who he married anyway. He began using the drugs that now circulated in the tiny town of Monroe, and soon he was strung out most of his days, except for when he reserved his strength for Leigh Anne's beatings. Unaccustomed to the pitiful life she now led, Leigh Anne ran back to her father, who wouldn't accept her back into his family, but did give her enough money to leave Alabama and keep from further upsetting her mother. This left a young Angela, a child of only three at the time, to become the objects of Calvin's rage at a life gone wrong.

The child attended local schools when the truant officer threatened Calvin, who would just as soon have given her up, were it not for the purposes she served. As soon as she was old enough he forced her to drop out, which saddened her more than anything. By forcing her to quit school he had killed both her body and soul. Learning was the one thing that came easy, and while most of the other kids ignored her, she always felt special because of her teacher's constant praise. She was the student who was always ahead and always prepared. Her instructors felt sorry for her, of course, but they also respected her intelligence. They taught her at school that if you wanted more out of life, education was the only way to get it, and when Calvin took it away, it was the same as slamming the iron door she now sat behind.

With the combination of her parent's skin and athletic genes, she was the most naturally beautiful girl in the entire county, but an outcast to both races. She had never been asked out on a date—not that Calvin would have let her go anyway. She had made a few friends in school, though she had been relegated to the misfit group of overweight girls and nerdy young boys, but she lost touch with them, too, when her father forced her to quit after her sixteenth birthday. Had she been all one race or the other, anybody would have naturally assumed her to be the head cheerleader. At five feet six inches tall, she had the body of a track star, long silky black hair and big brown eyes.

Her facial features included a small nose, high cheekbones and a slender neck. Her arms and legs were muscular, yet smooth.

And then there was the skin. Deep, rich, and creamy, it was the color of caramel. But her most beautiful asset was the very reason that few came near her. She was the lustful dream of many schoolboys, both black and white, though they dared not admit it. What would their friends say? Sell out? Nigger lover? From either side she couldn't win. And thanks to her father, she had already lost.

She had heard that her mother died of a heroin overdose in California, and now her father was gone too. According to the sheriff, thanks to her and a Louisville Slugger. But that was the part she couldn't remember. Oh, yes, she had thought about it a million times. How she would do it and where she would run when she did. She had never been more than thirty miles from her home in all of her nineteen years, but she knew there was a life out there, she had read about it. And she knew the only thing stopping her from finding it was her father.

She tried to run on two previous occasions. Once, after she turned sixteen and was forced to quit school, she ran to the paved road some five miles from her house and eventually waved down a deputy police officer. In school they taught her that policemen were your friends and could be trusted. The deputy took her back to the station where she began to tell her story of the abuse she was taking from her father. That's when Sheriff Watkins came back to the office and told everyone she was lying. He put her into his car and took her back to the little shack and her father, who didn't wait until the sheriff was gone before hitting her twice in the face. After that she knew there was no going to the police for help.

Her second attempt came a little over a year later. She managed to steal a grand total of one hundred dollars in dollar bills and lose change from her father, who stayed too high to know where his money went. One night while he was gone to work, she took the money and a change of clothes and ran into the woods. Her plan was to head deeper into the pine forest until she crossed a paved road and then she would try to make it to another town with the money she had. The first night she slept in the woods, shivering from the cold of the early part of winter. The next day she walked deeper into the forest, but never found a road. Later that night, tired, cold, and hungry, she decided to stay on a dirt road until it lead her to a highway. About an hour after dark she saw the headlights of a car and decided to take a chance that it was somebody who would help her. Blinded by the headlights, she couldn't see that it was a police car until it was upon her. She panicked when Sheriff Watkins stepped from his patrol car and ran into the woods. She tripped over a fallen tree and sprained her ankle allowing Watkins to catch up, otherwise the fat man would've never had a chance. Watkins took her back to her father, who quickly made her forget about the discomfort of her swollen ankle by giving her much more intensified pain to deal with. He told her if she ever tried to run again, he would kill her.

She was about to try again. She estimated that she was only about a month away from having two hundred dollars stolen from her father, and she had been waiting for him to buy some groceries to take with her. This time she would disappear so far into the woods that Sheriff Watkins would never find her, and she would not stop running until she found a place that knew nothing about her. But now she would never get that chance.

As she relived these thoughts, the paint chips from the wall began collecting on the floor at a much faster rate. The underside of her fingernails became red with irritation from her task, but she continued to peel at the wall. Her thoughts of him, even after his death, made her feel sick inside and her anger showed in her work.

A tear developed in the corner of her eye and then rolled over the high check bones of her face and across her chin. Her lip quivered. She could no more fight back the tears than she could the memories. She did not know a lot about the world, but she knew daddies didn't treat their little girls that way. But then Calvin was not her daddy.

He was just a man who had slept with her mother and then stole every dream his only daughter ever had. She hated him.

Maybe they were right.

Maybe she did kill him.

FIVE

SAM DIDN'T SEEM the least disappointed in Spence for leaving her in the back of the truck for the entire afternoon. She could feel his excitement over their new vehicle as he called her into the Explorer where she gladly claimed her spot in the passenger seat, sliding around on the new leather. She sniffed the console and dash, then turned to examine the backseat, her wagging tail wiping the inside of the windshield.

Spence found a note on the windshield of his old truck with directions from Kathy. It instructed him to join Americus at the Chamber of Commerce building at eight o' clock to meet some of their clientele at the Friday night social. He wondered how Kathy had known which vehicle was his, because in Monroe there seemed to be a black Ford truck behind every tree. And there were a lot of trees. It was already 7:08, so Spence threw his things into the Explorer and headed back to his new house.

Inside the house Spence gave Sam the grand tour and watched her excitement as she ran from room to room, paws clicking on the hardwood floors. Realizing he was wasting time, he dashed to the bathroom for a quick shower. The plumbing didn't have nearly enough water pressure to suit him, and he made a mental note to ask if there was anything he could do about it. There was no soap or shampoo, but the warm water still felt nice after a full day of traveling. Americus had thought of towels, or at least Miss Ophelia had, and Spence claimed one of the two that hung on a rack next to the bathroom door. He rubbed the towel over his face and head, dried the beads of water that formed all over his body and then hung the wet towel over the shower rod to dry. He rummaged through his shaving kit for his deodorant and hairbrush, which he ran through his short black hair. There was no hairdryer, but he never used one anyway. It would be dry in a few minutes.

He laid his only suit on the bed, grateful that Americus had supplied at least this one piece of furniture. He dressed quickly, left Sam with instructions to guard the house and headed out the door to the Chamber of Commerce, following Kathy's map.

When he arrived at the little brick building in the center of town, the meeting was already in progress. He found Americus in a full rendition of Walt Whitman's "Song of Myself," slurring most of the words to a delighted crowd, who would occasionally take a few steps back to keep the bourbon, which overflowed freely as Americus waved his glass, from spilling on their shoes. When he saw Spence, Americus completely dropped his glass in a dramatic fashion and, still holding his arms out, rushed through the crowd with fresh bourbon on their footwear, which followed him as if he were further acting out his interpretation. He tossed his arm around Spence and announced, "Ladies and Gentlemen, I give you my newest associate, Mr. Spencer Michael Thompson."

There were only about fifteen people in the room, but to Spence it seemed like a hundred in a very small place, and he suddenly felt crowded. They were all mumbling to one another and though only a few feet away, Spence couldn't understand what any of them were saying. Spence had heard Americus say that small town inhabitants have the ability to talk about someone standing right in front of them while that person is unable to understand what was being said. But

Spence was finally able to make out a few words from two middle-aged women who stood just to the side of him and remarked to each other about his pleasant appearance. When he decided the mumbling had gone on long enough, Spence announced to the crowd, "It's very nice to meet you all."

Then Americus announced: "Spence is going to be handling some accounts for all of you, so I hope you will take it easy on him."

"Don't take it easy on me," Spence replied "make sure I make it easy for you."

Americus gave Spence a little nudge with his arm, feeling that was exactly the type of response a business-lawyer should've made. He liked his nephew and it was obvious.

Having broken the ice, Spence worked the room like a seasoned politician, shaking hands with everyone, setting up lunch dates with the ladies and hunting trips with the men. His uncle watched him with a close eye the entire night and could tell he'd done a very good thing by bringing his nephew to Monroe. The crowd adored Spence. His manners were perfect as always, and it was easy to see he was going to be a very valuable asset.

To Spence, the gathering was not much different than a fraternity party, where he had learned how to scan the room for the people who could be of use. When he was sure he had introduced himself to everyone, and guests were starting to leave, he made his way to Americus, who was talking to Marc Wilson, a loan officer at the First National Bank of Monroe.

Mr. Wilson was a funny shaped man who looked liked he was always slumped over and whose choice of clothing did nothing to help his appearance. His suit was at least a full size too big, causing his coat to sag and his pants to bunch up around his ankles. He was a rather short man with a large belly, balding head, and apparently poor eyesight, judging by the thickness of his glasses. Spence stuck out his hand and greeted him.

"So Spence, how are you liking our little town?" Wilson asked.

"I like what I see so far. I'm just worried about having enough places to eat. I'm a single man you know."

"Well, you're always welcome to come over to my house. If you'll eat some of my wife's cooking, that'll be less that I'll have to force down. I was just talking to your uncle here about how it's a shame you didn't get to meet Richard Powell. He was one of the nicer lawyers in town."

"What happened to Mr. Powell?"

"Hunting accident," Americus quickly interjected. "Back during the hunting season last year. They still don't know exactly where the bullet came from. All they know is he was shot with a 30-06 at over a thousand yards. Given the land he was hunting on, it could've come from anywhere. What's worse is every redneck in Monroe has at least two 30-06's in his arsenal."

"Yeah," replied Wilson, "they really ought to watch who they let hunt out there."

"Hunt out where?" Spence inquired.

"Some of NAPCO's land south of town," Wilson replied. "They'll give a permit to hunt on it to anyone. There are so many people out there with rifles they ought to know somebody's gonna get hurt. Unfortunately for Richard, it'd be too late to do anything now,"

"What type of law did Mr. Powell practice?" Spence asked.

"Everything at first," Americus huffed. "All small town lawyers practice any kind of law they can get their hands on when they first start, but most recently Richard handled most of the town's appointed case work."

"I sure hope you didn't practice every thing at first," said Spence to his uncle. "Please don't tell me some poor old jury had to listen to your drama for afternoons at a time."

"You mean you don't know about the great Americus Kirkland, trial lawyer?" Wilson spurted back. "Your uncle has never been defeated in a trial."

"Civil trial," Americus retorted, raising his finger and glass to

Wilson. "I've never had the unfortunate circumstances of having to argue a criminal trial."

"What happened?" asked Spence, surprised. He knew Americus hated courtroom practice. "Did the judges in town refuse to hear your cases? If you never lost a trial you had to be making some pretty good money. Why'd you quit?"

"Well, you see, Spence, you're not too far off the mark," replied Americus. "James Hamilton, who is now the circuit judge in town, was only two years ahead of me in law school, even though he's probably ten years older. He had to work for a living while daddy paid for mine. By the time I got out, he was defending most of the insurance companies in these parts. The first case I had against him, I burned him for thirty thousand dollars, which was an awful lot of money back in those days. It raised quite a ruckus in the local print. From then on, I think the townspeople just kind of assumed I was supposed to win and kept deciding in my favor. It got to the point where I could sue for anything and, in fact, I just about was. I won thirty-one cases in a row, 'cause God knows Hamilton refused to settle a damn one. Of course, this meant that he hated me and figured the only way to keep me from winning all my cases was to get elected as the judge, which he did. So to keep from giving him the satisfaction of throwing my cases out of his court, I started practicing the type of law that didn't require going to court, but I'll bet he's still waiting on me to try one. I'm surprised the sum-bitch hasn't had me appointed to do some sort of public defense work. He knows how much I hate criminal law."

"So you never do anything that requires a judge's approval?"

"Hell no. If something comes up I refer it out to one of the other lawyers in town. Of course"—Americus wrapped his arm around Spence's shoulder—"now I won't have to because I have this stud of a new associate that I can throw to the wolves."

"Thanks!"

"So, did you guys hear about Calvin?" Wilson asked.

"Yes, I did," replied Americus. "I still can't believe that poor little fragile thing had the strength to do it. Calvin was the best athlete I ever saw back in his day, and even strung out on drugs he'd have been quite a match."

"Hold on, fellows," Spence held up his hands. "I'm still new here."

"Oh, just a story out where the pavement ends," Wilson replied. "Calvin was one of the town's best athletes about twenty years ago. The whole town treated him like he was a favorite son, even though he was black. He got a scholarship, went off to college and got a white girl pregnant. The school boosters, of course, took his scholarship away, and he's been mad at the white world ever since," Wilson finished.

"And he decided to punish us all by keeping himself strung out on drugs and alcohol," Americus said. "Sure is a shame. His mama was fine people." Americus took another sip from his drink.

Spence seemed agitated. "Well, get to the good stuff. What the hell happened?"

"Well," said Wilson in a confidential tone, "Calvin worked out at NAPCO. When his ride came to pick him up yesterday for work, they found his head beat in with a baseball bat. Sheriff Watkins found his half-breed daughter in the pine trees behind their shack. No telling what Calvin had done to the child—or woman, I guess it would be now. For trial purposes, I mean. Huh, Americus?"

"Oh yeah, they would try her as an adult if she were only twelve, but she's got to be at least nineteen or twenty by now."

"Any chance she can use self defense?" Spence wondered aloud. "From the way you guys are talking it sounds like Calvin used her as a sparring partner."

"Oh' I'm sure he did that and much more," declared Americus, "but in this town she doesn't have a chance. Whites aren't going to be sympathetic to a half-breed and the blacks, despite all of his short-comings, still considered Calvin a god. They're not going to take kindly to the killer of their fallen hero, even though none of them associated with the bastard anymore anyway."

"C'mon Unc, we're in the twenty-first century you know. This isn't 1940. Are you saying that a young girl who's been physically abused by her father can't get a fair trial no matter what color her skin is." Spence surprised himself. He sounded as if he were defending this girl.

"Oh no, son," Americus defended his statement. "We all work and play fine with each other, when we know what we're dealing with. A young black girl, raped by a white man would do fine with an all white jury, if she were truly black. Just as a white girl would be alright with an all black jury. We all know what's right and wrong, even though we all have our separate places and thoughts. But you see, you can't always be sure what goes on inside a person's head, since he may be saying one thing and thinking another. As long as we can clearly place someone in one category or another, our minds let us justify our lives. It's when we can't make the classification that we began to be nearsighted. As time goes on we become more accustomed to different things and we can live and work together as long as everyone knows where they, and everyone else, fits. It's when we don't know where to categorize someone, that we, like all animals, become scared. In that sense, small towns are no different than the biggest cities on earth, it just shows more clearly here because we're not as immune to as many different lifestyles. The fear of the unknown will always be the greatest fear for all men, no matter where they live."

"Will she have a good lawyer, now that Mr. Powell is gone?" Spence inquired.

"Don't matter," Americus stated, still washing the bourbon over his tongue. "She doesn't have a snowball's chance in hell."

SIX

THE THIRTEENTH BOXCAR. That's what they told him. Unload all the other cars over the drop bins numbered two and three, but make sure the thirteenth car was unloaded over the first drop bin into the dump trucks below. When he worked on the day shift they told him never to drop anything into the first bin, making him wonder what the first bin was used for—why the grating that covered its opening was always clean, while the grating over the second and third bins were filthy with the remains of slurry.

The thirteenth? Wasn't that what Little John said?

Or was it the eighteenth?

Dubo Wilson fidgeted with the controls to the sort bins hanging underneath the railroad tracks just a few feet away from him. He sat in the control box, an eight by twelve rectangular room inside a much larger warehouse structure and positioned beside the incoming railroad tracks of NAPCO's paper mill facility just outside of Monroe, Alabama. Dubo had worked sparingly at NAPCO for the twelve years he'd been out of high school. He hadn't graduated, but he was out, which was all the same to him.

A painfully skinny man, Dubo looked sick most the time. And because of the drugs and alcohol he kept pumping through his veins, most of the time he was. His eyes were usually bulging and bloodshot and his matted hair was never combed or neat. He was lucky to bathe twice a week, which made his presence hard to tolerate. His arms and legs were frail with veins that bulged through the skin, especially in his forearms, which made them easy targets for the needles. Dubo was only twenty-nine years old, but his withered skin, rotting teeth and over all sad looking appearance gave him the looks of a man twice his age. A man living a sharecropper's life, even though work was something in which Dubo seldom participated.

Dubo had been in the mill's employ before, but lost his job after arriving drunk for his shift three days in a row. Little John, the night shift supervisor, questioned his refusal to report sober, to which Dubo gleefully informed him that drinking gave him the confidence to work. Then he passed out. But Dubo was right—drinking did give him confidence. Sober he was scared of his own shadow and spoke with a stutter. He avoided people he didn't know and scurried around with a nervous twitch, refusing to make eye contact. Drunk he was a different man. Drunk he would attempt to extinguish hell's fire with a water pistol. Such as one night at the local roadhouse called the Nightstand, when Dubo called out a cut-throat thug known as 'Jail Time' because of his fondness for the Alabama penal system. Once in the parking lot, Dubo threw all of his one hundred thirty-six pounds at the much larger Jail Time, who severely beat Dubo until he could no longer stand and left him lying face down in the gravel and mud of the Nightstand's parking lot. The following night the two men were back at the bar drinking together.

"No, no," Dubo said aloud, "it was definitely the thirteenth." He had heard it clear. He was nervous, but then how could he not be. His entire future was riding on this. To succeed meant a new position at the mill, more money in his paycheck, and more importantly, a free bag of blow. Not to mention the fact he got to stay out of jail for the next twenty years.

It was the thirteenth. Definitely the thirteenth.

This was his big opportunity and he could ill afford to blow it and face the wrath of Little John or Sheriff Watkins.

"Thirteenth" he mumbled, "I know it's the thirteenth."

It was three o' clock in the morning and Dubo was halfway through his nighttime shift. A train was expected any minute with a load of cargo vital to the mill's existence. Dubo took careful notice of his surroundings to make sure he was ready for its arrival. The mill was loud and most of the workers wore earplugs so the continuous hum of the paper machines did not rattle into their heads and follow them home when their shift was over. The mill's three large paper machines caused such a heavy and continuous vibration that Dubo could feel it in the tracks that flowed through the building as he sat in the control box. The rails running over the drop bins were inside a large warehouse with an opening big enough for three trains to enter simultaneously. Through the opening Dubo could see the entire mill in the glow of florescent lights, bright as day, but with the familiar greenish-yellow tint they cast on every object illuminated. Smoke stacks towered out of the ground, some as high as one hundred fifty feet into the dark Southern sky where white smoke bellowed from their tops. The night air was humid from the Alabama heat, but Dubo sweated even more profusely from the combination of his body pushing out its latest intake of alcohol and the heat created by the manufactured steam the mill used to turn the huge turbines that never stopped.

As he stood next to the control booth door talking to himself, Dubo was suddenly startled by Little John, who came from up the tracks behind him. With the constant noise of paper machines echoing in the building next door, there was no way for Dubo to hear him coming.

Little John was anything but. He stood six foot five inches, weighed two hundred and eighty pounds and was called 'Little' only because he shared the same name as his father, an equally impressive figure. Little John always wore overalls, was never in a good mood and hated ineptitude, so he had very little patience with employee Dubo Wilson. But he knew well that for the job he had to do, and for the payment terms they had agreed upon, there was no doubt that Dubo Wilson was the most qualified person in Monroe for the recently opened position of nightshift bin operator.

"Train should be here soon. You ready?" Little John asked, reaching his large hand to the side of his head and pulling the earplug from his right ear to hear Dubo's response.

"Yes, sir, I'm ready," Dubo answered.

Little John nodded his head and began to walk off with the big lumbering stagger that was inevitable for a man of his size.

"It's the thirteenth car, right?" Dubo shouted to Little John, just to be sure.

Little John wheeled around, "Look you dumb son of a bitch! We've been over this a million times! It's the thirteenth! You got it? The thirteenth!"

"I just wanted to make sure!"

"Are you sure you can count to thirteen?"

"You know I can, you watched me do it for Sheriff Watkins."

"Well, for your own sake, you'd better get this right. Personnel told me today that I can't build up anymore vacation time and that I'll lose what I've got if I don't take it now. So next week I'll be gone and you'll be on your own. You sure you can handle this?"

"Yeah, yeah, I got it."

Little John walked off shaking his head and rubbing the back of his neck with his large hand. Dubo again played with the controls of the drop bins, opening the doors and then shutting them to make sure they had not malfunctioned since the last test he conducted just five minutes before. He watched as Little John disappeared around the corner and then whispered to himself, "Big dumb redneck."

Underneath the first drop bin sat three large dump trucks and their drivers, who also waited on the train carrying their cargo. The function of the drop bins was to funnel the product from the boxcar into its destination either into the trucks or onto a conveyor belt carrying the product up to a large holding tank used for the mills own production of paper. Product loaded into the trucks would be taken to one of NAPCO's other mills located in the U.S or Canada. Once the train was worked into the proper position over the bins, the doors would open from the bottom of the boxcars and the product would fall into the bins below. Dubo's job was to make sure that the proper car's cargo ended up in the right place. He had worked the bins before on the dayshift and had been Calvin's assistant on the nightshift. But now Calvin was gone, and it was up to Dubo to keep the production of NAPCO's most profitable product in full swing.

As Dubo sat at the controls, down the tracks about fifty yards a man in a green John Deere baseball cap walked from one side of the rails to the other. He had seen Dubo and Little John talking, but he couldn't hear their words because of the noise in the mill. He removed his cap and wiped his forehead with the shoulder and sleeve of his shirt. He had watched Calvin and Dubo unload the boxcars before and didn't understand the importance of their position, although everyone in the mill knew that the two men had been singled out to perform this task. He replaced the cap on his head, spoke not a word to Dubo, but continued to pay close attention to what was going on. He just wished he knew what it was.

SEVEN

SPENCE'S WEEKEND HAD been spent moving his belongings into the new house and buying furniture at the store where Americus arranged for his credit. His interior decorating skills were novice at best and he was still thrifty with his money, unaccustomed to a retailer giving him free reign of a store and its contents. He purchased a kitchen table, a couch—the cheapest in the store—a 29" television and a stand to place it on, a mattress, box springs and frame for the spare bedroom and a dresser for his own room that did not match the bed given to him by his uncle. The store's owner was glad to deliver his furniture the same afternoon since Spence had made such a large purchase and even threw in a lamp as a way to say thank you.

Once everything was in place at the house, Spence discovered plenty of necessities still to be purchased. There were no dishes or silverware, no pictures for the walls, and even though he had a bed for any overnight visitors, he had no sheets for them to sleep on. A quick trip to Wal-Mart produced the items he was looking for, including pictures and sheets. But every time he began to organize the house, he realized he had forgotten something, such as a trash can or paper towels. With only thirty-seven dollars in his checking account, he was forced to put everything on his one and only credit card, already dangerously close to its limit. His last trip to Wal-Mart had been nerve-racking. Standing in the checkout line as the clerk swiped his card, he worried that it could be rejected. He wanted to call Visa before leaving the house to see how much available credit was left on his account, but realized he'd forgotten to purchase a phone on the previous trip.

Monday morning Spence walked into his new office not really sure what to expect. It was 8:05. He wanted to make sure he gave Kathy time to get to work so he wouldn't seem too overanxious. And there she was, in a dress two sizes too small and an over-application of eye make-up. When she heard the front door bell, she ran to the lobby to greet Spence. From the second floor handrail, she leaned over to expose as much cleavage as possible, but it was more than the top two buttons of her dress could hold. They burst from their stitching and fired towards the bottom floor and Spence, exposing her lacy red bra.

"Dear God!" she shouted, quickly gathering herself back in and running to her office.

Spence found her buttons on the floor and yelled behind her, "Are you going to need these?" When no answer came he decided not to pursue the incident anymore since he was just as uncomfortable as Kathy.

He walked up the stairs to his office and rounded the corner to find a man already sitting in one of his blue leather guest chairs. Startled, Spence said nothing, while his guest stared at him solemnly as if he were scolding a child, with his chin pressed hard against his chest. The man couldn't have stood more than five-four and seemed even smaller sitting in the large chair where the tips of his shoes barely reached the floor. He was dressed in a short-sleeved white button-down shirt with food stains at the stomach and wore tennis shoes at least ten years old.

Spence finally mustered a "Hello."

"I hope you don't think you're going to start running things around here, because you're not," Huey Crance stated in an authoritative voice that sounded a lot like Barney Fife.

"Excuse me?" Spence replied, setting his briefcase on the floor and extending his hand in front of Huey. He felt awkward but somewhat amused at this little man's attempt at intimidation.

"I run things around here," was Huey's quick reply. He did not rise from his seat, but he did take Spence's hand and gave it a very feminine handshake. The little man was trying to make a point, not be rude, and in the South there was a difference. "I run your uncle, run Kathy, run everything. If it weren't for me this place wouldn't make a dime and you lawyers wouldn't have so much money to spend. I've earned the right to be respected after thirty-three years and respect is exactly what I'm going to get. Are we clear?"

Spence recognized the line. He had seen Jack Nicholson's performance as Colonel Jessup in *A Few Good Men* as well, but he did not oblige Huey with "crystal" as his response. "Okay," he said, "but do you mind telling me who you are?"

"I'm the H-M-F-I-C, and sonny, that's all you need to know." Having made his point, he jumped to his feet and strolled past Spence, staring at him on the way out of his office. Americus was coming down the hall to Spence's office and spotted Huey in the hallway just outside Spence's door.

"Hello, Huey. How the hell are ya?" Americus was wearing his biggest smile as he greeted his employee. Huey responded with a "Huh," as the two met in the hall. Americus, who hadn't been looking for a response anyway, said a well rehearsed, "Fine. Fine," and strolled passed Huey into his nephew's office.

"Hello, ma' boy," Americus was still wearing the politician grin and held a folded newspaper in his hand.

"How's it going?" Spence responded with curiosity on his face for his next question. "Does that guy work here?"

"Oh yeah, that's Huey. He'll be doing the title work down at the courthouse. You didn't think I was going to drag your ass down there, did you?" Americus replied.

"Don't you just order the title from a title company?" Spence asked with curiosity.

"Dear God, son," Americus huffed, "This is Crawford County, not Birmingham. We don't have a title company. Someone actually has to go down to the courthouse and look up the title record to the property and make sure that whoever is selling the timber or the land, really has the right to sell it. Since I'm certainly not going down there, I hired Huey to do it."

"Is Huey a lawyer?" Spence inquired.

"Christ no. I'm not even sure if Huey graduated from high school. I hired him away from another lawyer in town eighteen years ago, and he's become the best title searcher in this part of the state. He's at home in any county courthouse south of Montgomery and he only works for me. Not bad considering I only pay him seven dollars an hour, huh?"

"How does anybody live on seven dollars an hour?" Spence asked and then quickly realized that he'd actually been living on less than that for the last several years and had been quite happy. Now all of a sudden it seemed impossible to do.

"This is a small town," Americus answered back. "People here have simple needs. Besides, money is relative. Most folks don't know anybody with a lot of money, so they have nothing to compare it to. That's the way it is in most pulp wood towns."

"They know you, and you seem to be doin' okay," Spence replied.

"They don't know how much I have, and I don't flaunt it in front of them either. I do all of my extravagant living in either Atlanta or New Orleans or vacation spots in the gulf so none of the town's people will see me blowing it. They all know that I'm richer than most, but it's bad for business if they think you're really loaded. Speaking of business, you ready to meet some bankers in town?"

"Sure. That's what I'm here for."

"We've also got to go out to NAPCO and introduce you to Smitty. He's expecting us." Americus turned to walk out of the office and

Spence followed behind.

"Oh, I almost forgot. Here's the morning paper." Americus tossed the rolled newspaper in the center of Spence's desk. "You need to start reading it so you can become more familiar with the people in the county. There's also a story on the girl who killed her father with the baseball bat. The one Wilson and I were telling you about Friday night. You can read it when you get back."

Americus began his usual brisk pace down the hall. Halfway to the lobby he spun around to face Spence following just behind. With a concerned look he asked, "Do you have any money?"

Spence blushed, embarrassed at how broke he was. "I've got a five dollar bill in my pocket. Do you need to borrow it?"

Americus laughed, "No, that's okay." He reached into his right front pocket and produced a wad of cash, neatly folded in half, the faces on the bills turned outward. "Here," Americus said, then counted out five one hundred dollar bills and handed them to Spence. "You can't walk around without money in your pocket."

"I don't think I'll need this much."

"Nonsense. You might have to bribe somebody."

Spence smiled at what he thought was Americus' attempt at a joke. But when Americus turned around without returning the smile, Spence realized that he just might have been serious.

They headed out the back of the office to the Mercedes in the alley. Remembering Americus' driving skills, Spence pleaded for the keys. He finally convinced his uncle that in order to learn where NAPCO was he needed to drive. Americus relented and tossed him the keys.

NAPCO was the acronym for the North American Paper Company, an aggressive conglomerate quickly becoming one of the largest paper producers in the nation. With sales now exceeding $18 billion per year, it trailed only the likes of International Paper and Georgia Pacific within the industry and was gaining ground ever year. Even greater things were expected from the company that entered the

Fortune 500 for the first time in the previous year. NAPCO had the whole industry—and Wall Street—abuzz. Profits were soaring and share prices increasing while the rest of the industry struggled along.

Following Americus' directions, Spence guided the Mercedes to the outskirts of town and then headed south. Outside the city limits he turned on County Road 78 and immediately noticed a shocking difference. Most of the roads throughout the county were old and in bad need of repair since they depended on the county budget for upkeep. Some were even so badly riddled with potholes that it would have been better to leave them as dirt roads. But County Road 78 lead to NAPCO and it was as smooth as Tennessee whiskey. The surface looked as if it had been paved only yesterday and the yellow lines painted in the center still seemed wet. NAPCO had agreed to pay for half of the road's building cost, as it needed an adequate ingress and egress for the hundreds of trucks coming to and from the plant each week. But halfway through the construction of the four-lane road the county ran out of money, and NAPCO was forced to pay for its completion. Having done so, it now considered 78 its own private driveway and made sure that it remained the best road in the county.

Just a mile down County Road 78, Spence could see the smoke generated by the plant. Another mile and he could smell the all too familiar sulphuric stench associated with paper mills. The smell of sulfur in the ponds supplying water to the mill was almost nauseating to strangers, but residents no longer complained—perhaps because that smell provided for their livelihood.

"Ah," Americus remarked, "smell all that money."

"Doesn't smell like money to me," Spence replied. "Smells awful."

"Nonsense, ma' boy. That smell's gonna make you and me a lot of money. Dump trucks full. You see, the pine trees around the county get bought by the mill, but NAPCO doesn't want to take trees off of property until they're sure they know who has the right to sell the timber. Someone could own a piece of land and still not own the timber. So that's where you and I come in. When the mill buys trees, it hires me to make sure the seller has a right to sell them," Americus explained.

"So then you send Huey down to the courthouse to make sure the seller actually owns the timber rights" Spence replied.

"Exactly, and Smitty—or Paul Smith—is the timber buyer out here at NAPCO, and he sends me all of his work."

"I see," said Spence. "Y'all must be pretty good friends."

"Not really," Americus responded. "He's kind of an ass, but I pay him a thousand dollars a month in cash to get all of his business and then I charge NAPCO a premium to do the work. Smitty could care less what I charge. It's not his money."

The ponds generating the awful sulphuric smell were a mile and a half away from the entrance to the mill, and as Spence drove closer, he noticed the smell was either fading or he was getting used to it.

He turned the Mercedes onto the entrance drive leading to the mill's offices and drove to the security gate. The guard inside recognized the black car and barely looked up from his paper while opening the gate. Spence was still waiting for the guard to ask for a pass when Americus said, "Hell boy, we ain't on a pier fishin', go on through." Spence hit the gas a little too hard and the Mercedes stalled in the middle of the gate. Americus placed his head in his hands and gave a resounding "Dear God."

Spence, soundly embarrassed, restarted the car and drove on through the gate waving at the guard, now staring at Spence as if he were an idiot.

Spence drove through the mill following signs that read "Offices." As he drove past a large fenced area, he realized he had never seen so many trees in his entire life. There were thousands of them stacked in a single circular row. All the limbs had been stripped, and the trunks looked like forty-foot toothpicks. In the middle of the circle was a crane at least ten stories high. It was hauling up twelve to fifteen trees at a time and feeding them into a huge mulching machine that shot wood chips out the other side. The wood chip mountain, several stories high itself, was slowly being reduced by a huge, bright yellow earthmoving piece of equipment.

On the other side of the road large turbines steadily turned and moaned, apparently driven by steam as smoke and water occasionally shot into the air. Like everything else in the mill the turbines were painted pale green, except where the paint had been scraped off showing rusted metal underneath. The turbines sat fifty feet off the ground and fed huge pipes nearly six feet in diameter into a concrete building at least three hundred yards long. Spence had never seen such a large operating facility. It was absolutely overwhelming. And to think, it was in the middle of nowhere.

They finally reached the mill offices located in a silver walled building about a hundred fifty feet long. Spence parked the car in a space marked "Guest" and he and Americus walked up the stairs leading into the offices. Immediately facing the door was a receptionist desk with an attractive young lady sitting behind it. She did a double take when she noticed Spence.

"Hello, Mr. Kirkland," the young lady greeted Americus.

Spence guessed she was in her early twenties, brunette with big brown eyes. Brown eyes just happened to be his weakness in women, if it could be said he had one, and this girl's were inviting. She was wearing a tight red blouse that showed her figure.

"Now I told you to call me Americus, Amy. My father was Mr. Kirkland. I'm just Americus."

"Okay, I'll try to remember," Amy responded with a smile, trying not to make eye contact with Spence.

"Now, Amy, I want you to meet my nephew and newest associate, Spencer Thompson. He's going to be working with us and living here in Monroe," Americus explained.

Amy sat up a little straighter in her chair. Spence picked up on it. Could it be that she was happy to learn he wasn't just passing through?

"Glad to meet you Spencer," she said.

"Please, call me Spence," he replied, "and believe me, the pleasure is all mine. I didn't know there were actually people my own age in town."

"Amy here just graduated from Auburn University," Americus stated, "and she's going to be working in the personnel department when that old hag Leslie Burch retires in the winter. Until then, she's passing time by answering the telephone."

"Mrs. Burch is not that bad," Amy replied with a grin, as if to say 'shame on you Americus.'

"Trust me. I've known her a lot longer than you have, ma' dear, and if she doesn't ride a broom to work, its just because she's saving it for Halloween. Now, Amy, I see there are some messages back there for Smitty. If you'll hand them to me, I'll take'em to him on my way back."

"Oh, that would be great," Amy said, then rose from her chair and walked to the counter behind her. When Americus looked at Spence and raised his eyebrows, Spence realized the old man had asked for the messages just so Spence could see Amy's full figure. Spence was grateful too; the back was every bit as good as the front. She was wearing a tight black skirt, which fell just above her knees showing her muscular calves and slender ankles. Americus whispered just low enough for Spence to hear, "Pine trees ain't all we're good at growin' round here."

Amy returned, "Here you are Mr. Kirkland. I mean, Mr. Americus."

"Thank you, Amy," Americus replied, "and I want you to know that I expect you to show my nephew here around this wonderful town of ours."

"I'd be happy too," Amy responded and turned to face Spence, this time making direct eye contact. He wanted to say something cute and witty, but the big browns caught him off guard and all he could muster was, "I'll hold you to it."

Spence and Americus turned toward the hallway that led to Smitty's office. After a few steps he glanced back to take one last look at Amy and caught her watching him walk down the hall. She didn't try to hide it. Spence smiled and she returned the gesture. This was going to be fun.

EIGHT

P. THOMAS KENDALL sat behind the large mahogany desk in his Chicago office and stared at himself on the cover of Fortune magazine. He was forty-nine years old, but the picture made him look much younger. Six foot three inches tall, lean, with thick black hair, he looked every bit the powerful executive. Of all the magazines and publications that had written recent stories about him, he liked the Fortune article the best. It made him look like a genius. He especially liked its title, "NAPCO's Kendall finds Profit Where No One Else Can." It was a special edition of the magazine ranking the top companies in each industry. With profits the previous year of nearly 1.3 billion dollars and a 21 percent return to shareholders, no other paper product company came close to Kendall's NAPCO. A phenomenal feat, especially considering the previous year was only the second time in the past decade the company managed to show a profit.

As Kendall continued to admire himself, his computer screen ran a continuous ticker across the bottom, giving him the latest share prices from Wall Street. He looked at his watch and realized that his NAPCO price would be coming across the ticker within the next few minutes, just like it did everyday about this time and twice an hour until the market closed at 4:00 p.m. eastern. He laid down the magazine and stared at the screen.

"C'mon you bastards. Show me you love me," Kendall said.

He knew NAPCO's price would only go up if the stock was active and if those who bought and sold for a living had a good feeling about his company. And to believe in NAPCO was to believe in Kendall. He needed that faith, not for the money, he had plenty of that, but for the glory of having Wall Street's trust. A man like Kendall needed such glory. He—the modern business warrior—needed to conquer, and fair play was not a requirement. By any means necessary would do just fine.

The price strolled past the bottom of the screen as Kendall fixed his eyes on the 'NPCO' ticker symbol and the price that followed. $42.07 per share, up four cents from the previous day. He leaned forward on his desk and punched some numbers into his calculator; 110 million shares at four cents a share. He was 4.4 million dollars wealthier today. Kendall sat back in his chair, placed his hands behind his head and smiled.

"Suckers."

He was satisfied for the moment having been given purpose and praise. He relished in it. He needed it like an alcoholic needed a drink, and Wall Street had just handed Kendall a bottle of liquor.

All the credit for NAPCO's recent success was given to Kendall, its CEO, whose father help start the company over forty years ago. The son was a Harvard-trained lawyer, who had assumed control over the company after it fell deep into financial trouble only half a decade before. Under his control, the paper giant made a resounding comeback. His years of training as a Wall Street securities lawyer had created quite a savvy business mind, and it was complimented by his drive to be rich and powerful—his most dominating feature. He loved money, and more importantly, recognition. It was the glamour of being on top that lured him to wealth and power. He not only wanted people to know he was rich, but also that it was he who had created such great wealth. Money without the recognition was an insult. It would mean he was like those he attended law school with, who were worth more money before they were born than most towns. He had always considered himself different from the bluebloods, even though the similarities were more than a few.

Steve Ricter, NAPCO's Chief of Operations, lightly tapped on Kendall's door.

"Come in," Kendall responded.

"Good morning, Thomas," Ricter said, entering the spacious office and noticing the magazine on Kendall's desk. "I see you've already got a copy of the article."

"Have you read it?"

"Yes, I have," Ricter responded with a smile on his face.

"So, what did you think?" Kendall prodded, as he leaned over the desk. The glare on his face intensified with curiosity.

"I liked the one *Success* did on you last week. It showed your personal side more." These are the words that came out of Ricter's mouth, but he was thinking how good it was for the company that the article had not shown an accurate Kendall to the public.

"Yes, I thought so too," Kendall answered back. He relaxed and fell back into his chair, pleased with Ricter's answer. Kendall was a Harvard trained lawyer running a 'Fortune Five Hundred' company. His ego was often unbearable, and Ricter was glad to see he had satisfied it for the moment.

"How are things down in hick town?" Kendall inquired.

"Everything went fine." Ricter replied, "The Miami office is expecting a new shipment any day now, maybe even as early as Thursday. I called the hicks and they're ready to make it regular. New man did fine. They say there's nothing to worry about."

"I told you there wouldn't be," Kendall said as the smile grew on his face. "Nobody cares what goes on in those small towns. Place is probably better off without him anyway."

"I just never thought we would have to be a part of something like this," Ricter said, looking down at his shoes.

Kendall held up the magazine so Ricter could see the cover. "You also never thought we would be a part of this, did you? Believe me, it's worth it. Nobody that mattered got hurt and they're singing our praises on Wall Street."

It was Wall Street that mattered. Always had to Kendall, and he
finally felt like he belonged.

His father had stressed the importance of education from the time
he was born, even though he had little formal education of his own.
Kendall Sr. was a scrap metal dealer in Chicago before World War II,
and by the time the Japanese surrendered he was a wealthy man—
thanks to lucrative contracts he had made with Uncle Sam. Like most
newly rich, however, he was snubbed by the aristocratic families of
Chicago and always blamed his lack of education for their indifference.
His third son from his second marriage, a relationship he did not enter
into until the age of forty-five, shared his uneasiness for the idle rich,
even though he received the corpus of a million dollar trust upon his
graduation from Harvard Law School. Still, in many ways Kendall Jr.
considered himself different, if only for the reason that his grandfather
had actually been poor and that his father never socialized with
Chicago's elite, although his fortune was considerably larger than many
of their own.

Kendall had loved Wall Street ever since his father taught him
how to read the financial page. On the world's most famous avenue a
new millionaire was created everyday. There a man with a good idea
could cash in and watch as his fortune grew. Corporate CEOs and
money managers were worshiped as the gods that drove capitalism.
People watched their every move and listened to their every thought.
Reporters wrote articles about their lives and lifestyles and prayed to
someday be them. The Rockefeller's, the Morgan's, and even simple
men from Bentonville, Arkansas, were considered geniuses. They
were loved by those who worshiped at the altar of gold, and Kendall
sought this admiration with a fevering passion.

Kendall despised being a securities lawyer, even though as one of
the best, he was paid five hundred dollars an hour for his services.
But he still had to work for his earnings, while corporate fat cats flew
on private jets and stayed in plush hotels for morning meetings on

the west coast. As a lawyer, compared to these CEOs he was just a common hourly laborer—even if he did have a Harvard education.

Upon his father's death in 1985, Kendall inherited his share of NAPCO, a company he started with two other newly rich entrepreneurs. The company made steady growth for the first two decades of its existence, primarily through the manufacture of paper products like disposable diapers and newsprint. Its crown jewel, however, was its line of high quality papers, known as 'Silksheets', a common sight in law firms and executive offices. The company went public in 1979 because the demand for Silksheets created the need for a considerable amount of new capital. It was at the time of the IPO that plans for the Monroe facility were announced, to be built especially for the production of the high quality Silksheets.

Even after its initial public offering, the company was still controlled by its three original investors until Kendall Sr.'s death. At that time the company headed for the red for a number of years due to poor management. Kendall had inherited 16 percent of NAPCO's voting stock. He studied the company's financial statements, took notice of its vast infrastructure, and formed a plan to make it profitable again. He immediately began to acquire more stock and resigned from his job at the securities firm to learn more about the company. After three years of running NAPCO's legal department, he leapt into the CEO's chair by skillfully lobbying at corporate board meetings. His stake had risen to 31 percent of the company by the time he became the chief executive, and by 2001 he owned 53 percent, giving him outright control. Now he could put his plan into full execution. Ever since he could remember he had dreamed of being the CEO of a Fortune Five Hundred Company—even if it killed him. As of the morning Ricter entered his office with the *Fortune* article, death had eluded him, but two failed marriages and a flirtation with alcoholism had not.

Ricter was still shamefully looking at the ground when he said, "I just hope this is the last time we have to do this. It's just not my nature to do business this way."

"C'mon Steve, I would have thought someone with an MBA from Harvard wouldn't be so squeamish when it came to making money. Didn't they teach you how to play hardball over there?" Kendall asked, lifting an eyebrow.

"Hardball, yes. Criminal behavior, no," Ricter replied.

"What's the difference?" Kendall retorted, thumbing through some papers on his desk.

Ricter still stood behind one of the two luxurious wing chairs that faced Kendall's massive desk, and now his fingers sank like teeth into the soft leather on the chair's top. "They must have been saving all of the lectures on common thuggery for use over in the law school."

Kendall raised his head to look at Ricter. He interlaced his fingers and cracked his knuckles, a habit he indulged in when he was irritated and wanted to show it. He wanted to hammer away at Ricter for such blatant insubordination. It took very little to irritate Kendall, and open disrespect by a subordinate was usually a good cause for a complete verbal undressing. His breathing thickened as he found it hard to contain his anger. But now, more than ever, he needed Ricter, and he urgently needed Ricter to keep their secret.

Kendall took a deep breath. "I know you have things to do and so do I. Come back this afternoon and we'll talk some more about the latest shipments."

The two men stared at one another for a brief moment, then Ricter nodded and turned to leave. Once at the door, he opened it and paused there, wanting to say something to break the tension. But the best he could do was look back at the CEO and attempt a quick grin.

After Ricter closed the office door, Kendall turned in his chair and scowled at Chicago from his sixty-eighth floor window. He slowly rubbed his forehead, digging into his scalp with the pressure from his fingers, still fuming. Suddenly and violently, he kicked the mahogany baseboard at the bottom of his wall. "He'd better remember who he's talking too," he snarled.

NINE

THE MORNING WENT well for Spence and Americus. Smitty's welcome to town seemed sincere, and the bankers around town were already making bets on who Spence would take to lunch first. Americus took Spence by the old courthouse in the middle of town and showed him where the probate records were kept. He also introduced Spence to the secretaries in the probate office, doting over a shorthaired blond of about fifty in particular. Spence suspected that she and Americus were more than just friends, even though she wore a gold wedding band on her left hand. He inquired about it later in the car, to which Americus answered with a smile.

While in the courthouse records room, they ran into Huey, already busy pouring through heavy deed books in search of chains of title. Huey acted annoyed at having to show Spence how he did his work, but he actually enjoyed the attention. There were few visitors in the county's records room. Huey tried to continue his act of pretending to be hampered by the firm's new lawyer, but began to warm a little after a few praises by Spence, ever trying to sharpen his ability to win people over. In a few more minutes, Huey was showing off his vast knowledge of the county's property with such enthusiasm that Spence and Americus were hard pressed to escape.

When Spence returned to his office he unrolled the newspaper Americus had given him earlier that morning and read the story of the local girl who allegedly killed her father with a baseball bat. The article said she was nineteen years old and there was a good chance the district attorney would ask for the death penalty. She had been arrested last Friday morning around 8:30 in the woods near her home. By Alabama state law she had to appear before the court within seventy-two hours of her arrest, and she was given her first appearance on Friday afternoon to satisfy the requirement. She was being held without bond and the judge was going to appoint her an attorney because she couldn't afford one. Spence realized she had been arrested and charged on the same day he arrived in town. She was in custody over the weekend and would remain in jail for at least another week until the Grand Jury met the following Monday to see if there was enough evidence to indict her. The county sheriff who found her said she was cuddled up at the base of a large pine tree and made no attempt to run. She still had not spoken to the sheriff's department and it was believed that she might be in shock. Spence questioned the accuracy of the newspaper story because it didn't seem well written. He shook his head and turned to the sports page to see if the Braves had won the night before. On a solo homerun by Chipper in the eighth, they had beaten Houston 4 to 3.

At 11:15 Spence pushed himself away from his desk and headed for the conference room at the end of the hall to witness his first official closing as a member of the Alabama State Bar. It was a residential loan closing for the new Methodist minister in town and Americus was already in the room shuffling papers and making small talk with the Reverend and his wife. The Methodists did not provide their pastor with a house, but they did provide him with a housing allowance, so he could live anywhere he wanted. He had chosen a small three bedroom, one-and-a-half bath just two doors down from the church. Reverend Jones had already mentioned that he had three daughters and Spence was concerned that one-and-a-half bathrooms would never be sufficient with three young girls in the house.

Americus explained the documents, and the Reverend dutifully signed them without asking any questions. The entire procedure took about thirty minutes, and at the end Americus informed Reverend Jones that he would be cutting his fee and the title insurance premium in half—to $520.00—since the loan was for a man of the cloth. Spence and Americus walked the Reverend and his wife to the door, where they shook hands and the Reverend invited them to service on Sunday. When the new homeowners had exited, Americus turned to Spence.

"So, you think you can handle a loan closing now?"

"I think so. It doesn't seem to be that difficult," Spence answered.

"Good. You have another one at 1:30 this afternoon. I won't be here, so I expect you to handle it. If you have any questions, ask Huey." Americus turned and walked away before Spence could argue.

Spence decided to grab a quick lunch so he could return to his office and study the loan closing documents for his first closing as the lead attorney. He drove down the street to the Hardee's, Monroe's only fast food chain, and bought a burger and some fries with one of the bills Americus gave him earlier that morning. The young girl behind the counter, surprised to see a one hundred dollar bill, struggled to find change, eventually calling the manager to bring her some twenties from another register. Apparently, Americus didn't eat at Hardee's regularly. Spence ate his lunch in his Explorer on the way back to his office. When he entered his office, for the second time in his first day there was a stranger waiting for him.

The stranger identified himself as Deputy Sheriff John Reeves as he stood up to shake hands. A tall man with long arms and legs, Deputy Reeves' skin was dark black and his eyes even darker. His uniform was neatly pressed and he was well groomed with a close haircut and a clean shave. Though Deputy Reeves' looks were intimidating—even to Spence, who himself was not a small man—he was universally considered one of the finest human beings in the county.

Deputy Reeves was a native of Tuscaloosa, Alabama, and held a degree in criminal justice from the University of Alabama. He and his wife, a fourth grade teacher at the local elementary school, settled in Monroe when it became the only town they were both offered jobs in their fields of study. At thirty-three years of age, Deputy Reeves had two children, a six-year old girl and an eight-year old boy, already one of the stars of the Monroe Dixie Youth Baseball organization. The citizens of Monroe, both white and black, respected Deputy Reeves. While on duty he was stern and refused to show favoritism, yet he was fair and understanding. He listened to everyone's side of the story, laughed at the townspeople's jokes and greeted the men with a smile and the ladies with a tip of his hat. His little white house, located downtown on Main Street, got a fresh coat of paint every other year whether it needed it or not. The grass in his yard never rose above two inches high, shrubs were kept tidy and trimmed, and his patrol car was usually spotless.

Most citizens assumed that Watkins was supposed to be the sheriff because his family had been in Monroe since the town was settled in the early 1800's, and his uncle had been the sheriff before him. He was elected before many of the townspeople could vote, and like many small towns, Monroe was not fond of changing its political guard, obvious by the fact that most of the town's elected officials had been in office for the greater part of twenty years. However, it was because of Deputy Reeves that the majority of the people in Monroe felt safe at night, leaving an outsider to wonder why he was not the county's top cop.

The difference between sheriffs in small towns and police chiefs in larger cities is that the former doesn't necessarily have any law enforcement experience, nor does he need any to assume his post. Sheriffs are elected by the general populace, while police chiefs are appointed by the mayor or city council. When he was born, Watkins' uncle had just been elected sheriff of Crawford County. Twenty-one years later he hired his nephew, fresh out of the army and with no prior policing experience, as a deputy sheriff. At the age of twenty-seven, Watkins became sheriff when he was the only candidate to appear on the ballot, after his uncle threatened anyone who dared run against him. Once elected, an incumbent small town sheriff is practically impossible to unseat, because to run against him and lose would mean an uphill battle for anyone needing a political favor within the county. An experienced deputy sheriff wouldn't dare run against his boss, simply because after announcing his candidacy he would have to report to the unemployment office. But even with the electoral system stacked against him, there was perhaps a chance that Reeves could have beaten Sheriff Watkins in a general election, if the decision of each voter was public record. In the politically correct world of the twenty-first century, even small town voters wouldn't dare admit that they refused to elect a man because of his color. But ballots were still secret, and a black candidate for sheriff in a predominately white county had about the same chance of winning as a WASP congressional candidate in the inner city districts of Los Angeles. It simply wasn't going to happen.

"Spencer Michael Thompson?" Reeves asked in his no nonsense voice.

"Yes, sir," Spence replied, still standing in the doorway of his office.

"Judge Hamilton requests your presence at the courthouse this afternoon," Deputy Reeves handed Spence a summons and turned to walk out of his office.

"What's this about?" Spence inquired as Reeves was walking down the hall.

"I don't know," Deputy Reeves answered, "I don't read 'em. I just deliver 'em." He stopped at the end of the hall and turned back to Spence, who still studied the envelope. "But I suggest you don't be late," he added. "And by the way, welcome to Monroe." Reeves trotted down the stairs and out the door.

Spence flipped the envelope over in his hand, opened the summons and read it. A simple yet official looking typewritten note on Circuit Court letterhead, it instructed him to be at the judicial building at 4:00 later that afternoon. From his law school studies, Spence

remembered that a subpoena is an official letter from the court
demanding that a person appear to give testimony and held negative
consequences for anyone choosing to ignore it. A summons was
along the same lines and was usually served to defendants of lawsuits
by the sheriff's office demanding that the defendant come to the court
at a specified time to defend himself or else lose the case by default.
But in many jurisdictions, a summons was sometimes used by the
judge to inform a lawyer that his honor wanted to see the counselor
for official court business. Were it personal or of a matter off the
record, the judge would have called on the phone or had the clerk
give the attorney a note the next time he was in the courthouse. But
a summons was official and gave an attorney no choice but to appear,
and even an attorney wet behind the ears like Spence knew its importance. Spence quickly sat down at his desk and called Americus' car
phone.

"That sum bitch!" Americus exploded into the phone, "He's
screwing with me, I know it." The old man's voice was filled with
anger and Spence could imagine the Mercedes veering out of control.

"If he's just screwing with you, does that mean I don't have to go?"
Spence asked.

"He may be a slimy bastard," Americus responded, "but he's still
the judge. You'd better go see what the hell he wants." Americus managed to get in another faint "sum bitch" as he was hanging up.

At 1:30 Spence's first clients showed up. After a few minutes of
small talk, Spence learned that the young couple was buying their
first house and Spence was relieved. He assumed they had never been
in a closing, so they would never know if he screwed up. Huey, who
not only researched the titles, but also prepared all of the important
loan documents, came to the conference room on the second floor,
dropped the file on the table and gave Spence a reassuring pat on the
shoulder. It had only taken a half a day for the Spence Thompson
charm to win Huey over.

Mike and Laura Staten were born in Monroe, and at twenty-four years of age Mike was already a five-year veteran at NAPCO. A hard working young man, Mike had enough intellectual ability to have gone to college had someone encouraged him to do so. But when his uncle thought he could get him hired at the mill, his parents told him to take the opportunity, never dreaming there was more in life. He had done well at his job, steadily making advancements in responsibility and pay. He was recently put in charge of the storage facilities at the mill and his salary increased to $22,000 a year, meaning he and Laura could finally get out of the trailer park and buy a home.

Spence explained the documents as the Statens signed, going over escrow accounts, mortgage insurance, promissory notes and settlement statements. Surprisingly, the closing went smoothly, although Spence realized after Mike and Laura had left that he had failed to get them to sign an attorney disclosure statement stating that he represented the lender in the transaction. He would have to get it signed later. It was now 2:30, and though he was not expected at the judicial building until 4:00, he decided to arrive early and at least get a look at Judge Hamilton. He told Kathy where he was going and headed outside, where the intense heat of the Alabama summer struck his face like a fist. He walked down the street making a conscious effort to keep his arms away from his side, trying not to sweat through his white starched shirt.

The judicial building was two blocks from the town square. It was built in the late 1970s after the original courthouse's space became too inadequate to handle all of the county's affairs. Now only the Probate Court, Revenue Commissioner and drivers license divisions were still housed in the old courthouse, and all other county affairs were conducted at the judicial building. Spence, a little scared and a lot nervous, walked down the street with the summons in his hand, wondering what the county's highest-ranking judicial official could want with him. He noticed the many cracks in the sidewalk, the age of the buildings and the cars passing by, and how few people were actually on the street. Such a sleepy little town. No surprises. He would always be able to see them coming. He could handle anything this judge decided to throw at him. There was nothing to worry about. At least that's what he told himself.

TEN

THE JUDICIAL BUILDING was a three-story concrete structure occupying an entire city block. The building's plastered surface was in need of cleaning as green mildew stains oozed down from the eaves and over the walls, making their way from the roof to the ground. As Spence approached, he noticed a work crew of county prisoners in bright orange jumpsuits preparing pressure washers to clean the judicial building when it closed at 5:00. They were arguing about who had to climb the ladder with hose in hand and clean the roofline. The guard keeping watch sat in a van next to the curb with the windows up and the engine running. Undoubtedly, the air conditioning was on. He didn't care about who had to climb the ladder; he just wanted his shift to end so he could go home. The sight of prisoners around the building had a certain irony to it. Certainly all had received their prison sentence in the very building they were about to clean. Had it been in the middle of a field and surrounded by barbed wire, the building would have even looked like a prison.

Spence pulled open the loose front door of the building and immediately found his path blocked by a metal detector. He instinctively reached for the change in his pocket and the pen in his shirt, placed them in an empty plastic bowl to the side and passed through the tall metallic frame before realizing his keys were in the other pocket. His key chain had always set off the detectors at the airport, so he stopped expecting to hear a siren. But the machine must have been turned off since nothing was happening. It wouldn't have mattered if it had been buzzing anyway. There was no guard around to question the contents of his pockets.

Immediately to the right after entering the building, the Circuit Court entrance was through a large pair of wooden double doors with a bronzed plaque that hung over the doorway stating the room's purpose. The doors were fully opened and a judicial hearing was taking place as Spence made his way inside. The courtroom was large for such a small town. Enough rows of dark-stained benches fanned out on either side of the center aisle to accommodate 200 people. With a set of benches on each side of the courtroom and the aisle directly in the center facing the bench, much like church pews and pulpit, the entire setting was more ecclesiastical than judicial. The wall coverings matched the dark wood of the benches, but the floor was a white and charcoal colored vinyl tile, making the stain in the wood seem that much darker. A swinging gate divided the bench and the seating section of the courtroom. There were only about ten people in the room and they all sat on the first or second row.

Two attorneys argued in front of Judge Hamilton, who sat at the bench with his glasses on, in deep thought about whatever issue was in front of him. A very skinny man was arguing for the defendant and Spence decided he must have been from Monroe. The defendant's counsel was wearing shoes in bad need of a shine and his suit was very old and faded, the pants much more than the coat, showing that they had been put to additional use. His hair looked uncombed and his glasses were huge on his face, giving him the appearance of a fly. He was arguing on a *motion in limine* on why the deceased plaintiff's reckless behavior, in previous work situations, should be admitted during trial. He was doing a very good job at arguing his case.

The plaintiff's attorney was the polar opposite of his rival counsel.

Well groomed in a new dark suit, he sat with his legs crossed at his table, listening closely. If Spence had to guess, he would have said the plaintiff's attorney was not from Monroe and that his firm's television commercial had paid off by working up clients in the county. Spence assumed he was from Birmingham or Montgomery. He had the arrogant look of a big city lawyer.

Others in the courtroom varied in looks of importance. There was a woman taking notes in the witness box and two other men in the jury box. Both seemed to be attorneys waiting for their turn in front of the judge. Two old men sat in the middle of the second row on the left seating section, there just to pass away the afternoon by listening to the public record of the court. On the other side in the second row, a deputy sheriff sat talking to a lady of about thirty-five. And then there was Hamilton, sitting in his chair with a plastic cup on the corner of his bench to spit the juice from the tobacco he worked vigorously in his mouth. Everyone seemed to notice Spence as he walked in. The attention made him feel uneasy.

Spence sat down in the third row of seats. He would watch the hearing until it was over, and then, if the judge went to his chambers he would follow him in and inquire about his summons, even though it would probably not be 4:00. He sat on the hard wooden bench and watched, trying to get a feel for the judge. But Hamilton spoke very little and mostly just nodded as the two counselors argued in front of him.

When the hearing was over, the judge made some comments to the woman in the witness box taking notes and asked the two attorneys if there was anything else. They both said no and began to pack up their belongings on the desk in front of them. This stirred the two attorneys in the jury box who stood up and proceeded toward the tables. Spence was shifting his weight, attempting to get comfortable on the stiff seat when he heard the loud voice.

"Young man, may I help you?"

Spence looked up and found every person in the courtroom staring at him. They had all wanted to know why he was there and all of them stopped to find out, now that Judge Hamilton had pushed the issue.

The question caught Spence off guard as he looked around the room, searching for a kind face. Finding none, he finally answered, "Uh, sir, I was, uh, hoping to see you in your chambers."

"I'm going to be busy most of the afternoon and don't know when I'll get to my chambers, so you had better say what's on your mind now," responded Hamilton, picking up the cup and spitting in it.

Spence could feel everyone lean a little closer to find out what his presence was about.

"Well, sir," Spence began, "I'm Spencer Thompson and you sent this—"

"I thought I asked you to come at 4:00," Judge Hamilton interrupted, glaring in Spence's direction.

"Well, yes, sir," Spence started again, "but you see-"

"Young man, are you not an attorney?" Judge Hamilton interrupted again.

"Yes, sir, I am," Spence answered cautiously, wondering what the rhetorical question was setting him up for.

"Well then, it's 'Your Honor,' not 'Sir' and for God's sake stand up when you address me in my courtroom," Hamilton demanded.

Spence jumped to his feet. All of the attorneys in the room had huge smiles on their faces and the thin defense lawyer was unable to stop his chuckling. Embarrassed, Spence stepped out from the benches and walked down the aisle, stopping at the gate that divided the bench and the courtroom seating. He cleared his throat and tried to collect himself. Grabbing the gate in front of him he asked, "Your honor, I was just wondering what my summons to your courtroom this afternoon was about."

"I guess you couldn't wait until 4:00 to find out?" Hamilton barked.

"Shall I come back, Sir—I mean, Your Honor?" Spence asked.

"Well, hell no," answered Hamilton. Now everyone in the courtroom was chuckling except for the young lady talking with the deputy sheriff. She was the kind face Spence had been looking for.

Hamilton started again: "Now that you've disturbed my afternoon I might as well tell you. You've been appointed to represent the defendant in *The State of Alabama vs. Angela Chauncey*.

Spence smiled as a wave of relief washed over him. He recognized the girl's name from the newspaper article and knew her case was serious, far too serious for an attorney wet behind the ears and only licensed to practice for a few days. This was obviously some kind of joke that Americus was playing on him, and the judge, regardless of what Americus had said, was in on it. The story about Judge Hamilton hating Americus was simply part of the set up. They were probably old fraternity brothers and had been planning this gag for some time. The other lawyers must have known about the scam, since they were all greatly amused. Spence figured they probably went through the same initiation when first admitted to the bar.

"And I guess, I can't expect any help from Americus either," Spence answered back, his smile increasing.

"I don't know if you can or not," Hamilton said, raising his eyebrows in a bemused expression. The courtroom grew quiet.

"So, what should I do now?" Spence grinned even wider, waiting for the next step in the charade.

Hamilton was becoming greatly irritated and his face flushed red. He could hardly contain himself physically and could feel the anger in his throat, ready to scream. After all, he was the judge and unaccustomed to being addressed in such a jovial manner. With his hands on the bench, the judge raised himself slightly out of his chair and fired back at Spence, "I suggest you go talk to your damn client!"

Nobody was laughing now. They could feel the anger of the judge and so could Spence. A new wave of emotion poured over him for the second time in a single minute, but this time it was a tidal wave of fear.

"Your Honor, you've…," Spence paused and cleared his throat. "You've got to be kidding."

"I assure you, young man," Hamilton replied severely, "I am not kidding."

"But Your Honor, I just passed the bar," Spence answered back, "I don't know anything about criminal law and certainly nothing about a murder case."

"Well the Code of Ethics says you better hurry up and learn. If you screw this up for your client, you can be disbarred," Hamilton retorted.

"This is ridiculous." Spence felt his own irritation rise and his voice increased in volume. "I'm not qualified to try a murder case."

Judge Hamilton raised his hand to his face and removed his glasses. Still holding them in his left hand, he leaned over the bench and asked, "Son, did you sit for the Bar exam?"

"Yes, sir—I mean, yes, Your Honor."

"And did you pass that exam?"

"Yes, Your Honor."

"Well then," Hamilton began with an irritated grin on his lips, "The State of Alabama considers you qualified to try a murder case. And since the county's usual appointed counsel is recently deceased, and all the other attorneys in town have real jobs and real cases, and being that you are the low man on the totem pole around here, the case is yours. Do you understand?"

Spence stood at the railing, speechless. Everyone was staring at him again. He seemed to be growing smaller.

Judge Hamilton finally broke the silence, "Now then, young man," he solemnly declared, "I suggest you go and see your client. You'll find her in the county jail."

Spence could think of no response. The courtroom, which had looked so large when he entered, was now closing in around him. With a look of disbelief, he finally let go of the rail and turned his back to the bench and the judge. Slowly, he began his way back down the aisle, but stopped about halfway and turned around. The skinny Monroe lawyer and the big city plaintiff's attorney were also quickly proceeding down the aisle, passing Spence as he stopped.

Spence looked toward the bench and saw Hamilton furiously

scribbling on a legal pad, growing increasingly irate until he finally threw his pen down on the courtroom floor and yelled at the woman in the witness box, "Damn it, Shirley, find me another pen!"

The judge then noticed that Spence had stopped in the aisle and turned to face him. He picked up the cup from his bench and spat in it, never taking his icy stare off Spence.

Spence hung his head in disbelief. This couldn't be happening.

ELEVEN

IN HIS TOUR of the town Americus had neglected to show Spence the county jail, so Spence stopped an elderly man on the sidewalk outside the courthouse and ask him the whereabouts of the county lock-up. It was a block behind the courthouse, opposite Americus' office, hidden by a row of storefronts and the sheriff's office. Spence walked to the courthouse square, crossed the street and parking lot, and headed to the jail.

The county jailhouse was a solid-looking one-story building that had all of its holding facilities built under ground. Its entrance was a poor design, as Spence walked up six steps to get to the front door and then immediately after passing through, proceeded back down six steps to get to the front desk. A stern-looking woman in a county deputy's uniform sat behind the counter writing a report. Without looking up she asked, "Can I help you?"

"Yes," Spence said, still stumbling for words in disbelief. "I'm here to see the girl they brought in for murder."

The clerk stopped writing and put her pen down on the counter. She removed her reading glasses and looked up at Spence. "And you would be?"

"Spence Thompson."

"Well darlin, your going to have to do better than that if you want to see a prisoner charged with murder," the clerk answered back.

"Ah, yes. I'm an attorney," Spence replied.

"Well, sweetheart, we're getting closer. Now tell me, are you her attorney or just any old attorney?"

Spence hesitated. He didn't know how to answer her question. He knew what the judge had told him, but certainly no one actually expected him to defend a murder suspect. He was still searching for words when she asked again, "Are you her attorney?"

"Yes," he answered quietly.

"Well, then, sign this and follow me," the clerk instructed.

Spence signed the register and the clerk led him to the end of the hall where a large white steel door with a small window stood facing them. She inserted a key and opened the heavy door, which revealed the stairway to the county's holding facilities on the bottom floor. She walked down the steps and Spence followed. The stairway was narrow—only about two and a half feet—with solid block walls on either side, white-washed with paint. As they descended to the lower level, Spence felt the air becoming cold and damp like the musty atmosphere of a cellar. The floor at the bottom was bare concrete, and as she led Spence to the first set of bars, the clerk's shoes echoed down the corridor. The only escape to the outside world was the stairway and a small window about one foot square with heavy bars that allowed a tiny amount of sunlight from the alley behind the jailhouse.

"Open up, Tom," the clerk moaned. "Angela's lawyer's here to see her."

Tom was sitting on a stool behind the first set of bars, reading the paper. He looked to be in prison himself, completely enclosed in iron. The first set of bars separated him from the hallway where the clerk and Spence were standing, and the next set separated him from the actual jail cells. He didn't say a word, but slowly got up and unlocked the first set of bars. Spence cautiously walked inside Tom's cage, and the guard slammed the door behind him. Spence had never been inside a jail. He began to feel lightheaded and the entire scene became surreal. His nervousness caused sweat to appear around his face, even more noticeable in the cool environment of the cellblock. Tom opened the second set of iron bars that lead to the cells and began walking down the center aisle.

There were eight cells, four on each side. Each was divided by a cement block wall separating the prisoners, while the front of the cells were fortified by iron bars. In the first cell immediately to the left, a man slept on a cot protruding from the back wall. He didn't stir from his slumber even as Tom slammed the iron door behind Spence. Tom walked down the hall as Spence followed taking a good look at the solidarity of the cellblock, which gave him an eerie feeling of hopelessness.

"Relax," Spence told himself. "They're not going to keep you here." Trying to appear casual, he reached out his hand and allowed his fingers to strum the steel bars as he walked past.

Clearing the last cement wall that separated the cells, Spence first cast his eyes upon Angela Chauncey. She sat on the very back corner of her cot, hugging her knees. She looked at him curiously through a tear stained face, this man she had heard the clerk say was her lawyer. Spence was equally curious and immediately became absorbed by her face. He had expected her to be dirty, trashy and obscene. She was anything but. She was beautiful.

Tom opened her cell, grabbed a folding Samsonite chair sitting at the end of the hall, walked inside and placed the chair in the middle of the cell. He turned to look at Spence, still standing outside the steel bars, staring at his client.

"Are ya comin' in?" Tom asked.

Spence broke his momentary fixation on Angela, entered the cell indecisively, and stood just inside the door. Tom walked out and slammed the door, gave it a yank to make sure it was locked, and retreated back down the hall. Spence turned to watch him until he was out of sight. He felt like crying for help, like an animal that had just been caged. When it was obvious that Tom was not coming back to save him, he turned to face her. She was still staring at him.

He surveyed the cell. The gray paint on the walls was fading and the concrete floor had large black stains on it. The cot hanging out of the wall sloped slightly downward, apparently accustomed to holding heavier prisoners than her. Around her toilet was a temporary makeshift curtain wall to provide the female prisoner with privacy. Spence looked around for a long, awkward thirty seconds, then finally summoned the courage to speak. He wasn't afraid of her, but he had no idea what an attorney should say to a client suspected of murder.

"I'm Spence Thompson," he said, still looking at the wall. He slipped his hands into his pockets, walked around the chair, and slowly lowered himself into the seat. When he looked up, she was still staring at him with an expression between fear and wonder. He removed his hands from his pockets and leaned forward with his elbows on his knees. He cleared his throat, but suddenly forgot what he wanted to say. They made eye contact and another awkward moment passed. She had a large bruise on her left eye, and Spence feared that looking at her would make her feel uncomfortable. But then, he found it hard to turn away.

"Are you a lawyer?" she asked.

"Yes, I am," Spence answered, thankful for a question he knew the answer to. "I am a lawyer."

"Are you my lawyer?" she asked.

Spence did not know how to explain what had just happened in Judge Hamilton's courtroom. Certainly he couldn't tell her that the county had just appointed someone with no criminal law experience to attempt to save her life. He was contemplating his answer when she said, "They told me I didn't have to talk to anybody," and then dropped her forehead onto her arms, covering her bruised face.

"That's right," Spence answered. "You don't have to talk to anyone if you don't want to." He did at least know that much about criminal law. "But you will need to talk to a lawyer, so he can help you,"

Spence finished excitedly, happy to be giving valuable advice.

"Are you going to be my lawyer?" she asked again, raising her head to look at him.

Spence's voice cracked, "Uh, no. I don't think I can be your lawyer."

"Why not?"

"Well, you see, I'm a real estate attorney," Spence said, adding under his breath, "and I've only been doing that for a day."

"So why are you here?" She kept one thought ahead of him, and his mind was working too slowly to catch up.

"The judge—Judge Hamilton, that is—wants me to be your attorney. But I don't think I can," Spence was talking more to himself than to her. "I don't know anything about criminal law or murder cases. I'm just..."

"I don't think I killed him," she interrupted.

"What's that?" Spence asked, though he had heard her clearly.

"I don't think I killed him."

"Well then, who did?" Spence was suddenly intrigued at the chance of knowing the facts before anyone else.

"I don't know," she said softly and placed her head back to its resting position on her arms.

"Okay," Spence said, then hesitated. "Maybe your attorney can help you figure it out."

She didn't look up. Spence could hear her began to weep.

He had never felt more awkward. Few girls had cried in front of him, even when he was breaking off their relationship. What should he say now? Several times he made an effort to speak, but couldn't. He needed time to collect his thoughts. He wished he hadn't come to see her so hastily. But that had been the judge's suggestion, who was he to disagree with it. Finally, he rose from the chair and walked to the cell door. He had forgotten the guard's name, so he just shouted, "Guard".

Tom came back down the hallway and unlocked the door. Spence stepped outside as Tom went in the cell and retrieved the chair. As Tom placed the chair against the wall, Spence stood at the cell door and looked at Angela Chauncey. Softly he said, "Goodbye." She did not answer. Spence followed Tom out of the cellblock. He could still hear her sobbing as he walked away, and suddenly a part of him wanted to comfort her. But how could he? The best way to help would be to not get involved. He couldn't help her. He wouldn't even know where to start.

Tom had to lead Spence back up the narrow stairway to unlock the door and let him out of the dungeon. Spence quickly walked up the stairs, afraid to look back, fearing that he would be sucked back down into a dark world he knew nothing about. When he reached the top and Tom opened the door, he slid past and began to hurry for the exit of the jailhouse, for once losing his manners and not thanking Tom for his help. In fact, it was not until the female clerk at the front desk said, "Bye" that he realized the omission. But then, how could he have thanked Tom? He could hardly breath.

He quickened his pace as he walked past the lady clerk and answered her with, "Goodbye." Outside the front door he jumped down the stairs two at a time and broke into a jog across the street and past the old courthouse. He was already sweating from the fear inside, and now he had to deal with the stifling heat. He ran around the side of the building that housed his office and accelerated to a dead run on the way to his Explorer parked in the alley. He fumbled for the keys in his pocket as the sweat began to pour down his face and seep into his shirt collar. He unlocked the door and got in. After starting the car, he leaned back against the leather head-rest and tried to think about what to do now. He threw the car into gear, sped out of the alley and onto the street heading out of town. Something was telling him to never slow down at the city limit sign.

—

Spence picked up a six-pack of Bud Light on his way home. When he got to his house, he looked at the beer on the seat beside him and wondered how it got there. He sat on the back porch steps with his beer and watched Sam play in the late evening sun. He could think of nothing but Angela. He wondered what she was doing, what she was thinking. Was she cold? Even in this heat? Did she have plenty of blankets? Why did he care? The loneliness had to be unbearable for her. He knew it was for him. She was pretty. She had been beaten up badly, but he could tell she was very attractive. Could she have really killed somebody?

He had been in town for scarcely seventy-two hours, and already he had found a new hell.

TWELVE

THINGS ARE NEVER as bleak in the early morning sun as they are in the evening light of the night before, but nevertheless, Spence found himself at the office early the next morning. He waited until seven A.M. before he called Wes and, more importantly, Wes' father, Jack. He wanted to talk to Mr. McCain before speaking with Americus, so he could convince his uncle that he had actually gone to a criminal law class while in law school. He knew Jack would be in his office before 7:00, but Spence wanted to wait until business hours before disturbing him. He waited until it was 8:00 in South Carolina and then punched the numbers on his phone. He asked the receptionist for Wes, who, just as Spence had figured, found his situation hilarious.

"You're kidding me!" Wes boomed into the phone. "You're going to try a murder case? You went to Crim class fewer times than I did."

"I'm not going to try the case, you dumbass," Spence retorted. "That's why I'm calling Jack, to see how I can get out of it."

"This is great," Wes was still laughing, "When it's time for the trial let me know, so I can come down there and watch those rednecks whip your butt."

"Just shut the hell up and get Jack on the phone," Spence

answered back. He loved Wes, but sometimes he didn't know when to give it a rest.

Wes went to his father's office where Jack McCain put Spence on the speakerphone. "What's the trouble son?"

Spence explained the situation, while Wes made derogatory comments in the background. When Spence finished his story, he heard Wes holler, "Isn't that hilarious?"

"Probably not hilarious to Spence's client," Jack said in a pointed reprimand. Jack McCain was a fun-loving man, with a passion for martinis and deep-sea fishing, but he took the practice of law and the well being of his clients very seriously.

"Can he make me defend her?" Spence inquired.

"Oh yes," replied Jack. "He has to appoint somebody from the local bar. In a larger city you could probably appeal it on the grounds that it's not your field of practice. However, being in such a small town, where most lawyers do a little bit of everything, it's unlikely that you could get out of it, especially if he is the only circuit judge in the county. It's doubtful that local attorneys will want to confront him. Remember, they make their living in his courtroom."

"But I thought you had to sign up and volunteer to be appointed to defend indigents."

"In larger jurisdictions that's usually true, and a lot of attorneys seek appointed cases. It helps pay the bills. But it sounds like your town's kind of small. If no one volunteers, he can appoint anyone he wants. Is there a lawyer in town who usually does these things?"

"There was, but he got killed in a hunting accident."

"Well, son, sounds like you've got yourself a client."

"So what am I going to do?"

"Your best bet is to find another lawyer to help you, but in the meantime, you better start putting a case together. You do have an obligation to defend her, and should you not do that to the best of your ability, you could lose your license to practice."

"So I've heard."

The conversation ended with Wes making a few more jokes and Jack giving Spence an immediate game plan on how to defend his client. Spence told Jack what few facts he had—including the bruises on Angela's face—and Jack suggested he explore the option of self defense, which meant the first thing to do was to have the girl examined by a doctor to record any signs of abuse.

When Americus arrived at ten, Spence went to his office and informed him of the latest developments.

"That sum bitch," muttered Americus through clinched teeth. "I'll see what I can do about getting you some help, but in the mean time, you'd better not allow this to interfere with your new duties here. I feel sorry for the girl, but she doesn't have much of a chance, so don't waste a lot of time on this. Hell, even I probably couldn't get her off." Americus smiled, lit a cigar and opened the paper. It was time for Spence to leave.

Spence had his second closing at 10:30, so he stepped into his office to review the documents. He stopped to call Americus on the interoffice phone to ask him which doctor he should call to have the girl examined.

"Call Doc Simpson," Americus shouted into his speakerphone, his usual tone when talking without the handset, "If you actually have to go to trial, he'll have the best rapport with the jury. Just hope he lives long enough to make your court date."

Spence had Kathy find him the number to Doc Simpson's office. He called and explained to the receptionist what he wanted. She placed him on hold, then came back a minute later to say that Doc Simpson would meet him at the county jail at 11:30, which meant his closing could not run long. Luckily for Spence, Huey stayed in the office that morning, so he was able to give him a fast review of the file. There was only one document that Huey omitted in the closing package, so the entire procedure went rather smoothly. Spence was already feeling quite the expert on real estate closings.

He beat the clients out the door and headed for the county jail.

He felt completely unprepared. He hadn't explained to his client what his plans were, but then he really didn't have a plan. As he walked he tried to ease his nerves by reminding himself that she wouldn't know the difference anyway. How many times could she have been charged with murder?

THIRTEEN

TUESDAY MORNING MEETINGS were something Kendall had grown to despise and today was no exception. When he took over NAPCO's top position, he had made these meetings absolutely mandatory. Now, he hated making himself available for them.

He sat at the end of a large marble conference table, slumped in his chair and barely conscious of the vice president of production standing at the opposite end of the room making a presentation on a power-point screen. Kendall had been hands-on when he first became the CEO at NAPCO, demanding reports and follow-ups; but now he left most of the day-to-day functions to Ricter, who sat just to his right at the table. Kendall occasionally glanced his way. Ricter had his eyes glued to the screen, giving full attention to the presentation. Kendall was still upset from their last meeting in his office and frowned every time he thought about Ricter's insolence. Still, Ricter was more than competent at his job and would be a hard man to replace. Besides, with all that he knew, there would be only one way for him to leave the company. And Kendall knew that it would be much more difficult to give the order on someone he knew personally, rather than some redneck from nowhereville.

With every meeting they now held, Kendall became further

detached from the task of making paper products and would have preferred to let Ricter run NAPCO completely. But the company's operations had become complicated and its corporate secrets extremely sensitive. Not to mention the fact that Ricter's loyalty was in question. Kendall rubbed his face and began to click the pen in his hand as he swiveled back and forth in his chair. Others around the table glanced furtively at the distracting noise, but he didn't care. Why should he?

Kendall did not make an effort to hide the reality that his mind had drifted. Never satisfied with his success, he needed a more prestigious challenge and recently launched *Kendall & Company*, an investment house in New York. Men like Charles Schwab and Peter Lynch were in the glamorous world of stocks and investing, creating much more excitement on Wall Street than Kendall's dirty old paper company. Even though he generated billions of dollars each year, he wasn't getting the respect he deserved. There just wasn't anything sexy about the paper business. At least that's how Kendall viewed it. He wanted to be in the limelight and meeting in high-profile places like New York and Los Angeles, not taking tours of rusted paper machines in ignorant little hick towns like Owensboro, Kentucky; Catawba, South Carolina; and Monroe, Alabama. NAPCO owned seven mills throughout the United States and Canada, but all were in hellholes, as far as Kendall was concerned, built on cheap land near the trees needed for their production. NAPCO owned nearly two million acres of timberland worldwide, but Kendall had seen enough trees.

And now he sat wasting his morning by listening to some thirty-five-year-old junior executive, who actually had the nerve to imply that his efforts had profited the company two billion dollars last year. What a joke! He was rich only because Kendall wanted him to be—part of the facade Kendall wanted the rest of the world to see. But Kendall knew that if it were not for his ingenious side business, the company would actually be losing money at an astronomical rate and would be bankrupt within a few months. Yet, this arrogant young prick truly thought the company's success had something to do with how fast their machines were able to dry paper. "What a loser," Kendall thought to himself. "Where the hell do we find these idiots?"

Kendall continued to fidget with his pen, still not making an effort to conceal his impatience. When the presentation was finally over, the young VP sat down and Ricter asked, "Is there anything else we need to think about?"

No one answered. "Okay," he said, "we'll see you all next week."

Kendall sat silently and chewed on the end of the pen. He watched as some stood to leave, while others rustled papers back into their folders and brief cases. None dared speak to Kendall on their way out. When all were gone, Ricter walked over to the conference room door and closed it.

"You were awfully quiet today," Ricter said.

"I hate employees. They're all a bunch of idiots who don't have a damned clue about how to make money."

"How can you say that, Tom?" Ricter seemed genuinely puzzled. "We've got some of the best people in the industry working for us. Real professionals."

"Oh Yes," sneered Kendall. "They're so professional that we could have lost as little as a billion dollars last year had it not been for our side interest."

Ricter gazed at Kendall but said nothing. He had run the numbers. He knew it was true.

"I think we need to up our shipments," Kendall stated, still coldly staring at the far conference room wall with the pen in the corner of his mouth.

"Tom, we've already talked about that," Ricter answered softly, with real concern in his voice. Leaning closer, he half whispered, "Let's not get greedy and spoil this thing. We need to make sure that we stay under the radar screen."

"The customer wants more," Kendall replied, "and I think we need to give it to them. It's just good business."

"But it's illegal business."

"What's that got to do with anything?"

Ricter put his elbows on the conference table and dropped his face in his hands. Kendall's mind seemed to be made up. Still, Ricter hoped to keep things from spinning out of control. He looked up at his boss.

"You know we've got to be concerned with who's running things down there. You said yourself they're nothing but a bunch of ignorant hicks," Ricter said, finding himself degrading the boys from Monroe, when normally he was the one defending them from Kendall.

"I'm not so worried about them anymore. I've got somebody keeping an eye on things down there. Real competent fellow."

Ricter's face lit up in surprise. "Were you planning on telling me about him?"

"I just did."

"Anybody else I need to know about," Ricter asked sarcastically, "or are they watching me and I'm not supposed to know."

"Of course not," Kendall answered and then asked, "Why? Do you need to be watched?"

Ricter did not feel like justifying the question with an answer. At the moment he just wanted to talk Kendall out of what he saw as a potentially dangerous move. He calmly folded his hands together on the table. "Tom, let's just be content with what we've got. We're already beating our competition. Let's just ride this thing out for a little while and then get out and spend our money."

Kendall threw his hands in the air, "Content? Content?" He could hardly contain himself. "You know, if people like me had attitudes like yours, we'd still be living in caves. No wonder you haven't become a CEO yet." Kendall stared at Ricter, daring a response.

Ricter's face flushed red, but otherwise he hid his anger. He knew the comment was just a retaliation from the 'common thuggery' remark he made in Kendall' office. He took solace knowing that he had been offered two CEO positions in the past two years, but he was concerned about Kendall's reaction to such a move. His boss was becoming increasingly paranoid, and Ricter knew too much. Right now Kendall wanted to argue, but Ricter didn't have the mental strength to oblige him in something he knew would be a futile attempt at convincing Kendall to show some restraint.

Ricter bit his bottom lip and said "Fine, Thomas. Fine." He gathered his papers, stood abruptly, and walked out of the room.

Kendall slouched in his chair. He wanted to go home for the rest of the afternoon and relax by his pool. Let those other idiots put in a full day at the office, he smirked. He was smarter than them. He knew how to make money.

FOURTEEN

WITH ONE LOOK Spence figured that Doc Simpson's grandchildren probably got everything they ever asked for. He was the kindest looking old man Spence had ever seen. He was at least seventy, according to Americus, but he looked like a man in his mid-fifties. He had a comfortable slouch that made him seem shorter than his six feet, and he had snow-white hair and deep blue eyes. He wore a soft gray suit, a matching yellow tie, and black wing tips shined to a high gloss. His broad smile was infectious, and Spence felt the warmth in his hand when they introduced themselves on the steps of the county jail. Doc Simpson was the kind of man that could make a child smile even while getting a shot. He looked the part of an old Southern doctor and spoke with an even stronger Southern accent, always accompanied by the broad grin. Spence wondered if the old man was going to start quoting William Faulkner right there on the jailhouse steps.

"Dr. Simpson, I can't tell you how thankful I am for you taking the time to help me," Spence said.

"Oh certainly, glad to do it. I'm here to help in anyway I can," Doc Simpson replied.

Spence started to ask if he would try Angela's case, since he seemed so willing to help, but the doctor was not through talking. "I don't know if you know this, but your grandfather was a good friend of mine."

"Really?"

"Oh yes. We were old bird hunting buddies. He gave me the loan to start my practice."

Spence recalled that his grandfather started out as a banker.

"As a matter of fact," Doc Simpson continued, "your mother was the third baby I delivered after I began my practice here in town."

They entered the jailhouse and continued talking cheerfully as the desk clerk checked them in and lead them to the door descending to the cellblock. As the large door closed behind them, the noise from the busy first floor of the building was suddenly shut off, and the silence of the stairway brought an end to their cheerful conversation. Spence could tell that Doc Simpson didn't get down to the cellblock very often because the old man seemed to be as uncomfortable as he was.

Nevertheless, Tom and the doctor knew one another, and they exchanged pleasantries while Tom opened the iron doors that lead to Angela's cell. The three men walked to the end of the hall where she was being held. Her position hadn't changed much from the night before—still on the bed, knees in her chest, head on her arms. Her head lifted when she heard Tom rattle the keys in the cell door lock.

"Angela," Spence said in a reassuring tone, "I'm Spence Thompson. I was here last night. Do you remember?"

As soon as he said it, he wished he could take it back. He didn't mean to imply that she might not remember what had happened to her in the last twenty-four hours. She had been sitting in a jail cell. It wasn't like a whole lot of activity could have taken place. Even from his brief visit yesterday, he knew she wasn't stupid. Her questions had come quickly—and logically. There was something about her that stirred him—a strange feeling from someone he had only spent a few moments with. Perhaps it was because she had been thrust into his care and for the moment was totally helpless without him. The rest of her life depended on how well he handled her case. He knew this scenario was bound to stir conflicting emotions to either run and hide, or stand and fight. And at this point he was still deciding which emotion to follow.

Angela looked at him, then at Doctor Simpson.

"We've got to start putting a case together for you," said Spence. "This is Doctor Simpson." He put his hand on the Doctor's shoulder. "He needs to examine you for any signs of physical abuse. I think our best case at this point is probably going to be self-defense, so we'll need some evidence—that is, if it's okay with you." He added this last part for her. She hadn't said a word, and he had no idea how comfortable she was with the idea of a physical examination.

"I thought you weren't going to be my lawyer," she said, uncurling her legs and lowering her feet onto the floor as her hands gripped the edge of the mattress. She leaned forward with an inquisitive arch in her brow. For the past twenty-four hours Spence had been thinking that this poor creature truly needed his help, but all of the sudden she didn't look so defenseless. In fact, Spence was the one who felt trapped. He knew at that moment she was a stronger woman than even he had given her credit for.

"Well, you… you see," Spence stuttered. Some great trial attorney he was. Even questions from his own client made him nervous.

"You see, I'm not going to be your attorney, but until I find someone else to defend you, I'm obligated to defend you to the best of my ability." In his mind he added, "Which isn't much."

Angela Chauncey didn't know any lawyers or many people around Monroe, for that matter. Her father made sure of that. The only person to ever show her affection was her grandmother, who died when Angela was twelve. But on Sundays before her death, the elderly lady had taken young Angela to church, and as her Sunday school teacher, she always made sure the other children included her in their activities. Angela never understood why the children she played with on Sunday morning would ignore her the next day at school. It made it hard for her to trust anybody. But somehow this young attorney was different. She felt it. Maybe it was his nervousness, like he was afraid to let her down. No one had ever expressed that feeling for her before. It made her uncomfortable, yet she liked it. She did not want him to go away. She wanted him to be her lawyer.

When the county jail was remodeled in 1962, the last cell on the block had been designed specifically for the privacy of female prisoners—on the remote chance that a female from Monroe might one day deserve imprisonment. But the designers had television sets and knew the world, and the women that inhabited it, was undergoing some drastic changes out past the county lines.

At the top of the iron bars sealing the cell's front was a track with a curtain folded on the right side and held back by a lock and chain on top and bottom. Tom, curious about Doc Simpson's presence, had not left the hallway and listened as Spence introduced him to Angela. Now that Tom understood why the doctor was at the county jail, he entered the cell and opened the locks that held the fold out curtain. He pulled the curtain along its track until the front of the cell was completely secluded. Once the curtain wall was fully extended, Tom instructed Doc Simpson to call when he had completed his examination and headed back to his own little cage.

Doc Simpson walked to the cot where Angela sat and placed his black bag on the floor. With his hands folded in front of him and still wearing his biggest grin, he introduced himself to her. His bedside demeanor was excellent, always making sure that the female patients in particular were comfortable with what was about to take place.

"Angela, I'm Doctor Albert Simpson. To help Spence prepare your case, I'm going to give you an examination and document what we find. If at any time you feel uncomfortable, please let me know and I will stop. Okay?"

Angela nodded. She had become outwardly nervous, as if she were hiding something, scanning back and forth from Spence to Simpson. Men made her nervous. The only one she had really ever known was her father, and he had been anything but kind. She felt she could trust this doctor. After all, he was an old man and doctors were supposed to be nice. But then, so were sheriffs. Plus, the doctor was going to be touching her, something that in her past had not been a pleasant experience. Still, she said nothing.

"I'm just going to wait outside. I'll be right out here if you need me," Spence said, and he turned to find the end of the curtain.

"Please stay," Angela whispered. She was staring at him helplessly now, so different from the confident expression she had had just moments before. Her brown eyes were uncertain. They were all Spence could focus on. They captivated him, made him unable to turn away. But why did she want him to stay? Doc Simpson was one of the sweetest old men he had ever met. Certainly she wasn't afraid of him.

"Doc?" Spence asked.

"If your client wants you to stay, I think you should stay," Doc Simpson replied.

Spence once again turned to Angela, who had yet to take her eyes off of him. He found himself sliding to the corner of the cell and finally settling into it. He leaned a shoulder against the cement wall, crossed his arms, and tried not to look at her.

She took her eyes off of Spence and watched nothing in particular on the ground. She did not know why she wanted him to stay, saying it almost instinctively as he was leaving. Somehow his presence was reassuring.

Doc Simpson removed a chart from his bag. On one side was an outline of a female torso, as viewed from the front and the flip side showed the same torso from the back. Simpson laid the chart on the cot and then began to pull his examining equipment from the bag. Once all of his tools were in place, he pulled a pen from his coat pocket and at the top of the chart he wrote "Angela Chauncey, July 26."

"Okay, Angela," Doc Simpson said, "let's have a look at that eye."

Her left eye had clearly been bruised by something, and Spence could already see himself arguing it was the result of a beating. To him it looked worse today than it had the day before, puffy and swollen all around, and much darker than the rest of her mocha skin. Doc Simpson shined a small examination light into the injured eye.

"Angela, have you had any trouble seeing out of this eye," Simpson asked.

"No, sir."

He then gently touched the bruise. She winced when he probed just below the socket, where the pain was the most intense. Doc Simpson examined her face thoroughly, pausing also over a small laceration under her lower lip, and occasionally made notes on his chart.

"Okay, Angela, do you have any other areas with bruises or cuts?" Doc Simpson asked.

"Yes, sir," she replied, "on my legs."

Spence noticed how she called the Doc "sir" and wondered if she was always so polite or if Simpson's gentle nature had begun to win her over. Spence was a firm believer in the value of manners. He knew they had opened doors for him and wondered if she was smart enough to know their benefits as well, or was she simply that scared.

"Well, then," Doc Simpson began, "let's take a look at those."

Angela's eyes turned toward Spence. She was embarrassed. For Doc Simpson to examine her, she would have to pull her pants down below her knees. She wished she had let Spence leave the cell, but to ask him to do so now might hurt his feelings, and that was the last thing she wanted to do. For some reason, she trusted him and wanted him to know it. Their eyes met when she reached for the drawstring holding her orange county-issued pants. With the motion of untying her pants, Spence's eyes fell to focus on the floor immediately in front of his feet. He wanted to be professional, but he didn't know how. Would a seasoned lawyer stay in the cell? Would he inspect her legs? Would he need to view the bruises to defend her better?

She turned three-fourths of her back toward Spence and lowered her pants below her knees. Spence tried to resist, but his curiosity would not let him. He wanted to see how badly she had been beaten.

When he was sure she could no longer see his eyes, he turned his head up so that he might observe her. On her right leg, beginning just above the knee and running all the way up the back of her thigh was a dark blue discoloration. Doc Simpson bent down to take a closer look and then grabbed his chart to make some notes. Spence could see him draw a line to the back right leg of the figure on the chart, and then pencil in his comments. Spence was finding it difficult to look away. Americus said her father was a great athlete, and she had definitely inherited his athletic body. Her legs were smooth with muscles and her calves well defined, springing into action when she rotated on her toes. Spence felt himself begin to sweat.

"Okay, Angela, I've seen all I need to see from here," Doc Simpson said. "You can pull your pants back up."

Turning to pull up her pants, her eyes met Spence's again, and again he quickly glanced away. Again the questions entered his mind. As her lawyer did he need to be watching? As a man why was he so afraid of seeing her bare legs. He wished she had let him leave the cell.

"Is there anywhere else I need to look?" Doc Simpson asked.

"Yes, sir," she replied, "I think I have some bruises on my back."

She looked down at her issued blouse and began unbuttoning it. Spence studied the floor again. Should he be taking notes? Asking the doctor questions? The girl was beautiful and the man in him was curious, but this uncomfortable moment was not the way he wanted to start their lawyer-client relationship. Was this the way all lawyers did it? He had so much to learn, and didn't even know where to begin.

When she unfastened the last button, she turned and dropped her shirt to the small of her back. Spence glanced up. At this moment he realized—just from seeing her back—what a special creature God had made in this woman. Her shoulders were broad, and her torso narrowed toward her waist in exquisite proportion. Her skin was silky smooth, and the muscles in her back glistened in the low florescent light of the cell. He had seen beautiful women before, but none like her. There had never been one like her.

Spence continued to unwillingly stare. He tried to collect himself and he suddenly felt the room getting hotter. He screamed at himself inside his head to get control. And then he noticed it. It was Doc Simpson. The little old man was also entranced with the beauty of this woman standing before him. He stood behind her, admiring the muscles in her back. Spence was convinced by Doc Simpson's reaction that he was not just caught up in the moment—she really was something special.

All at once Doc Simpson snapped out of his trance, shook his head and began to examine the bruises on her back. He furiously wrote on his chart and tried not to look at Angela unless necessary. A tiny bead of sweat began at Doc Simpson's temple and ran down the side of his face toward his chin. At seventy-three years of age, even the good doctor was finding the cool jail cell a touch warmer.

FIFTEEN

JUDGE HAMILTON ENTERED his chambers and found Sheriff Watkins and Patrick Seaver, the county's district attorney, waiting for him in the large leather chairs facing his desk. They were there for the informal Tuesday meeting that the three held every week. The subject matter was not about county business or judicial functions, but it was important to keep a firm grasp on what each other was doing. They said they needed communication, but each in his own mind knew it was because he did not trust the other two. After all, when men collaborate to do evil things, paranoia sets in. They trusted no one, not even each other. Especially not each other. From now on, everybody they came in contact with would be regarded as a criminal. And why not? They were. They could never turn their backs, even on men they had known and trusted their entire lives. Days were spent with the apprehension of feeling like a fish in an aquarium. There was nowhere to hide. When they went to bed at night the anxiety never left them. What if one of the others told? What if the Feds were closing in a little more each day? The pressure never left. No longer just ordinary men looking forward to retirement, they were now reluctant business partners, growing to despise their associates because of the secrets they shared. Their nerves were on edge, and every move was magnified by a thousand degrees. But the money. How the money made it all seem worth it.

Watkins was especially a cause of concern for the judge and district attorney. After all, he was not a lawyer and therefore a lesser species. Of the three, Seaver was the brightest, and the better trial lawyer between the judge and himself. He was in his fifteenth year as the county's top prosecutor, and merciless on criminals—unless they were on his side. He was not a natural born politician like the judge and despised campaigning, but it never showed in the county's election results. In all of his races he had never really been challenged. In Monroe, the judge was more respected, but the DA was more feared.

"I heard Dubo did fine with Friday's shipment," the judge said, turning to Sheriff Watkins after closing the door to his chambers.

"He did just fine," the sheriff answered.

"Can we count on him to keep his mouth shut?" asked the judge.

"Damn right," Watkins answered matter of factly while looking down at his tremendous belly and straightening his slender black tie. "Me and Little John made him understand that if he wanted to stay out of jail—or out of the grave for that matter—that he'd keep his mouth shut and talk to no one about his job. Besides if he don't keep quiet, we'll just get rid of him like we did the last one."

"I guess you figure he's expendable," Seaver said sarcastically.

"They're all expendable," the sheriff answered back with a stare.

The district attorney had made it clear at an impromptu Saturday night meeting at the judge's house that he didn't approve of the way Watkins deviated from the plan. He was to have killed Calvin *and* the girl and then, of course, to eventually give up on finding the killer. But Watkins never liked the original plan because it made him look incompetent. And when he saw the girl lying on the floor, unconscious from an obvious struggle, he conceived his own plan. Watkins thought it was brilliant. Everyone would certainly believe the girl killed her abusive father and the judge could sentence her away until the murder was forgotten. The matter would be closed, without endless speculation as to what really happened.

Seaver, however, looked at the whole matter differently, through the eyes of a lawyer. Twenty years of experience had taught him that anything could happen at a trial, and while he had agreed at the meeting that the judge could control his courtroom, he still viewed a trial much too risky. The original plan, with no trial, was much safer.

"I still don't like the thought of involving a courtroom on this matter," he reiterated.

"What's a matter with you Pat? You scared of this new kid or somethin'?" Watkins asked, smiling at Seaver.

"Now stop it you two," the judge interrupted. "We went over all of this Saturday night. Pat, I told you that I had his records checked and the kid barely passed his Criminal Law courses. Hell, he barely passed law school period. He knows nothing about a trial or how to prepare for one, and Americus certainly isn't going to help him. The trial will be over before he knows what hit'im, and he'll once again be knee deep in deeds and settlement statements and totally unconcerned with what happens to a girl he doesn't even know."

"James, I know you feel you can handle anything this kid might dig up and maybe you're right," Seaver answered, "but there's something about this guy that makes me nervous. I saw the way he handled himself in front of you yesterday, and I just don't know that we can run over him like you think we can. It concerned me so much that I've done a little checking myself this morning with some friends that I have at the State Bar, and it seems that our kid here may not be as dumb as we think. Out of the five hundred and ninety-three applicants that took the bar exam in February, our boy scored better than five hundred and ninety-one of them. And he missed having the highest score in the state by two questions. Hell, every woman in town has heard of the new guy, including my thirteen-year old daughter. If we get a jury full of women, we could get screwed."

"Relax," the judge replied. "Think about all of your past experiences as a lawyer. At any point in time, do you think that if the judge had it in for you or your client, you'd have won?"

Seaver answered back, "I understand what you're saying, James, but don't forget that you won't be presiding over the appeal, and if we convict her, there will certainly be an appeal."

"And I'm telling you, Pat, I can make the record so that she won't have a prayer at an appeal either. What's that saying—'If God be for us, who can be against us?' If the trial judge is against you, God or not, you're going to lose."

"I hope you're right, James. I just hope you're right," replied Seaver.

"Think about it Pat," Watkins interrupted. "When you wanted that kid that was following your daughter around last year thrown in juvenile, we didn't have any trouble doin' it. And you know as well as I do that he didn't slash them school bus tires. But when the little punk woke up this mornin' at the detention center, he had to take a piss in front of thirty-five other juvenile punks."

"But guys, this is murder," Seaver argued. "Its not that simple."

"Pat, it's precisely that simple," the judge said. "I don't know why we're arguing about a trial anyway. All we've got to do is make this kid plead guilty and there won't be a trial or an appeal. We convince him that we'll give him the deal of a lifetime and he can't refuse."

"What if he doesn't plead guilty?"

"He will. I've heard you say a hundred times that plea bargaining is just like playing poker, and in this game you're holding all the cards. You'll just have to convince him that avoiding a trial is the only proper thing to do. He's been practicing law less than a week, so he ought to be willing to take a little well-meant advice."

"Yeah, Pat," Watkins chimed in, "just make sure there's no trial." The sheriff was starting to understand that his revised plan was not so foolproof.

"I hope it's that simple," Seaver said. "I mean, I know we've got to do something now. The whole town knows we arrested her. It's not like we can just turn her loose."

The judge stood up to leave the room but turned to give one last instruction to Seaver. "Pat, you just concentrate on getting the kid to plea bargain and tell them boys in Chicago not to worry. We'll handle our end down here. And believe me, we can handle it. Mr. Spencer Michael Thompson will never know what hit'im."

SIXTEEN

ALL OF THE bankers in town lost their bet on who Spence would first take to lunch. His first lunch date—Wednesday, his fifth day in town—was with Amy, the receptionist he met on Monday with Americus. He called to remind her that she promised to show him how to act like a local. She informed him that as his host, her first duty was to initiate him into the world class cooking of Pinkney, the cook at Miss Sarah's Lunch Stop, located on the town square.

Spence insisted that he pick her up for their lunch date, partly so he could show off his new Explorer, and partly so they could get more familiar with each other in the car. He drove out to the mill to pick her up, and while there, made sure he spoke to Smitty. He knew Americus would be pleased.

When they got to Miss Sarah's, Spence could tell that the little restaurant was indeed the most popular place for lunch in Monroe. The dining room was crowded from wall to wall and he wondered how they'd ever get a table. Amy recognized her aunt and uncle sitting at a table and went over to say hello. Spence stopped to shake hands with a few bankers he met earlier in the week, and then joined Amy at their table. Amy's aunt and uncle were just about to leave, but stayed a few more minutes to inspect the company their niece was keeping. Satisfied she was alright, they walked to the counter, paid their bill and left. Spence was pleased to be alone with Amy again and began to take notice of his surroundings.

Like all of the other structures around the square, the restaurant was aged, with countless layers of paint on the walls. The building was much too old to have central heating and air, but four ceiling fans and two window unit air conditioners worked to keep the temperature bearable. Their task was hindered in that the front door stayed open the entire lunch hour. Two black women waited on tables, one in her fifties and the other in her twenties. They walked hurriedly around the tables and in and out of the kitchen, carrying pitchers of tea and plates of food. A skinny teenage boy was bussing tables as quickly as customers finished their meals. Spence assumed that Pinkney, the cook he had been hearing so much about, was behind the swinging double doors that led to the kitchen. Behind the counter at the cash register was a huge white man, who must have weighed at least three hundred pounds. He sat on a stool and steadily took money from paying customers. He said nothing to them, and customers spoke only to tell him how many meals they were paying for. He took their money and placed it in the cash register, which like the front door was never closed. It took a couple of glances, but Spence finally put his finger on what was different about the cashier. The large man was blind.

Amy began to tell Spence about the history of Miss Sarah's. Thirty some-odd-years ago, Miss Sarah's husband, a local sharecropper, died, leaving her with a young blind boy to care for. Unable to work the fields and with nowhere else to turn, Miss Sarah invited a local banker over to the house she was about to be thrown out of. Her plan was to convince him she could cook so well that he should give her a loan to start a restaurant. She finished the meal with her famous blackberry cobbler and that was all it took to seal the deal. She moved into the building currently housing the restaurant, hired Pinkney to help with the cooking and his wife Maddie to wait on tables. About ten years later Miss Sarah died, and it became the responsibility of Pinkney and Maddie to care for

Big Earl. They were the only family he had left, and from that day forward they did everything for him. The younger woman waiting tables was Pinkney's and Maddie's daughter and the young man bussing tables was their son, home from college for the summer and the only recipient to ever receive the Big Earl Scholarship. By now it was rumored that Big Earl was the second richest man in town, next to Americus, and Spence could see why such a story would circulate, and possibly even be true. The little restaurant obviously stayed packed and the customers almost always paid with cash—a restaurant owner's preferred, and the IRS's least favorite, form of payment. Besides, there was very little for a three hundred pound blind man to spend his money on in Monroe.

Spence and Amy ordered their lunch from a one-page typewritten menu that gave customers a choice of five meat dishes, eleven vegetables, two kinds of bread, and two kinds of desserts. Maddie took their order and expressed to Spence how glad she was to meet him, but she didn't stay long. She was extremely busy giving orders to the kitchen and keeping everyone's tea glass full.

Two and a half minutes later their food arrived, and Spence and Amy began to eat. Pinkney had lived up to his billing. It was wonderful.

"So where's the last girlfriend?" Amy asked, "Or are you the noncommittal type?"

"You don't waste much time do you?"

"When it comes to love in a small town, you have to be quick. The pickings are pretty slim."

Spence laughed. "So, should I latch on to you right away?"

Amy squinted her eyes as if she were trying to read something on Spence's face, "No, I don't see you as the 'latching on' type."

"That predictable, huh."

"Well, your past gives you away."

"And what do you know about my past?"

"I know you were a football player in college. A good-looking guy like you—on the football team? I would imagine you're pretty experienced—or at least had a lot of opportunities to be."

"How did you know I played football?"

"This is a small town. Word travels fast. If you're single and some-one who's available comes to town, the phone lines heat up."

"Is that right?"

"Like you wouldn't believe. By the time you and your uncle came out to the mill, I had already gotten calls from my mother, two of my aunts and my third grade teacher telling me about the new single lawyer in town."

Spence was captivated by the pretty girl and her funny commen-tary. "You've got to be kidding me."

"Oh, I wish I were. At least this time the product was something worth looking into," Amy answered with a smile. "My family sounds the alarm at anything in pants."

"If that was a compliment, thank you. But it doesn't sound like it takes much to be considered a prize around here." Spence took a bite of his mashed potatoes. "So, go on, tell me more about my past."

"Well, after being the big man on campus in college, you went on to law school at the University, where I'm sure plenty of bowheads were chasing at your heals."

"Bowheads?"

"Sorority girls. You know the prissy type that wear bows in their hair."

"You got something against sorority girls?"

"Of course not, I'm an Alpha Xi Delta myself, and I've got a draw-er full of hair bows to prove it."

Spence nodded his head and smiled. He took a bite of his fried country steak smothered in white peppered gravy. He chewed his food carefully, since he was on sort of a date, and took small bites so he could keep the conversation going. The food was so good that he almost wished Amy wasn't there and he could eat the way he wanted too. He was trying to think of something to change the subject from his past, but Amy wasn't about to let him off that easy.

"So Mr. Thompson, how many?"

"How many what?"

"How many victims have you sent to the broken heart club?"

"That's a terrible way to put it."

"Oh, come on. I'm not that innocent. How many girls awoke to find you gone the next morning—or are still waiting for that phone call? I'm guessing it's a lot. How many? Ten? Twelve?"

The answer was more like twenty, but Spence was not about to let her know that. He liked her line of questioning, though, and her frank talk about one-night stands and lost innocence. Maybe he was getting somewhere. "Oh, I'm quite sure it's not that many," he answered.

"Well, you had better mend your ways if you are planning on getting married in this town."

"Married? My, you do move fast."

"You don't want to get married?"

"Sure, but I'd like to finish lunch first if you don't mind."

Amy smiled. Perhaps she had been a little too inquisitive.

They ate more of their lunch and then Amy started on her next topic.

"So I hear your going to be defending Angela Chauncey."

"Word does travel fast."

"You're going to have to do a better job of reading the local paper. It was in this morning's edition that you were the new appointed defender."

"I am not the new appointed defender." Spence leaned back in his chair, surprised to find himself already in the news. "And as a matter of fact, I'm trying to get out it as we speak."

"I always felt sorry for her."

"You know her?"

"I know of her, I guess you could say. She was a couple of years behind me in school, but she never finished. She was never really close to anyone."

"I've only talked to her a few times in her cell, but she seems to be a normal person. Why couldn't she make friends?"

"Oh come on, you know. The white boys wouldn't talk to her because of, well, she's a half-breed, and nobody seemed to know which crowd she was supposed to be around. And let's face it, she's beautiful and I think most of the girls resented that. Besides, her father was crazy."

"Why couldn't she just hang around the human crowd?"

"In a perfect world, maybe. We get along pretty well around here, and I have my share of black friends, but jungle fever is still frowned upon."

"Well, it makes no difference to me anyhow. The sooner I find her another lawyer, the better off the both of us will be. I have no idea what I'm doing in a murder case."

"Didn't they teach you what to do in law school?"

Spence smiled at this common misconception about law school graduates—that they actually could go out into the real world and start practicing law.

"Not quite," he replied, "They taught me what murder was. They never mentioned anything on how to get out of it."

"Well, I'm sure you'll figure it out. You don't look like the type that likes to lose, especially your first case."

"Does everybody in this town have a hearing problem? I already told you I'm not going to defend her. I'm trying to find someone else." It was starting to bother him that the whole community presumed him to be Angela's attorney.

Amy could see he was trying to be polite, but he didn't want to talk about Angela. But she couldn't let it go.

"Just seems a shame," she said.

"What's that?"

"All of her life, nobody's wanted her. And now, from what I hear, her life's about to be over and she still can't find anybody to help her. Just seems a shame."

Spence placed his fork down beside his plate. Suddenly, his appetite had disappeared.

SEVENTEEN

THE WEEKEND COULDN'T come fast enough to satisfy Spence. Friday morning he sat in his office, staring at the computer screen, thinking about how little he remembered from the day before. He had a date with Amy later that evening, and he hoped she could take his mind off of the case for a while. Or better yet, off of Angela. His client had dominated his thoughts the last few days and he wished he knew why. Was it the fear of his own incompetence? Or was it that body he witnessed with Doc Simpson?

He sat with his feet on the floor and spun his chair from side to side, tapping his pen on the desk, trying to think of something constructive to do. By design, Fridays were slow around the office so Americus could begin his weekend early. There were no closings scheduled, and although Huey and Kathy were expected to put in a full day, Spence was tempted to leave. But he had scheduled a lunch with Wilson at the Bank, and didn't want to go home and then drive back to town. But what to do with the next hour? He was quite certain there were plenty of things he could be doing to prepare for Angela's case, but he didn't know what they were. So far he had spent most of his time trying to find a way out of the entire situation.

He picked up his paycheck that sat on the corner of his desk and admired it for the fourth time. Americus had never discussed the amount of his salary and Spence had just been thankful to get a job. He certainly wasn't going to argue about money. There were classmates from law school still looking for employment four months after passing the bar, and their credentials were certainly more impressive than his own. Were it not for his uncle, Spence sometimes wondered what he would do. But then it was Americus who wanted him to go to law school in the first place and promised him a job when he graduated. If something were to happen to Americus now, at least Spence had a law degree.

He stretched the check in front of his face. Maybe the amount was a goodwill gesture to help him setup his house—yet another example of Americus' generosity. But what if it was the same each week? Fifteen hundred dollars a week before taxes; $78,000 a year. He couldn't suppress his smile. All his life he was the one with no connections or important friends, and now he made more than ninety percent of his graduating class only because he was the nephew of Monroe's wealthiest lawyer. Seventy-eight thousand a year in Monroe was the equivalent to a hundred and fifty in the hustle and bustle of Atlanta or Birmingham. And here he was, struggling to pass the time.

He placed the check back on his desk and relaxed in his chair, which made a squeak as he reclined back to its full position. Placing his hands behind his head, he closed his eyes. He could see her, the shirt wrapped around the small of her muscular back. The silky smooth hair over her shoulders and the skin—the most gorgeous skin he had ever seen. A dark tan, almost liquid, as though to touch it would create ripples. Spence wanted to see his own reflection in that water.

He opened his eyes and shook his head, then said out loud, "What the hell are you thinking? She's a client."

His attention would be better served by focusing on Amy anyway. She was a more realistic conquest and he would begin his pursuit at 6:30 tonight. But maybe he could go talk to Angela briefly before lunch. Maybe, if he went by and stayed only a few minutes, with another appointment pending, it would look like he was a real attorney with real cases. But why was he trying to impress her? She certainly couldn't help him get what he wanted.

He gathered up his briefcase from the floor and opened it on his desk to put his paycheck inside. He noticed that the pen normally in the pocket of the case was missing, so he pulled out the long center drawer of his desk to find another. Instead, he found an envelope with his name written in big letters across the front. It was Americus' handwriting. The envelope was not sealed, but did have the flap tucked inside. He pulled out the contents—a stack of one hundred dollar bills and a note:

I've seen the same suit on you three times in the past week. Go buy some more. Americus.

Spence placed the note in his briefcase and counted out the money. Twenty-five hundred. Where did Americus get all of this cash? And why was he willing to give it all to Spence?

He finished packing his briefcase, told Kathy he was leaving and walked outside to put his suit jacket in the Explorer. He could walk to the jail faster than he could drive and was going to meet Wilson over at Miss Sarah's anyway. The entire journey from where he stood now, to the jail, then the restaurant and back to the car would be less than a quarter of a mile. Spence draped his suit jacket across the passenger seat, closed the door and locked it. The heat was getting worse each day as the summer settled into the dog days of August. As he walked to the county jail to see Angela, he wondered just how much money his uncle made.

Curiosity caused him to keep a ledger of the fees generated over the previous week. He had done four closings, and with the attorney's fees and title insurance premiums, generated nearly four thousand dollars in revenue. He also signed eight timber right opinions for NAPCO. Huey created the documents and placed them on his desk for signature. He read the first two, thinking he was acting lawyerly,

but then realized he had no way of knowing if the opinion was correct
or not, so why bother to read it? Huey knew more about real estate
than he did anyway. From then on he just signed them.

Americus charged seven hundred and fifty dollars per opinion, so
that was another six thousand dollars added to the week's income. He
undoubtedly owned the building that housed his office and paid
Kathy and Huey peanuts. His only expensive overhead seemed to be
the monthly thousand-dollar kickback he gave to Smitty, NAPCO's
timber buyer. So he began to understand how Americus could throw
such money around. Spence alone had accounted for nearly ten thousand dollars in the past week, and none of this took into considera-
tion the income Americus received from his properties spread
throughout the state. Perhaps Americus just had more than he knew
what to do with and felt like sharing. As the beneficiary, Spence certainly wasn't going to argue.

The money was bulky in his pocket, but he liked its feel, never
having had enough at one time to actually feel its presence when he
walked. He had wondered what he and Amy would do on their date.
Now he guessed they could go to Auburn or Dothan and go shopping. Certainly a self-described bowhead would like to do that.

When he reached the jailhouse he realized he didn't have anything to write with, or on for that matter, so it was not like he could
really dig into his client's case. He thought about leaving, but could-
n't lie to himself. He wanted to see her.

After the ritual of signing in, he proceeded to the door leading
down the long narrow stairway to the holding cells. This time the
desk clerk did not follow him down the stairs, opening the door and
then closing it behind him. The clerk had become more friendly with
each visit and Spence felt important as she lead him to the stairway,
but he hated to hear the door shutting behind him. The stairway was
so confined and quiet that it echoed in his ears. It was a dreadful,
lonely sound.

He found Tom in his cage, reading the paper on the stool, just like always. They exchanged greetings as Tom opened the doors to let Spence through, closing them behind him and again creating the eerie sound of slamming iron. Spence noticed there were three new members to the cellblock, and that the inmates there on Monday and Tuesday were gone—except for Angela, whom they found sleeping on the bed.

Tom unlocked the door to her cell and turned to Spence. "Close it behind you when you're done," he said, and then began his stroll back down the hallway. Spence was a little surprised that Tom had become so cavalier about a prisoner accused of murder, but figured the guard knew she was an unlikely candidate to try an escape.

Even from a few feet away he could see the tear stains on her face. She was sleeping so soundly that even the noise for the steel doors closing could not disturb her slumber. He decided not to disturb her, having no particular reason to be there anyway, other than to see her face. Her shoes were placed neatly on the floor beside the cot and he could see her slender ankles as her pants ascended up her calves. Turning in her sleep had caused her shirt to wrap around her upper body, exposing her tiny waistline. The side of her face rested on the back of her hands, placed together on the pillow as if she were praying. Spence found himself caught in the rhythm of her breathing, in then out, while her clothing moved ever so slightly. He watched for a full two minutes, taking full notice of her entire body, then, quietly as he could, he closed the iron door.

Dear God she was beautiful.

EIGHTEEN

AMY'S APARTMENT WAS on the other side of town from Spence's house in one of only two complexes in Monroe. When she moved back from college, she knew it would be impossible to live with her parents after being on her own for the last four years. Not that she led a particularly wild life, but still, she was from a different generation than her parents and for her sake and theirs it was probably better if they didn't know her every activity. Like, for instance, the fact that Spence had spent both Friday and Saturday nights at her place.

On Sunday morning Spence awoke to find Amy lying against his back, her arms underneath his, her hands pulling his body closer. It was a few minutes past seven when she made her move. He pretended to be sound asleep. The sex the night before had been good, a two-and-a-half-hour escapade spread over the few rooms of the tiny apartment, but he wasn't in the mood at the moment. Last night's wine had not completely vanished from his head. Amy had had only two boyfriends in her lifetime, one in high school and one in college, so her sexual experience was limited to that point. She was more than willing to use Spence to make up for her lack of experience. That suited Spence just fine. But as beautiful as she was, and as willing as she had been to please, when he closed his eyes, it was another girl's face he saw.

"Good morning," Amy said softly.

"Morning. How do you feel?"

"Exceptional."

"Don't you think you could feel even better with another hour or so of sleep?" Spence was still far too sleepy to be in the mood.

"I'll admit, that would be nice, but I'm afraid you've got to go."

"Was I that bad?"

"Oh no, you were wonderful," she said, kissing the middle of his upper back, "but my parents and little brother will be here soon to pick me up for church and I didn't think this would be the best way for you to meet them."

"You and me naked? What's wrong with that?"

"You know, you could come to church with us."

"No thanks. I'd prefer to make their acquaintance in a little less intimidating environment."

He rolled himself over and the two of them wrapped themselves in each other's arms.

"I could get used to this," she said.

"Me too," he answered back, pretending.

"I'd better go get ready. You can stay here for a little while, but they'll probably be here in an hour."

"Don't worry, I'll disappear."

"I really had a good time last night," she whispered as she buried her head into his chest.

"Me too."

She kissed him and got out of the bed. Spence left his hands on her until the very last minute, rolling them over her arms, down her side and over her hips. He didn't stop touching her until she was out of his reach. She had been a little shy the first morning about being naked in front of him, but that awkwardness was gone as she walked to her dresser and pulled out a pair of silk shorts and a shirt. Spence watched as she dressed, still firm at twenty-two. Then she came to him again, kissed him on the forehead and walked into her bathroom. Now he was in the mood.

—

When Spence made it to his house, Americus was on the front porch waiting, cigar in mouth, reading the Sunday paper. He was the cleanest Spence had ever seen him, looking like a thinner Matlock, dressed in a seersucker suit with a light blue tie, clean shaven and combed back hair.

Americus looked at his watch and said, "Eight thirty and your night's just now ending? I take it you're starting to like our little Shangri-La."

"It's got its upsides."

"Glad to hear it. Now go get ready."

"Ready for what?"

"Hell, it's Sunday morning. Church for Christ's sake. No pun intended."

"I've already turned down an invitation to go with a beautiful young lady. What makes you think I'll accept one to go with an ornery old man?"

"Because I sign your paycheck."

"I see what you mean. I'll go get ready."

"Thought you'd see it my way." Americus stuck the cigar back in his mouth and reopened the paper.

Fifteen minutes later Spence was ready to go and ran outside to get in the car, still straightening his tie and running his fingers through his wet hair. As Americus wheeled the Mercedes down the country roads of Monroe, Spence only hoped that if they wrecked, it happened on the way back from church. He had never been a religious man, and figured he needed as much favor as he could get, if this was indeed the day he met his maker. And when Americus was driving, Spence always felt that meeting was just around the corner.

Never one to miss an opportunity for a business lesson, Americus was again talking as fast as he was driving—this time about keeping up appearances of a good Christian lawyer. Spence, partly hung over and partly exhausted, was having a hard time listening.

They turned off the paved road about ten miles from Spence's house and he wondered if there was anything outside of town, other than the NAPCO mill, that had a paved road in front of it. But his mind was soon back on the road in front of him. He could actually feel the old Mercedes sliding around the curves of the dirt surface as it left a huge cloud of dust behind them. Americus finally brought the car to a rapid stop in front of a small white building with a sign out front that read 'Shady Pines Baptist Church.' Spence stepped out of the car just in time for the red dust cloud following the Mercedes to sweep over him, and he made a mental note to let the dust pass next time before he opened the car door.

The Pines, as it was called, was just as most people would imagine a small country church to be—a perfect rectangle, painted white, with a large steeple in the shape of a cross that sat on the roof over the doorway. Spence could see part of the congregation still in the churchyard, shaking hands and giving hugs. All were dressed in their Sunday best with big smiles on their faces, which didn't surprise Spence, but the fact that they were all black did.

Americus, accustom to driving on dirt roads, had waited for the dust to settle, so Spence leaned back down into the car to ask, "Are you sure we're at the right church?"

"Of course I'm sure," Americus answered as he inspected himself in the rearview mirror. "This is the Shady Pines Baptist Church, and today is Americus Kirkland day."

"I didn't know you were the center of a religious holiday."

"Well, son, churches are not unlike most institutions. You give them fifty thousand dollars and they'll declare you a saint."

"Saint Americus, huh."

"Who says you can't buy your way into heaven," Americus said with a grin and a wink.

Americus got out of the car and they walked to the front steps of the church, where a large woman in a big pink hat and a short fat man were greeting everyone. When the man saw Americus he held out his hands. "Amer'cus Ki'kland," he said as the two men embraced in a hug. Once they had sufficiently patted each other on the back, Americus turned to introduce Spence.

"Reverend Huntley T. Stevens, may I introduce my nephew, Spencer Michael Thompson."

"Aw, ver' nice to meet ya, son, ver' nice to met ya," the Reverend said as he furiously shook Spence's hand. Reverend Stevens was a short man—practically a walking bowling ball. He looked just like a black snowman from the waist up, with a perfectly round midsection and a perfectly round head placed on top, with the seemingly absence of a neck. He was wearing a black shiny suit that looked like it was made of silk and a purple tie from the same type of material. His cheeks were so fat and his smile so big that when he extended it to its full width, it almost squinted his eyes shut.

"Spence," the Reverend said, "this is my wife, Sister Clara Belle."

Sister Clara Belle was a large woman, whom Spence could look in the eye when they spoke. She was a good eight inches taller than her portly husband and outweighed him by at least fifty pounds. She was wearing a bright pink dress with enough bosom stuffed inside to make Dolly Parton jealous. The dress was complemented by a matching hat with a white lace strip around the brim. She shook Spence's hand as hard as the Reverend and with an equally big smile and much excitement said, "Good mornin'!"

"Morning," Spence answered.

"O' it is a beautiful mornin' our Lawd has made, an' we gone be happy an' rejoice in it."

Spence's limited experience with church lingo made the situation uncomfortable, and he was thankful when Americus motioned him up the steps to introduce him to someone else.

Inside the church, Spence was impressed with its cleanliness. The pews were all brand new, as was the bright red carpet separating them, which led from the front door to the pulpit. Members of the congregation were shaking hands and taking their places. Americus stopped and exchanged pleasantries with most of the people and then introduced Spence, who gave up trying to remember names. On one side of the pulpit, a woman sat at an organ banging out gospel hymns while people continued to take their regular places in the pews. As Spence followed his uncle down the aisle, he noticed that the closer he got to the pulpit, the older the congregation became. The teenagers sat in the back with sleepy looks on their faces, still convinced of their immortality. The elders of the church, knowing perhaps that their time was much closer, stood in front so not to miss any of the grace that the good Reverend was sure to pour down upon them. Behind the pulpit was a choir section with three rows of folding chairs. It began to fill up with choristers, easy to recognize in their long white robes. When the last one of the fourteen choir members shook the last hand and made her way to her spot on the last row, Sister Clara Belle sat at a piano opposite the organist and joined in mid-song. The choir members began to sway back and forth, clapping their hands. Reverend Stevens made his grand entrance down the center of the aisle and took his place behind the pulpit. The tiny building exploded into song. It was time to give thanks.

Spence stood on the very front row, flanked by Americus on one side and an eighty-year-old deacon on the other.

"There's a sweet sweet spirit in this place."

The whole church was standing and singing, including Americus, and even though every pew had hymnals located in the pockets, no one that Spence could see was holding one. Everybody knew the words.

"And I know that it's the spirit of the Lord."

Every now and then, somebody in the choir would break out with an impromptu stanza to the song, but no one seemed to mind. 'Hallelujahs' were abundant and everyone raised their arms at least twice in praise. Spence knew none of the words to the song, but he had to admit, the music and all of its accompanying activity was very uplifting.

After about twenty-five minutes of singing, Reverend Stevens calmed down the congregation, asked them to be seated, and began to make the church's announcements. After the activities had been read, informing the church members of a pot luck supper on Wednesday night, the Reverend began to take prayer requests, a session where members of the congregation asked the other members to pray for persons in the community who had illnesses or other problems. Every so often a member of the congregation would stand up and, usually in a tearful speech, thank the members for all of the prayers he or she had received during a recent difficulty. One old lady behind Spence reminded everyone to pray for her third cousin, Calvin, who was killed last week by his own daughter and to remember that the girl needed praying for too. At the end of the prayer requests, which lasted for nearly thirty minutes, Reverend Stevens asked for unspoken requests, which Spence reasoned was to get prayer for those lost souls who were actually in attendance without calling them out by name.

Prayer requests were followed by one of the younger members of the church singing a solo, as the congregation vocally cheered her on with 'hallelujahs' and 'Praise the Lords'. She wasn't very good, but Spence admired her stage presence as she sang at the top of her lungs.

After her song, Reverend Stevens asked the congregation to be seated, pulled a handkerchief from his pocket and wiped his brow. He continued to hold the handkerchief in his right hand, knowing he would need it again soon, and placed both hands on the sides of his pulpit. Spence fanned the church program he held in his hand in front of his face, attempting to create a breeze. Most of the congregation did the same since the three fans in the ceiling did little to suppress the intense summertime heat. There were two window unit air conditioners in the middle stain-glassed windows on each side of the church, struggling to maintain the slightest bit of coolness in the large open room. Spence could hear them humming behind him, but they had no chance of drowning out the voice of Reverend Huntley Stevens.

"Now brothers and sisters, y'all all know what evil the devil's done in this world we live," Stevens began.

Everyone shook their heads in agreement and a few throughout the congregation added a resounding, "Praise God!"

"And we was all reminded of this evil last June, when some of his henchmen..."

"Tell it, Lord!" somebody sang out.

"Some of his evildoers set fire to this holy ground," Stevens finished, with increasing volume in his voice.

"Amen!" at least three people shouted.

"But, whenever the devil acts his evil...," Stevens paused a moment waiting for somebody to shout encouragement. No one obliged for a few seconds.

"Praise God!" Sister Clara Belle finally shouted from her piano seat so her husband could continue.

Leaning over his pulpit and speaking in a very slow, deliberate and loud tone, Stevens finished with, "God answers with his grace!"

The congregation exploded from their seats, standing and cheering the Reverend on. After a few moments he calmed them down and concluded, "And this time, God's grace came in the form of Americus Kirkland, who graciously gave to restore th' work we been doin' here at The Pines."

The congregation again rose to their feet, clapping and cheering, while Americus stood waving and smiling.

"Com'on up here," Stevens motioned Americus to the pulpit. Never one to avoid the spotlight, Americus went charging up the steps and stood with the Reverend, arm in arm, while the congregation clapped and shouted. For the next few minutes, Americus took over the pulpit, preaching like a seasoned evangelist, quoting scripture, pausing in all the right places for the congregation to respond, and working them into a frenzy. He would have received a standing ovation, but they had never sat down.

When he finished, Americus came back down from the pulpit

and took his place next to Spence, but the crowd kept on cheering and yelling 'hallelujahs.' After a few moments, the Reverend quieted his people. "Alright brothers and sisters," he began, "we gots to get started on the Lord's work."

He looked around the pulpit for his Bible. When he was unable to find it, he turned to Sister Clara Belle and asked, "Sister, have you seen the good book?" From about three rows back someone shouted "Praise God" and the Reverend quickly looked out over the crowd. The church members glanced from side to side as some of the elders frowned. Someone had not been paying attention.

Once Sister Clara Belle found his Bible, Reverend Stevens opened it on the pulpit and began to preach. Spence looked at his watch. They had already been there for an hour and a half, and as far as he could tell, they were just now getting to the good stuff.

For the next two hours Spence watched the special drama that was Reverend Huntley T. Stevens giving his congregation spiritual guidance. It was a very interactive affair, as members made their way up and down the center aisle whenever Stevens mentioned a subject dear to their heart. In all of the commotion, Spence was shocked that even the little old man who sat next to him had good enough ears to hear his stomach growling. It was after one thirty now, and he hadn't had a chance to eat breakfast before Americus hurried him out the door.

At 2:15 in the afternoon, the tithes had been offered, not once, but a second time, when the Reverend felt that the first passing did not collect enough money for a respectable congregation. At least two souls had been publicly saved, one of them for the third time. Reverend Stevens closed the festivities with a seven-minute prayer and the members proceeded out of the church and into the yard for lunch. All in all, Spence had to admit that the experience was inspirational, to say the least. He had often heard people make jokes about falling asleep in church. Those people had obviously never heard the Reverend Huntley T. Stevens bringing the good word to his congregation.

Spence sat next to Americus on one side and Sister Clara Belle on the other, at a folding table in the churchyard, with enough food on his plate to feed three people. He felt bad for a moment as he passed through the line overfilling his plate, until he noticed everyone else doing the same thing. There was no chance of running out of food anyway. The tiny congregation, sixty people at the most, had brought enough food to feed an army.

Sister Clara Belle had the same questions for Spence as everyone else in town. She asked him about his background and how he liked Monroe. She told him how much she loved his uncle and how thankful she was that he'd rebuilt their church after the fire. Then she broached the subject she really wanted to talk about.

"So, they tell me you're goin' to be defendin' Angela for killin' Calvin."

Spence was tired of arguing with people about being her lawyer and had decided to just accept it until he could get someone else appointed. "Yes, ma'am," he answered, trying to finish the potato salad in his mouth so he could speak legibly. "Did you know Calvin?"

"Oh Lawd, yes, child," she said. "Me and his mama was best friends, God rest her soul. That boy was practically raised on my cookin'."

"So you know Angela."

"Oh yes. Minnie, that was Calvin's mama, used to bring the girl to church."

"So I guess your families were pretty close."

"Me an' Minnie was. Calvin was kind of a loner when he come back from college. An' we tried to tell him, his mama an' me, that his thing with the white girl just wasn't goin' to work. But they done had the little girl, so it was kinda' too late."

"Did you see them much after your friend died?"

"Hadn't seen 'em in years. Calvin never come to church and we never went vistin'." Sister Clara Belle lowered her voice and leaned closer to Spence, "Truth is, some of the congregation didn't want 'em here anyway."

"Didn't want them at church?"

"Now I know that's bad to say, but ya know she was quite purty. I reckon some folks was worried about our boys takin' an interest in her."

"I guess that's a bad thing to happen in church?"

"It is if'n they white." Sister Clara Belle tried to stop before she said it, but it was too late. Her conversation had been going so well, she forgot for the moment whom she was talking to. She was not accustomed to watching her speech at church where she rarely, if ever, made conversation with any other race but her own. She looked at Spence, whose mouth hung open in surprise from the words he had just heard from the preacher's wife. "Not that there's anything wrong with bein' white, mind you," she quickly added with a smile, as if she had been joking."

"Of course not," Spence answered. "Of course not."

"I think I'll go get some more ribs. You want anything, honey," Sister Clara Belle asked, obviously embarrassed and trying to change the subject.

"No, ma'am. I'm fine," Spence answered.

She raised herself from the table and walked away. After refilling her plate, she did not return to sit beside Spence.

In the car on the way back home, Americus sat with the button to his pants undone and a toothpick dangling from his mouth. Every now and again he would give a quick hiccup and rub his slender stomach.

Spence sat quietly in his seat, staring out the window, watching the pine trees as they passed.

"You're awfully quiet, son. You eat to much?" Americus inquired.

"No, sir. I'm fine."

"Somethin' else botherin' ya?" Americus' already heavy Southern accent was even more dramatic on a full stomach.

Spence didn't answer right away. He searched for the right words and wondered whether he should talk at all. Still staring out the window he said, "The girl I'm defending, nobody seems to like her much. Nobody knows her. But still, they don't seem to like her much."

"You expect something different? She's a half breed."

"I guess I figured that whites wouldn't like her, but I thought she would have some friends in the black community."

"What made you think that? They're just as human as whites. They aren't going to like the white in her any more than the whites are gonna like the black."

"I don't know. I guess I never thought about it from their side."

"How could you? You're white."

Spence did not answer right away. Americus had a point he'd never thought about. The life in front of you can be hard enough. Why add to your burden by worrying about someone else's perspective?

"Do you have any black friends?" Spence inquired.

"Sure, Reverend Stevens is my friend."

"Ever dated a black woman?"

"Nope. Paid five dollars to have sex with one when I was in college, but I've never dated one."

Spence was surprised at his uncle's candor. "Would you ever date one?" he asked.

"In New York? Sure. In Monroe? Never."

"What's the difference?"

"Obviously, in one place people would never look at you twice. In the other, I couldn't make a living or sleep peacefully at night."

"So what's right?"

"Son, it doesn't have a damn thing to do with being right." Americus could tell that Spence was struggling with something, so he decided to take the initiative. "Son, right or wrong is decided by society, not you and certainly not me. Now, do I think you'd be any less likely to get into heaven for doing something that society frowned upon? Hell no, but then life's too short to waste on trying to change people's opinion. But I'll make it easy for you. You find someone you can't live without, regardless of their color, and I'll still love you. Deal?"

"Deal. But I don't think your going to have to worry about it."

"Why, you don't believe in falling in love with someone from a different race?"

"No, sir. I just don't believe in falling in love."

NINETEEN

THE MONROE KIWANIS Club met on the first Tuesday of every month at 4:00 in the Chamber of Commerce building. The group had been meeting for nearly fifty years, and although the membership was still a who's who among local city officials and businessmen, the group didn't carry the same clout it once had. There was a time when a man couldn't hope to survive in the local economy unless he was active in the club, but the arrival of NAPCO changed the way business was done. No longer were the townspeople's' lives dependent on the interaction of each other to survive now that an outside company employed more than half of the town's working citizens and directly effected the other fifty percent. But the Kiwanis continued to meet so the local lawyers and bankers would have an excuse to leave the office for fellowship among their peers. And the Club did contribute significantly to local charities and fundraisers, also giving an annual thousand-dollar scholarship to a deserving senior from Crawford County High School.

Although Americus paid his annual dues and was always dependable for a donation if needed, he hadn't been to a Tuesday meeting in over twenty years. Not that he thought they were foolish or beneath him; he simply had other pastimes he enjoyed more. And since he donated the entire thousand dollars for the annual Crawford County High School Scholar's Award, no officer of the club every pushed his luck by badgering Americus for his attendance. Still, Americus liked the idea of Spence representing the firm at the meetings, and when Wilson at First Bank personally called to invite the town's newest lawyer, he insisted that Spence go.

Spence was actually delighted to go to the meeting, wanting to become more familiar with Monroe's professionals and hoping that the afternoon social could take his mind off of Angela's case for at least a few hours. He met Wilson in front of the bank at ten minutes until four and the two men walked to the Commerce building. It was the second time Spence had been to the small brick structure, so he was at least familiar with what to expect and upon his arrival found the scene much like he anticipated. There were seventeen people in attendance—all white males and most of them sixty or older. Spence recognized a few people he'd seen around town, including the skinny defense attorney in Hamilton's courtroom when he'd been appointed to defend Angela. He also identified a stocky well-dressed man as one of the lawyers who had been sitting in the jury box that same afternoon. The man was talking to someone else, drinking Coke from a small plastic cup and smiling expansively. Spence had been wondering about his adversary ever since he'd been appointed to defend Angela. He'd learned that the county's district attorney was a highly respected man in this part of the State, and known for his integrity while practicing his profession. Americus had told him that if there was a silver lining to his appointment, it was that at least he would be defending the girl against Pat Seaver, who was merciless on criminals, but willing to help young attorneys learn their trade. Spence had no way of knowing for sure, but he felt like the man he recognized from the jury box was the district attorney. He just looked the part.

After a few minutes of mingling the Kiwanis were called to order by their incumbent president, Moody Johnson, a retired accountant who had turned his firm over to his forty-eight year old son just two years before. Mr. Johnson started the meeting by asking everyone to be seated. He then asked that they bow their heads and said a quick ninety-second prayer. After the amen it was time to rise once again and turn to the flag hanging in the back corner of the room for the pledge of allegiance. After the second amen of the meeting, Mr. Johnson again asked everyone to be seated. He took a moment to welcome Spence to the meeting and offered the hope that Spence would continue the tradition that his family had in the Kiwanis, since his grandfather had been one of the founding members of the Monroe chapter. He then asked Spence to stand and introduce himself to the rest of the members.

"Hello, my name is Spence Thompson, and I wanted to thank you all for making me feel very welcome in my first week here in town. As most of you probably know, I've recently graduated from the University of Alabama's Law School and I'm here in town to practice with my uncle, Americus Kirkland. I look forward to meeting you all and working with you here in town. Thank you very much."

As Spence sat back down into his chair there was a brief pause before Mr. Johnson stood back up. One of the elders of the club decided that the pause was meant to give Spence some applause and began to clap, being joined by the others once he started. Spence was embarrassed by the extra attention.

"Mr. Thompson we're certainly glad to have you," Mr. Johnson continued, "and I'm sure you'll do well here under the tutelage of your uncle. I understand that you already have a big case and want to wish you luck on that."

Spence smiled and nodded his head. He looked at the well dressed-man sitting at the next table, but there was no expression on the man's face.

Mr. Johnson spent the next few minutes giving an update on the club's activities and forthcoming events. He then turned the floor over to Joe Tidwell, a young man from Monroe who had been doing missionary work in Mexico and had been sponsored by the Kiwanis and several local churches. Tidwell gave a short five-minute speech about his progress of converting souls in some poor Mexican village that Spence had never heard of and then ask if there were any questions from the crowd. For the next few minutes, members painfully struggled to find questions for Tidwell to answer and there were often long pauses between inquiries. Once the questioning was over the crowd applauded politely and Mr. Johnson again took the floor. He asked if there was anything else that someone wished to address. When no one responded he again said a prayer and adjourned the meeting.

A couple of the members made their way to Spence's table once the meeting was over and introduced themselves. Wilson shook Spence's hand and told him that he had to leave. Once Wilson was gone and Spence finished his current conversation with Mr. Johnson's son, he headed for the door.

"Mr. Thompson," came a voice from behind.

"Yes, sir," Spence answered, turning to find the well-dressed man walking his way.

"Mr. Thompson, I'm Pat Seaver, the district attorney."

"Glad to meet you," Spence said holding out his hand, "and please, call me Spence."

"Very well, Spence," Seaver answered, shaking hands firmly. "Do you mind if I walk with you for a minute?"

"Not at all."

They walked out of the chamber building and headed towards the square. The DA pulled off his suit jacket and threw it over his shoulder. He'd only been out of the air-conditioned building for a few moments, but the sweat was already beading on his forehead. He removed a handkerchief from his front pants pocket and wiped away the perspiration.

"How are you liking the town so far?" Seaver asked.

"Well, to be honest," answered Spence, "I was so surprised about my appointment as the girl's defense counsel that I haven't had a lot of time to see it."

"Ah yes, the case. As you can imagine, I wanted to talk with you about that."

"I figured."

"Look Spence, I know you probably feel overwhelmed by being appointed. And I'm sure you're wondering why the judge appointed you when you have so little experience."

"More like no experience."

Seaver smiled. "Well, I think it's pretty simple. Including you, your uncle and myself, there are only eight attorneys in town. And none of them are as well off as Americus. They stay pretty busy trying to make ends meet, so Hamilton didn't want to pull anyone from their existing clients to work the case. And to be honest with you, Spence, it isn't going to be a very big deal."

"It's murder. How can it not be a big deal?"

"Well, the facts are pretty cut and dry. I'm sure you've heard what kind of situation the girl comes from. I don't know how far you've gotten with your own investigation, but believe me, everybody in town knows she's had it pretty rough."

"I get that feeling."

"I don't know what she's told you so far, but I think you're going to have a hard time finding any possibilities other than she finally had enough and killed him. Calvin was a loner, and I can't imagine that anyone else would have a reason to murder him."

"Would it matter if I told you that she said she doesn't think she did it?"

The DA chuckled. "Spence, I've been putting criminals in jail for over fifteen years now, and believe me, I've never found any of them who thought they were guilty at first. Has she told you anyone else who may have done it?"

"She said she doesn't know."

"Look Spence, don't get to caught up in this thing or her stories. Clients will tell you anything, but I'm going to shoot it to you as straight as I can. I'm willing to be lenient on her if she doesn't try to cause me any trouble. You convince her to strike a deal and I'll make sure she gets a fair sentence, considering what she's been through. But if she wants to turn this into a full blown trial, I'm going to hammer her."

The two men made it to the street where Spence's office was one way and the DA's another, so they stopped on the corner to finish their conversation. Seaver again wiped the sweat from his brow.

"So it's that simple?" Spence asked. "She pleads guilty and this whole thing goes away?"

"It's pretty much that simple. She pleads guilty and then you, I, and she can get on with our lives and put this behind us. That's why the judge appointed you, Spence. It ain't complicated and shouldn't take up too much of anybody's time."

"Then why am I so nervous about it?"

"Because you've never done it before. It would be odd if you weren't nervous. I didn't sleep for days before my first trial. Believe me, its common for every lawyer to feel the same way."

"Just the same, I was hoping to find someone who might at least help me with the procedures."

"You can try to find someone to help if you'd like," Seaver said, trying to make it sound as if it were totally unnecessary. "But procedure shouldn't be much of an issue. She had her first appearance within seventy-two hours like she was supposed to, and the Grand Jury met yesterday and sent me an indictment this morning. The arraignment's set for Monday. There's really nothing else to do except pester me a few times to see how good of a deal you can get for her," Seaver added with a smile.

"So I guess I've got to convince her to plead guilty within the next week."

"That's all there is to it. And I promise you Spence, if you save this busy man the trouble from having to prepare for a trial, I won't soon forget the favor. Besides, you can make three times the money over at your office working Americus' gravy train than what the State is going to pay you to defend this girl. You understand where I'm coming from?"

"Well, certainly. I'll see what I can do. To tell you the truth, I didn't realize it was that easy to put somebody away."

"Now's the time to start learning how real law is practiced."

Spence smiled. "Deals and favors sound much better to me than those legal theories anyway." He stuck out his hand.

Seaver took Spence's hand and returned the smile. "Son, you're going to make a fine attorney."

TWENTY

WEDNESDAY MORNING SPENCE woke earlier than usual. It had been a full week and a day since he'd been appointed to defend Angela. He had been unable to sleep most of the night, coming to the realization that he was defending a suspected murderer and yet he didn't even have his client's version of the story on the night the victim was killed. Fighting the restlessness as long as he could, he decided to take Sam for a jog before the sun came up.

He left Amy sleeping in his bed and was quiet not to wake her. It had been the third night she stayed at his house and the fifth time they made love. Spence knew it would probably be their last and he had a feeling she knew it too. Not that she wasn't a beautiful woman, and he certainly enjoyed her companionship. But he couldn't keep his thoughts from Angela and that wasn't fair to Amy. He felt like she understood he wasn't the one for her anyway and would probably move on without much complaint. He had been here before and there was little he could not see coming.

On the front porch he stretched his calf muscles on the steps while Sam waited impatiently. Skipping down the porch, he ran to the end of the graveled driveway and turned down the dirt road away from the paved highway, so they could run the entire time with little chance of passing a car. The morning was peaceful, the air was crisp, and though physically Spence felt really good, mentally he had the weight of the world on his shoulders. The last few days had seemed almost surreal, but the realization of what was happening continued to sink a little deeper as the hours passed.

He understood the rationale. He was the newest lawyer in town, and the man who normally served as the appointed counsel was recently deceased. But it bothered him that the judge would allow someone's life to depend on an inexperienced attorney in town for a total of one day when he was appointed. At least now the DA had made it easy for him. Get the girl to plead guilty and get on with his life. He just hoped he could convince her.

But perhaps his most troubling concern was the way he felt. He didn't know his client, or any of the people involved for that matter, yet there was something familiar about the girl. He tried to tell himself that he had nothing to lose in the outcome of the case and this was simply a sidetrack to his master plan. He would do the best he could until he found someone else to defend the girl, and even if no one came to his rescue, he would defend her to the best of his ability, hopefully convincing her to plead guilty, and whatever happened—well, it just happened. No one was expecting him to get her acquitted. Even Americus said there was no way she could win a trial. All he had to do was put up a defense and when they found her guilty and sent her to the state prison, some young associate from a big city law firm would handle her appeal as part of their pro bono obligation. And if by some strange twist of fate she was found innocent, he would become one of the most feared lawyers in town. Either way, it would be over soon and he and Americus could get back to the business of making money.

That was how he *wanted* to feel, but he was having a hard time distancing himself from the girl's problems and feelings. He had still only seen her three times, and yet he felt some connection, like no other he had ever experienced. She was beautiful, that was for certain, and he smiled thinking back to Doc Simpson's examination, and how the old man reacted when she undressed before him. But Spence had seen plenty of beautiful women in his life, including the one in his bed right now. None of them worked on his emotions like Angela did—without even trying. She was far too inexperienced and naive to be playing games with him. Maybe his feelings stemmed from what he knew about her mistreatment and abuse. After all, he had seen the bruises.

Or maybe she was a killer and knew exactly what she was doing.

Spence and Sam ran farther down the narrowing dirt road. Tall pine trees on either side of the road were just about ready for harvesting, and in fact, he had seen several logging trucks pass in front of his house, no doubt loading trees and taking them to NAPCO's plant. Americus told him that most of the land in this part of the county was privately held, which was good news for the two of them. NAPCO owned much of its own timberland, but to feed such a tremendous operation, the company was still forced to buy more than 50 percent of its trees from private landholders. When the mill purchased trees from individuals, Smitty hired Americus to research the deeds to the property and make sure that the individual who owned the land also owned the timber rights. For people who inherited land from previous generations, the sale of timber planted years before could become a windfall, although few people in Crawford County owned enough land, or timber, to retire rich. In fact, there were only four entities in the entire county that owned more than a thousand acres of property, and already Spence knew two of those—NAPCO and Americus. But still, the trees were an added bonus to many landholders' financial situation.

Spence looked at his watch and decided that after thirteen minutes he and Sam had ran about a mile and a half, so he turned back. As he headed home he focused on what he had to do in the upcoming day. He had a closing at ten o'clock for the First National Bank of Monroe. After lunch, he had a contract signing for the sale of some

timber purchased by NAPCO, and he decided afterwards he would
go see Angela and get her side of the story on the night of her father's
death. If he was going to convince her to plead guilty, he would at
least have to find some holes in her version of events to show her
what a jury was likely to believe.

He'd begun to hate thinking about her, since every time she
entered his thoughts, he got that uncomfortable feeling and struggled
to figure out why. Perhaps there was a special place inside of him for
battered women, because for most of his life he watched his mother
take verbal and physical abuse from her boyfriends, only to know
that he was unable to do anything about it. But over the years he
began to feel less sorry for Sandra, knowing her lifestyle self-inflicted
most of her own pain. But what had Angela done? He remembered
the comment Sister Clara Belle made by mistake, before she could
stop herself. Other than being born to interracial parents, in a time
and place that had no tolerance for such a practice, she could hardly
be blamed for her own suffering.

That had to be it. He was simply feeling sorry for her, and
although there was little he could do to help, it was normal to feel
sympathy for someone who couldn't help herself.

Suddenly there was a loud shriek as a sparrow hawk came flying
out of the trees beside him. Spence came to a sudden stop as Sam
passed in front of him chasing the bird. It was still early in the morning and the woods were silent. He paused to listen for something,
hearing nothing but the crickets and the first bird song as the early
morning sun was rising. The woods were quiet, absolutely devoid of
human sound. There couldn't have been anyone around for miles.

"You could get away with murder out here," he whispered to
himself.

TWENTY-ONE

WHEN HE GOT to his office, Spence saw that Huey had left the documents on his desk the day before, so all he had to do was review the names. It was amusing to Spence that he and Americus got the money and prestige for convincing their clients that they knew something about their piece of land, when in fact, Huey knew more about the county's property, and real estate law for that matter, than he and Americus combined.

Americus felt like a week of on the job training was plenty of time for Spence to learn how to run the office without him, so he departed to New Orleans for several days with one of his former secretaries. That left Spence with Kathy, who had already been to his office on several occasions, offering coffee and anything else that Spence might need or want. Her outfits were getting more and more revealing everyday

Spence did ask her to find him the coroner's phone number, so he could get the report on Calvin before he went to see Angela. The Crawford County coroner and the local funeral home owner were one in the same. When Spence called, the lady who took his request told him that the coroner was under the supervision of the district attorney, and that the DA would have to approve the report being released. Therefore, if the DA said it was okay, it would be after lunch before a report could be faxed to him. At least Spence would have it after talking with Angela, so he could begin to put a case together later that evening. He had begun to research his old law books for the elements of a murder and was surprised at how much he remembered from his classes. He knew Angela would have needed a motive and an intent to kill, but felt the DA would have little problem convincing a jury of those elements. He hadn't known Calvin, but just what he'd heard others say about the way he treated Angela, made Spence want to kill him too.

Spence grabbed a quick lunch instead of going to Miss Sarah's, which had become his ritual. He would be there for dinner anyway, so he wouldn't miss Wednesday's special of country fried steak and gravy. When the last closing ended at 2:00, Spence told Kathy he would be gone for the rest of the day, and walked to the county jail to see his only criminal client.

By now everyone at the jailhouse knew who he was, and no one bothered to look up until he made his way downstairs where Tom, the cell guard, was reading the morning paper. They exchanged greetings as Tom opened both gates at the same time, a violation of procedure, and allowed Spence into the cellblock. They walked down the hall to Angela's cell, and Tom opened the iron door. She was resting on her bed with a Bible lying on the floor face down. When she saw Spence, she sat up on her cot and straightened her hair and issued clothing. Tom brought in the Samsonite folding chair, arranged it on the floor in the middle of the cell and walked out.

"How are you today?" Spence asked, as he sat down in the chair.

"Not bad," she replied.

"Are they treating you okay?"

"They brought me a Bible. They said it would be okay if I read while I was in here."

"Yeah, I'm sure they don't mind you reading, especially that."

"Did you find me another lawyer yet?" she asked before Spence could say anything else.

"No, ah, not yet. But don't worry, I'm still looking." He figured by now she'd picked up on the fact that he had no idea what he was doing and it was starting to concern her as much as it did him. "But, anyhow we've got to start putting a case together, just in case I've got to do something before I can find someone to help."

"Do you get paid to defend me?" she asked, taking Spence by surprise.

He thought a minute, having not considered the subject until now. "Yes, I suppose I do."

"Will the lawyer you find to help, will he get paid too?"

"Well, um, I don't know."

"It'll probably be hard to find someone, unless they get paid too."

Spence was surprised at how well she seemed to know lawyers, but he wanted to change the subject, "Angela,"—he tried to sound gentle—"we're going to have to talk about your relationship with your father and what happened the night he was killed."

She put her feet on the bed, pulled them close to her chest and propped her chin on her knees. "Okay."

"Now, you told me the other day that you don't think you killed him. Do you still believe that?"

"Yes, I don't think I did it."

"Was there anyone else who would have wanted to kill your father?"

Angela thought for a moment and answered, "Other than me, no."

"So you did want to kill him?"

"I thought about it sometimes, wondered what it would have been like to be on my own."

"You don't think that maybe you finally had enough, and even though you don't want to believe it, you killed him?" Spence was hoping she would say 'yes' and he could easily convince her to plead guilty for a reduced sentence.

"No, I don't think so. I was too scared of my father."

"Alright, let's start from the beginning. Explain to me your relationship with your father. What kind of person was he?"

Angela stared at the wall next to her bed, visiting a far off place.

"He was very bitter," she said, "very hateful towards my mother. He blamed everything on her. She was white you know?"

" I've heard that."

"He said it was her who had ruined his baseball career, her and the white men. He said that if she hadn't come along he would've been famous."

"Did he drink a lot?" Spence knew the answer from hearing others talk about Calvin, but he wanted to hear her say it.

"Yes, and that was when he was really bad. He was very upset and cruel when he drank, but at least the powder usually calmed him down."

"The powder? What kind of powder?

"Powder, you know, the kind you suck up your nose."

"Cocaine? You mean your father took cocaine?"

"Just about everyday. You act surprised."

"Well, I don't know much about it, but I do know it cost money." Spence sat in thought for a moment. Cocaine was an expensive habit for anybody, but a mill laborer would probably have to steal to support such an addiction. When Americus and others told him that Calvin had a drug problem, he just assumed it was marijuana, crystal meth, or some other poor man's drug.

"Well maybe it was his drug dealer who killed him," Spence heard the excitement in his own voice. He felt like he was really getting somewhere. Perhaps Calvin was killed for not paying his bills. "Who'd he get the drugs from?"

"I don't know, he brought them home from work."

"Did anybody ever come to your house and do drugs with your father?"

"Occasionally Dubo Wilson would come over and they would take powder together, but they always ended up in a fight."

"Did anyone else ever come to your house?"

"Only Little John, that was his boss at the paper mill. Sometimes he would come pick him up for work." Angela paused to think. "And sometimes the sheriff came by. A few times he brought my father home."

"Sheriff Watkins?" Spence had not actually met the sheriff yet, but he had heard other people talk about him and knew who he was.

"Yes, Sheriff Watkins."

"Did your father have constant problems with the law? Did he stay in jail a lot?"

"No, I don't think so. He never told me if he did. When Sheriff Watkins came by, he usually wasn't angry or anything. Although lately I had seen him yelling at my father on the porch."

"So your father never called you from jail?"

"We didn't have a phone."

"Oh, I see." Spence was embarrassed for her. "Well, okay then, we'll try and figure out who else could have wanted to kill your father later. Right now let's talk about your relationship with him. What was your typical day like?"

"Well, um, when he worked, he worked the second shift, from three in the afternoon to eleven at night. He usually came home and went right to the powder. Sometimes he had already been drinking."

"Did he work every night?"

"He was supposed to work seven days on and three days off, but he skipped work a lot."

"Did he ever get fired?"

"I don't think so."

"So, what did he do during the day?"

"He slept a lot or watched T.V. Sometimes he would go outside and throw a ball against the side of the house or hit it with the bat that stayed on our front porch."

"And what did you do most of the time?"

"He wouldn't let me go to school. He said that I didn't need to hear anything from the white folks." Tears welled in Angela's eyes. It was clear that this was a great source of pain for her. "I cooked and cleaned mostly and read the books my grandmother had given me before she died. I had read them all. At least three times." She smiled through tears as she said this, proud of the accomplishment.

"Angela…" Spence had never been an emotional person. He hated goodbyes and awkward moments and hadn't had much practice at acting like he cared. But now he wasn't acting, and his next question tore at his fabric. He already knew the answer. He just wished it wasn't true. "Angela," he started again, "how often did your father abuse you?"

She wasn't sobbing, but the tears in her eyes were clearly visible. "Almost everyday."

"Did he do anything else to you?"

She nodded, and then placed her head on her knees.

"Did he sexually abuse you?"

She said nothing, but Spence could hear her beginning to cry into her arms. All of his life he tried to avoid situations like this, for fear they might remind him of his own misfortunes. He'd broken many girls' hearts and had his own broken a few times, but he always managed to get out of the moment without lasting damage. And yet here he was, prying into this young girl's life, wrenching her emotions and placing himself in the very center as her only comfort. And to his surprise he wanted to help. He waited before he said anything else, searching for the right words.

She continued to sob with her head down on her knees, which she held tightly against her chest. Spence was embarrassed for her and felt uncomfortable himself. Maybe she was not ready to talk about it, and at this point he certainly did not want to pry any further. He stood up from the chair and collected his pen and pad. He wanted to leave her alone, at least for a few minutes, so he thought he might find a glass of water and give her a chance to calm herself. As he started around the chair and out of the cell, he heard her.

"It doesn't count you know." Her words broke through the silence. "It doesn't count if you don't want it to happen. If somebody forces you to."

She was still crying. Spence stood in the bare cell and decided that maybe this session had gone on long enough and perhaps he should give her some time alone. But something inside of him didn't want to leave without offering her some kind of comfort. He walked over to her bed while she wept into her arms. Feeling his presence as he came closer, she lifted her head and looked up at him. He knelt down, gently took her hand from around her legs, and held it in both of his. She looked into his eyes as he gazed into hers. Even with tearstains soaked into her cheeks, she was the most beautiful woman he had ever seen. He raised her hand to his lips and gently kissed the top.

"You're right," he said softly. "It doesn't count."

TWENTY-TWO

"HELLO."

"This is Kendall. Where the hell are you?"

"I had to go out of town for a few days. There was something I wanted to check on."

"I'm paying you to watch that little hick town, not some vacation site."

"I'd hardly call Montgomery a vacation site. Which by the way, my phone doesn't get a good signal from here. If I lose you, I'll call you back."

"What's in Montgomery?"

"Our little fat sheriff. I think we've got a problem."

"What?"

"He's here with some other sheriffs on some kind of conference and he's throwing a little too much money around. They're starting to take notice. Bought about six of them a five hundred dollar meal and some drinks last night. When one of them asked him how he had so much cash, he told them he had a little side interest going."

"Damn it!"

"He's going to be a problem. Him and the big mill worker."

"Little John?"

"Yeah."

"Some people just don't know how to handle money."

"Some people just don't know how to keep their mouth shut."

"Can you shut it for them?"

"If you'd like."

"I think we had better."

"Do you want to talk with Ricter before I do anything?"

"I run the show. I don't have to ask Ricter."

"Just thought you might want to discuss it."

"I don't need to discuss anything. I'll send someone from up here to run Little John's shift for a while. You sure you can take care of both of them?"

"Piece of cake."

"What about the kid?"

"Doesn't seem to be doing much of anything. I think he's intimidated, doesn't know what to do. Don't worry about him. I think we'll get him to plea bargain."

"And if not?"

"Then I can take care of him too."

"Thank God."

"What's that?"

"Finally somebody who thinks like I do."

TWENTY-THREE

BACK IN HIS office, Spence read the coroner's report that Kathy placed on his desk. The DA must have approved its release. He'd never seen a coroner's report before, but it didn't take long to find what he was looking for. Halfway down the page, under the deceased's name, address and other information was the line for 'Cause of Death.' The explanation was short: "The deceased died from a severe trauma to the head, no other signs of bodily harm were evident."

Spence stuck the report in a file he had labeled "Angela." He looked over the next day's closings, then read some more on the elements of murder from an outdated criminal law book he found in Americus' office. He was about to leave for Miss Sarah's when the phone rang. Everyone else in the office had gone for the day, so Spence answered it himself on the first ring.

"May I speak to Spencer Thompson, please?" the voice on the other end asked.

"This is he."

"Mr. Thompson, I'm Jimmy Weeks, over at Weeks & Sons Funeral Home. I'm the coroner here in the county. I understand you're defending the Chauncey girl for the murder of her father."

"Yes, sir, that's right."

"Did you get the report my office faxed to you this afternoon?"

"Yes, sir, I did. Thank you very much."

"Oh, you're welcome, son. That's our job. Listen, I don't usually call lawyers or get involved in the cases unless they ask, but there's something that's been bothering me and I just thought you might want to know about it."

"Yes, sir, I'm listening."

"Well, I guess you saw on the report that Calvin was killed by a severe blow to the head. And from the best we could tell, it was just a single blow to the back of the left side. Now, I know your girl has pretty good genes. Hell, ol' Calvin was still quite a specimen. But I've seen a lot of severe head traumas—you know car wrecks and all—and I guess what I'm sayin' is that whoever whacked Calvin packed some more kind of a punch."

"Are you saying that you don't think Angela could've hit him that hard?"

"I can't make any kind of conclusion about that. I'm not a scientist. But I just thought you might want to know that to cause that kind of damage would take either a pretty good athlete or a rather large man, or maybe both. His skull was cracked like I'd never seen one before, and I've seen a lot you know—car wrecks and all."

"Is there anyone else I can talk to about this?"

"I don't know. I'll check around and see if I can't find you some kind of expert on these sorts of things in our files. We don't have a lot of murders around here."

"Mr. Weeks, I sure do appreciate this. I'll be in touch."

"Don't mention it. Like I said, it was just something that was bothering me. That girl didn't appear to be very big to me." There was a short pause and Weeks started again, "Oh yeah, one more thing. It was pretty clear from the wound that Calvin was hit from behind."

"Okay, so that means he probably wasn't in the middle of a struggle when he was struck." Spence thought maybe this was the direction Weeks was headed in.

"Well, even more than that. Like I said he was struck from the back on the left side of his head. Tell me son, is your girl a lefty?"

Spence tried to think if he had seen Angela do anything that would show her dominant hand, "Well, to be honest, sir, I don't rightly know."

"Well, whoever hit Calvin with that bat—if in fact he was hit with the bat they found beside him—whoever hit him was a lefty. A right-handed person would have damaged the right side of his head if they had hit him from the back. Just something to think about, Counselor."

—

Spence thought about what Weeks had said on his way to Miss Sarah's. He knew Angela was athletic just by what he had seen from Doc Simpson's exam, but, still, the way Weeks talked she would have to be a large man to cause so much damage to Calvin's skull. He decided not to tell her about the coroner right now. Instead he would try to find out if she was indeed left handed, but he didn't want to give her a false sense of hope until he knew more.

Miss Sarah's looked a lot bigger without the afternoon lunch crowd packed inside. Of course the regulars were there—Big Earl sitting behind the counter, Maddie waiting tables, and Pinkney, presumably, in the kitchen. Several couples waited in line to pay, but the only other patrons were two elderly gentlemen drinking a leisurely cup of coffee and another man in his mid-thirties, wearing a John Deere cap and sitting alone at a table near the window.

Spence sat down at a table near the center of the restaurant. Maddie came, took his order, and left him a glass of sweet tea. When the man sitting next to the window finished his meal, he stood up and tucked his shirt back into his blue jeans. Spence noticed how small his waistline was and how his shirt stretched across the muscles of his chest. Spence had been lifting weights ever since he was four-teen, and he knew the look of someone who systematically trained their body. People who did a lot of physical labor could get strong, but they were not usually as well-proportioned as someone who went about strength training scientifically, and Spence could tell the difference. He wondered where the man worked out since there was not a gym in town. In fact, Spence had already ordered himself a training station to put in his house because he was so tired of doing sit-ups and push-ups.

When the man reached into his back pocket for his wallet the muscles in his forearms rolled across one another in high definition, another sign of a person who took great interest in the performance of his body because the forearm muscles were used in almost every exercise. He left a one-dollar tip on the table, picked up his check and walked toward the counter. Suddenly, he stopped at Spence's table.

"Hi, I'm Greg Barnett," he said, extending his hand.

Spence shook his hand and answered back, "Spence Thompson."

"You're that new lawyer in town, right? The one with the murder case?"

"I tell you, word sure does travel fast around here."

Barnett smiled. "It sure does, but don't let it worry you. This is really a pretty nice town. You have to remember that lawyers in small towns are kind of local celebrities."

"So you lived here all your life, I suppose?"

"Nope, only about six months. I'm originally from Georgia."

"What brought you to Monroe?"

"I'm a mechanical engineer out at the plant," Barnett did not have to specify which plant. Spence knew it was NAPCO.

"Like it here so far?" Spence inquired.

"Sure, it's nice and quiet, and there's plenty of places to fish."

"How's your wife like it?"

"My wife probably would have liked it fine, problem was she did-n't like me very much. I'm divorced."

"Sorry to here that. But if you need a date here in town let me know, because my secretary is hot on the heels for somebody and I get the feeling anybody will do."

"You work with Americus Kirkland, don't you?"

"Yes, sir, he's my uncle."

"Then I'll pass on the set-up with your secretary. I've already met Miss Kathy. Besides, I don't think I'm her type. I keep to myself most of the time and committed the ultimate sin of not attending Sunday services, even after several churches came to see me at home. So, are you going to get the girl off?"

"I'm going to try, that's my job."

"I'm sure you'll be fine," Barnett declared as if he had some kind of stake in the outcome of the case. "I'll see ya around. Maybe we can go fishin' sometime." He straightened his John Deere cap and walked toward the counter.

"I'd like that. See ya around," Spence answered.

After he paid Big Earl for his meal, Barnett walked by Spence's table one more time. "You be careful now," he said quietly.

Maddie brought Spence his food and he began to eat. It took a few moments to sink in, but there was something that bothered him about Barnett. He talked with a southern accent, but it seemed almost manufactured. He also seemed to be much too neat for a single man. His blue jeans were just a little too new to suit Spence. The sight of a weight trainer in a town without a gym was also a little puzzling. And then there was the final comment. "Be careful" was not an uncommon expression in the South, but the way Barnett had said it, it sounded like he meant it.

When Spence finished his meal, he left a dollar on the table for Maddie, and proceeded to the counter to pay Big Earl.

"How are you tonight?" Spence asked pleasantly, knowing Big Earl would merely nod in answer. He'd eaten at Miss Sarah's enough to know that Big Earl rarely said a word to anyone.

Spence took out his wallet for what had become his favorite part of eating at Miss Sarah's, and for what was sure to be one of the reasons it stayed so crowded—though Pinkney's cooking needed little help. Spence had two twenties, a ten, a five and three ones in his wallet. His meal, like every dinner served at Miss Sarah's, was $5.75, including tax, and although he had six dollars, he placed the ten-dollar bill and the bill ticket in the blind man's out-stretched hand.

"Just one," Spence said, letting Big Earl know how many meals he would be paying for.

Big Earl took the bill ticket and placed it in a large stack with the other tickets that had been collected throughout the day. Then he took the money and rubbed the corner of the ten-dollar bill between his large thumb and forefinger. As opposed to the lunch hour when it was never closed, this time the big man punched a few keys on the register and the drawer flew open revealing the money slots. Big Earl dropped the ten in the slot with the others and counted out four ones and a quarter for Spence's change. He handed the money to Spence and closed the drawer. Perfect again.

TWENTY-FOUR

ON FRIDAY MORNING, just like the week before, Spence had very little to do in the office. Americus never scheduled closings on Friday, and in fact, if he had to do any work at all, it was done in the morning. Working Friday afternoons was completely out of the question. Spence had only to prepare some corporate papers for one of Americus' warehouses in Montgomery. The resolution named Spence to the Board of Directors, so he took a particular interest in preparing the documents carefully. As he worked on his computer, the phone page rang, and Kathy informed him that Americus was holding.

"So Unc, how's the Big Easy?" Spence inquired.

"Never better, ma' boy, never better," Americus' speech sounded slurred enough to cause Spence to glance at his watch. It was only 9:30 in the morning.

"Sounds like you're having a good time. Rough night?"

"I don't know yet. I'll let you know once it ends, but meanwhile I've got some good news for you. I've found a lawyer to take that murder case off of your hands—that is if that sum-bitch Hamilton will allow new counsel."

The news took Spence by surprise. The idea of another lawyer taking over Angela's case seemed strange all of the sudden. But he knew Americus didn't want him wasting his time on the case, and he didn't know enough about practicing criminal law to give Angela a good defense. He also wanted someone to confirm the DA's opinion that the case should be settled long before it goes to trial.

"Great," Spence answered. "Somebody here in town?"

"Nope, he's an acquaintance of mine. Fellow I go gambling with from time to time. He has a big firm down in Dothan. Said he'd send an associate over to help out as part of his pro bono work."

"Should I give this guy a call?"

"He said he'd have someone call you in the next few days. When is the arraignment?"

"It's scheduled for Monday."

"Well, you'll have to go and enter her guilty plea, and then maybe he can take over from there. After Monday you can enter a motion for new counsel. Certainly Hamilton will allow it. He could catch a little heat if he didn't, and it'd be good grounds for an appeal."

"How do you know she's guilty?" Spence asked.

Americus paused on the phone. He cleared his throat as if he were stalling and then began, "Well, son, I've heard the stories. Calvin was found dead at their house, head beat in with a baseball bat. She was the only one there and her fingerprints were found all over the bat still lying on the porch. Sounds pretty guilty to me."

"Yeah, I guess it would," Spence replied.

"Why? You know something I don't?"

Spence thought for a brief second of telling Americus about the coroner and some of the things that Angela had said, but decided now wasn't the time.

"No, not really," Spence answered.

"Listen, son, don't take this thing to heart. I'm counting on you to start running things and I don't want you involved in this stuff. It wouldn't be good for business. I'm sure the girl will have plenty of defenses, you know, physical and mental abuse and all, but let someone else take care of it."

"But what if she's not guilty?"

"Who the hell cares? You want to save the world or make a pile of money?"

"I'd rather make the money," Spence said in an attempt to convince himself as well.

"Well, good, that's why I brought you on. You're as greedy as I am, and don't let anybody ever tell you that's a bad thing. Just enter a plea of guilty on Monday morning and I'll be back to get this thing out of your hair. Don't let me down, son." Americus hung up the phone.

Spence hesitated a moment before he placed the receiver on its cradle. He wondered why Americus wanted him off the case so bad. Maybe he wasn't like his uncle after all. But then these days he didn't know who he was like. Angela's terrible suffering had stuck a chord in his soul, and everything he'd known only a few short days before was now in question.

He needed something to make him feel good, so he reached into his desk drawer and pulled out the check. Fifteen hundred dollars. Just like last week. Americus certainly had something figured out.

TWENTY-FIVE

SPENCE WAS PACKING his briefcase when he heard Kathy talking excitedly on the phone. He didn't know who she was talking to, nor could he understand what the discussion was about, but he could sense by her voice it was something bad. Of course, he did not know if it was something bad for Monroe or just Kathy, but either way he would know soon enough. Every afternoon before he left, Kathy enlightened him on the local gossip. Spence would stand in the hallway and nodded his head, pretending to be interested in Mr. Tyler's affair with the choir director or Mary Bryant's unfortunate situation of being with child and unsure who the father was. It was difficult for Spence to act interested in other people's problems, especially people he didn't know.

Spence finished packing his things and walked toward the front door. As he passed Kathy, who was still on the phone, he whispered, "Goodbye." She held up her finger, a signal for him to wait because she had something to tell him. Spence stood in the hall waiting for her to hang up and contemplating who she would tell him had fallen off the wagon and had been seen drinking. Finally, Kathy ended her conversation.

"Well, okay, girl, call me now if you hear anything else," she said and then hung up the phone. With a contrived look of disbelief on her face, she turned to Spence and said, "You're never going to believe whose car they found in the river."

Of course, Spence didn't know enough people in town to even make a guess, so after a brief pause, he tried to speed up the process by saying, "I can only imagine."

"Sheriff Watkins," Kathy said, eyes wide.

"The sheriff here in town?" Spence asked, suddenly interested. He'd been wondering about the sheriff ever since Angela told him that he was a frequent visitor to her house.

"Yeah. He's actually the county sheriff. Some of the men from my church found his police car washed up under a log in the river."

"Is he hurt?"

"Don't know. When they pulled the car out he wasn't in it. All they found were a couple of liquor bottles under the seat. He was bad to drink, ya know."

"No, I didn't know that. I never met him, just heard people talk about him. Nobody's heard from him? What about his family?"

"Well, he was supposed to get back last night from a sheriff's convention in Montgomery, but he never came home. Apparently, that's not a rare occurrence at his house, so his wife didn't even get concerned enough to call anybody. This morning they found his car. Took all afternoon to get it out."

Spence had heard Americus and others talk about Watkins and from his observations everyone knew him, but few in the professional community of Monroe appeared to respect him. It occurred to Spence that Deputy Reeves, the man who served him with the summons from Judge Hamilton, was much more appreciated. But Spence knew that sheriffs in Alabama were elected, and presumed that Reeves wasn't the sheriff because he was black.

"Maybe he'll show up then. He could've gotten out if they didn't find him in the car," Spence said.

"Maybe so," Kathy answered with a sigh. "Still, it doesn't look good."

Spence left his office and made his way to the county jail. When he opened the door, the ever-present heat struck him in the face. This time of year, even during a rainstorm, there was always the heat. And since Monroe hadn't seen rain for nearly two weeks, it was even that much worse.

As he moved closer to the jail, he noticed the commotion stirring out front. Still hanging on the wrecker, Sheriff Watkins' car had drawn a crowd of curious onlookers. A deputy Spence didn't recognize was guarding the car to keep spectators from actually touching it, but he wasn't making an attempt to disperse the gathering crowd and seemed to be enjoying the attention.

Spence made his familiar descent down into the basement of the county jail, exchanged pleasantries with Tom, and, as usual, found Angela sitting on her bed, Bible in hand. When she saw Spence, she marked her place and folded the pages together.

"You doin' okay?" Spence inquired.

She responded by nodding her head. She was actually ecstatic to see him, although she tried not to show it. She was more attracted to him than she had ever been to anyone else in her life. And somehow, although shy by nature, given the conditions she had been subjected to, she felt less helpless in this man's presence. She did not want to believe her emotions were from desperation, but the fact remained that in the story of her life, he was the only potential hero she had left.

"Listen," he began, "we've got some decisions to make. Your arraignment has been set for Monday morning, so we've got to decide how you're going to plead."

"I don't think I did it," she quickly interrupted.

Spence sat up a little straighter in his chair. "I know. You told me that before. But don't you think that maybe you were so angry with you father, I mean, given the way he treated you, that maybe on some subconscious level you might have done it?"

She turned her head and stared at the wall. She wasn't really sure what he meant by "subconscious level", but it sounded like he wanted her to say she killed her father.

"Angela," Spence tried to get her to look at him.

She abruptly turned to face him, her voice cracking with emotion. "You've never even asked me what happened that night. Just like everyone else, you just assumed that I killed him."

Spence realized she was right. He wanted to ask her the details of the night Calvin was murdered on his last visit, but she had gotten so upset he put it off. Now, three days before her arraignment, he still didn't know her side of the story. He'd been concentrating so hard on figuring a way out of defending her and getting a guilty plea to satisfy the DA that he really hadn't been concerned with her defense. Some attorney he was.

"Alright," he said, getting out a legal pad and pen, "let's have it."

"Where do you want me to start?"

"Well, I think I've got a pretty good picture of what your home life was like, so let's just start with that day. Did your father go to work?"

"He hadn't gone to work for several days. Little John, his boss, had come by the two nights before and tried to get him to go, but they just argued in the yard and Little John always left mad. My father would come into the house and go straight for the powder. He seemed like he was really upset about something those few days."

"Why was his boss so anxious to get your father to work?" Spence asked. "Did he have some sort of special training that they needed him for?"

"I don't know. I don't know what he did at work."

Spence made a note to find out what it was Calvin did that was so important to Little John and the mill. There had to be at least a thousand people who worked at NAPCO, and Calvin's importance didn't make a lot of sense.

"Okay, go ahead," Spence said, rolling his hand forward for her to continue.

"I think he finally ran out of powder and decided to go to work because Little John came by and they left about two that afternoon."

"You told me the other day that your father missed work a lot, so this was not unusual, right?"

"No," she replied. "Happened all the time."

"Was there anything out of the ordinary that happened that day?"

"Not really. Sheriff Watkins came by that morning and yelled at my father a little while on the porch, but that had happened a few times lately too."

Spence thought about telling her that Watkins's car had been found in the river and that the sheriff was missing, but he didn't want to interrupt her story.

"Did your father argue with the sheriff?"

"No, he never argued back to the sheriff. He always just stood there and listened, but he was always really mad when the sheriff left."

"Did you ever hear what Little John and your father were arguing about or what the sheriff was lecturing him on?"

"I never tried to listen. I knew better."

"So your father went to work. What next?"

"Little John dropped him off that night. I was already laying in my bed."

"Were you asleep?"

"No, my father hadn't been to the store for a long time. I kept telling him we needed food, but he stayed too strung out to get any. There wasn't any food left in the house. I was too hungry to sleep."

Every time Spence spoke with this girl she broke his heart a little more. Mentally, physically and sexually abused by her father and then starved on top of that. How could one person endure what she had gone through and still be as gentle and soft as she seemed. Every second he spent with her made him feel even more guilty for believing that his own life had been so hard. How could he sell her out to the DA if she really didn't do it?

"How did you know that it was Little John who brought your father home?"

"I looked out the window and recognized his truck."

"Did they argue?"

"No."

"Did he come directly into the house?"

"I heard him open the door and stumble when he came inside. He came to my room and stood in the doorway. He asked me where his supper was and I told him again that we were out of food. He told me to get out of bed and go to the kitchen." Tears began to well up in her eyes, but she continued with her story. "He stood at the doorway as I passed. He was very drunk. He…He smelled awful. When we got to the kitchen he told me to fix him something to eat, and I told him again we didn't have anything to fix. He became very angry and I begged him not to hurt me. I told him it wasn't my fault there was no food in the house."

She was openly sobbing now. Reliving the events of that night were taking a toll on her strength, a memory that was a constant reminder of how pitiful her life had been.

"He started at me," Angela went on, "and started pushing me around. I hadn't eaten in two days. I was too weak to put up much of a fight." The tears streamed down her face as she stared into the wall, not wanting Spence to see her.

"He slapped me a few times and then hit me really hard. I spun around and hit the table on my way to the floor. I tried to get up. I guess I blacked out." She hung her head.

Spence gave her a little time and then said, "I know it's difficult, but you've got to finish. I need to know what happened." He didn't want to tell her that his curiosity was killing him.

"When I woke up," she began again, "it was daylight." She wiped her eyes with her hands and took a deep breath. "Everything was quiet, so I figured he must've passed out. I looked around the house, but couldn't find him. I went to the bathroom to wash the blood off my face and then walked out to the porch. That's when I saw him. The bat was laying beside him. He was in a puddle of blood. I didn't know what to do. I screamed, but we live so far out in the woods, I'm sure nobody heard me. I ran off the porch and into the woods a little ways from the house. That's where the sheriff found me. I wasn't far away. He told me I had a right to a lawyer and then they brought me here."

"So you didn't call the police?"

"We didn't have a phone, remember?"

"Oh yeah, that's right. So the sheriff must have just come by again?"

"I guess so."

Spence took a second to collect his thoughts. Everything was really starting to confuse him and he felt a headache beginning at the base of his neck. A few weeks ago he had it all figured out. Then he got appointed to defend this beautiful young girl, who had spent her life as a punching bag. As annoyed as he had been with the appointment to defend her, at least his first thought was that everything would be cut and dry. Young girl abused by her father, finally has enough and kills him. He plea bargains her case as well as he can, she goes to jail and he gets back to his original plan of making money with Americus. But the last few days had confused matters and things were no longer clear. The coroner questions whether or not someone of Angela's size could cause so much damage. Then Little John seems awfully concerned about getting Calvin to work, when a boss would normally fire such a lousy employee. And to top it all, the county sheriff was a regular at the home of a cocaine addict, who never seemed to spend any time in jail. And now the sheriff was missing.

"Do you think I did it?" Angela interrupted his thoughts.

"I don't know. Without someone else having a motive to kill him, it's going to be hard to prove that you didn't. At least I thought with a guilty plea you'd have a pretty good chance of a reduced prison sentence."

"Even if I didn't do it?"

Spence took a deep breath. "I'll get back to you on that."

TWENTY-SIX

TO KENDALL A martini was a lot like a salad—they were only good if you could afford to have someone else prepare them. He held a stem in his hand and contemplated that he had two sips left in the glass. It was time to call Nicolas, his English butler, and have him make another round. He punched the button on the inter-com system and Nicolas answered.

"Yes, sir."

"I need you to come to the billiard room."

"Right away, sir."

Kendall relaxed in the suede leather chair, still holding a Joss pool cue in his hand. There was a half played game of nine-ball on the replica Louis XVI table, Kendall having stopped when the effects of the gin caused him to miss two easy shots at the orange five-ball. He only played nine-ball when by himself, playing billiards whenever he entertained other nobility. But when alone, he reverted back to the game that his scrap-dealer father had taught him as a young man, when the elder Kendall often took him to a downtown pub to play for a dollar a game against dockworkers and other laborers worth a tiny fraction of his own wealth.

The house was quiet on this particular Friday evening, and

Kendall liked the sound of its silence. It allowed him to clear his head and think about his next move. He hadn't seen his current live-in, Shelia, a thirty-two year old bombshell, in three days, but she had left a message that morning that she was in New York shopping and would be home Sunday afternoon. He'd been so busy he hadn't even noticed she was gone until last night, when he left the billiard room to look for her in the 13,000-square-foot mansion. After discovering that she was not there to satisfy his needs, he went back to the billiard room and drank martinis until he fell asleep.

He thought about finding some companionship for this evening, but he wasn't sure he wanted to go through the trouble. A barmaid at the club had been consistent with her advances, and he was tempted to call her bluff. She mentioned a few times how she heard about the exquisite decorations in his home and wanted to see them. He knew she was really looking for a sugar daddy, which tempted him even further. She had certainly picked the right place of employment, he had to give her that, because the Chicago Country Club was crawling with available non-bachelors. He almost called the club a few times to see if she was working and wanted to join him for a drink after her shift ended. That was the beauty of living in the Palisades, a gated neighborhood where she could leave her car parked out front all night long and Shelia would never know. Not that he cared if she did. He had come so far in his infidelity and could remember having to retreat to hotel rooms to be unfaithful to his first wife. Such were now the joys of being filthy rich.

A few minutes later Nicolas entered the room carrying a tray with a pitcher of martinis already mixed. He knew what Kendall wanted when he buzzed over the intercom, so Nicolas prepared the concoction beforehand. He placed the tray on the bar, poured a fresh martini in a new glass, and walked to Kendall in the leather chair.

"Will there be anything else, sir?" Nicolas asked, offering the drink.

Kendall turned up the glass he held in his hand and drank the last of his old drink. "If there is, I'll call you."

"Of course, sir."

Nicolas took the empty glass and left the room.

Kendall swirled the olive in his martini and thought about what he needed to do next with his company. The past twenty-four months were the best of his life, but the pressure was starting to mount again. At least this time it wasn't money problems. How far he had come in the past four years—from the depths of desperation to the pinnacle of his profession. It had been only forty-seven months since his bank gave the ultimatum: either turn NAPCO's financial misfortunes around, or they would call the loans and sell the company. The experience nearly killed him, since there seemed to be no way out. His paper company was ranked ninth in an industry at an all time low. Only the Monroe, Alabama, mill that made his signature line of Silksheet paper was managing a profit. The other six mills were rotting into disrepair and suffering from outdated equipment, while the company had no capital to invest in a much needed modernization. The internet had killed newsprint sales as more people were reading their newspapers electronically, and the paper companies ahead of him were sinking millions into renovations, bringing their cost down on other products like paper towels. Kendall was being squeezed out of the market. The stock price fell every quarter and the company had been in the red for eight years straight with nothing in the future promising an end to its troubles.

Kendall fired people everyday, brought in countless numbers of advisors and finally hired Ricter, the brightest young star in the industry. But in the end, they all came to the same conclusion: the company needed money and it needed it fast. He had worked so hard and sacrificed everything to make the company he inherited worthy of Wall Street's accolades. But the end loomed ever closer and there was nothing he could do to stop it. The humiliation of having to go back and practice law for a living would be more than he could bear.

But Kendall was a man of destiny, or at least that's how he saw himself. One Saturday afternoon at the club, only months away from a bank takeover, he was fortunate enough to be paired in a foursome with Gabriel Triboli, another man who had inherited the family business. Mr. Triboli had numerous legitimate enterprises, but they were all fronts for the one that no one ever asked about. That afternoon on the course, Triboli told a story about fixing a boxing match in his younger days when he bet against the boxer he was promoting and then had his fighter take a dive. Triboli declared that there was always more money to be made at the backdoor where no one was looking than at the front where everybody watched. Triboli had made twice the money for himself and his boxer by arranging the fight. His comments set the CEO's thoughts in motion. The story changed Kendall's life.

Over the next few weeks Kendall took inventory of NAPCO's transportation infrastructure and formed a plan. He looked at railroads, trucking, and the distribution of products, all used in abundance by the company. The problem of crossing the border from Mexico had all but been eliminated by the North American Free Trade Agreement, and his boxcars rolled over the Rio Grande everyday without being checked. The only logistics problem would be transferring the product from a railcar into packages, which would necessitate a lot of activity and create a greater risk of being exposed. But the beauty of Kendall's system was that his drop point would be in the middle of nowhere, surrounded by nothing but millions of pine trees.

His scheme would involve only a few: Ricter at his office in Chicago, a mill supervisor, and a drop man to separate the products. There would be no need for anyone else in the company to know, since the two products were indistinguishable by the naked eye. He felt Ricter would be an easy sell. Although his right hand man was morally sound, his reputation was also on the line, and NAPCO's position since his hiring had steadily become worse. The mill supervisor and drop man made peanuts working for Kendall's company, so a little money would surely do the trick for them, and if it didn't, he would fire them until he found the right men for the job. His only other concern was local law enforcement. He wanted to have the right officials in his pocket in case anything happened and he needed them to squelch out any trouble. His plan was to approach all seven mill towns until he found a few local officials who would cooperate, but he never had to make a second offer when the circuit judge in Monroe agreed to help and promised he could deliver the courthouse and the sheriff's department.

Once convinced he could pull it off, Kendall approached Mr. Triboli with his idea, promising to move more product faster and cheaper than the traditional methods—and with far less risk. He explained to the Italian how his company had everything in place to slip the goods through the backdoor, while everyone watched them make paper out front. He told Triboli he was looking for a partner. The Italian thought the plan was ingenious.

Within six months Kendall was ready to bring the operation on line. There were anxious nights, knowing what Triboli's response would be if Kendall failed to deliver the product. But within three fiscal quarters, Triboli had a surplus of goods and NAPCO was well on the road to recovery, having signed a very lucrative contract with 'Triboli's Office Supply' chain, which had new stores in every major city in the United States.

Everything was perfect until the Monroe drop man got greedy and tried to strong-arm the other conspirators. The problem had been solved, but now some were getting cold feet. Kendall especially didn't understand Ricter's qualms. Ricter had been in the corporate world all of his life and knew that sacrifices sometimes had to be made for the good of the company. Some sacrifices were just greater than others.

Kendall took a sip of his drink and leaned his head against the leather chair. The low light of his billiard room was comforting, and he focused on an oil painting of a black-maned lion that overlooked his bar. He had wanted to be that lion, the undisputed leader of the pride. But his situation was not what he had planned when he set out to build the perfect company. Here he was, half drunk and alone in a big house, wondering who he would have to kill next to keep it. The money was supposed to have solved everything, so why did he still need the martinis to go to sleep?

TWENTY-SEVEN

SATURDAY MORNING SPENCE decided it was time he took a visit to the murder sight. Since he wasn't familiar enough with criminal procedure to know if he could visit it by himself, he and Sam drove to the sheriff's department to see if he could get a deputy to take him there. Spence pulled up front, told Sam to stay in the Explorer, and went inside. He went to the counter where a deputy was writing something on a standardized form. The station was alive with activity as people scampered everywhere, including the Alabama Bureau of Investigation and a reporter from Montgomery. Watkins' body still hadn't been found and there were search and rescue teams constantly looking for him.

The deputy at the front desk barely glanced up to see what Spence wanted. Just behind the deputy at another desk was John Reeves, the tall black deputy sheriff, who was the acting sheriff while Watkins was missing. Spence explained to the deputy that he was defending Angela Chauncey and needed to see the murder scene.

"We're a little busy right now," the deputy stated, rolling his eyes around the room to show the activity. He put his head back down and started writing again.

Spence stood there a moment, wondering if he should demand

that someone take him, or just leave and come back at another time. He started to turn and walk away when he heard, "I'll take you."

Reeves never stopped what he was doing, but he stated again, "I'll take you out there. I need a break." He stood up and grabbed his hat from the desk, walked outside of the counter and proceeded to the door, where Spence followed him. At the door, a man in plain clothing with a badge attached to his belt stopped Reeves, and they spoke for a few moments. Spence assumed the man was with the ABI and the conversation had something to do with Watkins, but he didn't eavesdrop. When the two men stopped talking, Spence followed Reeves outside.

"You can ride with me," Reeves said, opening the door to his patrol car.

"I appreciate that, but I've got my dog with me and I can't leave her that long, so I guess I'd better follow you."

"Nonsense. I love dogs," said Reeves. "Put her in the backseat."

Reeves drove out of town and made a few turns down some extremely bumpy roads. He never said a word, but the car was filled with the noise of his police scanner as reports from the search and rescue teams filled the airwaves. About ten miles out of town he turned down a dirt road blanketed on both sides by tall pine trees. It was a lot like the road in front of Spence's house, except this road seemed more traveled and a river ran beside it on the other side of the trees. The road had been built wide so logging trucks and equipment could pass without fear of an accident. Crowned perfectly in the center for rainwater to run off, there was a well-kept drainage ditch on the opposite side of the river. The roadbed was a mixture of red dirt and sand and had recently been scraped, which left small ripples on the surface that could be felt in the car's suspension. For a dirt road it was remarkably well maintained, and the ride was better than on most of the paved roads in the area.

After fifteen minutes in the car without a word spoken, Spence decided to break the ice with Reeves.

"Any news on where the sheriff might be?" Spence inquired.

"Nothing positive," Reeves answered.

"I didn't know him myself. I had only heard people talk about him."

Reeves responded by nodding his head.

"From the rumor mill, it seems he may have had some personal problems, maybe even drank a little too much," Spence said, still looking for some type of response out of Reeves, who didn't answer. After a moment of silence Spence decided to be little more direct. "Did you and he get along?"

"We get along fine," Reeves answered back with an emphasis on the present tense.

As Spence searched for someway to keep the conversation going, Reeves surprised him by elaborating. "I respected him enough to work for him, but we didn't hang around one another socially."

"I see," answered Spence.

"I still hope he turns up, if that's what you were asking?"

"I'm not sure what I was asking," replied Spence.

They continued down the dirt road, neither saying a word. Spence had trouble reading the deputy. He was pleasant when spoken to, but rarely talked unless asked a direct question. Sam seemed at ease around him, though, which was always a good sign. Spence had long since learned that she was a much better judge of character than he was.

Reeves made a couple of turns down similar-looking roads until they came to a break in the trees—with a little yard of dirt, sand and crabgrass cut out of the pines. In the center of the yard sat a square-shaped shack on concrete blocks, about three feet off the ground. Four steps lead up to a porch, which extended the full length along the front of the house and had two old wooden chairs placed on each side of the door. The windows that flanked the door had cardboard patches that replaced broken glass, and the pair of windows on each side of the house were in similar condition. Silver tin sheets ran down the slope of the roof with rust spots on more than half its surface.

There was no paint on the entire structure, so the outside facade was made from gray-weathered plywood sheets, matching the floor of the porch. Trash, beer cans and an old rusting stovetop littered the yard. Perhaps knowing what had taken place in the shack added to his emotions, but the entire setting made Spence feel dirty.

Around the wooden square columns holding the roof over the porch was yellow police tape with the words "Do Not Cross" printed every two feet.

Spence told Sam to stay in the car and rolled a window down for her to get some air. He followed Reeves through the yard and up the rickety steps where the deputy held the yellow police line up for Spence to stoop underneath.

"This is where we found the body," Reeves said, pointing to the floor of the porch. Spence could see the bloodstains soaked into the wood. "The baseball bat was lying beside him," Reeves continued, "and over there is where we found the girl, sitting under that tree." He pointed off the left side of the porch.

"Was there any sign of a struggle?" Spence inquired.

"A dead body," Reeves answered with a frown.

"Other than that?" Spence inquired further.

"Not out here, but it did look like there had been a tussle inside the house."

The doorknob on the shack was broken, so the sheriff's office had padlocked the door after roping off the house. Reeves took out his keys and unlocked the door, which scraped loudly against the floor when he pushed it open. He reached his hand to the right side of the wall and turned on a light switch that offered very little illumination once it flickered on. The inside of the house was as plain and ugly as the outside. The door opened directly into the living room, with no wall separating the kitchen area in the back. The inside walls were also plywood, as bare and unadorned as the outside. There were no pictures on the walls or anywhere else in the room. The floor surface was uneven and Spence could feel his weight shift on the bumpy

linoleum tile that had large cuts and gashes throughout. In the center
of the living area sat a light green couch and a well-used synthetic
leather reclining chair. There was no coffee table, but an ancient looking television with two large antennas sat on a wooden box just to the
left of the front door. The only light in the room was the single
exposed bulb that dangled from two wires in the ceiling.

In the back of the room was a simple looking table surrounded
by three chairs. A fourth chair, obviously not a part of the set, lay
overturned on the floor. A counter ran the length of the back wall in
the kitchen, with a sink and cut outs for the stove and refrigerator.
Just past the stove top, the counter made a ninety-degree turn and
came out towards the center of the room. Between the counter and
the table were a broken glass and an iron pot lying on the floor.
Spence assumed the overturned chair, glass and iron pot were the
signs of the struggle Reeves had mentioned. He also thought the
items helped legitimize Angela's story about hitting the table after
Calvin struck her.

On both sides of the living room and kitchen were two doors. To
the right was Calvin's bedroom with a mattress lying on the floor and
stained sheets piled up in the middle. Again, there were no pictures
on the walls or any other furniture in the room. The only window was
covered with tin foil, so no light penetrated the glass. The door to the
left of his room led to the only bathroom in the house. It was small
with a wall mounted sink and a tub with a showerhead. There was a
cabinet over the sink and a mirror hanging over the toilet. The floor
was the same pitiful linoleum as the rest of the house.

On the other side of the living room was a small storage room
where the fuse box was located. Next to it was Angela's room. Spence
opened the door to her room and inspected it from the doorway. In the
center of one wall, there was a single bed with an iron headboard and
frame. A colorful quilt was neatly placed over the mattress and tucked
into the sides. Spence could see the impression of Angela's body on top
of the quilt, undoubtedly trying to stay cool in the summer heat, and

fighting off the hunger. Over the bed was a picture of two small children walking across a bridge in stormy weather, while an angel with large white wings looked over them. Over the only window in the room hung a pink sheet, placed in a manner to resemble a curtain. On the floor, opposite of the bed, was a row of books held up by two bricks used as bookends and organized so the tallest was in the middle and the others descended on each side. There was a small nightstand next to the bed and an old goose-neck lamp. A Bible lay next to the lamp. Spence went back to the living room and found Reeves.

"So what's the theory?" Spence asked, as he and Reeves stood looking around the living room.

"The same one I'm sure you've heard all over town. He comes home and beats her up like always. She finally has enough, follows him out to the porch and whacks him with the bat. His supervisor from the mill finds him the next morning and calls us. When we get here, she's sitting under the big pine tree outside. She never attempted to run. What's her side of the story?"

"Pretty much the same except for the part where she hits him over the head. She says she was knocked unconscious and when she woke up in the kitchen, she walked outside and found him dead. With no phone or car she had no choice but to wait for somebody to come by. She never mentioned his supervisor. She says the sheriff was the first to come, but maybe the supervisor came before she woke up."

"Do you believe her?"

"To tell you the truth, deputy, I don't know. There seem to be a lot of strange things about her father. Do you know if he was a cocaine addict?"

"Never met him, but I heard stories. I'm not from here originally, so I don't know much more than you. Here tell he was a pretty good ball player. Some of the old timers still talk about his heroics down at Miss Sarah's. But I never saw him out anywhere. He did get hauled in by another deputy one night, when he was at the courthouse whacked out on something and screaming at the top of his lungs. But the next morning the sheriff got him out of jail and I guess took him home."

"Was there a report filed?"

"I don't know. I guess I could look and see. I'm not supposed to, without going through the court, but I guess it couldn't hurt. You'll get it anyway if you want it."

Spence assumed Reeves was talking about some kind of procedure he could use to obtain the records, but since the deputy knew more about it than the lawyer, he just said, "Thanks."

"Seen enough?" Reeves asked, as he started toward the door.

"I guess so." Spence answered. He followed Reeves to the door. Once they were out of the shack, the deputy turned and replaced the padlock. It was only a little after 9:00 in the morning, but the heat and humidity were already on the rise. Thinking about how hot it was for that time of the day, Spence suddenly had a revelation.

"Deputy, you said that his supervisor found him the next morning, right?" Spence inquired.

"Yeah. About eight o' clock. Little John called us. Why?"

"According to my client, Calvin worked the second shift, which wouldn't have started until the afternoon. I wonder why his supervisor was here to pick him up at that time of the day?"

"Maybe he got moved to the first shift."

"But he worked the night before."

"He still could've been moved to the first shift."

"Even so, that would mean he would have a new supervisor, wouldn't it?"

"I guess so. Maybe when he didn't come to work, the supervisor decided to call Little John to come and get him since he had worked for him in the past."

"You see, John—" Spence hesitated a moment when he realized that he had called the deputy by his first name, like the two of them were becoming closer, but when Reeves did not change expressions, Spence assumed he did not mind and continued. "What I don't get is, why would a mill supervisor, responsible for several hundred men, be so concerned whether a particular man made it to work or not? According to Angela, Calvin missed work all the time, but they never fired him. What could he have done at the mill that made him so important?"

"I don't know," Reeves answered back, "but I'm sure that there's an explanation for it."

Spence looked around the porch and yard one last time. "Yeah, I'm sure there is. I'm just wondering if it has anything to do with my client."

TWENTY-EIGHT

SPENCE TOOK SAM home for lunch after he and Reeves arrived back in town. He wanted to talk to Angela about her arraignment on Monday and couldn't leave Sam in the car because he had no idea how long it would take. It was the first weekend in August, and in South Alabama, the heat index inside a parked car could be life-threatening for a dog.

As he made his way to the jail, he could still see the activity in front of the sheriff's office. There were few parking spaces left at any government facility in Monroe, a rare occurrence on a Saturday. Most of the cars had a state issued tag. The report on the late news out of Montgomery last night said Watkins was believed to have drowned in the river, and with every passing hour the chances of finding the body were diminishing. Spence didn't necessarily care about the fate of the local sheriff, whom he'd never met, but for his client's sake he was curious about the incident. He wanted to know why a sheriff would make regular visits to a cocaine addict's home in the middle of the woods. With the sheriff gone, he would never get to ask him that question. Maybe Watkins and Calvin played ball together, and maybe the sheriff had a soft spot for his friend and tried to keep him out of trouble. There were a lot of explanations, but how would he find the right one?

When he got to her cell, he found Angela doing pushups on the concrete floor, adding to his understanding of why her body was in such great shape. She stopped as soon as she saw Spence and rested on her knees.

"Don't let me stop you," he said, hoping to watch.

"It gets a little boring in here sometimes. I have to do something to pass the time," she said, catching her breath.

"Do you exercise a lot?"

"I grew up watching my father do push ups and run down the dirt road. I guess he thought he was still a great athlete. When he left, I would run down to the river. It helped clear my head."

"Yeah, it seems to do the same for me."

Spence placed his legal pad in the chair and his hands in his pockets and leaned against a cell wall. She stood at the opposite wall, shrugging her shoulders, still stretching from her workout.

"I went out to your house this morning with Deputy Reeves."

"Not much of a home, is it?"

"I've seen worse," Spence lied. "Your room looked pretty well kept."

"I had a lot of free time on my hands. You didn't bring my Bible or any of my books did you?"

"I thought you had a Bible here. I saw you reading one."

"They were real nice about giving me one, but I wish I had my own. It has my notes in it."

"I'll see if Reeves will clear it for me to bring it to you, and maybe I'll find you some new books to read."

"That would be nice."

The two stood awkwardly in the cell, hesitant over what to say next, and glancing across the cell and then to the floor in front of them. Each felt the silence was too long and wanted to continue the conversation, but the right words wouldn't come. Finally Spence remembered to tell her about Americus' friend.

"Good news," Spence began. "I think we've found you another lawyer."

Angela stopped moving her arms and shoulders and looked directly at him. "So you got rid of me."

"I think the more appropriate statement would be that you finally got rid of me. My uncle has a friend who has a big law firm in Dothan, and he's agreed to send someone up here to defend you. He won't be here until later on in the week, so we'll have to go through the arraignment by ourselves." Spence attempted a little smile. "We've got to decide how you are going to plead. Now, I know you have some doubts as to whether or not you did it, but we've got to remember that you could have a pretty good self-defense case—or maybe even temporary insanity."

"You think I'm crazy?" Angela tilted her head down and looked upward at Spence.

"No, no, of course not. Temporary insanity doesn't mean your crazy. It means that because of your abusive situation, you took temporary leave of the senses that let you know the difference between right and wrong and killed your father," Spence was stumbling to explain something he knew very little about. "It certainly doesn't mean you're crazy. It has to do more with your situation than with you." He didn't feel like he had done a very good job explaining the elements of temporary insanity, but when she didn't ask any more questions he moved on.

"On the other hand," Spence began again, "there are probably some things I should tell you that don't make much sense. Some recent occurrences that may be of some interest." Spence walked over to the folding chair and picked up his legal pad. He'd made some notes when he took Sam home at lunch. He sat down in the chair and flipped the first page over.

"Which hand do you write with?"

"This one." Angela held up her right hand.

"Would you swing a bat with that one as well?"

"Yes, I'm not a switch hitter." When Spence looked up, she added, "We watched a lot of baseball around my house, Spencer." She smiled and he smiled back. It was the first time she called him by his first name.

"According to the coroner, whoever killed your father was more than likely left-handed. Of course, that's with the evidence we have right now." The lawyer in him never wanted to sound too conclusive. "A large left handed person at that."

"That's got to be good news for me, doesn't it?" There was a little hope in her voice.

"We'll have to get some experts to verify it, but it certainly doesn't hurt. Also, there's the relationship between your father and Sheriff Watkins. Is there anyone else who might have known he was visiting your place so often?"

"Not that I know of. He always came alone."

"And you don't know what they talked about when he came?"

"I never stayed around. He always gave me the creeps—the way he would look at me and say things like 'you sure are a purty young thang.'" Angela did her best redneck impression. "Besides, he knew I didn't like him because he was the one who brought me home when I tried to run away.

"You tried to run away?"

"Twice."

Spence made himself a note to come back to that.

"Do you know what time you found your father on the porch that morning?" Spence asked.

"It was about 6:50. I remember looking at the clock in the kitchen and wondering where he was. The door to his bedroom was open and I could see he wasn't in it."

"According to Deputy Reeves, Little John found your father sometime around eight and called the sheriff."

"That's impossible. I was only a few yards away from the house. I would've seen anybody who came by. The sheriff was the first to come."

Spence thought this seemed strange. If she did in fact have her times correct, then Little John would have had to come before she woke up at 6:50 and then taken more than an hour to call the police. He could have driven to town and back twice in the same amount of time.

"There's certainly something strange about a sheriff and a cocaine addict associating with one another, always in private," Spence went on.

"Can't you find out what the sheriff says about it?" asked Angela.

"Well, that's where it gets even more strange. The sheriff's car was found in the river yesterday by a couple of fisherman, and as of right now they haven't found his body."

"Maybe the person who killed my father killed the sheriff too. Maybe the drugs had something to do with it."

"Maybe, but we're just speculating. We don't know if the two are related or not. Were your father and Watkins old baseball playing buddies or anything?"

"I wouldn't think so. Sheriff Watkins was a good bit older than my father. Angela leaned toward Spence from the side of the bed. "I know that him missing has something to do with this. Watkins was a bad man, I just know he was."

"Well, even if the two are related, we would have a very hard time proving that the local sheriff was involved in some sort of drug deal, especially now that he's gone and there's nobody else who knew he was visiting your father. Maybe you and your new lawyer can figure something out. Heck, maybe it's better that Watkins is gone. If he were still around, it would just be your word against his."

"So, I guess you won't be around."

Spence hesitated a moment and then answered, "Sure, I'll be around. I just won't be your lawyer anymore."

"What if I don't want another lawyer?"

Spence slowly stood up and walked back to the opposite wall, "Now Angela, we've talked about this. I think it would be better if someone else handled..."

"You said yourself they'll pay you to defend me. Why don't you want to?" Spence thought he could hear disgust in her voice.

"It's not that I don't want to," he said, "I just don't think that I can properly..."

"You're just like the others," she interrupted, and turned to face the wall.

"What do you mean, I'm just like the others? What others?" Spence's tone was that of a man cornered. All of the sudden he found he was defending himself.

"All the people I've ever met in my life. That's 'what others'. You may be nice to me to my face, but you really don't want anything to do with me because you don't know if I'm white or if I'm black. Just like all of those kids that I used to go to school with!" she said, raising her voice in anger.

"I don't care if you're white or black. That's got nothing to do with it."

"Then why won't you defend me? You're a lawyer, aren't you?"

Spence's voice rose. "Look, lady, I'm a real estate lawyer. So unless you're buying or selling a piece of property, I can't help you. Do you understand? I don't know what the hell I'm doing! When we go to your arraignment on Monday, that'll be the first time I've ever been in a courtroom as an attorney. Damn it—can't you understand that I can't help you! I don't know how!"

"Damn it—can't you understand that for once in my life I would just like somebody to try! Somebody who cares whether I live or die!"

"Look, I've tried to do everything I can to help you, and believe me, having a new lawyer will be the best thing for you."

"Why won't you just try?"

"I'm not going to be pushed into this," Spence insisted. "I'll see you Monday morning and we'll enter a motion to get you a new lawyer. Now that's the best I can do!" Spence walked to the folding chair and grabbed his legal pad.

He started for the cell door when suddenly she ran to his side, grabbed him, and said, "Please don't go."

She put her arms around his waist and buried her head into his chest. She was crying. Spence stood there with his hands in the air. Slowly he put them down and dropped the legal pad on the floor. He wrapped his arms around her and pulled her closer. His face pressed into the side of her head, and he took a deep breath. He stroked her back gently as she squeezed him tighter. They stood in their embrace until her sobbing slowed. Spence leaned his head back; she lifted hers, and stared into his eyes. She wanted him to kiss her. He knew it. He had seen that look from a woman before, but for the first time in his life, he felt he would never be complete until his lips touched hers. The moment was killing him. A thousand thoughts were running through his mind. He wanted her so bad—but he was her attorney. Besides, Americus would never allow him to become involved with a racially mixed girl. It would kill his business in Monroe. All of his life Spence had been fighting an uphill battle, and now that things were heading in the right direction, the one fear that was never a problem in the past was raising its head and demanding that he deal with it. He wanted to be selfish and not care about Angela or her problems, but suddenly that wasn't possible. He was more worried about Angela's future than his own, and he wanted to scream at the heavens for their injustice. For once, everything he ever wanted was within his grasp, and now he was willing to risk it all to have the girl in his arms.

Finally, he eased his embrace and rubbed her upper arms. "Listen," he said, "We'll figure something out. Don't worry."

She hugged him again as he ran his hands up and down her back. He knew there was no turning back. She had his full attention.

TWENTY-NINE

JUDGE JAMES HAMILTON'S house was in the heart of downtown Monroe, only two blocks from the county courthouse sitting in the main square. A large old Victorian style home with a veranda wrapped around all four sides, the home's exterior was painted yellow with white wooden columns encasing the porch at eight-foot intervals. A white banister made from wooden pilasters circled the porch's perimeter and ran between the columns. The roof sagged a little and the gingerbread trim needed painting, but the house was otherwise solid, especially since it had been in the judge's family from the time it was built in 1912. Dark green zoysia covered the yard, and a prize-winning rose garden—his wife's favorite pastime—lay at the east end of the porch. A huge oak tree, four feet in diameter, dominated the west side of the house, providing evening shade for the judge's favorite pastime—sipping bourbon.

This Saturday afternoon the judge had company for happy hour. But the county's district attorney was far from happy, and it showed on his unshaven face. He hadn't slept in days, and even the whiskey he drank from the judge's Waterford crystal glass failed to steady his nerves.

"Just like that, huh?" Pat Seaver asked the judge. "They just decided to kill him without asking us or giving us a chance to fix things first?"

"They were unhappy with the way he changed the plan when he killed Calvin," the judge answered. "The girl was supposed to die, too, and there was never supposed to be a trial. I tried to talk them out of it, Pat. You know I did. Hell, I even argued with you in my chambers that the trial wouldn't be a big deal. But, the fact is—and you know this as well as I do—Watkins was stupid. Eventually he would have done something to blow this thing for all of us, especially had he ever found out that you and I were making ten times the money he was."

"Yeah," said Seaver, "but has anybody taken the time to think about the situation we've got now? Reeves will be the acting sheriff, and there's no way he's bribable, and what's more, he's pretty damn smart. With a few clues, he could figure this thing out."

"The boys in Chicago knew that before they decided to kill Watkins, but they still wanted him out. We'd made a mistake by letting him in and he was far to reckless to be allowed to stay, given the knowledge he had."

The judge rocked forward in his chair and poured another splash of bourbon over the ice in the bottom of his glass. He held the bottle up, and Seaver offered his glass.

"Besides," the judge began again, "we've only got to keep Reeves in the dark for one year. Next year is an election year, and Chicago promised to send enough money to get whomever we want elected. Even said they could fix it if they had to."

The DA stood up and walked to the railing that encased the porch. He sat his glass on the top rail and leaned on his hands as he looked down the street.

"I still don't like it, James," he began. "I mean, I can see a pattern forming here. First, it was Richard Powell and his hunting accident when Calvin started to talk after we refused to give him more. Powell was supposed to be the only one. They said Calvin would shut up when he found out we meant business. Then it was Calvin, when he didn't shut up. Then Little John, because who knows why? And now it's Watkins, whom I didn't trust either. But the fact they did it without even discussing it with us scares the hell out of me. What happens when they decide we know too much? You think they'll have a problem killing us too? I think they've already proven that murdering a judge and a district attorney wouldn't bother them the least little bit."

"That's not going to happen and you know it," the judge answered, wanting to reassure himself as much as Seaver. "They know they've got a gravy train here, and they've got all the people needed to keep the tracks greased and the train rolling."

"I also know they could all spend the rest of their lives in jail, and we could, too. And if it comes down to them or us," Seaver declared, "Thomas Kendall will make damn sure it's us.

"Look," said Hamilton, rocking at his leisure, "all we've got to do is concentrate on what we need to do down here to help this thing blow over. We can control the kid enough to get him to plea bargain the case. Thompson's too much like his uncle to let this thing side track him for long. And as for the girl, she's better off anyway. Prison for a few years would probably be a welcome change from the life she's been livin'."

"I know that's the plan," Seaver had turned back around and leaned against the rail, "But I also know that here lately our plans have not been working. What if this kid decides that he wants the attention he'll get from trying to get this girl acquitted. He's not dumb, ya know. He may decide to snoop around a little bit before he sends that pretty girl off to jail."

"He won't try to be the hero, trust me. I know his kind. He's too greedy to let something like this—something he's only getting paid forty dollars an hour for—take up too much of his time."

"There's also the girl," retorted Seaver. "Neither you nor I had ever seen her, and we didn't know she was going to look like she came off the front of a Harlequin romance novel. You may say you know this kid, but I also know how men react to beautiful women, and it may not be as cut and dried as you think."

"She's a nigger," declared the judge.

"She's still beautiful."

"I'm telling you, Pat, we can control this thing. Hell, say the kid did fall in love. He's not going to risk her going to jail for the rest of her life when we make him an offer that could set her free in just a few years. You said yourself that he practically threw himself at your feet when you told him to plea bargain the case."

"I just hope you're right, James. I'm really starting not to trust Kendall."

"Everything's going to be just fine. As long as we don't panic and do something stupid. Don't worry about Kendall. Ricter's running things these days anyway. If you need some reassurance, just call and talk to him."

Seaver picked up his glass and gulped the bourbon. He walked back to the rocking chair next to the judge's and sat down. Picking up the bottle of Wild Turkey, he refilled his glass, leaned his head back and closed his eyes. "It's not worth it, ya know."

"What's that?" inquired the judge.

"The money. It's not worth it. Four years ago we were already two of the richest men in the county. What made us think we had to have more?"

The judge didn't answer, but instead sat in his chair with his own thoughts on what he had become.

"I mean, hell"—Seaver started again—"I went to high school with Richard Powell, and now I'm the reason he's dead. And then Calvin, and now Watkins. I can't sleep at night for worrying that the Feds are going to bust down my door any second, and all day long I'm look-ing around for men in dark suits from Chicago."

"You're just saying that because of all this going on right now," said Hamilton. "See if you still feel that way after we've gotten away with it."

Seaver opened his eyes, dropped his head, and looked at the judge. "If we get away with it, James. If we get away with it."

THIRTY

SPENCE DROVE DOWN the same dirt road that he and Deputy Reeves traveled earlier that morning, trying to remember where he was going and wishing he'd written down the directions. All the trees on either side of the road looked the same. He knew he had to make two turns. The first one was by the river, but the next would be a guess. The roads were well traveled because of the logging trucks that went in and out of the forest hauling trees to NAPCO—which meant that Reeves' tracks from this morning had been eliminated. If he found the shack it would be by pure luck, and he cursed himself again for not getting directions from Reeves.

The deputy gave him permission to go back to the house and get Angela's Bible and some of the other books once Spence promised not to touch anything. The sheriff's department and its five officers were spread thin by the ongoing search for Watkins, so Reeves really had no choice but to let Spence go by himself.

Spence continued to wander the endless maze of NAPCO's timberlands. He decided to try one of the minor roads to see if it was the one leading to Angela's house. He took a right turn on the next dirt road he came to, but soon realized it was not the road he was looking for. The road became increasingly narrow and eventually dead ended into a large lake. Spence turned his Explorer around, headed back out to the main dirt road, and drove deeper into the pine trees.

As he traveled through the trees he noticed gates with "NO TRES-PASSING" signs posted on the front, blocking off certain roads. Every now and then he would also see a "NO HUNTING" sign nailed to a pine tree. He knew NAPCO gave hunting permits for certain areas of its property because he had inquired about one for himself while at Smitty's office with Americus. He assumed the signs were in areas where they were going to be cutting timber soon and didn't want any-one on the property to potentially get hurt. He remembered Americus telling him about Mr. Powell, the lawyer in town who had handled most of the county's indigent clients, who was accidentally killed while hunting on some of NAPCO's property. The posted signs were surely in the interest of safety, but if someone were walking through the woods hunting, how would they know what part of the land they were on? All of the trees looked the same and this place was enormous. Thousands and thousands of acres with nothing but pine trees, over every hill and down through every valley, for as far as the eyes could see.

Spence decided he would take every dirt road to the right until he found Angela's house. He took the next right. No luck. He came back out to the main road and continued to the next right. He was beginning to get more confused and extremely frustrated. Why had-n't he written down those directions? Reeves knew exactly where the house was.

On the fourth dirt road, he came upon the little clearing. "Thank God," he said out loud, as he raised his hands off of the steering wheel and towards the heavens. Afternoon was becoming evening as darkness rapidly closed in. The sun was no longer above the tops of the trees to give him light. He wanted to get Angela's things and then hurry back to the paved highway before the night swallowed him. The forest was hard enough to navigate in the daylight and he cer-tainly didn't want to be lost out here at night, going through this end-less labyrinth of dirt roads and pine trees. He stepped out of the

Explorer and walked through the sandy yard to the steps of the porch. He took the key to the pad lock that Reeves had given him out of his pocket. They must have really bonded this morning for the deputy to trust him in such a short amount of time. He fumbled with the key and lock for a few moments, but finally got the door to open and turned on the light switch. In the late evening gloom the tiny room was even more depressing. What a pitiful life it must have been growing up in these conditions. How had she managed to stay so positive? She didn't seem to have any long lasting effects just by talking to her. Sure, she was a little timid, but her mind was sharp. She was quick-witted, sometimes even quicker than he. She hadn't been allowed to go to school, yet her vocabulary was excellent, Spence assumed from reading the books stacked on her floor, given to her by her grandmother. She spoke of her grandmother often—the only person to ever show Angela any kind of love. It was sad to think that Spence, an acquaintance for only a few days, was Angela's closest friend. He reached down and pulled his shirt to his nose. He could still smell her in his clothing from their embrace in her jail cell earlier that afternoon. He closed his eyes for a moment and could feel his hands on her back, her arms around his waist. The sudden hoot of an owl in the distance opened his eyes, reminding him to concentrate. It was getting darker outside.

He walked to Angela's room and turned on the light. The room was well kept, almost spotless, and it smelled clean. A vast contrast compared to the rest of the house. She must have never let Calvin in here, he thought. That is, when she was able to keep him out.

He took the Bible from the dresser and walked to the stack of books on the floor. He knelt down to read the titles. *To Kill A Mockingbird, Gone with the Wind*—strange books to be a black girl's favorites, but then she was half white. "What are you saying, Thompson?" he said aloud. Why does it matter what color you are to enjoy classic literature? He had to stop classifying her. From now on she would just be Angela.

He made a mental note to find her some books she hadn't read, but per her request he picked up five books and placed them under his arm.

As he made it out of the room and turned to close the door, he thought he saw a light through the window of the main living room. He moved quickly against the wall so not to be seen, but by the time he crept to the window, the light was gone. No sound but the early crickets chirping at the last orange color of the sunset rippling over the sky. Standing at the glass he surveyed the yard. Maybe it was just a fisherman leaving the river or a logging truck headed down the road. He knew he didn't want to be here in the dark of the night. He hadn't so much as a pocketknife to defend himself and the shack gave him strange feelings.

He decided that the light had only been his imagination getting the best of him. He tried to humor himself. A big, strong, young man scared of owls and moonlight. But he couldn't convince his mind that he was just in some ordinary forest. Ordinary forests were not encircled in yellow police lines.

He held tight to the books and walked to the door. Turning off the light, he closed the door and replaced the padlock. As he turned around, he saw the figure sitting in one of the porch chairs. He threw the books in the air and readied himself for an attack, too startled to run.

"Relax, Mr. Thompson," the man said. "It's just me."

When the man stepped out of the shadows Spence recognized his face. It was Greg Barnett, the man he'd encountered eating alone at Miss Sarah's. The divorced engineer that worked out at NAPCO. The man that for some reason didn't quite fit in with the rest of the town.

"You scared me to death," Spence said. "What the hell are you doing here?"

"Probably the same thing you are," Barnett replied. "Looking for answers."

"Answers to what?" Spence said nervously as he studied Barnett from head to toe. He had nothing in his hand, and it didn't look like he was carrying a gun, at least readily available. He seemed to be perfectly relaxed, though he had to have known that his sudden appearance would scare the hell out of Spence. Still, if he wanted to harm him, he would've already done it.

"Answers to who killed Calvin," Barnett replied.

"Are you just a concerned citizen, or was Calvin a friend of yours?"

"Never knew the man," answered Barnett. "Only heard about him. I did watch him out at the paper mill a few times. Didn't seem to me like he was a very good employee, but he didn't have trouble keeping his job."

It struck Spence that Barnett's Southern accent was missing. He seemed to know a lot about Calvin, and Spence wondered if this man held the key to Angela's defense. But at this moment he had no idea whose side Barnett was on.

"Did you work with Calvin? Do you work the second shift at the plant?"

"Yes, I normally work the second shift."

"So you know Little John, his supervisor?"

"Of course I do. He's my boss too."

"Then maybe you can explain to me why Calvin never lost his job. What the hell did he do that was so important to the mill?" Spence squatted down and gathered up the books he had thrown when Barnett surprised him.

"He was just a bin operator."

"You're going to have to forgive me," Spence said, "I'm not an engineer for a paper company. Exactly what's a bin operator?"

"Right," Barnett replied. "Trains come in bringing boxcars of slurry to the mill. Slurry comes in several different forms, sometimes a liquid, but mostly a powder. It's crushed calcium carbonate products, mainly marble and limestone, and it's mixed with the pulp from the trees to make high quality paper products. The difference between your newspaper and the paper you write on in your office is that the good paper has slurry added to it. When the trains bring the boxcars to the mill, they come to the holding bins—the large tanks that hold the slurry to be used in the production of paper. The tracks are elevated over the bins," Barnett said, using his hands in his description. "The boxcars are centered over the tanks and empty the powder through bottom doors into the bins. There are three bins at NAPCO. Two of them drop into tanks for the mill's own production. The third feeds the powder to trucks, which park underneath the track to catch their cargo and take the slurry to different mills. All Calvin did was open the bay doors on the boxcars so the powder could fall into the bins."

"Is this machinery that difficult to operate? Why was Calvin so important? The days that he didn't show up, who opened the bin doors then?" Spence had a thousand questions.

"Any three year old could do it. All you had to do is know what car dumped into what bin. But the trains don't come every night. The tanks are large enough to hold enough powder to last the mill for a week. But strangely enough, Calvin was always there when they came. He had other duties when he wasn't operating the bins, but he never seemed to do them. Little John's a hard-ass too. He rides everybody pretty hard, except Calvin. The rest of us never knew why."

"And I guess now we will never know Calvin's side of that story. Will we?"

"Sounds that way to me," Barnett replied.

"Well, what about Little John?"

"I don't think you'll get the answers out of him either."

"I can certainly subpoena him and ask him why Calvin never lost his job, which is what I guess I'm going to do. You say he's a hard ass. Do you think I'll have trouble getting my questions answered?"

"Well, you might have a hard time finding him at the moment. A couple of days after Calvin died, Little John went on vacation. He'd been at the mill for seventeen years and had a lot of vacation time built up. He was going to take a month off, but no one's heard from him. A new man from Chicago came to take his place while he's on vacation, some Italian-looking fellow. Little John might be back in a couple of weeks or he might not. The way things are looking around here, I'm starting to believe we'll never see him again."

"You seem to know a lot about the people of this town, especially for a man that's only been here a few months." Spence was sure now that Barnett was not there to harm him. He would have done it by now, rather than engaging in conversation on a porch in the middle of nowhere at night. But something brought him to Angela's house and Spence wanted to know what. "Do you mind telling me what your interest in all of this is? Why do you care about the death of a black man you've never met?

"Well, let's just say things aren't always as they seem," said Barnett with a sly grin. "I really came out here just to get your attention. That's the reason for the ambush here on the porch. I've been following you and you didn't even know it. You should've seen me two or three times just today. I saw you turn down every wrong dirt road coming out here, and I'm warning you now, you've got to start being more careful."

"What the hell is that supposed to mean?" Spence practically shouted. "Things are definitely not as they seem. Things are never as they seem. You want to give me a few more clues here? Whose side are you on anyhow? Are you a friend or is this supposed to be some kind of a threat?"

"Oh, I'm a friend," said Barnett, "but I can't tell you what's going on because I don't know myself. All I know is there's a few people in this town that seem to have a very expensive habit, and they seem to be supporting it on paper mill wages. I do know that whatever is going on, involves Sheriff Watkins who's missing, Little John, who's gone, Richard Powell, who was killed months ago, Calvin, who's now dead, and maybe even a few more people who work at the mill. But as far as what they're doing, where they're doing it, or how it all fits together, I don't know. What I do know is, willingly or not, you and your client are involved, and since I can't question her, maybe you can enlighten me."

"How the hell am I supposed to know?" asked Spence, shrugging his shoulders. "All I know is I'm in town for one day and get appointed to defend a girl who killed her father. I can say this, though. A lot of things just don't add up. Everybody in town wants to believe that the victim abuses this poor girl for years, and finally, one night she has enough, follows him out here on the porch and clubs him over the head with a baseball bat. Case closed. But—to me at least—it doesn't seem to be working out that way."

"Mr. Thompson, it will probably get worse before you find out the truth, and in the mean time, I hate to scare you, but you and your client could be in a lot of danger. I'm going to be keeping my eyes on you, and her, to try and prevent anything from happening. But realistically, until I know more, you're on your own."

"Wait a minute," demanded Spence. "I can't be this paranoid and defend the girl too. I've got to know more. Just who are you?"

"Unfortunately, I can't tell you that," said Barnett. "I've already told you more than I should. You're just going to have to trust me on this. I know you don't know me, but if you want to live, you don't have a choice in the matter."

"Are you going to tell me to drop the case, try to get her new counsel, make her plead guilty, anything like that?" asked Spence.

"I can't give you legal advice. You'll just have to do what you think is best. My job is to try to figure out what's going on, and I guess yours is to keep putting your case together. I'm just telling you to be careful and keep your eyes open."

"What a lousy piece of advice, now that you've got me scared to look over my shoulder. People dying all over the place. The sheriff missing. What kind of damn town is this anyway?"

"From the best I can tell, it's a pretty decent place, but it looks like there are a few bad apples and I've got to figure this thing out before anyone else gets killed."

"Yeah, mainly me," Spence said.

"I'm going to give you my home number," Barnett said, as he reached for his back pocket. The move startled Spence, who jumped back when Barnett made the sudden motion.

"Relax, it's just a card," Barnett went on. He handed Spence a plain white card with no name, but two numbers were written in pencil, one with an "H" beside it and the other with a "C". "You can always get me on the cell phone. If you come across anything strange, anything at all, you call me immediately. You and your client could be in trouble, and I would hate to see you get hurt."

"How do I know you're not involved?" Spence asked, cutting his eyes towards Barnett inquisitively.

"You don't. Like I said, you'll have to trust me. While we're talking, is there anything else you've found, other than what we've discussed?"

Spence thought for a second. He didn't know if he should tell Barnett about the coroner's report. He didn't know if, as Angela's attorney, that would be violating his responsibility to her. He simply knew too little about criminal law or criminal procedure to make that decision. He did know that Barnett hadn't made an attempt to harm him and seemed to be willing to discuss the case openly. He decided to tell him, figuring Barnett could probably get the coroner's report anyway. "I did get a call from the coroner when I requested a report on Calvin's death. He told me he didn't think my client was strong enough to inflict that much damage to a man's head. He said it would have taken a pretty large man or a tremendous athlete to hit some-body that hard. He also said it looked to him like the murderer was left-handed, or at least a switch hitter."

"I've already read the report."

"I figured you had."

"I've got some real smart people looking into that. If I hear any-thing, I'll let you know. In the meantime, stay the hell out of these woods by yourself."

"Oh, don't worry, I will," said Spence. "But who else you think may be involved? There's a lot of people in this town I don't know yet. What about Deputy Reeves? He worked for the sheriff. He brought me out here this morning."

"I don't think he is. I've been watching him some. Seems to be a good family man. Does his job, goes home, plays with his kids. He and Watkins never socialized together, and to tell you the truth, I don't think that they liked each other very much. So, no, I don't think he's involved, not yet anyway. As for the rest of the town, just keep an eye out for anybody who has a lot to do with the mill and acts doped up or has more money than they should."

Spence immediately sensed a rise in his temperature. Americus was one of the richest men in town, and he made no secret, at least to Spence, that he knew everything about the mill. And as far as acting strange, well, Americus was a little strange anyway. But Barnett knew Americus was his uncle, and surely he wouldn't have talked so freely if he thought Americus was involved. Or could he be using Spence to get to Americus?

"I assume I'm not supposed to tell anybody we talked?" asked Spence.

"Of course you're not to tell anybody we've talked. Don't tell anyone you've even seen me or know who I am. If we pass each other on the street, don't even acknowledge my presence. Who knows, they could be watching me like I know they're watching you. It all depends on who's at the bottom of this and what it is exactly they're doing. Now it's time you and I got out of here. You never know who could be coming around."

Barnett turned and walked down the steps of the porch. When he got to the bottom, he turned around and looked back up at Spence, who still stood on the porch trying to collect his thoughts and nerves.

"By the way," Barnett said "have you decided how your client is going to plead on Monday?"

Spence smiled, "I guess I should've known that you knew her arraignment was Monday morning."

"I know everything about her."

"Well, according to her she didn't do it, and I'm starting to think she's right. But at the same time, I think she'd have a pretty good self-defense case, considering the way he treated her. The DA's already told me that he would be very lenient with her if I could get rid of this thing for him."

Barnett smiled and shook his head, "Lawyers. Making deals with other people's lives."

"Hey, don't blame me," said Spence. "The simple truth of the matter is that, given the circumstances, pleading guilty is probably her best bet. You got a better solution?

"I don't know about her day-to-day life—or how badly Calvin treated her," Barnett said. "But there is one thing that I can say with a 99 percent certainty."

"What's that?"

"Calvin's dead, but your client didn't kill him."

"Well then, who did?"

"If I knew that, Counselor, I wouldn't need you."

THIRTY-ONE

THE EARLY MORNING sunlight came through the old transparent curtains and struck Americus in the face. He rolled over in his bed, attempting to shield his eyes from the morning, and hoping to get a few more minutes of sleep. But the dawn was unrelenting and the restlessness overtook him, leaving him unable to gain any comfort from his bed. It had been a long week of late nights, and he'd hoped to rest for most of this Sunday morning. But he was getting older, and sleep didn't bring the pleasure it once had.

He rubbed his eyes as his feet dangled from the large four-poster bed that suspended him nearly three feet from the floor. He gave a quick shiver in the morning air even though the temperature outside was already 78 degrees. He slid off the bed and into the slippers that kept his bare feet separated from the cool hardwood floors and walked to the closet to get his housecoat for warmth. His knees hurt as he took the first steps of the day and it took a little longer to straighten his back than it had in years past. He pulled the housecoat around his small frame, walked into the bathroom and stood over to his sink. From the counter he picked up a bottle of *coumadin*, prescribed to him by Doc Simpson, and read the label. In big bold print underneath the prescription instructions was a warning that read,

"Do not consume alcohol while taking this prescription." Americus smiled.
"Doc Simpson should've known better," he said aloud.

The medicine was supposed to thin his blood and make it easier
for his heart valves to function. He didn't know if it was working for
his valves, but the thinner blood in his veins made him cold most of
the time, even in the summer heat.

He splashed his face with water from the sink and brushed his
teeth, a ritual he followed first thing every morning, even before
breakfast. He knew the value of a gleaming smile and often brushed
his teeth as many as five times a day. He may not have been the perfect heart specimen, but he was a poster child for dental health. After
brushing and a round of floss, he walked back through his bedroom
and down the hall. The big house had beautiful ten-foot ceilings and
wide halls, but it was also old and in need of painting. Americus had
tried to remind himself to call a painter, or to at least have Ophelia
call one, but when he got into his normal daily routine it always
slipped his mind.

The hardwood floors squeaked as he continued down the hall,
passing the library on the right and the billiard room on the left, on
his way to the large living room. He'd at least purchased new furniture for the aging house in the last several years, paying for all
$200,000 of it in cash. He only bought it so he could continue to
sleep with the interior decorator he met in Atlanta for a few more
weeks. She was now gone, but he didn't regret the purchases. At his
age he didn't need any more money, but he could never have enough
sex. And the furniture helped to fill the fifty-year old house, which
seemed so large and lonely with just Ophelia and him roaming its
halls.

At the corner of the living room just before he entered the kitchen,
he stopped at the built-in shelves that flanked either side of the marble fireplace and picked up a picture of Spence and him in his front
porch swing. The picture had been taken at a Thanksgiving dinner
when the lad first came to visit Monroe at the age of eleven. It had

been just six months after his second wife had left him. Just seven months after the baby had died. The son that never made it home from the hospital. The doctors told them the child had a good chance for survival, although he had been born eight weeks premature. But in the fifth week, after steady improvement, they lost him, and no one could explain why. He wasn't even sure if Spence knew about the baby.

Looking back on his life, he could see his need for women and alcohol increase after the trauma. Anything that could numb his mind from the pain of losing a child. He had always prided himself on the strength of his resolve. But how did anybody get through this? The loss of so many hopes and dreams. Of a chance to be a hero, even if only for a few years. Of a chance to be perfect in another human's eyes, if only for a little while. The gift of life, the gift of immortality, squandered on lesser men who took it for granted like Calvin Chauncey, but denied from those who needed it. At times he cursed the God he had spent a lifetime worshiping. He would never be the same.

Those seven months brought Americus to the brink. The bourbon could knock him out, but it couldn't give him a reason to get up again. Then, out of the blue, an unexpected guest at a family Thanksgiving gave him renewed spirit to carry on.

Looking at the picture reminded him that he still felt the same for Spence as he did when they first met. His first marriage had been a mistake and lasted only a year. He always liked the excitement of a "spirited" woman, but found out they didn't make very good wives. His second choice was a pure Southern debutante, who brought to their relationship the sophistication that he lacked with his first wife, although she was sixteen years his junior. After several years of marriage and many unsuccessful attempts, they paid the fifteen thousand dollars to a fertility specialist. It worked, but the pregnancy was a series of close calls from the beginning. Americus could feel his wife pulling away every time they visited the baby in the NICU, and he knew that if the child didn't make it, neither would his marriage. After the baby's funeral, she became even more distant and no longer found comfort or warmth from her older husband. Within a month she was gone, taking with her his last chance at a meaningful marriage and fatherhood. He feared growing old alone. But he was at least encouraged by the boy who seemed to need a father as much as he needed a son. The boy in the picture was smart and Americus saw his potential. He could also see the potential of him becoming the one person who could add meaning to his life, and perhaps keep his law practice and other business ventures in the family. He'd discovered the way to really make money in the past few years and he just hoped Spence would go along with his methods. Old age scared him. He'd seen men with Alzheimer's and strokes, and it wasn't a pretty sight. He knew he had done a lot for Spence, and he knew the boy was the kind of man that would continue to be grateful. A family member to look after him in his old age.

Americus wiped the dust from the glass, put the picture back on its shelf and headed for the kitchen. He found Ophelia, his maid for the past twenty-something years, already standing at the stove, preparing his breakfast.

"Mornin' Miss Ophelia," Americus said.

"Good Morning," she answered back. Ophelia—or Miss Ophelia, as Americus liked to call her—was somewhere in her middle sixties, although he did not know exactly how old she really was. She had been his mother's maid until her death, and when Americus moved into the house, he found that Ophelia came with it. She lived rent-free in a small home on the outskirts of town. The house was owned by Americus, as was the Buick Skylark she drove. As for payment for her services, she was compensated two hundred and fifty dollars a week, in cash, and given a five hundred dollar bonus at Christmas. She had not received a raise in fifteen years, and it never crossed her mind to ask for one.

Americus could smell the bacon when he stepped into the kitchen and hear it sizzle as he moved closer to the stove. On the right side of the room was the breakfast nook—a round table with four cushioned chairs in the middle and a large bay window look-

ing over the gardens in the back. Americus' coffee was already cool-
ing in the cup that Ophelia had set on the table when she heard him
coming down the hall. She brought him the cream from the refrigerator and slid the sugar closer to his place at the table. He thanked
her, just like he had done every morning he was home since moving into the house.

Ophelia went back to the stove to finish their breakfast. Her hair
was pulled up in a ball on top of her head, and she wore a large apron
to protect her pink dress from the bacon grease. When she finished
with Americus and breakfast, she would go to church and then take
the rest of the afternoon off. Americus had pleaded with her to take
Sundays off entirely, but she worried about him eating properly.
Before she left, both his lunch and dinner would be prepared and in
the refrigerator ready for him to eat.

Americus sat at the table and unfolded the newspaper Ophelia had
brought inside. He sipped from the coffee and waited on his breakfast.

"Did you have a nice trip?" Ophelia asked from the stove.

"Oh, it was fine, just fine," Americus answered.

"They brought you a new dog while you was gone. I told 'em to
take it out to the farm," Ophelia said.

"Oh, that's right," Americus said, "I forgot they were going to
bring him this week." Americus had purchased a new English Setter
from T&E Kennels in Prattville. He already had four bird dogs, but
both of this one's parents were champion field trial dogs, and he
thought he could always use another. "Did Pepe come get him?" he
asked.

"Yes, sir, he came and got him after I called to let him know the
dog was here."

"How did he look?"

"Pepe?"

"No, ma'am, the dog."

"Look like a dog. You expecting something different?"

"I don't know? For what I paid for him I was hoping he would at least look like an expensive dog."

"Look like just another dog to me."

Americus shrugged his shoulders and put his head back into the paper. A few minutes later Ophelia brought over his breakfast. Biscuits, bacon, and two eggs over easy fried in the bacon grease. She also had an egg for herself and a cup of coffee, but she wouldn't eat with Americus, no matter how much he begged. She would wait until he finished and she had cleared the table. Americus had once told her that Doc Simpson warned him to start eating better, which to an old Southern maid meant eating more. So she increased his eggs from one to two and bacon strips from three to four in hopes of stuffing him before he went to work where she had no control over how much he ate. Americus found the whole situation amusing and reported back to Doc Simpson. "You eat bacon every morning?" Simpson asked. "No wonder your heart's struggling. Cut out the bacon and you'll probably live ten years longer." To which Americus replied, "If I can't eat bacon, I don't wanna live ten years longer."

As Americus sat at the breakfast table and ate, Miss Ophelia stood at the stove and the two of them talked about times past and how things had changed around Monroe since NAPCO came to town. Of course, Americus couldn't complain, NAPCO had made him a very wealthy man, but he longed for the good old days right along with Ophelia, knowing the only reason they were good was because he was younger.

Of all the housemaids in town, Ophelia was the most famous. After all, she worked for Americus Kirkland, known to all as the richest man around. But Americus was known more for being Americus than he was for his money. To Miss Ophelia he was a plethora of contradictions. She was the only one who ever saw him limp down the hall or complain about his health. To the outside world he always felt perfect, even if he had to fake it. He was loud at parties and always good for a dirty joke. He drank whiskey everyday and more often than not had a cigar in his mouth. And he was never short for words.

But for all his brashness, Americus was a man that could be trusted. If you really needed something, Americus could help you. Down on your luck, Americus could get you a job. Behind on your bills, Americus could talk to your bank. Most people in Monroe knew that if you had a problem, go see Americus, and more often than not, he could, and was willing, to help. The pride for Ophelia lay in the fact that Americus' generosity did not stop at the color boundary. She remembered a time when favors were not done for black maids and their families. So many times in her past she had known the truth and was unable to speak her mind. She knew the admiration that Americus held for his daddy, but she had not been particularly fond of the elder Kirkland. After all, she'd been his maid too. She did the laundry. She noticed when the white sheets were missing.

But now, because of her position in the life of the town's most well known citizen, she was somewhat of her race's fairy godmother. For if you needed to see Americus, Miss Ophelia could get you in the door. And perhaps her favorite thing about Americus, being a devout Christian woman, was that he knew the Bible better than most preachers in the state. If she needed help with her Sunday school lesson, she could always ask Americus, who could send her to the exact scripture, right off the top of his head. She only wished that he would live the scriptures he knew so well, but he was the boss and she never questioned his lifestyle.

"When's Mr. Spencer going to come eat supper?" She asked.

"I'll have him come this week," Americus answered. "You know, Ophelia, you just gave me an idea. I think I'll have Spence meet me at the farm and he and I can try out that new puppy."

Americus drank his last sip of coffee and Ophelia cleaned the dishes from the table. He thanked her for breakfast, wished her a good day at church and told her that he would see her in the morning. He then walked to the living room and called Pepe, his Mexican farm hand, on the telephone and told him to put out ten birds and get the new puppy ready because he was coming by to try the dog out. He then called Spence on the phone, with Ophelia listening to the one side of the conversation she could hear.

"Spence, this is your uncle. You out of bed yet?"

"I know it's a Sunday, son, but you should still be out of bed by now. Hell, it's seven o' clock."

"Well, go on and get up. I want you to get dressed and meet me."

"No we're not going to church again. We're going quail hunting."

"I know its August, but I'm not about to pay five thousand dollars for a dog and then wait four months to see if he's any good."

"You let me worry about the legalities of hunting out of season. You just put on a pair of blue jeans and boots and meet me out at the farm in an hour. And, oh yeah, bring that dog of yours."

THIRTY-TWO

AMERICUS' FARM WAS a thirty-two-hundred acre spread south of town, with a lone small farmhouse, where Pepe lived. There was a county highway that divided the property almost in half, with fourteen hundred acres on one side and eighteen hundred on the other. Dirt roads cut through the landscape allowing Americus to drive through its fields and trees. The land would have made good farmland because of a river that flowed along the back property line, giving adequate water for irrigation. But other than the pine trees he harvested and sold to NAPCO at a premium, Americus used the property for his own enjoyment, mainly quail hunting.

Each side of the road served a different purpose for Americus' hobby. The smaller side was called "the preserve." Here he raised nearly two thousand quail per year to be set out in the fields when he wanted to guarantee he would find birds. It was on the preserve that he took most of his clients hunting, to make sure they did plenty of shooting. The preserve had also entertained both U.S. Senators from Alabama and the state's Governor, as well as Thomas Kendall, the CEO of NAPCO, when he was in town for a tour of the mill.

The larger tract on the other side of the road was sacred ground for Americus, and he seldom allowed anyone but himself and his father's old hunting buddy, Doc Simpson, the privilege of its use. It was here that Americus nurtured seventy-five wild coveys of quail. For an old quail hunter, wild birds were the only thrill. Pen-raised birds flew slower, and usually only one or two at a time. But wild birds were accustomed to flying from cats, foxes, and other dangers, using their speed as a means for survival. When flushed, a single covey might have as many as thirty birds exploding into the sky. The problem with wild birds, however, is that they're exactly that—wild—and a hunter never knows where to find them. A wild bird hunter may walk all day without seeing a single bird as opposed to hunting pen-raised birds, where he is guaranteed to find quail because they were placed in front of him only minutes earlier. Hunting pen-raised quail was sufficient for Americus when he wanted to entertain some clients or train a puppy, but in his mind, only wild birds were real hunting.

Today's objective, though, was to see if he'd made a good purchase in his new dog, and he didn't want to spend all morning looking for quail, so he asked Pepe to put out the ten birds. Before Americus arrived, Pepe took a small cage out to the large quail pen behind the barn and gathered up ten birds by placing the cage on the ground, with the door open, and corralling the birds inside. He put the cage in the back of his pickup truck and drove to a field located on the back of the preserve. Americus preferred to release the pen-raised quail as far away as possible from his wild bird land, fearing the pen-raised quail might spread a disease through his sacred hunting ground. When he arrived at the spot where he wanted the first bird, Pepe reached into the cage and, careful to have a good hold on both of its wings, pulled the bird out. The one he selected was a male bobwhite, distinguished by the pure white feathers that ran in streaks over its head. The bird made a continuous low "chirp" as Pepe gathered it into his hands. Careful not to break its wings, because a bird that couldn't fly was useless, Pepe put the bird in his right hand and placed his forefinger and index finger on top of the quail's head. In a big circular motion he spun the bird three times with his arm at its full extension and then placed the bird next to a clump of grass in the field. The bobwhite, dizzy from the spinning, did not attempt to run when Pepe placed it on the ground, but rather bobbed his head up and down as if he were too drunk to walk. Pepe had been careful not to spin the bird too much because to do so may have killed it. He'd killed a few when he first started to work for Americus seven years earlier, but he was a pro now and had found that three good spins was just about perfect to keep the bird from walking off before Americus and his friends arrived to shoot it. When he had repeated the procedure nine more times, he walked back to his truck and waited for his boss.

Americus and Spence met at Pepe's farmhouse and then took Americus' white Ford pickup truck out to the field. The new five-thousand-dollar puppy rode in an aluminum dog box on the back of the truck, while Sam rode in Spence's lap looking out the window. Americus pulled the truck beside Pepe and got out.

"Good morning," Americus said, taking a deep breath to fill his lungs with the pure morning air.

"Hola," Pepe answered back. Pepe still didn't speak very good English, although he'd been in the United States for nine years now, two of them picking peaches in Clanton, Alabama, and the remainder doing the upkeep on Americus' hunting property.

Spence opened the door to the truck and Sam jumped to the ground. Spence nodded at Pepe who smiled and nodded back. Neither knew the other's language, so neither spoke.

"Did you put the birds out?" Americus asked, to which Pepe nodded his head in the affirmative. Americus reached behind the seat of the truck, pulled his Browning over/under shotgun from its case and laid it on the front seat. He reached back again and produced a brown game vest and a box of twenty gauge shells. Standing with the door of the truck open and using the seat as a workbench, he began to fill the vest with the shells, placing each one in a separate pouch at the pockets.

"Can that mutt of yours still find birds?" Americus asked Spence as he continued to load the game vest.

"You bet your ass she can," Spence answered.

"Well, I just hope she doesn't screw up my dog," Americus returned.

"Oh, so I have the mutt and yours is a dog."

"Of course."

"And why's that?"

"For the same reason that makes some women whores and other women socialites. Money."

"I'll have you know, Mr.-owner-of-a-five-thousand-dollar-dog, that a man once offered me five hundred for Sam and I wouldn't take it because my poor old decrepit uncle gave her to me for my graduation from high school."

"I know that's supposed to be flattering, but I'd have been more impressed if you had shown some business sense and taken the money."

Pepe opened the gate to the aluminum dog box and out sprang Americus' five-month-old setter, whom he had decided to call Rufus, after one of his father's old dogs. Once out of the box the young pup went wild, running in circles and expending the nervous energy it had built up while confined. Americus and Spence just watched, knowing that most puppies require a little "sprint time" before they get serious about hunting. Sam, as the elder huntress, watched while Rufus tore through the weeds, but eased into the field at a much calmer pace. When Rufus noticed Sam, he ran to her and jumped around in excitement at having found a new friend. Sam was totally disinterested and even growled at the hyper pup to let him know she was all business.

Americus handed the gun and game vest to Spence, who pulled on the vest, buttoned it, and then placed the bridged shotgun on his shoulder. The quail would only get up one at a time, so there was no need for more than one gun. Besides, Americus needed his hands free so that he could train Rufus.

Pepe began to walk toward the first bird that he'd placed in the field while Spence and Americus followed.

"Keep your eyes open, son," Americus said. "There's some more kind of rattlesnakes out here."

Spence hadn't thought about snakes. It was not normally something he worried about when hunting because in the fall and winter it was too cold for them to be out of hibernation. But now that Americus had mentioned it, he was very much aware that in south Alabama, in the heat of August, around pine trees and fields, rattlesnakes were not only common, but in fact, likely. He was suddenly conscious of every step in the knee-high sage and moved a little closer to Americus hoping to follow in his path. Americus and Pepe walked seemingly unconcerned through the thick brush without even looking at the ground.

Spence watched as Sam and Rufus made sweeping runs through the fields, noses in the air, searching for quail. He was tired. Wondering and worrying about what Barnett had said had ruined his sleep. He wanted to tell Americus about his encounter with the curious outsider, but then he didn't know what he should tell. Barnett told him to look for someone tied to the mill who had more than their fair share, and Americus seemed to have everybody's share. But certainly he couldn't be involved in killings and cover-ups. Americus' behavior might be unethical at times, but Spence didn't want to believe that it could be criminal. Still, he chose not to tell him about Barnett until he knew more.

"How's your client doing?" Americus asked, interrupting Spence's thoughts.

"I guess she's fine considering her circumstances."

"The other day on the phone, you sounded as if maybe you thought she didn't do it."

"To be truthful, I don't know what I think."

"Who else could've done it?"

"I don't know. I really haven't done that much investigating."

"Good. Keep it that way and concentrate on the things that make us money. The lawyer from Dothan will be here next week and you can be done with this entire matter."

"Whatever happened though," Spence went on without registering his uncle's comment, "Calvin sure did have a strange situation out at the mill."

Americus suddenly stopped and turned to Spence, who was now afraid that he'd said too much. "What mill?" Americus asked, squinting, although he knew exactly what mill Spence was talking about.

"NAPCO," Spence answered.

"Son"—Americus shook his head—"I know you want to help this girl and I'm sure she could use a friend. But that mill makes us a half million dollars a year in billings, and notice that I said us because it's part your money too. So I don't think it's such a good idea for you to start poking your nose around in its affairs. If something strange goes on out there, so be it. I've seen strange things myself, but I've turned the other way and kept cashing the checks."

"But what if the girl's innocent?"

"Who cares?"

Spence wanted to tell him that he cared, but just then they heard Pepe shout from up ahead.

"Point!"

Pointers, Setters, and certain kinds of Spaniels, all of which are known as bird dogs in the South, are not taught how to point. It's instinctive. Young puppies may point grasshoppers, butterflies or small grass birds at first, but once they get the smell of a game bird and some encouragement from their master, that's all they'll point. What distinguishes a good dog from a bad one is its ability to find the birds by knowing where to look and the amount of ground they cover while looking. Another characteristic of a good dog is its accuracy in finding birds and not generating "false points," that is pointing birds that are no longer there. Once the bird, or birds in the case of a covey, has been found, the dog will freeze into its trademark "point" by freezing in whatever positions it finds itself and raising its tail into the air. The more the dog is hunted the stronger this instinct becomes. Once, Spence had seen Sam jumping over a fallen tree when the smell of birds caught her nose. In mid-air she lifted her feet and fell to the ground with a thud, where she remained absolutely motionless for fear of flushing the birds before Spence was in position to shoot.

Americus hurried to get Rufus into his grasp and caught him about fifteen yards from where Sam was pointed near the clump of grass and Pepe's first bird. He held the puppy by the collar and put him in a simulated pointing position in the direction of Sam. Bird dogs point instinctively, but they must be taught to "back"—that is, to respect another dog's point. Once it sees another dog in position, regardless if it smells the birds or not, the "backing dog" will stop and point the pointed dog. The benefit of this for the hunter is that he doesn't always have to see the pointed dog, for when birds are found, all dogs respect the lead dog by pointing and letting the hunter know that at least one of them has found birds. Americus had been quail hunting all of his life and the thing he liked most about the sport was the respect of a point. If a dog couldn't learn to "back" then Americus had no use for him, even if the dog was great at finding quail. He'd once seen his father's dogs tackle a puppy and growl on top of it for continuing to move after another dog had pointed. It was all about respect, and Americus demanded it.

Rufus didn't put up much of a fight, his training having begun at the kennel. He stopped and raised his tail when Americus showed him that Sam had pointed and stood at attention even when Americus let him go. Spence pulled two of the yellow 20-gauge shells from the game vest, slid one into each barrel of the gun and snapped it closed. He looked at Americus to make sure he was satisfied with Rufus' position.

"How long will your dog hold that point?" Americus asked. Inferior bird dogs will break points and flush the birds early if the hunter doesn't come soon enough. Good dogs don't flinch.

"All day if you'd like," Spence answered.

"Naw, that's okay. I haven't got all day."

Spence took a few easy steps toward Sam who was hunched down in a perfect point—nose straight out front, right front leg lifted slightly off the ground, and tail straight as an arrow to the sky.

"That's it girl," Spence said loud enough for Americus to hear. "You show that over-priced biscuit eater what a real bird dog looks like."

"Just get on with it, boy," Americus answered.

Spence couldn't see the quail, but he knew it was there. Sam said so. He took another step and in a flurry of sound the bird sprang into the air. It started out right, circled behind a sapling pine tree and then began its escape route, flying away from Spence from his right to left. He threw the gun to his shoulder and took aim with both eyes open. He allowed the gun to swing with the flight of the bird, placing his mark about two feet in front of the target. With the bird about twenty-five yards away, he squeezed the trigger. The bobwhite fell to the ground.

Sam sprang from her point and ran to the fallen bird. She sniffed for a few seconds, found the dead bird, gathered it into her mouth and brought it to Spence. Spence held out his hand and she laid the dead quail in his palm. Sam ran off to find another.

Spence rolled the bird over in his hand. He loved quail hunting— the gracefulness of the dogs and their amazing instincts, the excitement of birds "on the rise" when they had been flushed from their hiding place and their wings beat the air, and the beauty of their white and brown markings.

"Nice shootin'," Americus said, coming over to inspect the kill.

"Thanks," Spence answered, as he continued to look over the bobwhite. "Almost seems a shame."

"What's that?"

"This bird spent its whole life in a cage and for the few minutes it was free, people were looking to kill it."

"That's what it was bred for."

"Still seems a shame."

Spence placed the dead bird into his pouch and started to walk towards the next bird. Americus placed his hand on Spence's arm and turned to face him.

"Son, some things in this world just weren't meant for the good life. And even for those of us who have found it, it's hard as hell to hold on to. Sooner or later you're going to have to decide what you want in life. The choice won't always be easy, but sometimes you've got to be a little self-serving if you want to hold on to what you've got. If you can help someone along the way, fine. But you can't let them stop you from getting what you want. Do you understand?"

Spence said nothing. He knew Americus was talking about Angela. Americus had made it clear that he did not want Spence to get caught up in her case, or worse, implicate NAPCO, his best client, in any wrongdoing. But Spence didn't know how to answer.

"Son, do you understand?"

"Yes, sir."

—

Spence laid his mechanical pencil on top of the legal pad on his coffee table and rubbed his eyes. It was 1:09 in the morning— Monday morning. In a few hours he would tell the world how Angela Chauncey pleaded to the charge of murdering her father. In their last meeting she left the decision to him, saying only that she felt like he would do the best thing for her. He knew what Americus wanted him to do and he didn't want to disappoint the man who had given him everything. And he had all but promised the DA that he would plead guilty and be done with it. He certainly didn't want to upset the county's top lawyer his first few weeks in town, because he might need a favor later. But what about Angela? Barnett said she didn't kill anybody and there were just too many unanswered questions. He cared for her, even though he didn't want to, and he couldn't stand to think of her going to jail for a crime she didn't commit. Her life lay in his hands.

Something inside told Spence he was at a crossroads, and that whatever decision he made would effect who he was for the rest of his existence. For the first time in a long while, Spencer Michael Thompson didn't know who he wanted to be.

THIRTY-THREE

WHEN MONDAY MORNING came, Spence found
himself so nervous he could hardly stand. He had never been in a
courtroom as an attorney. The closest he'd come to courtroom experience was mock trials in law school. Now a person's life was at stake.

Two deputies brought Angela to the courtroom and sat her next
to Spence on the Judge's left side. They removed her handcuffs and
sat down in the first row of seats behind her. She rubbed her wrist
and placed her hands on the table in front of her. Spence smiled and
said, "Hello." She smiled and answered, "Hi." They were both feeling
a little awkward from their encounter on Saturday.

In an effort to keep his hands moving, afraid that someone might
notice them shaking, Spence reached into his briefcase and pulled
out his notes. He had spent most of his Sunday afternoon on the
phone with Jack McCain, Wes's father, going through the procedures
of an arraignment. According to Jack, it was all very simple. The district attorney would read the charges and Spence would enter a plea
for his client. After that, they would continue to put their cases
together and negotiating a deal, if in fact there was a deal to be cut.
Spence had never received a definitive answer from Angela on what
she wanted to plead. He read her the indictment—murder, punish-

able by death or life in prison in the State of Alabama. Spence already knew that the district attorney was willing to lessen the charge, maybe even to manslaughter, given the lifetime of abuse Angela had suffered. There would still be jail time, but presumably not for life. That was something he and Angela would have to discuss later. Right now, they were only entering her plea, and she'd left the decision to him. As of earlier that morning, he still hadn't made that decision.

The ladies who worked at the county jail had given Angela some makeup and a brush so she could prepare for her day in court. The bruises on her face were almost gone, and she looked beautiful—even in her orange uniform. Spence wondered, that if the male personnel at the county jail knew what he and old Doc Simpson knew, if they would've issued her a smaller size.

The courtroom began to fill up. A couple of older men entered through the main doors and sat two rows from the back. They were regulars at the courthouse, with nothing to do but watch the events of the county. A middle-aged black man sat in a suit on the very last row with a pad in his hand. Spence thought he might be a reporter. There were also a few black women, dressed in their Sunday best, sitting in the middle seats. Spence thought maybe they were friends of Calvin's when he was a younger man, perhaps even family members. He wondered if they knew Sister Clara Belle.

Angela never spoke or motioned to anyone in the courtroom, and nobody made an attempt to have their presence acknowledged. From the best Spence could tell, nobody was there on Angela Chauncey's behalf.

The district attorney entered the courtroom and strolled down the long center aisle until he reached the gate that separated the gallery from the bench. He swung the gate open, walked over to Spence, and stuck his hand out. Spence stood up to shake hands.

"Hello, Spence. How are you doing?" Seaver smiled broadly, carefully avoiding eye contact with the defendant. This was his job, and in this case, his life. He didn't want the defendant to seem like a person.

This was business, and a lot of money rode on whether or not he and the judge could pull it off.

"I'm fine, … considering," Spence replied.

Seaver motioned his head towards his table. Spence looked at Angela and then followed Seaver across the aisle.

"How's that nervousness," Seaver asked, setting his briefcase on the table.

"It's getting better," Spence lied.

"I've been a little surprised you haven't come to see me. I was hoping we could've had something worked out by now. There's really no sense in prolonging this thing."

Spence felt uncomfortable. He didn't know he should have already been in touch with the DA, but then, he didn't know much in the way of procedure when it came to criminal law, or any trial law for that matter. He was sure, however, that the DA made this comment to put him on the defensive and he wondered if Seaver actually knew how little help he would need. Spence had entered the courtroom on the defensive.

"I've been a little busy," Spence answered.

"That's okay. It happens." Seaver talked fast, especially for a Southerner. But his big broad smile and his ability to seem genuine was luring Spence in. Besides Deputy Reeves, Seaver was one of the few people in town whom he liked instantly. Of course Barnett had him scared of his own shadow and he was finding it hard to trust anyone, even Americus, but certainly the district attorney couldn't be involved in a conspiracy.

"Let's just get through this arraignment. We'll get her plea entered and you and I can sit down and talk." He gave Spence another grin, opened his briefcase and began pulling out folders and placing them on the table. Spence looked around and then walked back to his side of the aisle, sat down, and immediately began to shuffle his papers and read his notes. He didn't want to seem outdone.

Suddenly the bailiff announced, "All rise. The District Court of

Crawford County is now in session. The Honorable Judge James Hamilton presiding."

Judge Hamilton entered from his chambers, stepped up to his large chair behind the bench, straightened his robe and sat down. He took a small case off of the bench that awaited his arrival. Opening the case, he produced a pair of glasses and reached under his robe and into his pocket to find a handkerchief. Once he had produced the cloth, he leaned back in his chair and began to clean his glasses. "Okay Joan," he motioned to the woman who sat in the witness box next to his bench. "What do we have first?"

The bailiff instructed everyone to be seated. Only the district attorney remained standing.

"The State of Alabama versus Angela Chauncey," the woman in the witness box answered and then she sat down to begin writing something on the notebook in front of her.

"Alright, son"—the judge never looked up from cleaning his glasses—"would your client like to be formally arraigned?"

Spence looked over to the DA who was looking down at his notes. Formally arraigned? What was that? Jack never told him there was a difference in a formal and an informal arraignment. Spence did-n't know what to do, but formal sounded better than informal so he figured his client needed the best. He slowly stood up and said, "Yes, Your Honor."

"Very Well. Pat, read the indictment."

"Of course, Your Honor," the district attorney answered while looking through one of his folders to find the indictment. He cleared his throat: "The Grand Jury of Crawford County charges that, before the finding of this indictment, Angela Chauncey whose name is oth-erwise unknown to the Grand Jury, did, with intent to cause the death of another person, caused the death of Calvin Chauncey by means of a deadly weapon or dangerous instrument, to-wit: A base-ball bat, in violation of Section 13A-6-2 of the Code of Alabama, against the peace and dignity of the State of Alabama." When the DA finished reading, he placed the indictment back on his table and turned his head towards the bench.

The judge held his glasses up to the light, at arm's length, to make sure he had removed all the dirt and specs from the lenses. At last he put the glasses on his face, turned in his chair, placed his arms and elbows on the bench and said, "Okay, son, how does your client plead?"

The moment had arrived. He hadn't asked for it. He tried to get out of it. But here he was, standing to address the same judge who had lashed out so harshly at him at their first encounter, about to enter her plea and become the one lawyer in whose hands Angela Chauncey would place her life. There was no turning back.

"Not guilty, Your Honor."

There was a long pause as everyone in the courtroom looked at Spence and waited for the judge to speak. The DA felt his heart flutter across the aisle, and his smile deflated like a balloon. Finally, the judge took his eyes off of Spence and raised his head, as if he were looking at someone in particular in the back of the courtroom. Then his eyebrows narrowed and he looked at Seaver. The DA turned to Spence, still standing, scared of the long pause after his answer. Had he done something wrong?

At last Judge Hamilton asked, "Okay, son, not guilty by reason of insanity, or self defense, or…?" The judge turned his palms up.

Spence knees were shaking, and he wondered if everybody could see it. The question caught him off guard. He didn't think he would have to give a reason why he'd entered a not-guilty plea. He wanted to keep things going, the sooner this was over the better. He didn't know what to say, so he said the only thing that came to his mind, "Not guilty by the reason she didn't do it, Your Honor."

The judge leaned back in his chair and attempted a smile. His face turned red and Spence thought he knew what was coming. He had seen this reaction from the judge before, when he had been appointed to defend Angela. But the judge's demeanor was far from violent. Instead, he stuttered when the next few sentences fell from his lips.

Like something was making him nervous.

"By reason that she…didn't…do it," he repeated perplexed.

Spence sensed the momentum shift in the courtroom. He felt the same kind of rush he used to get when he blindsided a quarterback.

"Yes, that's right," Spence said in his most clear and concise voice. "She didn't do it." He did not even follow up his answer with a "Your Honor."

Hamilton's face betrayed his consternation: this thing was getting out of control. The kid was supposed to enter a guilty plea. He had all but promised Seaver he would. What could he be thinking? For God's sake, he couldn't have evidence to back this up. Or did he? Hamilton needed to force Spence's hand—and quickly.

"She didn't do it because of what?" the judge asked as he leaned a little further over his bench.

Spence could see that the judge was looking for a specific answer, but he had no idea what it was. But he was tired of skating around the issue and decided to give the clearest answer he could, whether it was correct or not. He looked down at Angela, who's smile was all the reassurance he needed. He flexed his jaw muscles and turned back to face the bench. It was time to start a fight.

"By reason that someone else clubbed the bastard over the head with a baseball bat. That's the only reason I've got."

"Okay, Counselor, let's watch our language," the judge answered back, still on the defensive and not completely composed. "So you're telling me there's someone else out there who killed your client's father, even with the evidence as it is, and you're prepared to tell us who?"

"Your Honor, I wasn't prepared to try the case today. I thought this was just an arraignment."

"Well, son, I just want to make sure you know what you're doing," the judge said. "In order to protect your client's rights, I have to make sure you're competent enough to try this case. I would hate for you to be giving your client improper counsel."

"Your Honor, you haven't heard one piece of evidence. How can you decide at such an early stage whether I'm competent or not?" Spence didn't miss the irony. He had argued on behalf of his own incompetence only days before.

"I just want to make sure you know what you're doing, counselor," the judge returned.

"The State of Alabama said I was competent when they passed my bar exam, and from the last time I read the requirements, that was good enough," Spence made this comment to refresh the judge's memory on what he said the day he appointed Spence as counsel.

The judge remembered and regretted saying those exact words. He also regretted the appointment of Spencer Thompson. It had been their whole scheme, his, Seaver's, the boys from Chicago. Ever since Watkins changed the plan and left the girl alive, everything depended on this kid taking the path of least resistance. He was supposed to enter a plea of guilty and they could send the girl off for a little while. But all of a sudden this brash young attorney, who never went to his Criminal Law classes and seemed to blow off the entire law school experience, decided he wanted to be the next Atticus Finch and save the world. This was not supposed to happen. The judge began to feel the sweat collect at his brow.

He looked at Joan, still writing in the witness box, and said, "Enter a plea of not guilty for the defendant." Turning to Spence he said, "Counselor, I'd like to see you and the district attorney in my chambers, please." The judge then rose, made another quick glance to the back of the courtroom and swiftly made his way to the door behind the bench to enter his chambers. He gathered himself up so quickly that the door had already closed behind him by the time the bailiff could announce, "All rise." The middle-aged black man in the suit at the back of the courtroom gave a frown to no one in particular, then got up and left the courtroom.

Seaver stood up, and again careful not to make eye contact, walked to the same door behind the bench. Spence, already standing, looked down at Angela, gave his best attempt at a smile and said,

"Everything's going to be alright." He started towards the judge's chambers staring at the door, not knowing what to expect. As he walked around the table she grabbed his hand and the butterflies in his stomach, the ones he had felt all morning long, began to flutter their wings.

"You did good," she said, her fingers stroking the top of his hand.

"We'll see," he answered.

The two deputies walked to the table and stood beside Angela. She stood up and held out her hands. One of the deputies placed the handcuffs on her wrist and stepped back, holding out his arm in the direction he wished her to take.

"I'll be over in a little while, but I'm going to see what they want first," Spence said and followed Seaver into the judge's chambers.

Once inside the judge's chambers, Spence's new found confidence escaped him. He'd never been inside a judge's chambers in his life. The thick books and mahogany walls seemed meant to intimidate him. "Smart move," he thought. The judge had moved the game from the public courtroom to the privacy of his own quarters, giving him himself a tremendous home field advantage.

Seaver stared at some imaginary place on the judge's wall, his thumb and finger spread across the bottom of his chin. A thousand thoughts went through his mind. None of them were good.

"Have a seat, Mr. Thompson," the judge said, motioning to the chair opposite of Seaver. Spence looked at the DA and sat down.

"Look, son," the judge started, folding his hands on his desk, "I realize you want to help your client, but I also want you to remember that the evidence is overwhelmingly against her. She had a motive to kill. The victim had been abusing her for years. She had intent to kill when she hit him over the head with a baseball bat that was found beside him with her fingerprints all over it. There were no neighbors, or anyone else for that matter, for miles and miles around to offer any proof that your client wasn't the only one at the house the night Calvin was killed. Are you sure you know what you're doing by entering a plea of not guilty, because it seems to me that she would have an awfully good self-defense case." The judge cut his eyes to Seaver. "I just want to make sure you know what you are doing. A young girl's life hangs in the balance."

So now the judge was trying to sound like he cared about what happened to Angela—even though he appointed a man who had been practicing law all of one day to be her defense counsel.

"Look, Spence," Seaver spoke up. "Like I told you before, I'm willing to lessen the charge against your client for a guilty plea. Right now she's charged with murder, which carries a sentence of death or life in prison. We'll reduce that to manslaughter, and we can talk to the judge here and see if he'll be lenient on her sentence. She's only nineteen, which means by the time she's twenty-five, she'd be out of prison. Maybe in a halfway house in less time than that. Her father's already out of her life, and I think we can all agree that's a step in the right direction. In prison she could finish school, maybe learn a trade, and have her whole life in front of her. Now, don't you think that's the best way to go? Because let me be honest, if you continue to try and prove she isn't the killer, then I'm going to have to pull out all the stops. You run the risk of her spending the rest of her life in jail—or worse."

Spence didn't know what to say. He really hadn't thought that far ahead. A guilty plea would at least guarantee some sort of life for her to look forward to. He could possibly even negotiate a deal where she didn't spend anytime in prison, but instead received counseling and went straight to a halfway house. These guys seemed to be extremely willing to close out this case. And whatever it was that Barnett was chasing, he and his client would be out of the picture. He didn't want to be killed over something he'd not willingly volunteered for. He also didn't like his chances against Seaver, a twenty-plus-year veteran of criminal trials, even if Spence could prove that the evidence was stacked in his favor. He still had no clue how to try a murder case and found himself wishing that Americus' friend had already sent help.

But then there was Angela. How would she react to a plea bargain? She had been a prisoner all her life—physically, emotionally, socially. Would she find prison a welcome change or face the chance of death rather than live one more day than absolutely necessary being held captive to something beyond her control? He knew he had fallen for her and couldn't suffer the possibility that she might go away for a couple of years, especially since most of the evidence he had led to the conclusion of her innocence. But could he place her life in danger? For the first time in his life he cared more about what happened to someone else than about what happened to himself.

"Gentlemen, I'll have to speak with my client and see what she wants to do. But I'll be sure to pass these concerns on to her," Spence said.

"Fair enough," replied Seaver.

Spence stood up and walked to the door. He thought he'd made a miraculous recovery. He was actually surprised at how well he thought on his feet. Maybe he wasn't such a bad lawyer after all.

THIRTY-FOUR

JUAN MIGUEL SAT next to a boxcar on an empty five-gallon paint bucket. A shotgun lay across his knees. On the other side of the car sat another watchman, also armed with a shotgun. Every now and then, the two men would converse in Spanish in an attempt to beat the boredom, but for the most part they watched the tracks and made sure no unauthorized persons approached the car. The heat was extreme and each of them sweated profusely through their T-shirts and blue jeans. Juan Miguel wiped sweat from his forehead with a cloth he kept in his pocket, then leaned back and rested his head on the steel side of the car. He wondered again if he should find another job—and again came to the same conclusion. He'd never find another job this easy, that paid this much, unless he went to the United States.

Juan Miguel and the boxcar sat in the middle of NAPCO's calcium carbonate facilities located about forty miles north of Monterrey, Mexico. The facility had been in operation for thirty-four years, but NAPCO had only purchased it six years earlier, when Kendall decided the company should concentrate on high quality paper products. The plant supplied NAPCO's paper mills with the powdery white product called slurry that was mixed with pulp to create the company's line of 'Silksheets' paper. When the demand for 'Silksheets' began to rise,

NAPCO purchased the plant to guarantee a steady supply of product. The way the plant could be operated outside of the United States was also an attraction for Kendall. The facility was certainly unlike any across the northern border, where men with shotguns were not allowed to roam the grounds. The enactment of the North American Free Trade Agreement made it easy to transport the product across the border at a much cheaper price than it could be produced domestically. Twenty years earlier, a major U.S. corporation would have balked at having its livelihood located south of Texas, but the world was changing and companies were forced to find new ways to generate profit. No one embraced this concept more than Thomas Kendall.

Juan Miguel and the other watchman had to shout to hear one another, even though they were several hundred yards from the machinery that pounded rocks into powder twenty-four hours a day. The noise ricocheted off the surrounding hills and echoed back to the valley, making it possible to hear the plant's operations from ten miles away. But no one complained. Except for a few chicken farmers, everybody in the area worked at the mill and lived close by in housing supplied by the mill, and they certainly were not going to complain about the very reason for their existence in the limestone rich region. No one would've listened anyway.

The atmosphere within a mile of the plant was a dusty white fog. The white dust in the air collected on anything remaining stationary for more than thirty seconds and made it difficult for the workers' lungs to separate the oxygen from the carbonate dust. Visitors to the plant could stand the burning in their nostrils for only so long before they were forced to start breathing through their mouth. In the United States, workers at such facilities wore respirator masks in areas of the plant where the dust was at its worst, but this was Mexico, and the rules for the proper way to treat a work force were entirely different.

Everyone in the facility did wear sunglasses. Not to do so would mean a sure headache after a few hours of hard squinting. The plant and its surrounding grounds were covered by pure white powder for as far as the eye could see, and the intensity of the Mexican sun's reflection could eventually cause blindness.

Juan Miguel sat on his bucket and watched the dust settle on the tip of his boot. It took about four minutes for enough white dust to top off at a quarter of an inch and start sliding down the sides of his footwear. Every hour or so, someone he recognized as authorized would come with a couple of sacks on their shoulders, climb a ladder at one end, and pour the contents into the boxcar.

Juan Miguel's particular favorite was a man he knew only as Pedro. A small old man with leathery dark skin, Pedro came once a week from his small farm about six miles south of the plant. He had only an old horse as transportation, so he always arrived late in the afternoon since it took most of his day to travel the distance from his home to the plant. Pedro checked in, recorded the weight of his sack and received his money at a small office closer to the plant and about four hundred yards from Juan Miguel and the boxcar. He left his horse at the office and carried the bag on his shoulder, a struggle for the skinny old man. When he made it to the boxcar, Pedro opened his sack and took out two small plastic bags of product. Juan Miguel surveyed the grounds to make sure no one was watching, then took the bag from Pedro and stuffed it into his pocket. He had been warned when he took the job that theft of product would not be tolerated. But they were in the middle of nowhere. Who would ever know? After Pedro had gone, the two men would sample the product and the afternoon wouldn't seem quite so long.

The white boxcar had big black letters that read "NAPCO 110 TONS" written on the side. After several days of empting sacks into the car it was full, with an actual weight of 107 tons of white powder.

Just up the track from Juan Miguel's car, there was a string of identical boxcars nearly a half a mile long, with two large engines to pull them at the front. Juan Miguel's boxcar was brought to the others and placed as the thirteenth in line. The rest of the cars were attached behind, creating a line totaling 44 cars in all.

It was late in the afternoon when the loaded car was buckled into line, which would be making an express run from the plant in Mexico to NAPCO's facility in Monroe, Alabama. Juan Miguel watched as the train pulled off at its designated time. He and the other watchman then separated another boxcar from the pack and began to stand guard. They watched the car being loaded, one sack full at a time, and waited for the shift change.

The train headed due north away from Monterrey, paralleling highway 35, for the shortest route to the U.S./Mexican border. It was pulled by the Texas Mexican Railroad Company—or the Tex-Mex RR, as it was more commonly called—also known as the NAFTA Railway. The railroad company had no idea it was carrying anything other than slurry. At Nuevo Laredo, Mexico, the train stopped at the U.S. border where its contents were inventoried and paperwork exchanged, and the train was soon on its way to Laredo, Texas. NAPCO used only the best Mexican and U.S customs brokers to guarantee there were no problems crossing the border. The train rolled through Corpus Christie, Houston, and Beaumont, Texas; on through Shreveport, Louisiana, and finally into Jackson, Mississippi. In Jackson the boxcars were disconnected from the Tex-Mex engines and replaced by engines from the Norfolk Southern Railway, who again had no idea what they were hauling. The line neither picked up nor unloaded any other box-cars, but stayed in one complete line, just as it had been loaded at the plant in Mexico. NAPCO paid extra for the line to be kept intact, so the train could be guaranteed to arrive on schedule. The company could not afford the risk of any delays in production.

The train's conductor rolled through the dark woods of the Southeastern United States, oblivious to his cargo, and continued his journey through Meridian, Mississippi; Birmingham, Alabama; and finally on to Montgomery. In Montgomery the train engines were switched and the line was placed on the tracks that would take it to Monroe. At aproximately six o' clock in the afternoon the train reached the mill property and was held just outside the gates to verify its contents. Taking inventory didn't take long because the mill workers knew the drill. All of the cars were owned by NAPCO, and they were all identical with somewhere between 105 and 110 tons of powdery white product.

The train was scheduled to enter the unloading area at the mill. Monroe was the distribution point for all product brought in from the Mexico slurry plant. The first two bins emptied into holding tanks supplying the mill's production of paper. The third bin emptied into trucks waiting just below the tracks to take the product to other NAPCO mills throughout North America. The first few cars entered the unloading area and were centered over the first bin. In an explosion of white dust, their bottom doors were opened and the product fell onto a conveyor belt, carrying it to one of the huge holding tanks. When the thirteenth boxcar, Juan Miguel's car, was lined up for unloading over the third bin door, Dubo Wilson gave the signal for the first of three large trucks to pull into position. It would take all three eighteen wheeled trucks to carry the contents of the single boxcar. Once the first truck was in position, Dubo Wilson, the newly appointed drop man, pulled the lever on the boxcar, and 107 tons of pure cocaine, with a street value in excess of two billion dollars, began to fall into the trucks below.

The boxcar hauling the cocaine had no markings that distinguished it from the other cars. It hadn't been cleaned or given any special treatment. It was merely the next car in line. The car had the remains of slurry powder from its other loads, and also mud, grease and grime from its cross-country travels. But the cocaine would be cut down and made street-ready anyway, mixed with baking soda and who knew what else. A little calcium dust would never make a difference.

When the last truck was filled with cocaine, it pulled from underneath the elevated rail and fell in line with the other two. The drivers got out and gathered in a circle to talk with one another. By now it was 8:15 in the evening, but the Alabama sky was still not entirely dark, and they were under orders not to leave the plant until darkness was complete. The drivers waited a full hour before they decided to proceed. They discussed their route, reminded each other not to let any cars between them, and climbed back into their trucks. At the NAPCO gate they were stopped by the scale master, who took the weight of their trucks one by one. After each truck was weighed, the scale master gave them their release papers and motioned for them to drive off of the scales. Although they were free to go after each one had weighed individually, the first truck waited just outside the gate for the second, and they both waited for the third. Once all three trucks were outside the mill, they began their convoy north on the smooth paved surface of County Road 78.

The trucks drove approximately three miles north and turned west down another county road, this one full of potholes and patches. The tight convoy continued for another nine miles, passing nothing but farmland and the ever-present pine trees. At a small green sign marking the ninth mile of the road, they took a left onto a dirt road. Relieved to be off the paved roads, their trip had been just as they had hoped, never passing a car on the paved highway.

At the gentle pace of ten miles an hour the trucks continued down the dirt road with the lead truck's headlights on high beam, careful of deer that might leap into the road. It took fifteen minutes to go the two and a half miles to their next turn.

The turn-off was blocked by a steel gate with a sign reading "POSTED KEEP OUT" written in big red letters. On each side, steel pipes eight inches in diameter protruded from the ground to keep anyone from driving around the gate. The steel pipes stood four feet tall, and at two-foot intervals, extended into the trees for thirty feet on each side of the gate.

A man on a four-wheeled ATV opened the gate, and the trucks pulled through, headed deeper into the pines. The ATV man closed the gate and locked it, then pulled around and led the way down a narrow road to another gate three miles from the first. The second gate was made from chain links, reinforced by steel bars, and was considerably taller than the first. At the top it had rolled barbed wire to prevent anyone from climbing over and was covered with a green fiberglass material to prevent anyone from seeing inside. A large printed sign on the front read "NAPCO EQUIPMENT STORAGE No. 3 – Authorized Personnel Only". The ATV man unlocked the gate and slid it open so the trucks could enter the complex, then closed and locked it again.

The entire six-acre complex was enclosed by an eight-foot tall chain link fence with barbed wire at the top, just like the gate. The same green fiberglass material also covered the fence surrounding the entire perimeter. The yard was filled with standing pine trees to give cover from the air. Within the complex sat bulldozers, backhoes, scrappers and other logging equipment that was moved every two days to give the illusion of legitimate work being done.

In the middle of the complex sat an 80' X 150' warehouse with three large white roll-up doors across its front. The three doors were opened from the inside and a truck drove into each bay. Once inside the building, the doors were closed and the activity began. The three drivers got out of their trucks and checked the security of the complex. None of them were from Alabama, or the Southeast for that matter. Nor were they professional truck drivers. They were all from Chicago, and for the next few days they would be security guards. They would be closely watching the complex and the woods around it by means of TV monitors inside the warehouse that received the images from the twelve video surveillance cameras hidden in surrounding trees.

A team of six Mexicans, who had been in the building for six weeks straight, began to empty the contents of the trucks and take an inventory of the task ahead of them. Even Kendall was taking advantage of cheap, hardworking, immigrant labor. He never missed an opportunity to increase profits.

On one side of the warehouse were thousands of specially made packages stacked in crates with the words "Silksheets" written across all six outside walls.

Through a small door on the outside of the truck beds, a migrant worker began to shovel out cocaine with a large stainless steel shovel and place it into a wheelbarrow manned by another worker. Once the wheelbarrow was full, the second worker rolled it to the production area and another wheelbarrow was placed in front of the door.

At the production area two of the migrant workers packaged the product into "bricks"—six-inches square, one and a half inches thick—and packaged the bricks in plastic. The plastic packages were dusted with talcum powder to help cover the smell of the cocaine, then wrapped in plastic again. Each package was then boxed in a flexible cardboard casing, sprinkled with talcum powder one more time, and the whole assembly was placed inside a package marked "Silksheets"—a perfect replica of a five-hundred sheet ream of 8½" x 11" paper. After they were wrapped and sealed in their disguise, the packages were loaded on a pallet in a neatly organized stack. When the pallet was full, the entire bundle was encased in shrink-wrap to keep the packages from sliding around during transportation.

This process went on for several days as the Mexican workers rotated on eighteen hour shifts, with six hours of rest and fifteen minute meal breaks every three hours. Over the next few evenings, the trucks were taken out of the complex at night and three new trucks with van trailers were brought in their place. When a pallet was completed and wrapped, it was placed into one of the cargo vans until that truck was full. Once the product had been packaged and all three trucks loaded, one of the truck drivers sent an e-mail on a computer sitting in the corner of the warehouse. There were no phone lines running to the facility and cell phones were also prohibited. The e-mails, sent by a satellite system on top of the building, were the only form of communication. Once the e-mail message had been sent, the migrant workers began washing down the floors and equipment. The drivers waited for a response from the e-mail. Once it came, they met to discuss their route.

At midnight the following evening, all three trucks rolled out of the warehouse and followed the man on the ATV out of the gates and into the forest. They never turned on their lights, but the Alabama half-moon offered plenty of illumination. The trucks stopped several hundred yards short of the paved road, while the ATV man rode to the edge of the pavement. The dirt road had been strategically placed in the middle of a run of highway that was straight for two miles, so the ATV man could see what was coming for a mile in each direction. When he saw no cars on the road, he used a flashlight to signal that all was clear. They moved up to the paved road, turned on their lights, and began their all night trip to Chicago.

They arrived in mid-morning at a "NAPCO DISTRIBUTION" warehouse on the south side of Chicago. The place was a whirlwind of activity with a steady stream of trucks coming and going. NAPCO's larger trucks brought in pallets of paper from its mills, while its customers' smaller trucks and vans hauled the paper away to their stores. The warehouse itself was a million square feet, and forklifts ran on a bewildering maze of pathways between the pallets, filling up or emptying the trucks at the loading docks. The three Monroe trucks went to loading docks numbered 9, 10, and 11, just like they always did. Each driver got out of his truck, raised the door to his van, and stood beside the door guarding his cargo. Waiting at loading dock number 12 was a fleet of smaller vans with "Triboli's Office Supply" emblazoned on the side. A forklift operator unloaded the Monroe trucks directly onto the Triboli vans. The cargo never touched the warehouse floor.

Silksheets had been marketed for a special type of lawyer or executive who wanted to impress his clientele with high quality paper correspondence. But these trucks carried packages for another type of lawyer and businessman—one with a habit. These special trucks didn't always deliver to Chicago. NAPCO had distribution warehouses in

New York, Los Angeles, Miami, and Dallas as well. The customers who picked up the product were legitimate office suppliers in that they did sell office supplies, among other things. All of the accounting transactions were legitimate as well, and NAPCO paid taxes on everything it sold. The IRS wasn't concerned with how many pallets of paper were sold, just the money that NAPCO generated from their sell. If someone wanted to pay three million dollars for a pallet of paper, so be it. The IRS would never notice, as long as taxes were paid on the three million dollars.

NAPCO didn't make two billion dollars off of each shipment, of course. It had expenses—such as buying the product in the first place, transporting it, and general overhead. The company actually lost money on the paper products it sold, but the "supplemental" business certainly made up for the losses. While other paper product companies were lucky to make a one percent profit from their volume, NAPCO was holding a hefty seven percent, making nearly ten percent profit off of each boxcar it brought into the United States. In Kendall's mind, he'd managed to figure out how to get goods to the consumer with fewer hassles and quicker deliveries. To him it was just good business, and except for the nature of the product, all other aspects of his operation were legitimate. Accounting was accurate, suppliers were paid, income was claimed, taxes forwarded, and another two billion dollars of illegal cocaine hit the American streets. All in the name of commerce, and all concealed behind the corporate veil of one of America's largest companies.

THIRTY-FIVE

MONDAY AFTERNOON SPENCE had done the unthinkable—pushed back a loan closing with the bank so he could get a few things prepared before he visited the district attorney. Spence knew Americus would be furious, for both pushing back the closing and for pleading not guilty in Angela's defense. But Americus hadn't been to the office all day and would never come this late in the afternoon, so at least Spence wouldn't have to deal with him until morning. He still worried with what Barnett had told him: watch out for people with ties to the mill and with too much money. Americus was knee deep in both, but Spence couldn't believe his uncle was involved.

Spence kept working after Kathy left the office, then locked up. He threw his suit jacket and briefcase into the Explorer and walked to Miss Sarah's for dinner. It was almost 9:00, the restaurant's closing time, but Spence knew Maddie would feed him if he got there before they locked the doors. As he crossed the courthouse lawn, he heard someone calling for him. It was Deputy Reeves. Spence waited for him to catch up, and the two men began walking towards Miss Sarah's. Reeves explained that his wife was at a PTA meeting at the Cedar Springs Elementary School, where she was a teacher, and his kids were at the First Baptist Church of Monroe for Vacation Bible

School. He was a bachelor for the night and was headed out for supper. Like Spence, he had worked later than he meant to.

Spence asked how the search for Watkins was going, and Reeves
told him they had all but given up hope of finding him alive and were
now dredging the river for his body. Spence was dying to tell Reeves
what he suspected about Watkins, but the warning from Barnett
stopped him. Reeves didn't seem like the type to be involved in criminal activity, but then perfect crimes were committed by those smart
enough to get away with them. Spence was suspicious of everyone.

"I'm sorry to hear about the sheriff. I know it's got to have an
effect on you, even if you guys weren't that close," Spence said.

"Of course it does. Me and everybody else in the department."

"Some of the other deputies taking it rough?" inquired Spence.

"'Bout like I expected. Some taking it pretty hard, and then others
are just upset that we lost a pretty good hitter on the softball team."

"Sheriff still had a little spunk in him, huh?"

"Not bad for a lefty. Not bad at all."

"A lefty? That's interesting."

———

When they got to Miss Sarah's, most of the dinner crowd had
already gone. A few older men—regulars—were still drinking coffee at
one table, and two other men in their mid-forties sat at a booth against
the far wall having supper before going night fishing on the river.
Spence had noticed their truck and boat parked on the street by the
front door in a no-parking zone, but Reeves never said anything to
them.

Spence felt as if he were with a local celebrity when he entered
the diner with Reeves. There were a few "Hey deputy" exchanges as
hands went up all over. Reeves gave a big smile and started acknowl-
edging the salutations, answering everyone by name.

Four teenagers were also in the restaurant, three white and one black. One of the white kids was Crawford County High School's current quarterback, who, as a sophomore last fall, had led the team to eight wins. Great things were expected of him. The lone black kid was already a superstar. At six foot three and two hundred pounds, he was the first player from Monroe to be named Alabama's "Mr. Football." Colleges across the nation had tried to sign him, but local power Auburn University had won the recruiting war. The old-timers in town compared him to the great Calvin Chauncey, but of course when Calvin was playing, "Mr. Football" in the state of Alabama was white.

Deputy Reeves walked over and shook hands with all four boys. They'd just finished a summer baseball game and were eating their second dinner of the night. Oh, to be young again, Spence thought, when you don't know what a calorie is or what it means to eat them. Reeves joked with them for a minute or two, standing there with one hand on the quarterback's shoulder and the other on the receiver's back, and Spence was pleased to see how respectfully they acted toward the deputy. Finally Reeves said, "Y'all be careful now," and came to Spence's table and sat down.

Spence and Reeves took the opportunity of this late dinner to get better acquainted. Reeves' children were his favorite topic of conversation. His son was a pure athlete, Reeves boasted, much better than he himself had been, and his little girl had to be the smartest child ever. The deputy mentioned that it was some of his children's friends from their youth baseball teams that had invited them to the week-long Vacation Bible School at First Baptist. Spence saw here both a sad vestige of segregation and a hopeful sign that times were changing: the membership of First Baptist was all white, and Reeves himself would never worship there. But black children were welcomed at the church's annual summertime youth revival.

They talked about the Atlanta Braves and about college football. They talked about their days at the University of Alabama. It turned out that Reeves had graduated only three years before Spence began law school in Tuscaloosa. They talked about hunting together when the season began in the fall. They talked about how good the food at Miss Sarah's was, and Reeves promised to bring Spence a piece of his wife's red velvet cake, which he claimed was the best in the world. When Maddie had cleared their empty plates, Reeves looked at his watch and explained that he needed to get home before his wife sent someone looking for him. Spence ordered a cup of coffee for dessert as Reeves stood up to leave. They shook hands and Reeves walked to the counter where Big Earl was keeping guard. He paid his bill and gave everyone in the diner a last goodbye wave.

Only the old regulars and the two fishermen were still in the restaurant. Maddie and her daughter were in the kitchen washing dishes, and Big Earl sat at his register behind the counter. Spence felt peaceful for the first time in weeks. The dinner with Reeves had taken his mind off his problems for the past hour, and he reflected pleasantly over the things they talked about.

It seemed odd that the two fishermen were still there. They looked to Spence to be about the same age, but one was considerably taller than the other. The shorter one had a mustache, a wider girth and wore a white cap that bore the name of a local feed store. The taller man was clean-shaven and balding. Spence hadn't spoken to either of them, but when he glanced their way he noticed both of them looking at him. When he made eye contact with the short guy, he got the distinct impression that the man wanted to talk about something. Spence nodded his head in acknowledgement.

"How ya doin?" the man in the cap asked.

"Fine. And you?" Spence replied.

The man got right to the question on his mind. "So that girl you're defendin', she pleaded not guilty to killin' Calvin?"

"That's right," Spence took another sip of his coffee. Talking to strangers about the case made him nervous. Barnett had him suspicious of everyone.

"So you don't think she did it?"

"I can't really talk about that."

"Well, we all know she did. Who else would've done it?"

"Can't say, even if I knew."

The man was not talking directly to Spence anymore, but rather to the rest of the crowd. "No tellin' what the hell was going on out there in them woods. Hear say Calvin was screwin' her. His own daughter. Can you imagine that?"

Spence's nervousness quickly turned to anger. He knew Calvin had sexually abused Angela, but he didn't like to think about it and he certainly didn't want people reminding him of it. He never answered back, but took another sip of his coffee.

"Them people do strange things sometimes," the man in the cap continued. The other patrons nodded in agreement.

It was more than Spence could take. "What people?" he asked, looking up from his coffee and not smiling.

The man acted surprised. "You know, black people."

"What about them?"

"Well, don't get huffy. All I'm sayin' is that they ain't like us in a lot of ways."

Spence didn't know about that. It was his opinion that most people were strange, black and white. Since his mother had squandered all the money she inherited from her family, he had grown up poor—and in racially mixed neighborhoods. In his experience, whites had always been outnumbered on the football field—almost ten to one in college—but it had never bothered him. They all wore the same color jersey. And when he had spent time with his black teammates, he found they were typically concerned about the same things as he—women, football, school. Usually in that order. If he didn't have any black friends now, big deal. Except for Wes, he didn't have any white friends either.

"She's half white, you know. Maybe that's where the strange things come from." Spence gave the man an even stare.

"If'n they got a little nigger in 'em, they all nigger as far as I'm concerned," one of the old regulars chimed in.

"Hell, son, you seem to have a likin' towards their kind," the man in the feed cap said menacingly. "You come into town defendin' this girl, and now you're in here eatin' with the nigger deputy."

Spence gritted his teeth and felt his jaw muscles tighten. Little more than an hour ago this same man was the first to greet Reeves with a big hello, a handshake and a "how's the family."

"I bet you wouldn't say that to his face," said Spence as he stood up. It had been many years since he'd been in a fistfight, but this man needed an ass-whipping.

"You damn right I would. I ain't scared of that badge and I sure ain't scared of no nigger." The man stood up to face Spence and so did his fishing partner.

Just as Spence started to step forward, a thunderous "wham" echoed through the restaurant and a loud booming voice shouted, "You stupid sons a bitches!" It was Big Earl. The man who never spoke had heard enough.

Maddie and Pinkney came running out of the kitchen when they heard the noise. Big Earl had slammed his hand down and knocked the cash register to the floor. Loose change rolled around and settled on the floor in the now silent room. Big Earl stared at where he had heard the voices, face red with fury and hands trembling. "Sometimes you people make me sick," Big Earl roared. "I sit here every day and every night and listen to all of the hypocrites in this town, black and white. They always real friendly whenever the others around, but as soon as they see it's just folks who look like they do, they start blamin' the other color for all their problems."

Maddie walked over and placed her hands on the big man's shoulder. "Now, Earl, just settle down. I'm sure they didn't mean nothin'." Spence wondered how many times she had come from behind to fill someone's tea glass and heard jokes or slurs she wasn't meant to hear.

Big Earl shrugged her hand off his shoulder and took a step out toward the middle of the room. "I guess y'all think I'm some dumb old blind man, just cause I don't say much, but the truth is, they ain't but a few folks in town worth talkin' to. Y'all think I'm blind, but believe me I see plenty. I see inside a person's heart. I don't have the luxury of judging people by their looks like y'all do. I've got to listen to how they talk and see if'n they're sincere. Got to see if they treat me fair, see if they respect me for being a person struggling through this world, just like they are."

Spence looked around the room. The older men were looking into their coffee cups.

"Maddie and Pinkney didn't have to take care of me when my momma died, but they did 'cause they good folks and they didn't care that I was white and blind. Hell, they could've been stealin' from me for years, but they don't 'cause they honest and hard-workin'. And you know it too! If'n you could ever see past color, you couldn't find a finer woman in the county than my Maddie, but you don't think that way 'cause then you wouldn't have anybody else to blame your problems on. All them blacks blamin' the white folk for takin' all the good jobs and never hirin' them. Well, ain't it funny how all the hard-workin' blacks in town got jobs. And all the white folk blamin' the blacks for bein' on welfare and spendin' all the gov'ments money, say they won't never work. Well, everybody that works here 'sides me is black, and I wouldn't swap a one of 'em for any of you."

The big man hesitated for a moment, daring anybody to answer him back. When no one accepted his challenge, he started again. "Ya' know, I guess I know this town better than anybody. God may have took my sight, but he gave me some more kind of ears. I can hear what people are sayin' clear across this restaurant even when it's full. And let me tell you this, there is some fine folks in this town, some real fine folks, and you won't find a better one than the black man who just walked out of here. But there is also some lowdown, back-stabbin', sorry trash, and believe me skin color ain't got a damn thing to do with it 'cause there's plenty on all sides."

Everyone stood in silence as Big Earl stared out into the room.

Finally Maddie took his arm. "Come on, Earl," she said gently, "let's go to the back."

Big Earl allowed Maddie to lead him toward the door of the kitchen where Pinkney was standing. But before he passed through, he turned to face his audience one last time. "Folks don't blame me for bein' blind," he said in a calmer voice, "and they don't hold it against me, 'cause God never asked me if I wanted to be blind. He didn't give me a choice. Well, you might not remember, but he didn't ask you what color you wanted to be either, and yet you hold color against each other every day. It's a damn shame how blind you are, just 'cause you can see."

Big Earl disappeared behind the door.

By now even the two fishermen were looking down at the floor. Then, suddenly, the tall fisherman jerked his head toward the door, and everybody else looked that way too. There stood Deputy Reeves, hat in hand, in the open doorway.

"I forgot my keys," he said, nodding towards the table where he and Spence had sat. Spence wondered how much he'd heard. Reeves walked over to the table, and as he leaned down to pick up his keys, he gave Spence a private wink. He'd heard Spence defend him.

The restaurant was still completely silent as Reeves made his way back to the door. Before he left, he turned back to face the short man in the feed cap. "Good night, Richard," he said, and waited.

The man glanced down and then back up. "Good night, John," he said.

—

Spence was sitting on his back porch watching Sam play in the moonlight when the cordless phone rang. He picked it up and looked at the built-in caller-ID screen. It was Wes, calling from South Carolina.

"Hey, buddy."

"What's up, dumbass?" Wes was never down or depressed, and Spence loved him for it.

"Just sitting on the porch, watchin' the dog. What're you doing?"

"Gettin' ready for a hot date."

"At 11:00 on a Monday night?"

"Old high school prom queen here in town. They just can't seem to get over me."

"Sounds like it."

"What the hell's a matter with you? You sound like you just lost your best friend, but as far as I can tell, I'm still alive."

"Ah, it's nothin'. Just this case I'm working on. Got me down a little."

"How's it going? You gonna win?"

"Don't know."

"Well, don't sound so defeated. You're scarin' the hell out of me."

"I think I'm falling in love with my client."

"How appropriate. Is she hot?"

"She's half black."

"Good. Maybe your kids won't be flat-footed and slow like you."

"That doesn't bother you?"

"Why should it?"

"I don't know. It seems to bother a lot of other people."

"To hell with 'em."

"Somehow I knew that would be your response."

"Listen, buddy, you do whatever it takes to make you happy and don't let them rednecks down there change your mind."

"I won't."

"Alright, you cheer up. I've gotta go get laid. I'll call to check up on you this weekend. Remember, don't let 'em get to you."

"I won't."

For all his brashness and imperfections, Spence knew he had one thing in Wes that the world needed more of. Unconditional friendship.

THIRTY-SIX

THE FOLLOWING TUESDAY morning Spence wasn't in a hurry to get to the office. He knew Americus would not be pleased that he allowed Angela to plead not guilty. Spence was hoping he could steer the conversation to Americus' friend in Dothan sending someone to help. He was still very conscious of his inexperience and wanted the guidance, although he had to admit he was doing a pretty good job of learning on the fly.

He arrived at the office about nine o'clock and pulled his Explorer around back to park in the alley. Although he knew it would be there, his heart beat a little faster when he saw the black Mercedes parked in its regular spot. He got out of his car and walked through the back door, hearing the bell that rang down the hall. Walking through the hallway and up the stairs, he never realized how quiet the office could be in the morning, before the phones started ringing. Even Kathy seemed subdued. She just said, "Morning," and handed him a message slip. The district attorney had called and wanted to see Spence at his office later that morning.

Spence made it to his office and placed his briefcase beside the desk. He was still standing at its side, reading his schedule for the week, when Americus' voice startled him.

"I hear you had quite a Monday."

"Yes, sir," Spence wheeled suddenly and replied. He hated how Americus could sneak up from behind without him knowing.

"Wanna talk about it?" Americus asked, leaning in the doorway.

"Sure," Spence said, walking behind his desk and sitting down. He really didn't want to talk about his decision to plead not guilty, at least not with Americus, but he knew he had to at least sound confident about his decision. He'd been back and forth on his viewpoint of Americus' involvement in Barnett's possible conspiracy, but he decided his uncle wouldn't place him in danger, and if in fact he were involved, he'd probably come clean and fill Spence in with the details.

"Do you really think she didn't do it?" Americus asked.

"She says she didn't and there's a lot of things that don't make sense."

"Do you care whether she did it or not?"

"Yes, sir, I think I do."

Americus straightened himself up and stood in the doorway. His suit was neatly pressed and he looked bright-eyed and well rested. He glided around one of the large leather guest chairs in front of Spence's desk and sat down.

"Okay, son," Americus started. "Let's hear about your case."

For the next two hours Spence explained everything he'd learned over the past two weeks. He told Americus about the coroner's suspicion that a large left-handed man had struck the blow that killed Calvin. He told him about Calvin's supervisor making sure he got to work, even though he seemed to be a less than satisfactory employee. He explained that it was the same supervisor who found Calvin's body and called the police the morning Angela was arrested, even though Calvin did not work the morning shift and Angela never saw the supervisor come to the house. He explained how the sheriff frequently visited Calvin's home, and now both he and Calvin's supervisor were missing. He told him about Greg Barnett, who had been following him, but wouldn't tell him anything other than to be careful. And, finally, he tried to explain how he had a feeling that Angela was being set up, even if he didn't have any other facts to prove it. He just didn't think she was capable of murder, no matter how badly she had been treated. He didn't mention his growing affection for Angela, since he didn't want it to look like he had been seduced into believing her side of the story.

The two men went over the facts and with every passing minute Spence felt more comfortable that Americus was on his side. His uncle asked questions like any good law partner, and played devil's advocate by offering logical explanations for the strange occurrences. But in the end, he usually came to the same conclusions as Spence— there were no logical explanations. He would disappear into his office and find books and law articles that could prove beneficial and he advised Spence on ways to proceed with the information he had. They talked about the DA and judge's advice and their willingness to strike a deal. Americus also advised Spence to plea bargain. "You never know what could happen in a trial," he kept repeating.

As the two men worked together it dawned on Spence that Americus was perhaps more like him than he'd originally thought. Americus had always been the hero Spence knew personally. He was rich and connected. Whatever he wanted was usually only a phone call away. He knew governors and senators, and, more importantly, they knew him. He knew how to hold his liquor, partied like a college student, and was always surrounded by attractive women. He had style, grace and manners, was never at a loss for words, and always said just the right thing at just the right moment. He could talk intelligently about hunting, fishing, golf, football, politics, and religion—or any other subject that made you a man's man in the Deep South. He was a true old school Southern gentleman.

But as they sat there at Spence's desk, Americus occasionally laid his hand on Spence's shoulder in a gesture that was both proud and fatherly. It suddenly dawned on Spence that he was the only family Americus had left. His parents, and most of his aunts and uncles, save one aunt, were deceased. He'd been estranged from Spence's mother for nearly thirteen years, when he decided the worst thing he could do was continue to send her money. He ceased his charity in an attempt to encourage her to help herself. Americus soon realized that without his money, she wanted nothing to do with her older brother. Spence knew his uncle had been married twice, but both wives were gone and the old gentleman was childless. Americus had no steady girlfriend, at least one he could take out in public. Maybe that was why Americus was so adamant about Spence going to law school and then joining his practice in Monroe: he simply craved some companionship. Then, for the first time, it occurred to Spence that, as things stood, he was the sole heir to Americus' fortune. The thought brought a small smile to Spence's lips, but then a second thought made the smile blossom. Knowing Americus, he might just up and leave his whole fortune to the Shady Pines Baptist Church.

After several hours of debate and strategy, Americus came to the same conclusion as Spence: it was highly unlikely that Angela killed Calvin. But then who did? It seemed probable that Watkins was involved. Americus had known the sheriff all his life, and he certainly didn't argue that the blatant racist was above committing such a crime, but how would Spence ever pin it on a recently deceased law officer? And what motive would he give for the sheriff's participation. Any local jury would probably crucify him for even suggesting such a theory. "Take the district attorney's offer," Americus counseled, "and call it a victory."

Americus rose from the leather chair and walked to the door of Spence's office, then turned back to look at his nephew.

"Whatever you've stumbled on to, I don't know what it is," he said. "And that scares the daylights out of me, because I know everything that goes on in this town."

"Believe me, Unc, just knowing that you don't know anything is a huge load off of my mind."

"Thought I might've been involved, huh?"

Spence's suspicions embarrassed him now. "I've been really scared and confused," he said, "and to be honest, I didn't know what to think. Like you said, I knew that you know everything that goes on in Monroe."

"Well, you just concentrate on getting the best deal you can out of Seaver, and I'll see what I can find out. Starting with who the hell is Greg Barnett?"

"Thanks, Unc," Spence started to make a note on his legal pad, but his uncle was still there, so he looked up.

"Son," Americus said, "I'm proud of you." Then he disappeared into the hallway.

Spence smiled. He couldn't think of words he'd rather hear.

THIRTY-SEVEN

THE DISTRICT ATTORNEY'S secretary was a mildly attractive forty-year-old divorcee with two kids. She introduced herself as Jaime and was clearly delighted to see that an eligible bachelor had landed in Monroe. Just as Spence assumed, judging from her looks, she was a good friend of Kathy's, and inquired as to why Spence hadn't accompanied them to Dothan on a Saturday night for a little heel-kicking. Her question gave Spence a visual thought of himself between she and Kathy, and all that cleavage, on some honky-tonk dance floor participating in a country line dance. He had a hard enough time keeping Kathy at bay while at work, and could only imagine that it would take a whip and a chair to hold her off if she were given the benefit of loud music and liquid courage.

Jaime offered Spence something to drink, but he politely refused. She asked him what he thought of the town so far, and he told her it was nice. Sensing she was not making progress, she rang the phone in the DA's office to let him know Spence was waiting for him. He came to the door and asked Spence into his office.

"Good to see you again," Seaver began.

"Yes, sir, you too." Spence made his way over to one of the chairs in front of the DA's desk and sat down. The office was cramped and in bad need of renovation. It was not the office Spence figured the county's top lawyer to have, but, then, it was the county's limited budget that supplied the space. It certainly didn't compare to the office Americus had given Spence. The white walls were sorely in need of a paint job, and the scuffed flooring was the kind of white tile usually found in grocery stores. The ceiling's acoustical tile had brown water stains where pipes in the roof had rusted and leaked. There were three desks in the room—one in the center where the DA sat, a credenza behind him, and a third along the right side of the wall. All were stacked with files and papers, making the room look cluttered and small.

The DA himself was looking a little worn. His short, salt-and-pepper hair showed more salt than pepper, and his smile seemed to have become a heavy load. He was short and powerfully built, and his dress shirt was rolled up over his bulging forearms. His deep-set eyes, under small, wire-rimmed glasses, had dark circles below them, and the red tie was loosened at the neck. He looked like he had been working hard since early that morning. Normally a very well-kept man, the stress and worry of his recent activities with Chicago gave him the appearance of somebody in severe debt, rather than someone making an extra three thousand dollars a week. But Spence didn't notice any difference in the DA's appearance, having no encounters before last week to compare him to. He hadn't known Seaver when he was the most impressive looking lawyer in town, next to Americus.

"I appreciate you coming to see me," the DA started.

"I want to try and get something worked out as soon as possible," Spence said. He was nervous facing the DA alone for the first time since he decided not to take his advice and plead guilty.

"As do I, son. Like I told you before"—the DA motioned around the room—"I've got a lot of other work going on."

"Yes, sir, it looks like it."

"Well, son, it's like I told you yesterday in the judge's chambers. I'm willing to bargain a good bit because of the situation I know your client's coming from. If she insists on going to trial, though, I'll have to throw everything I've got at her. You do understand where I'm coming from don't you?"

"Of course," said Spence. "I don't want to risk a long jail sentence either, but then it's not totally up to me. I'll tell you, though, it really bothers Angela that nobody seems to care whether she actually did it or not."

"Is she willing to risk life in prison—maybe even a death sentence—to prove a point? Seems like an awful big price to pay for principle."

"You'd have to know her. She reads the Bible a lot. I get the feeling principle is important to her."

"I'm sure she'll listen to you, though," said Seaver hopefully. "You've got to explain to her the consequences of pursuing a not-guilty plea."

"Well, sir, to be honest with you, I'm not convinced she did it either."

Seaver could feel the color leaving his face. He cleared his throat. "Son, do you mean to tell me you think she's innocent?"

Spence sat on the edge of his chair and leaned closer. Once again Barnett's words of caution held him in a bind. Could he tell the DA everything he knew—or suspected? He at least had to convey his doubts; otherwise he would look like an idiot. "There's a lot of things that don't add up, that's all I'm saying."

"Well, if your client didn't kill 'im, who did? Can you tell me anyone else who would have had a motive?"

Spence had never spoken his theory out loud, not even to Americus, not even to Angela. But he had little doubt that Watkins was involved in Calvin's death, and he didn't want to back down now. The DA was waiting for an explanation, and Spence felt an urgent need to supply one. Time was passing. Silence filled the room. He needed to answer. He had to say something.

"I think Sheriff Watkins did it," Spence blurted out.

The DA slowly leaned back in his chair. He was in the middle of a nightmare. His body felt numb, like he was another person looking down on himself in his office. He had to concentrate to keep his mouth closed. He took a deep breath. How had the kid figured it out? Seaver had never been so scared in all of his life. He wondered if Chicago knew Spence was hot on their trail. He stared at the young man across his desk in disbelief. Spence, already concerned that his response was the wrong one, was fully expecting the DA to bust out laughing at the very idea.

Seaver tried to recover. "Do you mean to tell me that the sheriff of this town went into the woods and just arbitrarily went to killing black folks?"

"Well, no, sir, I don't think it's that simple, but I do think he was involved."

The two attorneys stared at one another for a moment, neither knowing how to continue the conversation. Suddenly Jaime's voice came on the speakerphone at the corner of the DA's desk. "Mr. Seaver, Mr. Shelnutt's here for your 11:30 appointment."

Relieved, Seaver stood up and walked around the desk. "I've got to keep my next meeting," he said. "You and I can talk some more later."

"Yes, sir." Spence stood up, shook the DA's hand and turned to walk out of the office.

"Hey, kid," Seaver said before Spence got to the door, "maybe you'd better keep your theory to yourself until you and I can talk again."

"Yes, sir, I think I will."

———

As Spence made his way out of the county building, the cell phone on his belt started ringing. He pulled it from its case under his jacket and flipped open the receiver. "This is Spence."

"Thompson, this is Barnett. Can you talk?"

"Sure. I'm by myself."

"I need you to meet me this afternoon. Something has come up I think you should know about."

"Where do you want to meet?"

"Take Highway 78 out of town. Go to county road 354 and take a left. I'll meet you on the second dirt road to the right. It'll be about five miles on 354. About four o' clock."

"Okay, I'll see you there."

"Don't let anybody see you, and be careful between now and then."

"Don't worry. You've got me scared of my own shadow."

THIRTY-EIGHT

STEVE RICTER WAS tired. It was nine-thirty on Tuesday morning, and he had been up most of the night arguing with his boss, Thomas Kendall. Kendall was furious when his Monroe spy reported that Spence and the girl pled not guilty to the murder. He blamed it all on Ricter, who was supposed to be handling the situation, even though the entire drug scam had been Kendall's idea from its inception. "How could you let it get so out of control?" Kendall had raged. And now both men were desperate to figure out how much Spence knew.

They sat in a small conference room just off of Kendall's office in NAPCO's downtown Chicago headquarters. The room had been soundproofed, so no matter how loud Kendall screamed, as he was accustomed to doing, he couldn't be heard in the hallway. His security company swept the conference room and his and Ricter's offices once a week—just to make sure no one was listening.

"Thomas, we've been through all of this," said Ricter with diminishing confidence. "They'll get the plea bargain, it's just going to take a little time."

"And what if they don't and this thing actually goes to trial? How do we know how much this kid knows about our operation?"

"We've got to let them try, Thomas. What other choice do we have?"

"I think you know what other choice we have, and I say we've got to take it."

"No, Thomas. You said Watkins would be the last. Now this thing is getting way out of hand."

"Getting out of hand!" Kendall shouted. "It's already past out of hand! It's a damn nightmare is what it is!"

"Let's not panic now," urged Ricter. "We've got to keep our cool and let things run their course."

"I've never been one for waiting, and I'm telling you, I want to stop this thing while we still can. I'm giving the order."

Ricter jumped out of his chair and put both fists on the table. "Damn it, Thomas! I can't let you do that! I'm tired of this. You're out of control! I'm a lot of things, but a murderer isn't one of them!"

"I'll tell you what you are, Steve. You're too damn soft to go to prison is what you are! You took the money just like I did, and you know everything I know. You made most of the phone calls, for Christ sake! If this thing gets screwed up, you're going to prison for the rest of your life, and, personally, I don't think your candy-ass can handle it. And besides that, prison is the best-case scenario because I think you know what Triboli's response is going to be."

"I'm not going to be a part of this!"

"You're already a part of this!" Kendall screamed.

The two men faced each other furiously across the table. Ricter slowly sat down and rubbed his face with his hands. He was not physically scared of Kendall, but he thought his boss had gone crazy with paranoia, and Ricter had no doubt that some of the thoughts crossing Kendall's mind included killing his right hand man. It seemed so incredible that things had come to this. Where had his future gone?

"I'm not going to do it," Ricter said flatly. "I'm telling you I'm not going to do it."

"You're going to do whatever the hell I tell you to do," Kendall hissed. "You've got no choice, if you want to stay alive and out of prison."

Ricter sat in his chair and stared at Kendall. He was right. He really had no choice. He couldn't risk leaving his family by going to jail, and he knew who their business partners in the venture were. He was simply past the point of no return.

Kendall stared at Ricter, waiting for a response. When none came, he walked to the small table at the end of the conference room and picked up the telephone. He dialed a number, then stared back at Ricter.

"This is Kendall. Start the extermination."

THIRTY-NINE

AFTER LUNCH, SPENCE went to the county jail to see Angela. He needed to make sure she fully understood the DA's offer—and the risk of refusing it. She had also asked him to bring her some T-shirts, which would be so much more comfortable than the hot polyester county-issued prison clothes. Reeves had approved the request, and Spence had gone to Wal-Mart and bought three white cotton T's. He estimated that a men's small would probably be the most comfortable for her, but then thought how great she would look wearing a boy's medium. In the end he compromised and purchased a boy's large.

As usual, Angela was lying on her cot reading her Bible. Her face lit up when she saw him coming down the hall with Tom, and Spence returned the smile. After Tom ushered Spence inside and walked out the cell door, the two of them watched as he disappeared down the hall. When Tom was out of sight, she lifted herself from the cot and practically flew into Spence's arms. Spence held her close and stroked the back of her hair. He felt so warm and comfortable inside her arms. He wished the moment could last forever, but there was a reason for his visit.

Spence guided her back to the cot and sat her down. He handed her the T-shirts folded neatly in the Wal-mart bag, having been thoughtful enough to wash the newness out of them. Her eyes glowed in happy appreciation as she pulled one out and held it up against her body to see if it would fit. Then she glanced once again down the hallway where Tom had gone.

"Close your eyes," she said.

"Why?"

"Because I'm going to change, that's why," she said with a shy smile.

"Well, hurry up," Spence said, grinning like a kid at Christmas.

As she quickly unbuttoned her jailhouse shirt, she looked back over her shoulder to make sure Spence wasn't watching. He was, but he had his eyes closed enough to make her think he couldn't see. She pulled the T-shirt over her head and down over her body. Spence could only see her bare back, but it was enticing enough. Once she had the shirt all the way down, she said, "Okay, you can open your eyes now."

"How does it fit?" Spence asked anxiously.

"It may be a little tight, but it sure beats this old thing," she said, tossing her issued shirt to Spence. The T-shirt fit just as Spence had hoped. It was tight around her breasts and left little to be imagined about her figure. She was not wearing a bra.

She sat down next to him on the cot, close, and let her hand rest on top of his. Spence had picked up her Bible to make a place to sit and still held it in his other hand. "You sure do read this a lot," he said.

"It's inspirational," she answered. "Do you read a lot?"

"No, not really. Not if I don't have to."

"Do you ever read your Bible?"

"No, not really," Spence answered.

He did have a Bible ... somewhere. He had received it at his high school baccalaureate service—a gift from a local church to all of the graduating seniors. But he had never opened it. He could count the number of times he's been to church on one hand, including his recent experience with Americus. Angela didn't need to know that, but he thought he might mention his visit to her church.

"I did go to the Shady Pines Baptist Church last week, though."

"That's my church!" she said excitedly.

"I know. I saw some of your old friends."

"Did you meet Sister Clara Belle?"

"I did. She told me to tell you hello," Spence said, omitting what Sister Clara Belle had really said. She relaxed her body and Spence could tell she was visiting another place and time that brought her happiness. Going to church with her grandmother had clearly been a highlight of her otherwise unhappy life. Spence hated to take her from her daydream, but they had things they needed to discuss.

"Angela, I went by the DA's office this morning to discuss your case."

"What did he say?"

"He said he's willing to lessen the charge, given the circumstances you've come from," Angela's head dropped in shame at this reference to her past. "He said he'd charge you with manslaughter and talk to the judge about reducing your sentence."

"Does that mean I'm admitting to killing my father?"

"It does."

"Then what's the difference?"

"It means you killed him on the spur of the moment rather than thinking about it awhile."

"He's still dead. Why does it matter what you call it?"

"I know. It's a little confusing, but the big difference is the sentencing. If you're convicted of murder, you could go to prison for the rest of your life. If we settle for the plea bargain, you'll probably only be in prison for a few years."

Angela's tone was somber. Her spirits had flown high when she thought Spence believed in her innocence, and she had hopes of being set free, but now Spence was asking her to face the reality of prison once again.

"Do you want me to go away for a few years?" she asked, looking into Spence's face.

"No," he said, staring deeply into her brown eyes. Then he leaned closer until their shoulders touched. "I don't want you to go away for five seconds."

She turned her eyes to the floor and smiled, embarrassed by the beauty of his confession.

"But, the truth of the matter is," Spence began again, "it's a much safer proposition than pleading not guilty. If we take the deal, you've got most of your life to look forward to. If we don't take the deal and we lose, you go to prison until you're an old lady, and I'm not sure I could handle that."

"But you said yourself you don't think I killed him."

"I don't."

"I think the sheriff and Little John killed him."

"So do I."

"Then why can't we tell them that?"

"There's more to it than that. We can't just tell them, we've got to be able to prove it. And all we've got is your word against the DA's, and he's not on trial for murder. With the sheriff gone, it becomes almost impossible."

"I know this may sound stupid, but I don't want to say I killed him if I didn't."

Spence shook his head. "I know. There was a time when I would have thought it was stupid, but not anymore."

She smiled at him, pulled her knees up on to the cot and sat on them. She took his hand and squeezed it. "We can convince them," she declared. "I know we can."

Spence sat in the moment, captured by the enthusiasm in her eyes. He couldn't help but smile at her schoolgirl charm. The longer he stared, however, the more he thought, and his expression turned serious. "You're amazing. Did you know that?"

She smiled.

"All my life I've put up with heartbreak and pain," Spence started, "and I always thought it made me tough. But then I met you.

You've been through things that I couldn't possibly imagine and yet you're so much stronger and so much more positive than I am. How do you do that? How does life kick you every single day and you still embrace it?"

"I had to stay positive if I ever wanted to fly away."

"What does that mean?" Spence asked, puzzled.

Angela reached down and took the Bible from underneath Spence's hand. She flipped it open to a page with the corner folded down and began to read:

"Even the youths shall faint and be weary, and the young men shall utterly fall:

But they that wait upon the Lord shall renew their strength; they shall mount up with wings as eagles; they shall run, and not be weary; and they shall walk, and not faint."

"Dreaming of my 'wings as eagles' is the only thing that has kept me going all these years," she said. "I knew that someday I'd rise above my father's abuse if I kept believing and never gave up. Now that moment is here. My time to fly away. I know it might sound strange, but no matter what happens now, I'm free."

Neither one spoke. Neither wanted to say the wrong thing and ruin this moment. They simply stared into each other's eyes.

Then, abruptly, Angela broke the silence. "Spence, I don't want to say that I killed him, when I know I didn't."

Spence didn't answer her. He just kept staring into her beautiful face.

After a few seconds she asked, "What do you think?"

"I think," Spence started then stopped.

"Yes?"

"I think I've gotta find my Bible."

FORTY

IT WAS FOUR o'clock in the afternoon and Pat Seaver still hadn't eaten lunch. His meeting with Spence had made him physically sick, and he had already vomited from nervous stress. He kept his next appointment, but remembered it only vaguely. He'd had Jaime clear the rest of his schedule and had been pacing in his office ever since. Eventually he decided he didn't want her around either, and told her to turn off the phones and go home. He looked horrible, and she was worried about him, but he convinced her that he simply had a stomach virus and would soon be okay.

He wouldn't be able to see Hamilton until court adjourned after four-thirty. In the meantime, he paced and wondered what Chicago knew. He'd talked with Ricter the previous Sunday and had actually been calm going into the arraignment on Monday when he thought for sure Spence would plead guilty for a lesser sentence. Not only had the kid plead not guilty, he had actually fingered the real killer. Seaver wondered what kind of clues Watkins had left behind, and he wondered what evidence might link him to the operation. Maybe Chicago was right and Watkins was too stupid to be trusted. He had obviously done something to tip the kid off, and now Spence had the upper hand until they were certain how much he knew. Now that he was gone, maybe they could let Watkins' name surface as a suspect in the murder. But that would really stir up the Alabama Bureau of Investigation, and state officials were the last people they needed snooping around Monroe.

He was trying to decide whether or not to tell Chicago about his meeting with Spence and what Spence had told him about Watkins. He really wanted to speak to Hamilton first, but he figured Chicago had spies watching his every move and they would know what time Spence left his office. Besides, if he made the call now, it would at least appear that he was looking out for everyone's interest by passing along this information as quickly as possible. To wait might look like he was trying to hide something. On the other hand, if Chicago didn't know that Spence was closing in, to wait might buy Hamilton and him a little time to convince Spence and the girl to take the plea bargain and make the whole thing disappear. In the end, he decided to make the call to Ricter, a man whom he still trusted. If he'd had to call Kendall, he probably wouldn't have done it.

Ricter wasn't available when Seaver made the call at a quarter to three, so he left the coded message that Mr. Stanley Jay from New York wanted him to return the call on his cell phone. At seven minutes after four, Seaver's mobile phone rang and he quickly answered it on the first ring.

"Seaver here."

"Pat, this is Steve Ricter. I got a message that you called."

"Yes, sir, how are you doing?"

"Well, to be honest, we're a little disappointed that the girl pleaded not guilty."

"Ah, yes, sir, so were we, but we still think we can get them to plea bargain."

"Think so?"

"Yes, I do."

"I hope so. What do you need from me this afternoon?" Ricter never was much for small talk with his subordinates.

"Well," Seaver stumbled over his words, "I just wanted to call and tell you that I had a meeting today with the kid lawyer we appointed to defend the girl."

"And?"

"Oh, I still think we're only a matter of days away from having this thing behind us, but the kid made a statement to me that's a little troubling."

"What did he say?"

"Well, he mentioned to me that he thought someone else had something to do with Calvin's death."

"Who?"

"Watkins."

There was a long pause from the other end of the phone line. At his desk in Chicago, Ricter held the phone to his ear with his left hand and buried his face into his right. He moaned a faint "Oh God," just loud enough for Seaver to make out.

"I just thought you guys might want to know, but like I said, I still think everything is under control," Seaver tried to sound as convincing as possible. He knew these people held his life—or death—in their hands.

"Is that all?" Ricter asked.

Seaver desperately hoped for some reassurance. He needed Ricter's approval. He wanted to know what Kendall's plan was, and more importantly, what it had to do with him.

"That's all I know right now, but"—Seaver hesitated—"Steve, is everything okay?"

"Sure."

"What's Kendall saying about all of this?"

Ricter didn't answer.

"Steve?" Seaver asked again.

Ricter violently massaged his forehead. He knew Seaver had a teenage son just like he did. He knew Seaver, also like himself, was a good man who had made a bad decision and got involved in something he shouldn't have. Ricter's conscience, already plagued by dead men's spirits, couldn't take anymore. To hell with Kendall.

"Steve?" Seaver tried once more.

"Pat, get your wife and children out of town right now."

"What's going on?"

"Just get out, and make sure you're out before nightfall."

Ricter hung up the phone.

FORTY-ONE

WHEN SPENCE ARRIVED at the dirt road to meet Barnett, he found him already there with a small fishing boat hitched to his Chevrolet truck, which was pulled onto the shoulder of the road. Barnett recognized the Explorer and motioned for Spence to pull over behind the boat. Spence stepped out onto the ground, and a puff of powdery red dirt exploded around his black wingtip shoes. Maybe he should've suggested an indoor meeting. Monroe had been two weeks without rain and Spence knew that all the dirt roads were dry and dusty.

"Going fishing?" Spence asked as he approached Barnett. He didn't offer his hand, a Southern sin under any other circumstance, but he still didn't know where Barnett fit in to the scenario, and he was much too nervous to pretend that he wasn't.

"The boat's just in case anybody drives by—so it'll look like we're meeting out here to go fishing. Otherwise, the whole town would be speculating by suppertime about why you and I were meeting on a secluded dirt road."

"While we're on the subject, why are you and I meeting on a secluded dirt road?"

"First of all, I wanted to tell you that we've finished our investigation on you and came to the conclusion that you're clean."

"Well, thanks. To be honest, I wish I could say I knew the same thing about you. By the way, who's we?"

"Not so fast, Counselor."

"Just thought I'd try."

"Unfortunately for you, the fact that you're not in the loop, so to speak, probably means you're in much greater danger."

"Thanks. I didn't have enough to worry about already."

"Just want to remind you to keep your eyes open."

"Oh, they're open, usually at about three in the morning. Is that all this meeting is about?"

"I was hoping you could tell me your client has given you some clues about how some of this fits together."

"I wish I could say she has, but unfortunately that's not the case. All I've got is that her father was a drug addict, who had some kind of relationship with the local sheriff, who coincidently is now missing as well."

"Would it help if I told you that yesterday in Los Angeles, somebody discovered a specially packaged box of Silksheets paper full of cocaine?"

"No, not really. What does that have to do with me or my client?"

"Silksheets are made here in town, by our friends at NAPCO."

"I still don't see where you're coming from."

Barnett licked his lips and looked into the pine trees, like he was thinking about how much to say. "Several months ago we began to see a pattern that connected some of the distributors of Silksheets to organized crime and drug trafficking. A few of these companies, in addition to being eye-poppingly profitable, seemed to have a lot of executives without college educations, but also with extremely expensive habits."

"I'm listening," Spence said, finally feeling as if he were getting somewhere.

"NAPCO's success also had us a little puzzled. At a time when the rest of the industry was struggling to break even, they were holding a hefty 7 percent in profit."

"So maybe they're just better businessmen than the rest of the industry."

"We've checked. They're not. Thirty-six months ago they were on the verge of bankruptcy. They made no significant changes to their marketing strategy and no large capital improvements to lower their costs. They just simply began making more money, and lots of it."

Spence squinted his eyes a little as if in deep thought. "Are you trying to tell me that y'all, whoever y'all are, think NAPCO is in the cocaine business?"

Barnett nodded.

A big smile came across Spence's face. "That's got to be the craziest thing I've ever heard," he chuckled. "Sounds to me like somebody's got an extremely vivid imagination."

"I can assure you, Mr. Thompson, it's not as crazy as it sounds."

"And I suppose that my client's father, an ex-baseball star, who was never sober and lived in a shack in the middle of the woods, with no phone, was the mastermind behind all of this."

"Of course not, but we do think he fit in somewhere. The problem is, to make it all fit together, I need to know how and where he was involved. Which is why I'm talking to you. There's got to be something the girl has said that could've tipped you off, given what you know now."

Spence lowered his head and shook it back and forth. This was all so overwhelming—and so farfetched. He tried to think back over everything Angela had ever said, anything that could shed some light on Barnett's theory.

"There's got to be something," Barnett stated again.

Spence still shook his head. "No, I can't think of anything."

When Barnett failed to respond, Spence looked up and saw the deep frown on his face.

"Look," said Spence, raising his palms, "all I know is what I've already told you." Then he lowered his arms and counted out Calvin's offenses one by one on his fingers: "He raped and beat his own daughter. He stayed strung out on drugs and alcohol. He was friends with the town's sheriff." Then Spence pointed directly at Barnett. "And fourth, according to what you told me the other night in the woods, he also emptied boxcars at the mill." Spence held his arms out and shrugged. "Hell, man, that's all I know."

There was a long pause as Barnett stood looking at the ground. This case had absolutely worn him out. Ever since the Agency first got the call from a local lawyer named Richard Powell over eight months ago, he'd been working sixteen-hour days. But Powell was killed before they had a chance to talk, so Barnett had little more now than the information he'd brought to town. He was frustrated. He could tell Spence wanted to help and could see the genuine concern that he had for his client. But Barnett was running out of time, and a murder trial was pending. He was convinced that the killings of Powell and Calvin were linked to the mill's activities, but he still couldn't prove it. He sighed and squinted his eyes in thought. Suddenly he looked up at Spence wide-eyed. Then he stared off into the woods on the other side of the road and said, "Oh my God."

"What?" asked Spence.

"Oh my God," Barnett repeated. "Right under my nose."

"What, man, what?"

"That's it. The boxcars. They're bringing it in with the boxcars. How could I have missed that?"

Barnett stood there in absolute amazement, like he had just discovered the cure for cancer. But Spence shook his head. It still wasn't making a lot of sense to him. "I don't get it," he said.

"What's that, Mr. Thompson?"

"Why would a paper company, a Fortune Five Hundred paper company at that, get involved with drugs in the first place. And even if they were, how in the world would they bring them into the country on a train in broad daylight? It just doesn't make any sense."

Barnett gave him a little grin. He looked around and then down at the road. Finding what he wanted, he walked to the side of the road where the red dust was at its thickest. He scooped up a handful and walked back to Spence. "On the street," he said, "if this were cocaine, it would be worth about five thousand dollars." Barnett separated his fingers and the dirt fell back to the ground. Spence watched it fall between their feet and then looked back up at Barnett. "Now, Mr. Thompson, can you imagine how much a boxcar full would be worth?"

Spence said nothing. The story was starting to make sense, except for the human motive. At least two people already dead? Cocaine by the boxcar load? "But why would anybody risk it?" he asked.

"Tell me, Mr. Thompson," Barnett asked. "What would you do for a billion dollars?"

Spence shook his head. "But it's a huge company, they're already rich."

"So was Enron, Spence. Like I said, two years ago NAPCO was nearly bankrupt. And the guys who run these companies, who live this kind of life, aren't going to give up their mansions and Mercedes without a fight."

Spence didn't answer, but it was beginning to sink in. Barnett was obviously certain that he figured out how the puzzle now fit together. His mind quickly turned to Angela. What about her safety? What did this mean to her case?

"Let me get this straight," Spence began. "NAPCO brings cocaine into the country on train boxcars, my client's father finds out about it so they kill him, pay off the local sheriff, decide he knows too much and then kill him. No offense to you and your comrades, Mr. Barnett, but can you imagine how much of an idiot I'm going to sound like standing in front of a local jury, three fourths of whom will work at NAPCO, and spinning a story like that?"

"First of all, you've got it wrong. Calvin was involved. He had to be to know which boxcar the cocaine was in. He probably asked for a bigger piece of the pie and that's why they killed him. It's also my guess that Richard Powell's hunting accident was no accident. He was the one who tipped us off, but he was killed before I could talk to him. And furthermore, Mr. Thompson, if I am right, and we can prove it, there won't be any trial."

"Finally. You said something I'm interested in. No trial."

Barnett gave Spence a big smile and held out his hand. "Mr. Thompson," he said, "you've been a great help."

He was turning to go when Spence stopped him. "Hey wait a second. Is there anything that you can do to ensure the protection of my client?"

"I'll need just a little more time to try and get some things in place," he answered. "But don't worry, Spence, I'm not alone here, and there's plenty of help just around the corner." Barnett walked to the door of his truck and opened it. "You just let everybody go on believing that she offed her old man and don't let on that there's another possibility."

Spence winced as he thought back to his meeting earlier that afternoon with Seaver. "I'm afraid that won't be possible," he said very slowly.

Barnett shut the door to his truck and walked back toward Spence, "What do you mean?" he asked.

"I had a meeting today with the DA, and I kind of told him that I thought someone else might have killed Calvin."

"Who did you tell him?"

"Watkins."

"Damn it." Barnett kicked up a huge cloud of red dust.

"I didn't know any of this stuff. I had to try and defend my client. That's what you told me to do. How was I going to do that without talking to the damned district attorney?" Spence asked defensively.

"Alright, alright. Relax. We don't know if Seaver is involved or not, so maybe it doesn't even matter. Just go home and stay out of sight for a little while, and don't tell anyone else!"

"Don't worry. I won't."

"I've got to get a few things set in motion, and then I'll go by Seaver's house and see if anything suspicious is going on."

"When can I come out of my house?"

"I'll call you." Barnett got into his truck.

Spence turned to walk back to his Explorer when he heard Barnett call out, "Hey, kid." Spence turned around and saw Barnett hanging out of the window of his truck. "Relax. You've done real good."

FORTY-TWO

JUDGE HAMILTON OWNED a cell phone, but he never turned it on. It had been a Christmas gift from his oldest daughter, who, now that he was getting older, wanted to be able to get in touch with him whenever necessary. But he only used it when he wanted to make calls and kept it turned off otherwise. After all, if he wanted to be reached, he'd stay at the office. Anybody who really needed to see him could call the office and get on his schedule. After all, he was the judge. He certainly wasn't going to get on theirs. He did keep a beeper on his belt, but only his wife knew the number.

It had been a long day in court, and Hamilton was exhausted from work, worry, and lack of sleep. It was nearly five o' clock now, and he wanted to relax for a little while to clear his head. His wife told him Seaver had been trying to get in touch with him for the past hour, but he didn't rush to call him back. He knew Pat wanted to talk about the kid and the girl and about how Chicago was going to react. But right now he didn't feel like talking about it. Everything would be fine. He would figure something out to keep the operation going and the money coming in. If nothing else in his forty years in the legal profession, he had learned the highs were never as high as you thought, and the lows were never as low. Things had a way of working themselves out.

He sat on the porch sipping his bourbon, his wife in the kitchen on the other side of the house preparing the evening meal. The sky was cloudy and the humidity in the air hinted at rain later that evening, but for the moment the cool breeze that flowed through the porch was a welcome antidote to the summertime heat. He watched a couple of squirrels play in the oak tree next to the porch and wondered—once more—how the hell he managed to get in such a predicament. Now in his early seventies, he should've been worrying about his grandchildren's next visit and not whether he would spend his retirement years in prison.

The money had been a great seducer. He had never been a smart investor and on more than one occasion had actually been on the verge of bankruptcy from failed business ventures. He'd blown his first nest egg—$250,000—by investing it all in a restaurant in Birmingham with an old college friend. Then he let his son-in-law talk him into building a strip mall in Montgomery. Of course, they hadn't done their homework, and when their retail space didn't lease quickly enough, they were forced to let the bank take it over. That one cost him $300,000—not to mention the extra $100,000 to bail out the sorry son-in-law, who had pocketed the proceeds from the construction loan. It was the closest he'd ever been to financial ruin. His relative affluence—by Monroe standards—came not from his astute business sense but because his profession allowed him to make enough money to overcome his ineptness. When Ricter approached him with a lucrative business proposal, he was immediately interested—even before he understood the terms of the deal. Later, when he realized what was expected of him, he still saw it as his last chance to become the wealthy old lawyer he wanted to be. He wanted to be admired. He wanted to be . . . like Americus.

Now he had plenty of money—both cash and NAPCO stock— but he still had the same life. There were only so many groceries you could buy with cash and so many vacations you could take. He had bought his wife some expensive jewelry, but she never wore it.

Extravagant balls and parties were non-existent in Monroe, and she didn't need emerald earrings to piddle around in the dirt of her rose garden. The last few days made him think about what Seaver had said at their meeting on his porch, and he was becoming more convinced that the DA had been right. The money wasn't worth what they had to do to get it. But, somehow, you never realize that beforehand.

He sat in his old rocking chair, sipping from his whiskey glass and watching the dark clouds roll in from the west side of town, when he was suddenly startled by a man standing at the bottom of the porch steps. He was a tall man, dressed in dark slacks, a white dress shirt and a black sports coat, even in the intense heat. His dark sunglasses, useless in the cloudy weather, were as black as his combed-back hair.

"May I help you?" the judge asked as soon as he had caught his breath. But he was startled all over again to realize that a second man—dressed just like the first—had somehow made his way up onto the porch and stood not two feet from the judge's rocker. His glass shook in his hand before he could rest it on the arm of the chair, and his other hand instinctively gripped its arm-rest tight. In the next instant, though, a deep calm came over him. He knew who they were. He knew why they were here.

Looking back to the first man, who had now made his way up the four steps and was standing on the porch, the judge begged, "Please, don't hurt my wife."

"Is there any need to?" the first man asked.

"No, she doesn't know anything."

"I hope not, Your Honor. I hope not."

The second man flew into action, wrapping a thick piece of plastic cellophane around the judge's head. The first man caught the judge's glass before it hit the porch, then stood up and looked around to make sure no one was watching. A third man the judge never saw helped pull him to the floor of the porch. All together they held his arms and legs to keep him from banging the boards for help, and the second man kept wrapping the plastic to make it airtight. The judge inhaled the first bit of air trapped between his nose and the plastic, but he had no way of exhaling as the plastic stretched tight and covered his mouth completely. The men tried to be as gentle as possible. Bruises or contusions would suggest that there had been a struggle.

When the judge's body stopped convulsing, the first man took his pulse and then nodded to the second man holding the plastic. They removed the plastic and inspected their work. Finding no visible damage, they laid the body carefully in front of the rocking chair and turned his glass over to give the impression that he had fallen out of his chair. They straightened his hair and clothes, and satisfied with their work, shook hands over his lifeless body.

When his wife found his body twenty minutes later, it looked like he had a heart attack so sudden that he was unable to call for help. The men were professionals and careful not to allow anyone to see their work. Their method of murder was perfect for killings on quiet streets. Years in the business had taught them one lesson every good hit man should know. You can't scream if you can't breathe.

—

Spence's heart skipped a beat when he grabbed his front door knob and the door cracked open. He'd locked the door earlier that morning, and he knew it. He hadn't worried about it when he first came to Monroe, but now he always locked it. He didn't want whoever might be watching him to be looking around while he was gone.

He slid the door open and looked inside. He was glad now that he had finally oiled the hinges. The door opened in perfect silence. His first instinct was to leave the house, but not without Sam. The fact that she hadn't greeted him at the door was the most disturbing thing of all. He eased his briefcase and suit jacket down onto the porch and slipped inside the door. He saw a few magazines on the coffee table he didn't remember leaving open, but otherwise the living room looked untouched. He tiptoed to the corner and pulled the five-iron from his rarely used golf bag. Then he heard paper rustling in the kitchen. His heart was about to explode, and again he wanted to run, but it was too late. Whoever was there was coming his way. He pressed his back against the wall beside the kitchen door and raised the club over his head. When the intruder came through the door and caught sight of Spence, golf club drawn back, he hollered "Jesus!" and threw potato chips and a ham sandwich into the air. It was Wes.

"What the hell are you doing?" he shouted.

Spence collapsed in relief. "Man, you scared me to death."

"I scared you? Is this how you treat all of your guests?"

"I didn't know it was you," said Spence, still trembling. "What're you doing here?"

Sam came bounding in from the kitchen. She had her two favorite people in the house and a ham sandwich on the floor. For her, life didn't get any better.

"You sounded like hell last night on the phone," Wes said. "I thought I'd better come see about you before you did something stupid."

"How did you find out where I lived?"

"The fat chick at your office gave me directions. I think she wants to do me. She gave me a key too."

"Great." Spence knew he couldn't get mad at Kathy for giving keys out to his house. She had no idea what was going on. "Where's your car?"

"I parked around back. Why are you so jumpy, man? What the hell's going on?"

"Believe me, you don't want to know."

"If it bothers you this much, I think I need to know."

Spence knew he had promised Barnett not tell anyone else about Watkins and NAPCO, but Wes was different. He was like an extension of Spence. Plus, Spence would just feel better if Wes knew. For the next hour, Spence explained the whole story, culminating with Barnett's theory about NAPCO and the cocaine train line. Wes sat amazed.

"Dude, we've got to get you out of here. You could be in real danger," Wes insisted. "Let's get in the car and just leave town for a little while. We'll go to the Island for a few days and let Pops do some checking on this thing."

"I can't leave Angela."

"She's in a jail cell. Nothing can happen to her there. She'll be fine."

"I've got to know that she's alright."

"Man, you really are hooked."

"You have no idea how bad."

FORTY-THREE

SEAVER CALLED HIS wife from the office and told her to get their son and daughter and go to her mother's house in Mobile. He would call her later and tell her what to do next. She heard the anxiety in his voice and demanded to know what was going on, but he told her to just please go, he would explain later. She refused—she wasn't going anywhere until he got home. Seaver had never raised his voice at his wife before, but now he screamed at her to get in the car and told her she better not be home when he got there. Thank God—her Volvo was missing from the garage when he pulled in the driveway.

As he entered the house, he could see that his threat had at least some effect on his wife. The TV was still on, as was his son's computer. He went to their bedroom and grabbed the handgun in the top drawer of his bedside nightstand. He checked to make sure it was loaded and stuck it in his pocket. He noticed, too, that his wife had not been too scared to leave without her make-up. He didn't bother to pack anything. If there was something he needed, he could buy it.

He reached under the bed and slid out a small gray lock box. He pulled his key chain out of his pocket and found the small gold key that unlocked the box. He opened it and moved papers around until he found another key. He closed the box without locking it and slid it back under the bed. He ran to the back door and out through the yard.

Seaver lived on a small sixty-acre farm on the outskirts of the county. He had lived there for twenty years and had made quite a few improvements to the property. His latest was a barn, about two hundred yards behind the house, which he built himself, paying cash for everything. The barn was a typical square building with a tin roof, housing his tractor and other equipment in the middle, with two horse stalls on one side for his wife's favorite animals. Two large doors, big enough for the tractor to drive through for storage, closed off the front of the barn. A chain and a lock secured them shut.

Seaver hurriedly unlocked the doors and swung them open, throwing the chains to the ground. Just to the right of his tractor sat a wheelbarrow with a beige canvas cover over it. He pushed the wheelbarrow to the side to reveal a small door in the barn's interior wall, fastened by only a simple hinge lock. On the other side of the door was a red safe, secured by both a key lock and a combination. Seaver stuck the key he had retrieved from the gray box into the keyhole and turned it, then spun the combination knob clockwise, counter-clockwise, then clockwise again until the final number rested on 53, his old high school football number. He pulled the safe door open and dragged out two heavy black duffle bags. He didn't need to check. He knew it was all there—$2.3 million and change, in crisp, new hundred-dollar bills. He threw the bags over his shoulders and ran for the garage. The barn doors still yawned open behind him.

He opened the front door of his new Buick Le Sabre, threw the bags into the front seat, and climbed in behind them. He backed out, spun around, and sped down the long driveway. The scuppernong vines on either side of the drive that he and his son had planted thirteen years earlier were in full foliage, and he realized that this would probably be the last time he traveled the gravel driveway of his home.

It was nearing dark when Seaver passed through the two brick columns at the end of his driveway, a quarter of a mile from the house. But he could still see without his lights on, and he turned right at the end of the driveway and drove two hundred yards to where the county road dumped into the highway headed back into town. At the stop sign he had to wait for an unfamiliar black Lincoln that was slowing down to turn beside him. As the black car turned, Seaver pulled onto the highway, but when he glanced at the occupants of the car, his heart stopped. He didn't recognize them, but he knew immediately who they were. One man was motioning frantically to the driver, and Seaver watched as the big black car continued to turn around at the mouth of the road. He put his foot down on the gas.

—

Barnett sat in his truck two miles from Seaver's house checking his equipment. This was the part of the job he loved and the reason why he joined the DEA in the first place. The first part of an assignment was always the worst, trying to put a case together and remembering who you were supposed to be. But now came crunch time, which made the mundane stuff worth it. It was dark enough to check his night-vision binoculars, so he turned them on and read the highway marker a quarter mile down the road. They worked perfectly.

He needed to find out what Seaver knew right away. Already another agent was investigating at NAPCO, getting a sample of the powder remains on the bin doors that dropped over the truck loading area. Barnett had a good idea what the lab analysis would find in the sample. As soon as it was dark, he would pay a visit to the home of Monroe's district attorney, tap his phone line and see who he was talking to. It wasn't an "official" wiretap because he didn't have a warrant. The evidence wouldn't be admissible in court, but that didn't matter right now. Right now he needed to find out how much time was left before he had to get Spence and the girl out of town and call in his reinforcements.

Suddenly, he saw lights coming toward him from the direction of

Seaver's house. The car was coming fast, faster, and Barnett recognized Seaver's car as it blew past, doing at least eighty miles an hour.

"Looks like he knows something," Barnett said aloud as he started his pickup truck. The second pair of lights was upon him before he had time to pull out, and when the black Lincoln barreled past him, Barnett got worried. There weren't many late model Lincolns in Monroe. He pulled his binoculars from their case and watched the car as it pulled away in pursuit of Seaver. Illinois license plates. He was out of time.

He grabbed his cell phone off the seat, flipped open the receiver, and hit speed dial #7. At the same time he turned on his headlights and stomped the throttle. A bloom of dust arose behind him, and the truck slid like a serpent out onto the blacktop.

———

Spence and Wes had been drinking a beer on the back steps, watching Sam frolic in the big back yard, but the mosquitoes were too much. They were just about to go inside when Spence heard the phone ring. He was still chuckling over the lurid tale Wes had just told when he got to the telephone in the kitchen.

"Hello."

"Get out of town, now!" Barnett screamed into the phone.

"Barnett, is that you?"

"Of course it's me! Who else would it be? Just shut the hell up, go get in your car and leave!"

"What's going on?"

" I don't have time to explain it right now! Seaver definitely knows something! NAPCO's boys from Chicago are in town, so you've got to leave now! Don't tell anybody where you're going! Just GO!"

"I can't leave Angela."

"What are you going to do, bust her out of jail? She's in the safest place she could be!"

"I've got to know she's alright!" Spence hung up the phone. He was walking around in a daze, trying to find his car keys, when Wes walked inside.

"What's going on buddy?"

"The NAPCO people are in town, and Barnett says I could be in danger," Spence answered, too agitated to find what he was looking for.

"You mean the drug people are here and they could be looking for you?"

"That's what he said." Spence spun in another circle, then screamed out, "Where the hell did I put my keys?"

"Forget your damn keys, man. We'll go in mine. Where do you want to go?"

"I've got to go see Angela."

Wes put his hand on Spence's shoulder and turned him so the two men were facing each other. "Let me see if I can get this right. There's a bunch of murdering drug dealers here tonight looking to kill you, and our plan is to drive into town to see if we can get some girl out of jail?"

"She's not just some girl, and you don't have to go."

Wes stood there rubbing his chin for a moment and then threw out his hands. "Hell, I'd like to meet a woman that's worth all of this. Count me in."

FORTY-FOUR

SPENCE AND WES were a lot alike, but in at least one way they were very different: Wes was rich. He'd always been rich. His father was a rich lawyer and both his grandfathers had been rich lawyers. The day he graduated from law school, there was a job waiting for him at one of the largest firms in South Carolina, a firm his grandfather had founded. His starting salary was two thousand dollars a week, over one hundred thousand dollars a year, plus perks. He had no student loans to pay off, and his grandmother had willed him her five-thousand-square-foot house in one Columbia's nicest neighborhoods. With his pocket full of disposable income, Wes decided to buy a car. Not just any car—a black GTS Dodge Viper, one of the fastest production cars ever made.

Coming to the house, he'd driven two miles an hour on the dirt road where Spence lived, trying to keep his car clean. But now they were in high gear, leaving a cloud of dust behind them on their way into town. When the car came off the dirt road and onto the pavement, the dust turned into black smoke as the car fishtailed sideways, and Wes struggled to gain control of the four-hundred-horsepower machine. The county road had gaping potholes every couple of feet, but at the speed the Viper was traveling, they scarcely noticed the condition of the pavement.

From Spence's house to the courthouse square was 6.7 miles—a ten-minute drive for Spence. The Viper made the trip in less than six, and Wes skidded sideways to a stop in front of the sheriff's office. It was 7:47 on Tuesday night, and the town square was empty.

Spence had been thinking about how he could get to Angela ever since Barnett told him on the phone that they were in danger. He figured Deputy Reeves was his only chance. But first he would have to find Reeves, and second, he would have to convince the deputy that Angela had to be moved to another location. Of course, there was the risk that Reeves was just as deep as the sheriff and the DA in NAPCO's drug operation, which meant he could be the very one out to get them. But if he wasn't involved, then he probably knew nothing about it, and Spence would have a long, complicated, and incredible story to tell in just a few minutes. At least no time would be lost looking for Reeves. He came running through the front door of the sheriff's office as soon as he heard the Viper come to its screeching stop.

"What's going on here?" Reeves asked as Spence and Wes barreled out of the car.

"John, thank God you're here. I've got to talk to you."

"Spence, you can't drive through the middle of town like that. What're you thinking?"

"John, just listen to me. We've got to get Angela out of the jail. She could be in a lot of trouble."

"She's on trial for murder." Reeves answered with a frown. "I'd say she's already in a lot of trouble. Now, I'm having a busy night and don't have time for this right now."

Wes had been looking around the square to make sure he didn't see anything suspicious. The only thing that struck him as odd was that there were only two cars visible from the street, and one of them was his. The other was Reeves' cruiser. Wes listened to Spence and Reeves and then chimed in with his own question, "I know this is a small town," he said, "but where is everybody?"

"The paramedics and the other two deputies on shift are over at Judge Hamilton's house. Who are you?"

"Wes McCain," Wes held out his hand. "Damn nice to meet ya."

Shaking Wes's hand, Reeves answered back, "The judge had a heart attack tonight, so everybody's over there. I stayed here to field some of the calls I know will come."

This new development sent Spence's mind into a whirl. He had never believed the judge's story that he appointed Spence to defend Angela because all the other lawyers in town had real cases going on. This was a murder case, and certainly somebody could've taken a little time off from collecting unpaid bills for the local tire store to defend one of the town's own citizens on trial for murder. The sheriff and the DA were involved. Why not the judge? He had been just as interested in keeping Angela's case from a trial as the DA.

"Is the judge dead?" Spence asked.

"What?" The question caught Reeves off guard. He was still busy sizing up Wes.

"The judge. Did the heart attack kill him?"

"Yes, it did."

"Oh my God." He saw it in a flash. "They killed him too."

"Who killed who?" Reeves asked.

"NAPCO. They killed the judge."

"The mill killed the judge? Spence, what're you talking about?" Reeves squinted in consternation. He liked Spence, liked him more all the time, and wanted to give him the benefit of doubt. But Spence's suggestion was way out of line.

"NAPCO," Spence started, then stopped, trying to figure out how to start the story. "NAPCO brings cocaine into the country by train. The judge, Watkins, the DA and Calvin were all involved. Apparently NAPCO got nervous. That's why they killed Calvin and Watkins, and they're here tonight. They killed the judge, and I'll bet by now the DA's nowhere to be found either. Please, John, you've got to believe me. I think they'll come after Angela next."

Reeves stood there, considering it. He had to admit that the theory would fill in a lot of the missing pieces to the current local puzzle, but it was a lot to swallow. NAPCO trafficking cocaine? And practically everybody in town in on it?

"Please, John, you've got to help me. We've got to get her out of here," Spence pleaded.

Reeves didn't say a word, but turned and walked into the sheriff's office. He could make a phone call, at least. He owed Spence that much anyway. Spence and Wes followed him inside, and Reeves walked behind the receptionist desk, opened a drawer and took out a list. He ran his finger down the list until he found Seaver's home phone number and dialed. Looking up, he stared at Spence, who stared back, wondering who he was calling and what he would say when they answered. The phone rang once. Second ring and still no answer. Third ring. Fourth ring. Fifth ring. Still nothing. Reeves was trying to decide how long he should let it ring when he saw the headlights come around the other side of the courthouse and shine through the glass on the sheriff's office door. The car came skidding around the corner, just like Spence and Wes had done in the Viper, and Reeves slowly pulled the phone away from his ear. "What the...?"

Spence and Wes looked just in time to see the car go out of control coming out of the turn. It was now headed straight for a brick wall next to the street that protected the Courthouse dumpster from oncoming traffic. The driver hit the brakes hard, but the car still crashed into the wall, which collapsed down on its hood. Just then a second pair of lights came around the same side of the courthouse. Wes, Spence, and Reeves ran out of the office and watched in disbelief as the district attorney grabbed a big black bag from the front seat of the wrecked car and ran behind the hardware store on the courthouse square.

The second car, a black Lincoln, screamed to a halt at the side of Seaver's wrecked Buick. Three men jumped from the car, and two of them chased Seaver behind the store. The third man spotted Wes,

Spence and Reeves standing on the office landing and immediately pulled a handgun from his waistline. Before he had time to react, Spence heard the bullet whistle past his head and explode through the glass on the sheriff's office door. Reeves and Wes jumped back in the office, and Spence took cover behind a small brick wall to the left side of the landing covered by holly bushes.

With his targets no longer visible, the shooter hurried after his accomplices. Reeves stood just inside the office doorway, handgun drawn. "Thompson, you okay?" he shouted out.

"So far."

"I'm starting to believe your story."

"I hope I don't have to get shot before you're completely convinced."

"I don't think that'll be necessary."

Spence darted into the office and stood on the other side of the doorway, with Wes right behind him. A third pair of lights came racing around the courthouse.

"Who the hell is this?" Wes asked Spence, who was still panting. Spence recognized Barnett's pickup truck.

"Believe it or not, he's actually on our side…I think."

Barnett opened his door, stood behind it for protection and pointed his gun towards the Lincoln, which still had three doors hanging open. Seeing no movement, he slowly moved out from behind his truck door, his pistol still aimed at the Lincoln. He glanced around the square and noticed the shattered glass on the Sheriff's office door.

"Barnett, it's me, Spence," Spence yelled from inside the sheriff's office.

Startled by the voice, Barnett crouched behind the hood of his truck. He saw Spence's head in the office doorway.

"Anything I need to know about?" Barnett shouted back.

"They ran behind the store in front of you."

"I'm coming over. Stay where you are."

Barnett made his way around the back of his pickup truck then sprinted toward the sheriff's office.

"I don't like the fact that a man with a gun is running toward my office," Reeves said to Spence.

"I've had no choice but to believe him," said Spence, "and I think you're going to have to, too."

Barnett made it inside and hugged the wall behind Spence and Wes. "They ran behind that little hardware store on the right?" he asked Spence as he surveyed the street.

"I know this is an unorthodox situation we've got here," Reeves interrupted, "but do you mind if I see some ID? This is still my town, you know."

"Excuse me, Deputy," Barnett answered. "I meant no disrespect. Just caught up in the moment," Barnett said with a smile. Spence could see that he was actually enjoying this. He reached into his back pocket for his wallet and flipped it open, "Special Agent Chris Landers, DEA."

"So that's who you're with," Spence said.

"Yeah, kid, that's the 'we' you asked about earlier." Then turning to Reeves he said, "Deputy, I've got some other agents on the way, but it's going to be at least another fifteen minutes before they get here. I'm guessing that Seaver ran behind the building and the men in the Lincoln chased him. Is that right?"

"That's correct," Reeves answered.

"Yeah, I'm sure they've punched his number. You hear any shots since they got out of the car?"

"Only the one that whizzed by my head and busted the glass here," Spence answered, nodding at the glass pieces on the floor.

"Well, deputy," Landers went on, "I guess since he hasn't been convicted of anything yet, we've got to try and help him. Am I right?"

"That's the way I see it," Reeves answered.

"Good," said Landers. "Besides, if we can keep him alive, it'll sure make my life easier."

"Let me get this straight," Wes interrupted. "There's a couple of guys out there with guns, you don't know where they are, it's completely dark, they want to kill us, and you two are about to go looking for them."

"That's what we get paid for," Landers answered back.

Wes rolled his eyes. "Well, whatever you get paid, it ain't enough."

Landers looked at Deputy Reeves. "You got a couple of shotguns around here?"

"They're in the gun cabinet. I'll get a few." Reeves slowly backed away and disappeared through a doorway behind him.

"What are we supposed to do?" asked Wes.

"I'm going to see if Angela's alright," Spence answered.

"You stay right here until I get back," Landers demanded. Then he shook his head and smirked, "Something tells me I'd have to handcuff you to the floor for that to happen."

Reeves came back holding two shotguns and a box of shells. He handed one of the guns to Landers and then began loading the other.

"Deputy, our hero here says he's going over to the jail to check on his client. What's your opinion on that?" Landers asked.

"I hate putting citizens at risk, but it's probably not a bad idea to let the guard know what's going on." Turning to Spence, Reeves asked, "Do you know how to use a gun?"

"Oh yeah," Spence answered.

As Reeves headed back to the same room from which he had retrieved the shotguns, Wes shouted out, "Hey, bring me one too!"

Reeves returned with two handguns. "They're loaded," he said. "Now you two hold up your right hands."

They held up their hands while inspecting their guns.

"Promise me you will only shoot bad guys and that you won't get killed yourself."

"I promise," said Spence.

"Hell, I hope," said Wes.

FORTY-FIVE

A COOL BREEZE blew through the courthouse square and rattled leaves on the oaks and sycamores. A summer storm had been building throughout the afternoon, and now thunder rolled toward town. Suddenly a streak of lightning split the night, and for an instant the sky was bright as day.

Landers and Reeves went in opposite directions around the square. Their plan was to walk the back of the stores and meet in the opposite corner, across from the sheriff's office. The blast of their shotguns would be distinctive, so if either one heard the other fire, he would know to come help. Landers first had Reeves cover him as he made his way to the black Lincoln and removed the keys from the ignition. He also took something small out of his pocket and put it underneath the seat.

Landers then ran to the corner of the hardware store where Kendall's exterminators had followed Seaver. Lightning was crashing all around the square now, and the thunder was only seconds behind. The wind picked up. Landers peered around the store's brick veneer and saw an overgrown vacant lot about fifty yards square. Beyond that were two rows of houses divided by Maple Street, one of the town's original avenues. Landers could see into the nearest houses where Monroe's citizens relaxed for the evening. Apparently the crash of the car and the single pistol shot had gone unnoticed in the constant roaring of thunder that invaded the town, and he was thankful that nobody had been drawn outside, into a street where armed gunmen hunted for the district attorney.

He studied the back of the stores for a moment, then decided to trek across the vacant lot. There was no movement along the back of the stores, but he was at a distinct disadvantage. The three gunmen had probably split up and could be anywhere. A few drops of rain hit his face as the storm rolled closer. He ran in a crouch across the lot and saw what he was looking for. Two houses down, a figure passed in front of a lighted window. Landers quickly took cover behind a big sweet gum tree at the corner of the vacant lot and the first house. He saw two figures cross the street in front of the house where he'd spotted the first figure, then suddenly someone appeared from around the side of the house and headed back toward the stores and square. Landers wheeled and pointed his shotgun at the runner, who, oblivious to his presence, was struggling with a large bag hung over his shoulder. Landers could tell it was Seaver, who had apparently circled back around the houses and was now looking for a hiding place along the rear of the stores.

It didn't look like Seaver had a gun, at least not in his hands— both were clearly visible during a lightning strike that exploded in the sky as Seaver ran through the vacant lot. But Landers couldn't assume he didn't have one on him somewhere, and if he did, he'd probably be just as likely to shoot a DEA agent as he would the thugs chasing him. He wanted to be careful not to corner Seaver or scare him into doing something stupid before he could get him to surrender. He watched to make sure the goons weren't following on Seaver's heels, then ran to the opposite side of the stores from where Seaver was headed.

Seaver hid on one side of the stores, two hundred yards away, while Landers readied himself on the opposite side. Still unaware that he had company, Seaver began to creep across back of the buildings, looking for safety. Storm clouds had obscured the half-moon, and the night was dark, but Landers could still make out the DA's white dress shirt as Seaver moved in his direction. It was perfect. If Seaver continued along the back of the building until he got to Landers, then maybe the agent could take him without firing a shot. He watched as Seaver made it to the middle of the stores, where he stopped at an inlet for the air conditioning units.

Landers could hear the rain coming across the courthouse lawn, and from the sound it made as it grew closer, it was heavy and thick. He felt the cool rush of moisture overcome him in the wind. Seaver was only about a hundred yards away now, as Landers waited patiently at the end of the building, peeking around the side, waiting for Seaver to come closer. The rain was perfect. It would provide even more cover for Landers to overtake him.

Suddenly a third figure sprang from behind an air conditioning unit—one of the exterminators, waiting near the stores in case Seaver came back. He had watched both the DA and Landers coming back across the vacant lot and he knew their positions. He fired a shot at the corner of the building where Landers was hiding, forcing him to seek cover. Hearing the shot, Seaver instinctively jumped into the air-conditioner inlet—where he found himself completely trapped. In the turmoil of the car crash and escape, he had left his gun lying on the front seat of his Buick, and now the exterminator revealed himself, blocking the only way out between the two walls. He dropped the black bag and raised his hands in surrender, and just as quickly the exterminator raised his gun and fired twice. Seaver never heard the shots. He was dead before they registered in his ears, his limp body falling against the wall with the black bag at his side. The rain thundered to the ground.

Landers wheeled around the side of the building and fired his shotgun at the assassin, who was already sprinting to the other side. At over a hundred yards, the pattern of the shotgun was too wide to do any damage, and because he didn't know where the others were, Landers had no choice but to let him go. In the rain he could barely see his hand in front of his face. He eased from the side of the building and deliberately made his way along the back to the place where Seaver had been shot. He kept scanning the vacant lot, the houses, the buildings, but saw no one. When he got to the inlet he could see Seaver's body lying face down with the bag beside him. He heard car doors slam and tires squeal, and he knew the murderers were gone. That they had extra keys didn't surprise him.

The inlet between the buildings was partially covered by a roof, so Landers could shelter himself from the rain and he turned Seaver's body over. There was no need to check his pulse. Two shots in the chest at point blank range will end in the same result most every time. He picked up the bag, unzipped it, and stuck his hand inside, where he found just what he expected. Even with their life on the line, they always went back for the money.

"Landers, you there?" It was Reeves at the end of the building where Landers had been hiding.

"Yeah, I'm here," Landers answered back, not attempting to lower his voice. Reeves ran along the back of the stores until he got to where Landers stood over the body and the bag.

"I heard you shoot. Everything alright?" Reeves asked. Rain poured from the brim of his hat in front of his face.

"It is for me, but I was too late for him," Landers said, indicating Seaver's body.

"I saw them drive away, but I couldn't get back to the square in time to stop them."

Don't worry. I've got a little surprise. We'll find 'em."

"Is that what I think it is?" Reeves asked, nodding his head at the bag.

Landers pulled a stack of hundred-dollar bills from the bag and thumbed it. "If you think it's a bag full of money, you'd be right."

—

Nick Howard was just twenty years old and had been a cell guard for only two months. He was still a little skittish about his job, and far from aggressive to begin with. His uncle Tom, the day-shift guard, assured him that he had no reason to worry. The Monroe County jail hadn't seen an attempted breakout in over forty years. However, most of the time Howard was scared of his own shadow, and even a gun at his side did not give him courage. Unfortunately for Howard, he drew the late shift on the night the exterminators came to town.

Spence and Wes waited a moment at the front desk of the jail-house for someone to appear, but county budget cut-backs made the night guard the only person present from the hours of 9:00 p.m. to 6:00 a.m. Howard knew to call the sheriff's office if he needed anything, but except for the officers who were a block away, he was all by himself. When no one came to the front desk, Spence and Wes finally decided to show themselves down the stairs to the cellblock.

The Monroe jail was particularly crowded this night. Two drunks shared a cell directly behind Howard—the remnants of a two-day poker game that had ended in a fight. Across from the drunks was young Mark Johnson, the local car thief. Mark never left town with the merchandise, nor did he ever try to sell it. He just liked driving new cars, and since he couldn't afford one of his own, he regularly borrowed somebody else's. Judge Hamilton, fed up with his antics, had given Johnson sixty days in the county jail to kick the habit.

In the second cell behind Howard, next to the drunks, was Jared Grant, a hot-head who liked to beat up on his young wife. She had called Reeves out to get him two days ago, and so far no one had come to bail him out.

And of course, all the way at the end of the cell block, with par-titions to give her privacy, was Monroe's most famous prisoner,

Angela Chauncey.

When he heard the door open at the top of the stairs, Howard didn't immediately panic. He assumed it was somebody from the sheriff's office bringing in another prisoner. But when he saw the two strange men running down the stairs with pistols in their hands, instinct took over. He threw himself up against the iron bars, raised his hands and shouted, "Don't shoot! Don't shoot!" Wes and Spence looked at each other. Any other time, it would have been funny.

"Relax man," Spence said. "We're on your side."

Howard now recognized Spence. "Aren't you Angela's lawyer?"

"That's right."

"What's with the guns?"

"We've got a little situation out on the street and Deputy Reeves thought I'd better come and let you know about it. Besides, I wanted to check on my client."

"What..."—Howard stuttered in his anxiety—"what kind of situation?"

"There's a bunch of killers in town trying to kill the DA—and Spence, too," Wes answered matter-of-factly.

Spence frowned at Wes. "We think Angela might be in danger and we just need to keep our eyes open," he said, hoping to ease the jailer's fears.

"Killers?" Howard stood frozen, his scared eyes glancing back to Wes.

"Can you open the door, so I can see her?" Spence asked, waking Howard from his trance. The jailer finally turned around and opened both iron-barred doors, and Spence and Wes moved quickly down the cellblock hallway. Howard tagged closely behind, looking over his shoulder.

Jared Grant let out a laugh. "You' s scared of 'em, wun't ya, Howard," he said.

"You shut up, Jared Grant, or you'll stay in that cell forever," Howard cried, his high voice cracking. Grant made a sudden lunge toward Howard, like he was going to attack him through the cell bars, and Howard jumped forward and bumped into Wes's back. Grant laughed even louder.

At the end of the cellblock, Angela was standing at her iron door, trying to see what the commotion was about. Spence put his hands on hers as they rested on the bars. She saw the gun sticking out of the front of his blue jeans.

Spence looked into her eyes. "Something's come up," he said quietly.

FORTY-SIX

UNDER A RAPIDLY clearing night sky, Landers barked orders to his fellow agents on the courthouse lawn. The summer storm had blown through town, leaving behind a much-needed half-inch of precipitation, along with the lingering scent of nocturnal rain.

A couple of agents were going over Seaver's Buick, from which Landers had already removed the other black bag. He wanted to keep the bags to himself for now, and had thrown both of them in his truck. Another agent was busy assembling a satellite receiver to locate the tracking device Landers had left under the driver's seat of the Lincoln. Mr. Weeks, the coroner, had come to deal with Seaver's body. Satisfied that everything was under control, Landers made his way to the sheriff's office and found Reeves headed out the door. He waited for him at the bottom of the steps.

"Are you going to check on the girl?" Landers asked.

"Yeah," answered Reeves. "I want to make sure Spence hasn't busted her out and fled to Mexico. Besides, the night-shift guard is probably one heartbeat away from cardiac arrest. He's a little skittish."

"I'll go with you."

When the two men made it to the cell floor, Howard heard them coming and jumped behind Wes, who couldn't stop himself from asking, "What the hell were they thinking when they hired you?"

"Shut up," mumbled Howard.

"How are y'all doing down here?" Landers asked, grabbing the bars to Angela's cell and testing them with a sharp yank.

"Pretty good so far," answered Spence. "We heard some shooting. How are you?"

"We're fine. But I can't say the same for Seaver," Landers answered.

"Did you shoot him?" Wes inquired.

"Nope. They beat me to it."

Spence shook his head. "That's so weird. Just this morning I was in his office talking to him about this case. I never dreamed he could be involved in something like this. And the judge too? It's just too incredible."

"Well, believe it, kid, because it's happening," Landers answered back. He folded his arms and leaned against the cell bars.

"Does somebody mind telling me exactly what is happening?" Reeves asked. "Because all I'm hearing so far is that one of the largest paper mills in the country is trafficking drugs through my town."

"That about sums it up, deputy. And the judge, your old boss, and the DA were in on it," Landers answered.

"What's Angela and Spence got to do with it?" Reeves asked.

"Calvin was the drop man," answered Landers. "Apparently he started to scare them or made some threats, and they killed him. Our hero here"—Landers nodded toward Spence—"was supposed to settle the case and let the girl go to prison for a little while. Case closed, everybody goes back to making money."

"I guess it didn't turn out like they wanted?" said Reeves.

"Never does," answered Landers.

"So what's with all the fire power tonight?" Reeves asked.

"Only thing I can figure," said Landers, "was that the Chicago office wasn't real pleased with how the case was going. They probably figured that Seaver and Hamilton had lost control and might blow the whole operation. Hopefully we'll know more in a few hours. As we speak, we're getting warrants in Chicago for every executive that's a vice president and up at NAPCO. If somebody knows something, my experience is they'll be singing like a canary before morning."

"You that confident?" asked Reeves.

Landers shrugged. "Actually, there's still one thing I have a problem with."

"The girl," said Reeves.

"That's right, deputy," Landers answered with a smile. "We could use you at the agency."

"No thanks. I like my family too much."

"Tell me about it," said Landers.

"What about the girl?" Spence asked, looking at Angela.

"It's unlikely that NAPCO knows that Landers has put it all together," Reeves began. "Which means they're still following their plan—not only killing the DA, the judge and Watkins, but also preventing the murder trial and getting rid of Angela. Especially now that they've killed the folks who were going to control the trial for them"

"That's right," said Landers. "But certainly they didn't plan on coming down the jailhouse stairs, guns blazing."

"Why the hell not?" asked Wes. "Barney Fife here certainly wasn't gonna stop them."

"Oh, shut up," Howard mumbled again.

"It's easy to believe the judge had a heart attack," Landers continued, "and maybe the sheriff drowned. You could even believe the DA was involved in something he had no business in—something that backfired on him and got him killed. As a matter of fact, that's what happened. But how would you explain gunmen coming inside the county jail to shoot a female prisoner?"

"So they gotta kill me?" Angela asked.

"I'm afraid so, ma'am. But they've got to do it in a way that doesn't point the finger back at them. But don't you worry." Landers gave Angela a wink. "Your boy Spence and I ain't going to let that happen."

"You notice anything strange tonight, Howard?" Reeves asked.

He pulled his hat from his head and shook the last drops of water from its brim.

"No, sir, there was a car earlier in the back alley, but they turned around and left. Other than that, I ain't seen a soul."

Reeves and Landers stood there, both staring at the ground, running scenarios through their minds.

"What were they thinking?" Landers wondered aloud.

At almost the same exact instant Landers and Reeves raised their heads and looked at each other with absolute terror on their faces.

"Howard, get the handcuffs out of the closest!" Reeves shouted.

Howard jumped. "But, deputy, I don't wanna leave."

"Just shut the hell up and do it, before I shoot you myself!" Reeves snarled back.

Howard raced out of the cellblock and up the stairs. Both Landers and Reeves drew their guns.

"What's going on?" Spence asked with a concerned voice.

"We've got to get out of here," Landers said. He turned to Angela and tried to give her a smile. "Don't worry, it's going to be alright."

Reeves shouted upstairs at Howard, "Hurry up! You've got the only keys to the cells!"

Howard, already a nervous wreck, came fumbling down the stairs with a pile of handcuffs in his arms. He ran to Reeves and dropped them on the floor. Keys and cuffs scattered on the cement surface.

"Did you bring the keys to the cuffs?" Reeves demanded. Howard didn't answer.

"Where we gonna take 'em, deputy?" Landers asked excitedly.

"We'll take them over to my office," said Reeves. He grabbed the cell keys from Howard and opened the door to Mark Johnson's cell. Johnson came to the cell door, and Reeves cuffed him. "You just stay right there," he ordered.

"Let's get the two drunks next," Reeves said, and moved to unlock their cell door. Neither had stirred during all the commotion. One was asleep on the cot in the corner, the other passed out on the concrete floor. Reeves threw the cell door open, clanging them against the cell bars, and still the drunks lay comatose. "Here," Reeves said, handing two pairs of handcuffs to Landers and Wes. "You'll probably have to carry them out."

Reeves' long legs strode quickly back down to Angela's cell, where Spence was still standing beside the door. He unlocked the door and opened it, and Angela offered her wrists. "Am I going to have any trouble out of you?" he asked.

"No, sir," she answered.

"I didn't think so," he said, and tossed the handcuffs to Howard.

"Thank you," said Angela. "You don't know how much that means to me."

"Damn, this son-of-a-bitch stinks," Wes complained from the drunk's cell. Having got the cuffs on the two prisoners, Landers and Wes were now attempting to throw them over their shoulders to carry them out.

"Alright, Howard," Reeves said to the fidgety, ghost-white guard, "I want you to pull your gun, and if anybody tries to run, you shoot 'em. Understood?"

"Yes, sir," Howard stammered. Reeves doubted that Howard would actually shoot a fleeing prisoner, but he wanted to say it out loud for the prisoners to hear.

"Okay, let's go," instructed Reeves.

"Hey, what about me?" Jared Grant shouted from his locked cell.

"Keep down," instructed Reeves, "I'll come back and get you when I've got a free hand."

"You'd better come back," said Grant.

"Don't worry," said Reeves. "You just sit down and shut up until I get back."

Howard walked backwards up the steps out of the holding cells, his gun shaking in his hand. No one else was too concerned about the danger posed by the prisoners. Angela didn't even warrant handcuffs. Mark Johnson, despite his odd activities, had never been a threat to anybody, and wasn't likely to make a run for it. And the two drunks were still unaware they had been in jail, much less that they were now being carried out.

Howard waited at the top of the landing for Landers and Wes, who struggled to carry the two prisoners up the narrow steps. Wes banged his prisoner's head on the door at the top of the walkway, but the man still never came to. Once up the steps, Howard led them out the front door and down onto the sidewalk in front of the jailhouse. They crossed the street to the corner of the sheriff's office building.

"This is fine," Reeves instructed. "Just prop 'em against the wall." Wes dropped his prisoner to the ground, and the man landed with a thud, rolled over, scratched his head and then fell right back asleep.

"Watch Mr. Johnson," Reeves said to Landers. "I've got to go back and get Jared."

As Reeves turned to go back to the jail, Angela grabbed him by the arm. "Thank you for giving me a chance," she said.

Reeves patted her hand. "I think it's about time life was fair to you," he said, then trotted back across the street and into the jailhouse.

Wes rubbed his aching back, which had already been sore from the long drive in his low-slung automobile. Landers walked Johnson a little closer to the edge of the building so he could watch his agents working in the town square. Spence and Angela stood side by side, his arm around her shoulders.

"I know this is a strange time to say this," she said, "but I just wanted you to know that I've never been happier in my life."

"Me either," he answered and squeezed her closer. "Me either."

It was the wind created by the explosion that Spence felt first. By the time the blast registered in his ears, the reverberating air was already full of debris. He grabbed Angela and pulled her to the ground, covering her on the side of the explosion. He turned to see the fire coming out of the six windows on the first floor of the jailhouse. At that moment, the whole right side of the building collapsed to the ground and smoke billowed everywhere.

"John!" Spence screamed and ran toward the burning building. Then a second explosion went off at the base of what was left of the building, and he instinctively dove to the ground. The whole building was engulfed in smoke and fire. When he tried to stand, Landers tackled him and held him to the ground.

"It's too late, man," Landers told him. "It's too late. He's gone."

Spence lay on the grass next to the street and buried his face in his hands. "It's not fair!" he sobbed. "He's got a wife! He's got kids!

Landers patted him on the shoulder, " I'm sorry, kid. I'm so sorry."

FORTY-SEVEN

STEVE RICTER DIDN'T have to ask the agents from the DEA and FBI why they rang his doorbell at 1:30 in the morning. At first he answered their questions generally, revealing little knowledge of the internal workings of NAPCO. But as the interrogation continued, he realized they already knew too much. He sweated through the questioning for an hour, increasingly aware of how slim his chances were. At 2:30 one of the agents took a call on his cell phone, then dropped the bomb on Ricter: the DEA had apprehended the exterminators in the Lincoln, and they had spilled their guts. Ricter decide to negotiate while he could. He asked to speak to someone who had the authority to deal and called his lawyer.

Kendall remained arrogant to the end. When the DEA, FBI and local Chicago police arrived at his mansion with a search warrant, he threatened to have every last one of them fired. He would make them regret harassing the great P. Thomas Kendall. He refused to cooperate while he waited for his attorney to arrive, and made sure the agents were as uncomfortable as possible in the meantime. When the news came of the exterminators' arrests and Ricter's break down, the FBI agent in charge informed Kendall he was under arrest and would be accompanying them to the local precinct for further questioning.

Again Kendall refused. Two Chicago policemen accompanying the
agents were instructed to place him under arrest. One took his arm,
but Kendall pulled away and took a swing at the officer. And there,
in the middle of the marbled foyer of his Chicago mansion, P. Thomas
Kendall, the man who answered to no one because of his money and
prestige, got his ass whipped by a big Irish Chicago cop making thir-
ty-eight thousand dollars a year.

—

Landers was still working furiously at three o'clock in the morning—and it had been one hell of a night. He was giving orders, collecting evidence, and frantically making notes on a legal pad so he
would have all the details he needed to write up his report.

Spence stood with Angela and Wes, leaning against a patrol car
and watching red and white fire truck lights bounce from the pile of
fallen concrete and steel that had once been the Crawford County
Jail. With his arm around Angela, Spence waited until Landers told
them they could leave. He was emotionally drained—ecstatic that
they could no longer hold Angela, but grieving the loss of the man
who had so recently become a friend. He told Wes to keep an eye on
Angela and walked over to Landers, who was still handing out
instructions to subordinates.

As soon as he had dismissed his agents, Landers turned to
Spence. "How's she doing?" he asked.

"She's fine. Just glad its over."

"And how are you doing?"

"I guess I'm okay. It really hasn't all sunk in yet," Spence
answered, looking around.

"You must really care about her."

"Yeah, I guess I do. The more I got to know her, the more I could-
n't help myself."

"I guess the fact that she's some kind of looker didn't hurt either."

"No, probably not."

The two men turned to look over the square. They leaned against an agent's car, quietly observing the scene.

"I'm sorry about your friend," Landers said. "From everything I saw, he seemed to be a good man."

"Yes, he was."

"He's got a couple of children, doesn't he?"

"Boy and a girl."

"Sure is a shame when kids have to grow up without a daddy."

Spence sagged, thinking about it.

"Gonna be tough for his young wife to manage," Landers added. "What does she do?"

"She's a school teacher."

"Yeah, that's right."

"I just hope the State or County has some sort of insurance for the families of officers killed in the line of duty," said Spence.

"Probably do, but I'll bet it ain't much."

"Probably not."

"What about the girl? What's she gonna do now?" Landers inquired.

"Don't know. Probably stay with me awhile. She'll want to go to school. I can promise you that."

"That'll be expensive. You up for it?"

"I don't know. I've got a world of student loans to pay back myself."

The two men stood in silence for a few moments while Landers contemplated his next move. It would be risky, but he knew it was the right thing to do.

"Did I tell you what I found on Seaver tonight?" Landers asked.

"No, sir"

"A bag full of cash."

"Oh, really? Trying to make his getaway, huh?"

"Yeah, something like that. Looks like it's a hell of a lot of money. Probably a couple of million anyway."

"Wow. I guess that'll really help—with evidence, I mean."

"Oh, I don't know. I think I've got plenty of evidence. Sad thing is, it'll probably just sit in a warehouse somewhere until all of the trials are over and then it'll be destroyed."

"Millions of dollars. That's a shame."

"Yeah," Landers took a deep breath. "I'd keep it myself, especially since I threw it in my truck and haven't told anyone else I have it yet." He stood up from leaning against the car and looked around quickly while he tucked his shirt into his jeans. "But unfortunately, I'm a little too honest. Wouldn't be able to sleep."

Spence didn't know why Landers was telling him this, but said the only thing he could think of: "I know what you mean."

"Seems to me that money could be better used by a young widow with two kids and a girl who hasn't gotten a whole lot of breaks in life."

Spence didn't know what to think. Did Landers have a plan, or was he just indulging in wishful thinking?

"Wish there was some way to get the money in their hands without any trouble," Landers went on, looking everywhere but at Spence.

Spence saw now that the agent was perfectly serious. "I think I probably know somebody who could make that happen," he said slowly.

"Oh, really?" Landers nodded his head. "I tell you what—why don't you take the girl home and you all get some sleep. I'm going to send an agent over to watch your house tonight, so you can feel safe. Just have her back here at the sheriff's office in the morning so we can clear her from the state record and get her released."

"That sounds great," Spence answered, but he still had the feeling he was missing something—something Landers wanted him to do. He leaned on the car for another minute, but when Landers offered no further suggestion, he pushed off and turned to walk away.

But Landers stopped him. "Hey, kid," he said quietly, "I'm about to call a meeting in the sheriff's office with all the other agents. Just in case you were wondering, my truck's unlocked."

Spence walked back to Wes and Karen and told them to get into the Viper and he would be there in a moment. He strolled towards

Lander's truck, and before opening the driver's side door he took one last look around. Just as he had promised, Landers had cleared the street and Spence had it all to himself. He opened the door and spotted the two bags in the passenger side floorboard. He leaned over the seat and tried to hoist one of the bags off the floor. He couldn't believe how heavy it was, and he staggered backward with it as he dragged it out of the car. When he had his footing again, he heaved the bag over his shoulder and turned around. The figure on the other side of the door scared him to death. Then he realized it was Americus.

"I hate it when you do that," Spence said, gasping for breath.

"Kathy called me at home and told me about all the commotion. When I couldn't get you on the phone, I got worried and decided to come down here. Are you okay?" As far as Spence could remember, this was the first time he had ever seen his uncle upset.

"Yes, sir, I'm fine."

Americus opened his arms, and Spence dropped the bag so his uncle could hug him. "Oh, ma boy," he said, sighing in huge relief, "I was worried sick. You should've called me."

Spence patted his uncle on the back. He couldn't help but chuckle. "I know," he said, "but there hasn't been a whole lot of time."

"Well, I'm just glad its over. Go home and get some sleep. You can fill me in on the details in the morning." Americus gave Spence another hug and then turned to walk away.

"Hey, Unc."

"Yes, son?"

Spence picked up the bag again and patted its side. "I kinda need your help with something."

—

He was hoping she would be able to stay awake so they could talk, but she hadn't had much sleep in jail, and this night had been long and exhausting. Spence carried her up the front steps and into his house, like a father carrying a child, while she wrapped her arms around him. He could feel her warm breath on his neck. Wes, who was also exhausted, parted with them in the living room and went straight to the second bedroom. He dropped onto the bed, still in his clothes, and slept till morning.

Spence carried Angela into his bedroom and laid her down on the bed. He took off her shoes and helped her underneath the linens. She pulled the blanket tight around her neck and whispered, "Thank you . . . for everything."

Spence watched as she quickly drifted off to sleep. He kissed her on the forehead, got up from the bed, turned out the light and left the room. He slept on the couch with Sam.

FORTY-EIGHT

THE NEXT MORNING Spence was up before daylight, remarkably refreshed after just three hours of sleep. For the first time since his appointment to defend Angela, he knew everything was going to be all right. The first thing he wanted to do was go into town and get Angela some new clothes so she could get out of the county-issued uniform. He left a note on the kitchen table in case either Angela or Wes awoke before he returned, offered a happy "hello" to the agent guarding his house, and then he and Sam hopped into the Explorer and headed for town.

The only store open in Monroe at 6:00 a.m. was Wal-Mart, but something gave Spence the feeling that Angela wouldn't care where the clothes came from. He picked out a couple of pairs of shorts, again guessing at her size, then picked out a couple of cotton shirts that he hoped would match. Next, he located a young sales clerk named Cindi and explained why he needed some help. She appreciated Spence's difficulty and told him to follow her. As they headed down one of the aisles, she turned back and asked, "Are these things for Angela?"

"Yes, they are. Do you know her?"

"I went to school with her, at least while she got to go. I should be able to pick out her sizes."

"How did you know they were for her?"

"Just guessed. I mean, I knew you were her lawyer."

Spence had never seen Cindi before, and yet she seemed to know everything he had done since he arrived in Monroe. He would never get used to small town life, he thought.

Cindi helped him buy some lace panties, matching bras, makeup, a toothbrush, deodorant, shaving cream, razor blades, hairbrushes, lotion, Keds shoes and lipstick. She seemed to enjoy the shopping spree, even if it wasn't for her. When they couldn't think of anything else, she walked Spence to the cashier.

"I hope everything works out for Angela," Cindi said. "I always thought she was nice—a little quiet maybe, but nice."

"I think she's going to be fine. I'll tell her you said hello."

Spence knew there was nothing to eat in his house other than sandwiches and beer. He also knew Wes would have the personality of an annoyed grizzly bear without something to eat. He stopped at Hardees on his way back back home and bought five sausage biscuits and five cartons of orange juice. He had no idea what Angela liked to eat, but again, he figured she wouldn't complain.

When he arrived at the house, he found Wes and Angela at the kitchen table. Wes was drinking coffee. She was wearing one of Spence's T-shirts. They were both laughing.

"Why do I have the feeling you guys are laughing at my expense?" asked Spence, as he put the bags down on the counter.

"What makes you think that?" Angela asked.

Spence nodded toward Wes. "Because anytime he's around and people are laughing, it's at my expense."

"I was just telling her about some of your law school study habits," said Wes. "I wanted her to know just how close she came to spending life in prison."

"Did you really only go to some classes one time?" she asked.

"Don't believe everything you hear," said Spence. He held up the flimsy plastic Wal-mart sacks. "I bought you some clothes. I hope they fit."

Her eyes lit up as she jumped from the table and ran to the counter. When she saw the shorts, shirts, and Keds sneakers Cindi had chosen for her, she gave Spence a huge hug. Then she kissed him on the cheek, grabbed up the bags, and rushed off to take a shower.

"Well, I guess you made her day," Wes said.

"Yeah. Kind of like you would be if I brought you a naked Demi Moore." Spence handed over the Hardees sacks.

"I still don't think I'd have been that happy. She's a sweet girl. I can see why you like her."

Spence pulled out a chair and sat down. "Then you can see why I didn't want to leave you two alone together very long."

"Oh, how well you know me."

Spence unwrapped one of the biscuits, but paused before he began to eat. "Tell me I not weird," he said to his best pal. "I mean, I'm not doing something totally bizarre, am I?"

Wes was devouring one of the biscuits. "Well, I'm afraid I can't tell you that you aren't weird, perverted, and sick, because you are." He swallowed and licked his fingers. "But just from the little amount of time I've spent with her, I don't think I can blame you this time. Besides, she's a babe."

Spence took a bite and chewed thoughtfully. "I know that I don't have to," he said, "but I wanted to thank you for last night."

"Are you kidding? Hell, I thought it was wonderful—now that it's over and I'm alive. Besides, what a story I'll have to tell my grandkids, not to mention the little hotties down at the beach house."

"Funny you should mention the beach house. I was hoping to take Angela there for a few days. I think we could both use the rest."

"Say no more. It's yours."

"Have I told you lately that I love you?" Spence said, looking doe-eyed at Wes over his biscuit.

"I know you're just using me for my father's money," Wes replied.

Shortly after breakfast, Wes had to leave. He had a date later that
night in Columbia and figured that if he couldn't get the girl into bed
with a story about being in a shootout between drug dealers and the
DEA, he'd have to retire from womanizing and get married.

Spence hated to leave Angela home alone, especially in her new
clothes. She had chosen the pink shorts and they were even shorter
than he'd hoped. They stood at his front doorway and hugged goodbye. The sexual tension was killing him. He wanted to touch her, to
kiss her, to pull her body tight against his. But he also wanted her to
feel comfortable, to know that her days of being abused were over, to
trust Spence with all her heart. He told her he would be back shortly and to get ready. They would be leaving that afternoon.

The agent on guard told Spence that Angela didn't need to come
back to the courthouse square after all. In light of Ricter's confession,
she was free to go. But Landers did leave a business card and a note
for Spence to call him in a few days when things calmed down.
Landers might need their testimony, the note explained, and he wanted to know where they were going to be. Landers must have had a
feeling they would be leaving town, at least for a little while. He
ended his note with a reminder to be careful and to talk to no one
about the past few weeks' events. By the time Spence read the note,
Landers was already on a plane for Washington to begin compiling
his case against Kendall and NAPCO.

When Spence got to his office, he found Kathy ravenous for the
details. Spence was in no mood to gratify her curiosity, so he told her
he couldn't talk about the case until the DEA cleared him to do so.

He went to his uncle's office and was surprised to find the door
closed and locked. He listened on the outside for a moment and then
tapped lightly on the thick wood.

"Unc, you in there?"

"That you, Spence?"

"Yes, sir."

Americus unlocked the door and opened it slowly until he was sure Spence was alone. Then, once Spence was inside, he looked both ways down the hall, shut the door and locked it again. He seemed to be having the time of his life.

On a table in the corner of the office, Spence saw the neat stacks of currency—two big ones and a much smaller third one. The black bags lay on the floor next to the chair Americus had been sitting in.

"How much is it?" Spence asked.

"About 2.3 million," Americus answered in glee, "in stacks of twenty thousand, all brand new one-hundred-dollar bills."

"Any chance it's counterfeit?"

"Oh no, ma' boy, I've already checked. Besides, Mr. Franklin and I are old friends. I know what to look for."

"So how do we get some of it to Reeves' wife?"

"That's already been taken care of. I called a friend of mine at Sawgrass Mutual Life Insurance and he's going to back-date some documents and paperwork, take the money and write her a check for a million-dollar insurance policy."

"Just like that?"

"Just like that. When he's done, it'll look like Reeves signed up for the policy about two years ago. There'll even be a record of his premium payments."

Spence thought about NAPCO. He thought about the insurance company. Then he asked his uncle, "Are there any big companies out there that do things by the book?"

"Of course not," answered Americus. "Too much money involved. And it's a good thing too. I wouldn't be nearly as rich if they did."

"So it looks like Reeves was smart enough to take out a big insurance policy, and she doesn't have to pay taxes on the million because it's insurance proceeds."

"That's right," confirmed Americus, still grinning. "But of course, my friend isn't going to do all of this for free. It's going to cost us fifty grand."

"I think that's reasonable. Now what about Angela's share?"

"I've already taken care of that, too."

"I wouldn't have expected anything less."

"As for her, I transferred a million dollars from my offshore account in Nevis to an account with her name on it, and I'll just keep the cash."

"What are you going to do with a million dollars in cash?" Spence laughed.

"Well," said Americus, as if the answer was obvious, "some of it I'll spend wisely on wine, women and song. The rest I'll probably just blow."

Spence chuckled in admiration. "Is Angela's money safe down there?"

"As safe as it would be up here. Safer actually. You don't have to worry about the IRS, unless of course she tries to bring it into the country. I've even got it invested for her, in the same thing it's been in for me. Should pay her around 120 grand a year. She'll have to pay taxes on that."

"And what's that going to cost me?"

"You said yourself that fifty grand sounded fair."

"You set me up."

"Of course."

"And what about the rest of the money?"

"I'm going to insist that you take a hundred grand yourself for risking life and limb in the pursuit of justice."

"Okay, I won't argue with you, but that still leaves about a hundred grand."

"Well, I've thought about that, too," said Americus. "And here's how I see it. You and this girl seem to think that you're in love, if there is such a thing. So I think you need to take the next few months and show her the things she never got to see. She's been cooped up in a cage since she was born and needs to spread her wings a little. See how she likes the world, and you for that matter."

"Does that mean you're giving me permission to miss work?"

"It does, but I expect you back in a few months. And if things should work out between you two, maybe we can look at starting an office in Atlanta or Birmingham."

"Sounds like you've got it all figured out."

"Of course I do. I'm the smartest man you know. Just promise me you'll take it slow."

"I promise."

"Here." Americus handed Spence one of the twenty-thousand-dollar stacks. "Call me when this runs out and I'll wire you some more."

"Thanks, Unc. I mean, for everything."

"The pleasure's all mine."

They walked to the door and Americus unlocked it. Spence went through and then turned to look at his uncle. "One million dollars. That's a lot of wine, women and song."

"Yeah, you're probably right," Americus answered. "I think I'll just put some of it over there in my safe. Along with the other millions." He put a cigar in his mouth and gave Spence his signature smile.

FORTY-NINE

EVERYTHING WAS DONE, and it was still only ten-thirty in the morning when he made it back to his house. Angela was waiting for him with open arms and hugged him as he came through the door. She had already found one of his gym bags and packed it with all the things Spence had brought her from Wal-Mart. He asked if there was anything she wanted from her house, but she said no. The only possessions she ever cared about were her books, and they had been destroyed in the explosion at the jail. As for the shack in the pine trees, she never wanted to go there again.

She played with the dog in the living room while Spence packed his bag. She was already winning Sam over—not easy for a female. Spence loaded their bags in the car, and the three of them set off for the beaches of the Atlantic coast.

Spence decided to route their trip through Atlanta, so he could take Angela by a mall to buy some more clothes. Going through the Georgia capitol would add miles to their trip to Edisto Island, but at least the roads were interstate most of the way. Besides, she couldn't live with only two outfits, especially ones he had picked out. As they drove up Interstate 85, they held hands and listened to the radio. She had a million questions—about all the places he'd been and things he'd seen. She couldn't wait to see the ocean and insisted on driving with the sunroof open to feel the wind in her hair—which also pleased the other female in the car.

As they got closer to Atlanta and the mall, Spence began to caution her about the experience she was about to undergo. He laid down a few ground rules: in Atlanta they would still be five hours away from the McCains' beach house, and he wanted to be there by ten that night. Angela promised not to shop too long if he promised to bring her back later. He promised.

Spence really didn't want to leave Sam in the car during the shopping expedition, so he decided she could have some pampering, too. He dropped her by Buffy's Pet Grooming Service for a bath and treatment. Buffy, the little old lady who owned the pet boutique, was obviously accustomed to having shih tzus and poodles as patrons and was surprised to see a pointer, but she was a professional. Besides, Spence knew Sam would make it easy on her.

Spence and Angela pulled into Lenox Mall in Atlanta's famous Buckhead section at three-thirty. Angela was overwhelmed—at the sheer size of the structure, at the people running around like ants on a demolished anthill, but most of all by the clothes. Spence watched with enormous pleasure as salesperson after salesperson helped her try on different styles, colors, and accessories. He had never enjoyed shopping with a woman before, and never expected to. When she found something she liked, Spence paid for it in cash. At the makeup counter at Macy's, the beautician pampered her for an hour, picking colors that worked best with her hair and skin. Their scheduled departure time came and went, but Spence couldn't bring himself to make her hurry. He even suggested that she get a manicure and a pedicure.

As he sat out front while she got her nails done, he picked up a copy of *The Wall Street Journal* and skimmed the headlines. On the front page was a large photograph of Thomas Kendall in handcuffs, trying to cover his face but failing to conceal a nasty bruise over his right eye. Spence read the article, relieved to find no mention of

Angela or him. According to Ricter's confession, NAPCO was even deeper into the drug trade than Landers had suspected. Their network included supply and distribution, and their reach was nationwide. The article went on to note that once the news of his arrest hit Wall Street, NAPCO shares dropped from forty-two dollars a share to a dollar fifty, a net loss for Kendall of nearly four and a half billion dollars.

Angela looked absolutely stunning after her afternoon of pampering, and Spence wasn't the only man to notice it. It seemed like everybody in the mall turned their heads as they passed. Of course, she was oblivious to it all—too busy looking at merchandise than to notice people looking at her. Finally she said, "I guess we need to go so I don't spend all of your money."

Spence knew he was going to have to find a way to tell her that she was a hell of a lot wealthier than he was, but he decided to wait until later. He figured that wasn't the kind of information you tell a beautiful woman on her first trip to a mall.

Sam, of course, had had the run of the boutique. "I couldn't keep that sweet puppy in a cage," said Buffy, obviously smitten. But she let her go, and the Explorer once again headed east, leaving the city behind. Angela's questions resumed as they drove through the Georgia darkness. When they passed through Augusta, Spence explained to her about The Masters, green jackets, and how people came from all over the world to watch professionals play golf. She wanted to come back and watch, too, and suggested that they stop off now and buy tickets. Spence realized he needed to be more careful. There were some things in life even Americus couldn't get, and Spence knew it would break his heart to ever tell Angela no.

It was late when they finally pulled up to the McCain family beach house on Edisto Island. As soon as they stepped out of the car, Angela heard the ocean from the backside of the house. She grabbed Spence's hand to hurry him up the stairs to the front door, and as soon as he got the door unlocked, she ran straight to the back of the house—Sam at her heels—and pulled open the sliding glass door.

She stepped onto the deck and there it was. She spread her arms wide, closed her eyes, and let the midnight breeze blow through her hair. She tasted the salt in the air and in the light of the half moon watched the white combs lift up and then crash down on the sandy shore. It was everything she had ever imagined. She was finally free.

Spence quickly unloaded the car and then joined her on the porch. He had never felt so good, so happy, so alive. Americus was wrong. Love did exist, and Spence knew where it was.

"I'm glad you came to Monroe," she said taking his hand.

"I'm glad I didn't find you another lawyer."

She turned to him and he stared into her eyes. She placed her arms around him as he pulled her closer. He put his fingers gently on her cheek and raised her face to meet his lips. There in the moonlight, as ocean waves crashed on the beach just a few hundred feet away, came the kiss they both had been waiting for since the first time Spence walked into her cell.

"Do you want to go back inside?" she asked.

"I think I'd like that," he answered. "You know, in all of our shopping today, we forgot to buy you any pajamas."

"That's okay," she whispered into his ear. "I won't need any."